When the Swan's Neck Breaks

by
Marilyn MacGruder Barnewall

When the Swan's Neck Breaks
by Marilyn MacGruder Barnewall

Printed in the United States of America

ISBN 978-1-60647-443-3

Unless otherwise indicated, Bible quotations are taken from The St. James Version. Copyright © 1924, 1925, 1929, 1930, 1932, 1933, 1935, 1939, 1940 by A.J. Holman Co., Philadelphia, PA.

www.xulonpress.com

When the Swan's Neck Breaks was written to...

. . . Celebrate things of which we see too little these days: truth, common sense, personal commitment, responsibility, and honor.

I will forever be grateful for the opportunity I had to spend a happy career in the banking industry! Done properly and without political interference, banking is an honorable industry filled with honest, hard-working people. They are undoubtedly some of the nicest people I have ever known.

The job of the Federal Reserve is to protect the currency of the United States of America. It is to manage the currency in a responsible manner so inflation does not occur. When the Federal Reserve was founded in 1913, the dollar was worth one hundred pennies when using gold as a comparative. In 2008, the dollar is worth about four cents, using the same comparative.

It was 1991 when I first saw what was happening in the mortgage market. I knew then a "housing bubble" would result from the manipulation of the credit markets by the Federal Reserve. No one has to understand economics or quantum physics to grasp a basic fact: the more the marketplace is saturated with a product, the less value the product has. That is true whether the product is television sets, computers – or, money. Why do you pay more for things today than your parents did? The dollar is worth less because too many have been printed and thrown into the marketplace. It's not that a gallon of milk has increased in value. It's that the money you are using to purchase it has gone down in value.

Know this: When the Federal Reserve creates money and floods the marketplace with it, injecting liquidity into America's banks, inflation will follow. When the money supply is increased, taxpayers pay via inflation and a devalued currency for one or another of the mistakes made by bankers and/or brokers. To increase the price of gold, print dollar bills. It works every time.

The Federal Reserve is not part of the federal government. It is a private cartel of bankers – much like OPEC is a cartel of oil-producing nations.

Remember that, please...

When the Swan's Neck Breaks is Dedicated to...

Herb, Jay, Dick, Bob, Steve, Rae, Ollie, Sue, Lori, Don, Dean, Jim, Mary, Judy – all of the wonderful bankers I have enjoyed knowing – and, to Bob MacGruder and Dede Hunter, my brother and sister, who told me to "keep writing; it's good." Thanks to Bob who, with a good heart and no blood ties motivating him, willingly read the text and gave me editing help and encouragement. Thanks to my mother and stepfather for the birthday present that made publishing this book possible.

After writing all of those non-fiction books thinking it was work, I can say after writing my first work of fiction... non-fiction is child's play.

Chapter 1

He let his shoulders relax a bit. She was right. He was tense. Aleksandr Plotnikov eyed Tatiana carefully. Though of sturdy Russian stock, there was nothing rough or masculine about her. Her curves were soft and perfect. That, he knew, was precisely why the Moscow bureaucrats had sent her. Her job was to keep him happy and she was normally very good at her job. But Aleksandr's conscience was troubled, and moreover he preferred his lovers to be volunteers. Her hot breath in his ear did nothing to warm his heart or arouse his desire. There was no emotion, no lust... only calculation. And Plotnikov was an expert at calculations. He liked them true and accurate, like facets in a diamond.

He was a handsome man if a little bearish around the edges. Logical, humorless, relentlessly honest – and lately more than a little dissatisfied with himself. She found the intensity in his dark eyes unsettling. It made her feel as if he could see through her.

Serious brown eyes met her blue, playful ones. "I'm sorry, Tanya. You know how having to tour the nursery – those fetuses." He rubbed his brow and lowered his head, moving it slowly from side to side.

"Dorogoi," she said and then frowned. He did not like for her to call him darling. "I don't see why going there upsets you so. The rodilnyi dom – the nursery – cradles your work for the people! You are a great man! A brilliant scientist! You will give the Soviet people the respect of the world! You should be proud of the nursery..."

"Proud?" he asked, interrupting her. "Of scientifically-created wombs filled with scientifically-created fetuses swimming in scientifically-created seawater?" Plotnikov slowed his thoughts, recognizing the danger of where they were taking him. He usually did not have difficulty controlling his emotions. He was a logic-dominated person who, though he felt things deeply, rarely expressed his feelings. He had to remember that he was playing her. He could not afford to let his emotions get in the way so she could play him.

He understood the games used by the whores sent by the State to keep him... relaxed and focused on his work. The State provided for his every need. They sent women like Tatiana. This woman, however, was better placed among the intelligence community in the U.S.S.R. than the others they sent.

Tatiana might be a gorgeous, provocative and alluring woman, but like everyone else in his world her soul belonged to the Party. He could share his secret with no one. He wanted her to use her contacts in Moscow to aid him in step one of an escape plan.

"You're right, of course," he said in a voice as humble as he could make it amid all his anger and disgust. Her eyes narrowed a bit as she evaluated the sudden change in his mood. She thought back over recent experiences with other Soviet scientists and decided they were all too intense. She watched him sip his vodka martini, eyes cast down. The only time scientists ever seemed volatile was when they discussed their work.

"To bring these babies to life ... what if I make a mistake with the cells and eggs and they are born with serious defects? When we first began, it happened." His tone of voice exemplified the shame he truly felt.

He had found humility an effective tool in past dealings with Tatiana. He knew the answer to his question. The State would kill the infant and bring him more cells from that experiment's clone file and insist he start over. These were not human beings to those who wanted to benefit from their existence. They were weapons of the cold war. They were expendable – as long as he could replace them.

Plotnikov did not know when he stopped looking at the fetal bags and their contents as something more than an experiment. He just knew that one day after a walk through the aisles of his life-giving experiments he left the building and became physically ill. He claimed loudly that he thought he was "over this damned flu," refused medical care, and asked instead to be taken home so he could go to bed and take the rest of his medicine.

There was no "flu" and that was his first lie. It would not be his last.

"Having to keep your discovery secret from the rest of the world doesn't bother you?" she asked.

"No. No. Do you really want to know what bothers me, Tanya?" He sat down on the sofa, beckoning her to join him. Now, he thought to himself, I can bait my hook... casting it into the waters will come later.

Plotnikov did not offer many insights into his personal feelings and she, sensing an opportunity, smiled warmly and sat beside him. She was paid extra for providing personal information about clients if it was unavailable from other sources.

"Of course I want to know what bothers you, Miliye," she said, smiling at him. He didn't like her to call him honey, either. "Share with me. Let me help."

"It's silly, really," Aleksandr began weakly, letting his insecurities show through an otherwise hard, logical countenance. Women loved men who let their insecurities show... trusted them, even when they were unworthy of it. He figured that out during his playboy days in Moscow.

"It makes me feel insecure to know that what I'm doing for the State is the result of an accident. It's... it is not based on scientific knowledge." He hesitated, hoping to appear as if he were reaching for truly meaningful words so he could share the experience with her. His dark eyebrows came together and for a brief moment his face looked older than his 35 years. "True progress is based on scientific knowledge, Tanya. When I think of how much I might accomplish if I weren't so isolated ... well, it's frustrating."

Tatiana blinked. Was that all there was to it? He felt alone? How could he feel alone when one of the most beautiful women in the Soviet Union was here with him?

"Alone?" she asked. There was a somewhat distant look on her face and a bit of hurt in her voice.

"Professionally alone," he corrected himself, smiling. "Tatiana, the mapping of human genes began in 1911. That was when they first realized that the gene for color blindness came from an X chromosome. In 1943, it was discovered that DNA was the 'transforming principle' at the base of the hereditary factor. In 1953, a couple of guys in London discovered DNA's double helix structure.

"Here I am in 1983 on Sakhalin Island cloning people but I have little insight into why what I do succeeds. One day I was studying proteins. I made a couple of mistakes and was suddenly able to clone a lab rat." Aleksandr took a sip of his martini.

He got up and began to pace, stretching his long, sturdy body, reaching his arms above his head and moving them slowly downward, behind him. He was a sexy man, she thought. Most of the scientists she shared her personal charms with were made of white putty... soft and flabby, even in their 30s and 40s. Not this man.

"I have no one to talk with, no way of knowing why what I do works. Thus, there is no way except experimentation to improve it. It makes me feel ... uncertain. When I visit the nursery, it is the worst possible reminder of my inadequacies. As long as I'm kept from those who understand DNA and the cloning process, I cannot provide a solution to my dilemma."

He bowed his head, resting his mouth on the fist of his right hand, his left arm folded across his body and the right elbow resting on his left hand.

"Are you saying you want to share your work with the outside world?" she asked, a tinge of brittleness entering her voice.

"Of course not! That's the last thing in the world I want to do!" His tone of voice left no doubt that he meant every word. And, he did. He prayed history would never associate his name and scientific credentials with this new kind of reverse holocaust. "How could you think such a thing?"

He continued before giving her a chance to respond. "I'm simply saying there is good science and bad science. Even though what I'm doing is working – for now, at least – it's not good science. I'm unable, through a lack of personal scientific skills, to validate my results. What if the clones I've created have some kind of mental or physical deficiency that doesn't show up until adulthood? What a waste to the state this little experiment of mine will have been! I need input from others who know more about Liniya Gzyzni ... this Line of Life." Would it sound logical to a non-scientist? Would she bite the carrot he offered, he wondered?

"You mean you want to learn more about what you are doing?" Tatiana asked.

"Put simply, yes," he answered. He furrowed his brow, letting his dark hair fall across his forehead. "If I could go to one of the many international DNA conferences, perhaps I could turn bad science into good science – something lasting and substantial for the Motherland." He smiled a bit wistfully at her. "An impossible dream," he concluded. He stopped his pacing and sat back down beside her and, breaking the tension, chuckled. "I don't think anyone in Moscow even knows where Sakhalin Island is."

There was a long pause. "But you're not an impossible dream." He reached out, taking her by the arms and pulling her to him, leaning back on the sofa pillows. He was strong and she enjoyed feeling the hard muscles of his body against hers as he pulled her to him, slowly moving her waiting mouth closer to his.

"You are real. Beautiful, and oh, so real," he said as his lips closed over hers.

Tatiana instantly relaxed. This was something she understood. It was an act she had performed on behalf of the state many times in at least as many ways. She enjoyed having sex with this scientist. He was a thoughtful lover and certainly not without skill. Her arms went about his neck and she let her hands run through his hair.

Passion flared within her heart and moved quickly to other female parts she knew from experience would soon be crying out for release. Her fast responses to sexual overtures combined with her quick mind were reasons why she had been recruited to serve her country in this manner. She unbuttoned his shirt, then his trousers, and slowly began a descent back down his body.

*****

He left her sleeping and walked to the beach. Aleksandr Plotnikov stared across the warm southern waters of the Sea of Okhotsk. It was only a brief train ride west to the Tatar Straights, then a few more kilometers by rail barge to Vladivostok.

But from the Island of Sakhalin, it might as well be on the other side of the world. The island was, of course, Soviet territory – no matter the centuries old Japanese argument of ownership to the contrary.

The Japanese argued that Sakhalin and the Kuril Islands were theirs. They pointed to an ancient Chinese geography book, published about the time of Christ's birth. It referred to the northern frontier of Japan as the Amur River. This, the Japanese said, proved their claim of first settlement rights. It held no weight in Moscow. The Soviet government recognized force, not prior sovereignty, to determine land ownership. That was, after all, how Russia became the Soviet Union.

"All of those years, all of that time, and both nations still fight for ownership of Sakhalin and the 59 Kuril Islands," Plotnikov said softly. He remembered that, in 1853, Russia had planted a flag at the northern limit of Sakhalin and declared ownership.

"It is 1983 and that flag is still there," he thought to himself. And the uniquely Russian persistence to win a battle once begun made him sure that if he left, they would look for him always and forever. There would be no place safe enough to hide for a lifetime.

Plotnikov thrust his hands into the pockets of his dark sweater and began to pace slowly.

Plotnikov: The superstar of Moscow University's Class of 1975. Plotnikov: The first bio-physicist in the world to use Liniya Gzyzni, to create life… a DNA accident of fate.

"Plotnikov, the great scientist, now in charge of cloning babies who will grow into adults used to swing world opinion in favor of the Soviets," he thought, outraged. He suddenly understood the full impact of the words of old people: "Is that all there is?" Is this all his work – what his life – was destined to achieve?

Visits to derevnya blezhetsov always left him feeling not just guilty, but desperate. And, though this camp where older children lived was bad, the nursery – the rodilnyi dom – made him ill. A few years ago when he first visited the place, it took months to get the vision of human fetuses floating in transparent sacs out of his mind. Those fetuses were now young children. Some were achieving adulthood quickly, the result of hormonal manipulation.

There was something other than hormones speeding the aging process of the clones, he knew, but he did not know what. He couldn't be sure because, while he might be one important part of the puzzle, he was only one part. The Science Committee was quite good at keeping the left hand from knowing what the right hand was doing.

All tyrants use secrecy as a means to keep secure bedfellows sleeping soundly, he thought. Secrecy… and fear, he added.

Growth hormones, discovered in another Soviet lab, one in Czechoslovakia and another in Hungary, began aging the babies at three times normal speed, starting at a tender six months of age. Years ago, the Hungarians had discovered an anti-aging hormone treatment process and were using it to help keep people from having to face their ultimate humility: old age. Russian scientists had merely reversed the anti-aging process into a rapid-aging one.

There had been mistakes and some clone lives lost, but it was for the good of the homeland. It became clear to Aleksandr that human flesh had little meaning to government bureaucrats. It was a fact he had to face. People were tools to be used to manipulate the social and political worlds in ways that resulted in power and more power. His participation, willingly or otherwise, was a kind of countenance of the behavior and policies of his country. Since something inside of him totally opposed what was happening, he was in conflict with the worst possible enemy: himself.

At the equivalent age of twelve, the clones would be sent to a physics lab at a secret location. Aleksandr did not know where or what scientific experiments would be performed on them. He only knew it was referred to as the "finalization process."

By age thirteen, it was said, some of the clones would have the physical attributes of thirty year olds. No one knew the long-term effects of these procedures, but everyone was willing to experiment with human life if it held political advantage. All they wanted was to start placing the clones in the positions of power now held – or, soon to be held – by real people.

There was no doubt in Plotnikov's mind that, hormones or no hormones, these little beings would still have to go through puberty. Some would probably get locked into a constant state of puberty, looking like adults but forever feeling the insecurities of childhood. That was a logical consequence of the age-inducing hormones that were a daily part of their diets.

Here on Sakhalin Island, in this unlikely place, their clones studied every public move the originals made. Known personal traits that made the originals uniquely "them" were observed and re-enacted as part of the clone's daily education. Or they were watched on video tape. Video cameras brought life to the biographies being rehearsed by these young students. From the time they were old enough to be taught, the area of expertise they would be replacing was included in the curriculum. If they were a clone of a banker, they were taught business and finance beginning with their third grade school year.

One day the famous originals would disappear. They would be quietly kidnapped. Maybe it would happen during the first day or two of a planned vacation or business trip. Telephone calls would be made to the right people by a clone who sounded exactly like the real thing. Excuses for the cloned person's disappearance would be accepted. Then, each person kidnapped would be quickly replaced by his or her clone. Any emergency could be created to call them away from family. The unsuspecting American news, movie, business or political hero would be hastily flown to Sakhalin Island for an intensive week or two of last-minute intelligence gathering about his or her personal life. It was then each man met his clone and was told to "Have a nice life here on Sakhalin Island" and they absorbed the bitter reality that they would never leave.

Part of Aleksandr's story to Tatiana had been truthful. He did hate feeling like he was functioning in a dark closet. What were his scientific cohorts doing, really? Was his intelligence contact, Colonel Yuri Malashenko, right? Were governments in other parts of the world trying to do precisely what he, Aleksandr Plotnikov, was already doing? Maybe they were already doing it, too.

The closed minds of the 1980s were not ready for science to usurp the powers of the Almighty in the creation of human life. They would have to be eased into the concept of cloning... perhaps they would start things off by cloning animals. A general disrespect for human life needed to be established... perhaps the legalization of abortion. Euthanasia could be positioned as a humane way to end the suffering of dying people. Plotnikov scoffed. Though most people were unwilling to accept it, from the day people were born they were dying. They would, he knew, have to challenge religious beliefs as bigoted and not worthy of the heart of true believers. The state would deal with all of the issues. It always did.

Like many scientific discoveries, Plotnikov's occurred in a serendipitous manner. He had been trying to solve another genetic puzzle when the mother of all puzzles presented its self. He had no idea precisely why the lab rat cells he placed in a culture media caused the cells to stop dividing while they remained quiescent and alive. He only knew they did.

He really wasn't sure why he excised an unfertilized lab rat egg and implanted it in the coat gathered around the cells. He had removed the nucleus from the egg to give the new cells their chance at life. He thought the experiment would come to naught. True, the result had been a freak of nature, but he had reproduced life.

His accident had really been nothing more than poor electrical wiring and a careless movement by him. He had shocked his experimental egg. He surmised later that his carelessness had induced fusion.

"I cannot do this," Plotnikov said aloud to no one, kicking a piece of rock on the beach. Though he had been raised in a nation with no God and no religion, every fiber of his being told him what he was doing was wrong. Some form of inherent moral law was gathering strength within him and was at war with the lack of moral law with which he had been raised. Plotnikov did not understand it, but he felt it.

He had made his decision: He had to leave. It saddened him, but walking on the Sakhalin Island beach always cleared his head.

It was his job to produce human cells to be cloned, transfer them to a minimal media, then, at the right time, add an egg without a nucleus and use electroshock on the mass until fusion was induced. There was a little more to it than that, he thought, but, frankly, not a lot.

After the appropriate time, an infant was removed from its seawater-based womb and delivered to the rodilnyi dom: The nursery. At that point, Plotnikov's work became someone else's responsibility.

His conscience, however, remained his own and quite hidden from view.

Plotnikov shook his head. He would have to be very careful.

Chapter 2

Colonel Yuri Malashenko listened quietly as Tatiana briefly suggested that Aleksandr Plotnikov be allowed to attend an international conference on scientific subjects of importance to him.

"He feels isolated, Colonel, I think that's why he is so depressed. We had a good conversation about these black spells of his. I will write about it in my report," she concluded. The train was waiting and this was not the time or the place for such discussions.

As she made her way to the narrow gauge train, he watched her swaying hips and had a sudden appreciation for the short skirt and knee-high boots. They added feminine clarity yet softness to her body. It reminded him of why it was necessary to enclose a Picasso in the finest of frames. It was ... fitting.

She wore a short fur jacket for warmth. It was early fall, 1983, in Sakhalin. The mod look, popular in parts of Europe and America, appeared out of place at a train station in a country where fashion appeared to have stood still for a century. Malashenko realized he could monitor her progress by watching heads as they turned to look at her.

She was as good as her word, however. Within two weeks, her letter arrived.

As Malashenko read the small, fine script, he was puzzled. Like most Russian men, he did not think of women who sold their bodies to the State as part of the intelligence community. Her report, however, was very thorough. He had underestimated her. He did not do that, often. He briefly considered taking her under his wing to help her progress up the ladder of military intelligence. Smiling at the thought, he knew he would return to it at a later time. He buzzed for a secretary, dictated a brief paragraph about Plotnikov and sent it off to the Department of Psychological Analysis.

Like most matters unimportant to him personally, once it was dealt with it was forgotten. Malashenko remembered his moment of compassion for Plotnikov only a few weeks later when a response was received. He was to report to Moscow for an interview over this matter.

"Nothing is simple," he said to himself, but he was smiling at the thought of a few days in a more civilized place than this little island.

The Colonel used the days before his departure to plan more time with his scientist. He wanted to observe Aleksandr Plotnikov, be able to talk about him as if he really knew him. Plotnikov was not an easy man to know. He kept to himself and did not talk much. He always said the right thing, though.

He rose and, after closing and locking the office door, walked to a recess in the west wall of his office. He pushed a black button that was well-hidden behind an oil painting and the wall panel slid open. From a set of keys he wore on his belt, Malashenko found the right one to open the filing cabinets located behind the hidden recess. His fingers flipped through a variety of highly confidential files. He found the one titled "Plotnikov, Aleksandr Mikhail."

Flipping through the pages, he was able to scan the material quickly. There was not much that he had not expected. Aleksandr Plotnikov, born in Leningrad, had no doubt adapted to the fierce winter winds and long, black nights for which the city was known.

Plotnikov's mother, Marie, was 24 years old when Germany attacked the city in 1941 and 27 when the siege ended. Plotnikov's father, Grigoriy, had watched his wife, a biology teacher, as she almost starved to death during the 900-day siege. He had been badly injured by Nazi shelling. Though Grigoriy Plotnikov worked to be the family provider, there were few alternatives available to him.

Aleksandr Mikhail Plotnikov was born August 6, 1947, three years after the human misery ended at Leningrad. His grandparents starved to death during the siege, so he never knew them.

"A lot of painful memories ..." Malashenko muttered to himself. The birth was too much for the already debilitated physical state of Marie Plotnikov and she died shortly after her son was born.

The scientist's father eventually became a curator at the State Hermitage Museum. He survived the war with Germany, remarried, and lived long enough to see his son attain his Doctorate. Like Andrei Sakharov in 1945, Aleksandr Plotnikov graduated from the Theoretical Department at the U.S.S.R. Academy of Sciences at Moscow University in 1972.

Plotnikov's outstanding grades at Leningrad University made attendance at Moscow University, where he could seek graduate degrees in science, a normal occurrence. After Aleksandr received his doctorate, his father finally succumbed to the wounds from which he had suffered since 1942.

"Well," thought Malashenko aloud, "this tells me a great deal about *what* scientist Plotnikov is, but not much about *who* he is." He wanted to understand the man's character. He scratched his head, thinking that the one dominant trait about Aleksandr Plotnikov was quiet determination.

He returned the file to its place, closed the safe, unlocked the office, then picked up the telephone and dialed the scientist's office extension. Thinking better of it, he quickly hung up before it could ring. Malashenko lifted his hefty frame out of his creaking chair and walked steadily – if a bit slowly and thoughtfully – to the Human Sciences building.

It had not yet snowed, but fall was definitely in the air. The rain would soon turn to snow. He would be grateful for the frozen ground. He hated what the mud did to his boots.

Plotnikov sat, feet propped on his desk, reading a copy of JAMA, the *Journal of the American Medical Association*. Like many Soviet scientists, Aleksandr was fluent in English.

"So you like the magazine?" Malashenko asked as he entered Plotnikov's office, smiling and using his friendliest tone.

Startled, Aleksandr's feet came down from the top of his desk. His surprised reaction to the interruption caused him to jerk back slightly in the chair.

"This damned chair!" he said quietly. "It will give me a broken leg one day!" He smiled back at the KGB officer. "I haven't seen much of you, lately," Plotnikov said, removing his reading glasses and tossing them on the desk, atop the magazine.

"I've been busy with the usual detail work ... you know, security clearances, family interviews, housing – medical care. But I leave for Moscow, day-after-tomorrow."

Malashenko lowered his head, the skin beneath his neck crinkling as his chin touched his uniform collar. He looked down, a big smile lurking under the otherwise unexpressive face. Malashenko paused. "I came by to see what you are doing for dinner. You are right. We have not seen much of each other, Comrade." Again, he gave the customary laugh.

Plotnikov struggled to understand what the man was after. The scientist didn't know what the game was, or the prize for winning – or, losing. His left eyebrow raised as that thought passed through his mind. It resulted in a questioning look that lingered on his face. After a brief discussion, the two men decided that fresh fish caught two days ago by Plotnikov would make a good meal for the two of them.

"I'll bring vodka and some borscht," Malashenko offered. His dark eyes, bushy brows and rather substantial mustache made him look somewhat foreboding.

"Sure," Plotnikov responded, mulling over this turn of events. In his almost ten years on Sakhalin Island, Colonel Yuri Malashenko had never offered any personal contact. "Bring a tomato, if you've got one. I have some salad greens, too."

"Da. A tomato I can handle. What time do we eat, good doctor?"

"Seven okay?"

"Da. Seven it is." And with that, Malashenko turned on his heel and walked briskly, confidently, away.

So, Aleksandr wondered, what was making his military intelligence contact act so strangely? A feeling in the pit of his stomach made him certain that something was afoot.

Aleksandr glanced at his watch ... only two hours until closing at five. He decided to leave a little early to prepare for company. He had not cleaned house for two weeks and dirty laundry was not something one aired in front of an intelligence officer.

*****

"Your tomato," said Malashenko, bowing slightly. "And your borscht. What kind of fish are you cooking?" he asked, heading for the small kitchen. He put his food contributions on the counter, walked to the stove and raised the heavy lid from the iron frying pan.

"Cod," Aleksandr replied.

A bottle of vodka appeared and the two men were soon seated in the small living room of Aleksandr's quarters.

"I will be leaving for Moscow tomorrow," Malashenko said. He raised the glass, half-filled with vodka, to his lips. "To your health!" he said before tilting his head and relieving the glass of its liquid content.

"And yours, Colonel" replied Aleksandr politely before drinking the contents of his glass in two gulps. He knew better than to ask why the Colonel was going to Moscow and just smiled quietly.

"This amuses you?" Malashenko asked, laughing. "And for tonight, the name is Yuri. We can go back to Colonel after I leave the warmth of your home, but for tonight... call me Yuri. We meet as friends."

"Yuri, then," Aleksandr said, smiling. "It makes me envious... your trip," Aleksandr said, also laughing. "But right now I'd better pay attention to our fish or dinner will burn." He got up from his chair and walked to the stove. He did not know if it was a good or a bad omen, but the fish was done.

All in all, it was not a bad dinner for two bachelors. Malashenko entertained Aleksandr with stories from his Moscow KGB days and

Aleksandr reciprocated, talking about his college years. He could not be sure, but in his gut Aleksandr felt a tension in the air.

"A cigar, another glass of vodka, and a message for you, Comrade Plotnikov," the colonel said, smiling. "Then I must be on my way."

"A message?" asked Aleksandr, brows furrowed. This was a first. It was a somewhat worrisome thought.

"I have received word that the National Physics College at Moscow University will be sending two people every six months to attend international conferences on certain topics of interest to the Motherland," Malashenko began. Though Aleksandr tried to contain himself, he knew his eyes opened a bit wider at the news.

"My job in Moscow for the next few days is to convince the powers that be that it might result in great project advances if you were allowed to attend such conferences. Can such a case be made?" A quiet demeanor came over the big man and he looked directly into Plotnikov's eyes, awaiting an answer.

"Why... yes, I believe such a case can be made," Aleksandr said quietly. He hesitated before continuing. He had to be careful, yet positive. He had to hide his excitement a bit. It was a difficult balance.

"Though I would love to say the cloning project is the result of my brilliance," he began, laughing, "I have openly admitted that my success thus far is as much a result of good luck as an understanding of genetics, biology, and physics." He smiled his boyish grin.

"I walk on unknown ground. There is no doubt in my mind that research about this Line of Life, as we call it, is under study in every advanced nation in the world. Access to information from other scientists would help me keep us in the race for the future of this important technology. The race to decode the structure of DNA and RNA is going on at top speed. Am I walking down the right road? Am I going up the wrong road? Will there be long-term consequences I might foresee if I had access to the latest data? In all probability, the answer is 'yes.'"

There was a long silence. Aleksandr held his tongue and remained quiet.

"I believe you have given me the information I need to argue your case. I am familiar with the purpose and scope of the project and its successes to date. I have your last report and the statistical data it provides. Has anything changed?" asked Malashenko.

"No," replied Aleksandr. "Nothing has changed. There are, perhaps, some concepts about which non-physicists remain uninformed. I, too, am uninformed because I cannot know all of the other possible applications of what I'm doing... like creating clones of politburo members to succeed themselves or growing new hearts or livers for transplants that are totally compatible with recipients' bodies because they are created from their own DNA." Aleksandr finished speaking in an almost casual tone.

It was Malashenko's turn for widened eyes.

"You have not spoken of this before," Malashenko said, his eyes piercing.

"No one has asked," Aleksandr replied. "How many times have I been told that the cloning project is of the highest priority and that I should devote all of my energy toward it? I have no wish to carry others into my world of little dreams."

"Are they just dreams?" Malashenko demanded.

"No. For other nations involved in DNA research, these are – from what I read – priorities around the world."

Malashenko was pensive. He folded his right arm across his chest providing a prop for his left elbow. Then, he proceeded to stroke his mustache with his left thumb and index finger in a well-practiced habit of contemplation.

"This is most interesting," he said. "What you are saying is that there are other avenues with great benefit to the state from this project of yours... benefits that could have a direct impact on those in powerful positions."

He rousted his burly frame from the overstuffed chair by Aleksandr's fireplace, still thoughtful.

"You have given me something very interesting to think about on my plane ride, Aleksandr. I'll call you when I return from Moscow." He reached for his coat, hanging on a peg to the left of the fireplace.

"Good fish. Good dinner... I hope you enjoyed the borscht. Good conversation. What more can a man ask of one dinner?" He smiled broadly.

"The borscht was delicious, Colonel. You must come again."

"Only if you promise to keep fishing," laughed Malashenko. The sound of his footsteps made clear the mud was still plentiful. Aleksandr closed the door. As he did so, he could not help but wonder if another door might be opening for him.

Chapter 3

In another four years, Dr. Aleksandr Plotnikov could see the final handwriting for the Soviet Union on the wall. He had seen the signs. By 1987, the country seemed like a decayed house barely holding together. It was then he saw clearly that the communist regime could collapse at any time. How many times must philosophers discover the same truth before people believed it? As Lord Acton once said, "Power corrupts. Absolute power corrupts absolutely."

He had to wonder. Did the politicians see the same impending disaster he saw? Were they keeping quiet about it because, like him, they did not know what to do or say about it? It was like watching a train speeding toward sure destruction and being unable to do anything.

Clones created by Plotnikov appeared grown to maturity, and beyond. The kid who was a banker looked to be in his 50s. Thanks to the special hormones, all of their bodies were those of adult males and females. How mature they really were was another matter. They were carefully trained to play the roles for which they had been created. When a very young person stopped behaving like a fifty-year-old, the punishment was so severe that the rebellion was quickly quashed. Aleksandr grimaced. The cycle would go on until someone discovered just how far into the pit of black deception the U.S.S.R. was willing to go to increase its power bases.

Aleksandr knew it was only a matter of time before someone got caught. Then there would be recriminations. People at the top would look for others to blame. They would seek those whose positions were lower on the chain of political command. It made them easy marks to suffer whatever penalties would follow. Aleksandr knew he was the perfect fall guy. He also knew Siberia held no appeal for him. The idea of appearing before a world court to defend himself for crimes against humanity haunted his dreams – or, more appropriately, nightmares.

The politburo was delighted with this success and the potential that lay beyond it. Other clones were ready to replace their originals. Over the years, more scientists had been employed. Aleksandr's staff had grown considerably. After he had worked out the cloning procedures for human organs, others were employed to clone new body parts for Russia's power elite. But this increase in personnel troubled him deeply. Secrets could not be kept when so many people knew them. Scientists were always seeking individual recognition. Some would violate any secret to achieve it.

As the need for cloned body parts increased, a plan of escape began to form in Aleksandr's mind. Only select people had access to cloned body parts, but many who did not qualify had heard of Plotnikov's secret laboratory on Sakhalin Island. Aleksandr started a very secret business on the side. Escape would be costly. He smiled grimly when he thought of this, his first entry into capitalism.

The decision to allow Dr. Plotnikov to attend at least two conferences of his choosing each year was step three for Aleksandr... step one had occurred in his dacha with Tatiana and step two over dinner with Colonel Yuri Malashenko in 1983. It was now 1987 and time to carefully plot step four and begin executing it.

The opportunity to do exactly that came unplanned... as had most of Plotnikov's life-changing successes. When in East Berlin, Alexander was not allowed to stay in hotels. He was too close to the wall and freedom. Rather, he stayed with a trusted Communist party member – Herr Doctor John Heinz. Heinz was periodically invited to social functions at the Russian Embassy in East Berlin. Being saddled with Aleksandr as a house guest did not slow Heinz down. He merely asked for and got permission to haul the scientist along with him to the party hosted by the Russians.

And that was how Aleksandr met Jake McGregor. He immediately recognized the man's face when Aleksandr saw him at a

Russian Embassy party in East Berlin. He knew McGregor was a covert agent for the Americans. A lot of other people in the room probably knew, too.

Aleksandr knew of McGregor only because, as chief scientist in his top secret laboratory, he coordinated security. He was regularly shown pictures of faces to report immediately, if seen. Malashenko told him these people were dangerous to the facility. The bulletin about Jake McGregor said he was a covert CIA intelligence operative functioning as an accountant at America's West Berlin Embassy. He had a price on his head in an amount that impressed Plotnikov.

Upon meeting Jake, Aleksandr recognized him from the intelligence bulletin photo. McGregor looked his 38 years. He was a year younger than Plotnikov, but looked a bit tired. He was slightly taller than Alex, square-shouldered, sandy-colored hair and blue eyes. It all matched the security bulletin description and photograph. The American looked a bit like the Ivy League preppy he was, Aleksandr thought, but his countenance also exhibited hardness. It started with strong, tanned hands and ended with intelligent blue eyes that added strength to an already strong face.

Aleksandr watched for the CIA agent to light a cigarette. The flyer he had seen said the man smoked Marlboro Cigarettes. He, too, pulled out a cigarette and used some of the Embassy matches, available on all of the tables, to light it. As most smokers do when they are at a public gathering, McGregor positioned himself by an ashtray. Aleksandr headed for the same ashtray and put the match he had used in it. Jake smiled at him and nodded. Aleksandr turned his back to Jake but stood almost shoulder-to-shoulder with him.

"Your name is Jake McGregor," he said softly. "Do not turn around, Mr. McGregor. The Soviets know you are not an accountant and there is a price on your head. I've seen the flyer." Alex paused. "You need to get out of here. Please give me your direct dial number at the Embassy. I will call at one o'clock tomorrow afternoon. Please answer your phone by saying: 'This is Dr. Mack'."

Jake was quiet for a full minute as he assessed the situation. He was in East Germany and had just been told there was a price on his head. He murmured his telephone number as he put out his cigarette. After a few moments, he quietly left the Russian Embassy.

The next day at one o'clock, Jake received a telephone call from the man… at least, the voice sounded the same. The man had been speaking so softly, it was hard to tell. He answered as the man had requested.

"Yes… this is Dr. Alex Plotnikov. I'm calling to make sure my food order is received for the DNA conference at the Waldorf Astoria Hotel in New York City on August 12th. You did say this is Dr. Mack?" the voice asked.

Jake shook his head and played along. "Dr. Mack… yes," he responded in Russian.

There was a quiet pause at the other end of the line before Plotnikov spoke again. "I want to make sure the forms I am completing are correct, Dr. Mack," the voice said, hesitantly. "I am to call 887-1145? The directions you sent are blurred and I cannot tell if this is a telephone or a room number at the Waldorf. It looks like 1145 is a room number…"

"It is a room number," Jake said. "I will see that you get another copy mailed to you this afternoon, Dr. Plotnikov. Do we have your correct address on file?" Jake hated these kinds of word games.

"Yes. That is what I thought. That is not my room number and so it concerned me. You have my correct address. Thank you and my apologies for any inconvenience my call may have caused," the voice said. "I look forward to seeing you in New York." The line went dead.

Jake thought about the man's words for a moment. What did they mean? It was obviously a secret message. Jake recognized 887 as the date the man told him he would be in New York City – August, 1987. It appeared the man was giving him a room number at the Waldorf… room 1145.

Jake quickly searched CIA records to try and get some idea of who Dr. Alex Plotnikov was. At least now he had a name. Jake surmised he was a scientist… why else would he be attending a DNA Conference? There was no information on file about Plotnikov.

He had to be pretty well respected to get out of the Soviet Union to attend conferences. Had Jake attracted someone who wanted to cross over the bridge from communism to capitalism? Or, was it a test to see if Jake was CIA and not a bookkeeper? Or was Russian intelligence trying to recruit him?

"So many questions, so few answers," Jake chuckled.

McGregor had been with the CIA long enough to become disgusted with the political involvement Washington thrust upon its primary international intelligence-gathering agency. He was 38 years old and had spent the last seventeen years of his life telling lies and trying to remember them. He knew there was a mole inside the agency. One of his good CIA friends had been killed in Belgium the previous month. Jack Caldwell was one of the most careful agents Jake had ever known. If someone penetrated his cover and discovered his real occupation, it was because they got the information from within the Agency. He was sure of it. Maybe this Plotnikov was part of a KGB effort to get him isolated so he could be the next dead body. He didn't think so... otherwise why would he have told Jake to leave the Embassy reception in East Germany? He could have been a sitting duck had he stayed for dinner.

As fate would have it, the next day Jake was given two weeks to return to Washington for his annual "vetting." He would take a lie detector test and talk with shrinks so the bureaucrats could decide if he was spying for the Russians or was terribly unhappy and about to do so. He had never liked shrinks. It was nothing personal. Jake just could not figure out how studying and treating the mentally ill qualified anyone to evaluate and treat the mentally healthy.

As he thought it over, Jake decided he would stay in the States for a two-week vacation he had coming. He had not had time to file a report about his encounter with the Russian at the Embassy. Though he reported being approached by an unknown who he thought was Russian and was told his cover was blown, he did not yet have enough information to file a report. Doing a little intelligence work about the man was a good way to get what he needed to do the paper work. Down deep, Jake knew the reason he was keeping quiet about the incident was because it was his identity and his life that were at risk. At this point, he didn't trust anyone at Langley.

He checked and found the Waldorf Astoria was hosting an international conference on the fusion of human cells and the possibilities of cloning human organs for replacement parts. Jake's interest was somewhat kindled by the thought of a U.S.S.R. scientist who might want to move to America. That would be a feather in his cap. The only thing he did regarding what he now thought of as "his case" was to call the Waldorf and place a reservation in the name of Dr. H. Mack. He was able to reserve room 1145 during the two-day conference.

On August 12th, Jake sat heavily disguised in the lobby of the Waldorf Astoria hotel, watching for his mysterious Russian scientist. He saw Plotnikov arrive. Two men who looked to be intelligence operatives accompanied him. Jake waited for the three men to leave the registration desk before approaching the bell captain to send a bottle of Stolchy to the Russian's room. The message was simple: "I look forward to talking with you… Dr. Mack, Room 1145."

Jake went to room 1145 and paced nervously, awaiting a phone call. He hated to be the one to initiate contact, but would if Plotnikov did not contact him soon. When the phone finally rang, he picked it up and in his best German accent said, "This is Herr Doctor Hermann Mack speaking."

There was a delay in response. Jake could hear muffled sounds. Someone else had made the call and was handing the phone to Plotnikov, he surmised.

"How do you do, Dr. Mack?" the pleasant voice asked in solid Russian. Jake was fluent in the language… he'd run the Russian intelligence desk in West Berlin for the Agency for seven years. "This is Dr. Alex Plotnikov. I was hoping we could arrange to meet so I can thank you for your gracious gift."

CIA files had given Jake access to seminar attendees. He had scanned their photos until he found one from another Eastern European nation who, with a little face doctoring, he resembled. He became that person. He slipped a waiter a hundred dollars to put "Reserved" signs for a half-hour on the two tables closest to him. No one would overhear his conversation with the Russian scientist.

Jake approached Aleksandr and they shook hands. The scientist was a cool cucumber, Jake thought. He knew it was hard to see through his disguise, and initially Aleksandr's eyes showed surprised recognition, doubt and then concern.

"It's me," Jake said with a slow smile. Aleksandr shook Jake's hand and quickly asked what they would do if the scientist whose identity Jake was borrowing showed up in the lobby.

"Not to worry. He's meeting by special invitation with the President of America's largest pharmaceutical company as we speak. But we don't have long. Would you like tea?" Jake asked.

"Yes," Aleksandr responded in a quiet, serious tone.

Jake straightened the wire-framed glasses, an exact duplicate of the pair worn by the man whose identity he had assumed. He smiled at Aleksandr. In his half-opened palm there was a scrambler. No one would listen to them.

"I want to leave the Soviet Union," Aleksandr said. "I do not, however, want your government involved in my departure. I merely need help finding a place – probably in West Berlin – to hide when the deed is done."

Aleksandr smiled. He didn't feel like smiling, but he only had a half-hour. He had to make a friend of this man. He had no idea who was watching him. He knew someone was. He raised the cup of tea to his lips, covering them. From what he understood, KGB agents read lips from across the room.

"I thought if I helped you, you might help me," he said after a long pause. "After I'm out of Soviet territory, I need a place to spend some time. Probably in West Berlin... it seems most likely. Can you – you, personally – help?"

Aleksandr Plotnikov was not the only person with a problem. Jake had one, too.

"I... I thank you for the warning. It validated what I was already sure was true. I will be leaving Berlin and returning to the States. I've already lost one friend and my name could be next. Did they show you a list... is that how you knew who I was?"

"You have a mole?" Aleksandr asked, softly.

Jake nodded. "He or she is giving names of covert American agents to your side. My name's on that list."

Plotnikov shook his head. "They showed me a picture," he said, smiling. "You are not safe on U.S.S.R. soil. That is why I picked you. You will be leaving Berlin?"

"I have already left Berlin. I have to go back to the Embassy and pick up my things, but I'm staying in the States," Jake said. "I will have to give you another name once I know who my replacement is," he finished quietly.

"No. Do not involve anyone else!" Plotnikov said decisively. The scientist's piercing brown eyes left no doubt in Jake's mind that he meant what he said.

At the time he and Plotnikov had scheduled this meeting, Jake had no idea what would transpire. He had no idea that by the time of the meeting he, Jake, would be permanently back in the United States. He would be in hiding – analyzing intelligence reports involving the Soviet Union – while the Agency tried to find its mole. He thought of the alternatives available to him.

"Okay, okay," he said to the anxious Russian. He pulled a menu in front of his face and said, "You know I have to file a report about our meeting? For now, you can remain anonymous, but you will have to have an identity to get into the country."

"I understand. You must understand that until I am safely in your country, I want no contact with anyone. Not you, not anyone," he insisted. "What I am doing is so secret... I do not want my name used – especially if you have a mole. Let me remain anonymous until I need a place to stay. Then, I will need a Passport to get into your country," he said.

Like many covert agents, Jake had started putting money in various numbered bank accounts many years ago. As the Soviet desk expert in West Berlin, he lived on the grounds of the American Embassy. There had been rumors of a CIA mole for many years, but when his very careful friend was killed, Jake was sure of it. He began keeping his own secrets and doing his own intelligence work. It was a simple matter of survival.

Using one of several false identities, Jake had rented a small apartment in a nondescript area of West Berlin over six months ago. It was his personal "safe house." He always carried the key on his person... along with directions on how to get there. He'd only been there once. If he needed the place, he would have to find it fast. It was the kind of information he could not leave in an Embassy or hotel bedroom. He removed the small, folded envelope from his pocket. The time with the Russian scientist was drawing to a close. He wanted to make sure he knew where this Aleksandr Plotnikov was nesting when word came that he had flown the coop.

"You'll find directions in the envelope," he said, bowing his head as he spoke. "It's my personal apartment and the CIA has no record of it. The rent is five-hundred Deutschmarks a month. The lease is in the name of Jake Smith, but I won't be paying the rent after the first of next month. Can you handle it?" Plotnikov smiled almost grimly and nodded. "I'll have them put the lease in your name... and I'll sign it for you. I'll use the name Alex Smith. I'll tell the landlord you're my brother. It will save them having to adver- tise. The address where you send the rent is in the envelope, too," Jake finished.

As the two stood and smilingly shook hands with one another, Jake slipped the key and directions to his West Berlin apartment into Plotnikov's hand.

"I will let you know where to reach me," Jake concluded, then turned on his heel and left.

After his conversation with Plotnikov, Jake planned to file the appropriate paper work. In fact, he was working on that write-up when the call came telling him that another of his Agency friends had been killed in London. Once again, Jake felt Plotnikov had saved his life.

Using a different name, disguise, and Passport, Jake flew to Berlin to collect his belongings. He made one last visit to the apart- ment and its landlord. He really did not take the Russian scien- tist seriously, but Jake liked the guy and felt like he owed him. If Plotnikov came to the apartment, there would be a laptop – thanks to American taxpayers – and a United States Passport in the name of Alexander Smith awaiting him. Jake left a note telling the Russian he would have to add a current photo to the Passport. It was all Jake could do... that and leave a throwaway cell phone and keep his eye on any unusual activity in the Russian sector. After that trip, Jake did not have time to worry about Aleksandr Plotnikov. When he finally did get moved and settled, he never filed a report on the scientist. He didn't know why. He just didn't do it. Perhaps it was instinct.

*****

Maybe it was luck, or perhaps fate simply caused the seminar Aleksandr was attending to be located in East Germany on the night of November 9, 1989 – six years after he cooked dinner for Colonel Yuri Malashenko... over two years after his meeting in New York with Jake McGregor. It was the night the wall that separated East and West Berlin came down.

When the opportunity presented itself for him to walk into West Germany amidst all of the celebratory confusion that night, Aleksandr stepped into the freedom of the West.

It did not take long to find an alley and disappear quietly into its velvety blackness and welcoming emptiness. Even the KGB could not keep tabs on people during such social madness.

After stepping over the shattered cement of the Berlin wall, after celebrating and appearing to be deliriously happy, he knew which train to take to get close enough to walk the rest of the way to an apartment he had never seen. It left a cold trail for the KGB. He moved quietly into the apartment for which his Swiss bank had been paying rent and utilities for the past two years. He immediately let his dark beard grow. After a week and with dark horn-rimmed glasses added, he looked quite different... a little like a 40-year old Hippie, he thought.

Aleksandr did not question why fate had placed him in East Berlin at such a fateful moment. He just accepted his good fortune.

Escaping from East Berlin was the easy part, Aleksandr knew. Now he had to get out of West Germany. It was time to get himself to the United States. He had been saving for years to get the job done... getting bank accounts opened in foreign countries under phony names had been the most difficult part of the process. He would use the American Passport McGregor had left for him and travel to Central America. Then he would make his way through Mexico to the border and enter the United States via the Rio Grande River. From what the American papers said, millions of illegals entered that way every year.

From Arizona, where he would cross into America, he would go to property he planned to purchase in the name of the Smith Family

Trust. Jake had given him a common American name. Aleksandr Plotnikov would soon be Alexander Smith – his American Passport said he already was.

He smiled, realizing just how valuable all of his visits to the sessions that trained clones to become Soviet spies had been. He knew how to blend in and look American.

Chapter 4

September 2006, she thought. It had been almost three years since disability had turned her world upside-down. In the wind, silent tears dried on her cheeks almost as quickly as they fell from her dark brown eyes. It was a young face for someone approaching 60 years of age... almost wrinkle-free. She was tall and somewhat fine-boned.

Jake watched as the breeze coming off the Cherry Creek Reservoir in Denver blew the short, brown-and-gray hair away from her face. It was combed back into a "duck's tail." She softened the style with slight curls on top.

Meredith Morgan brought her over-sized Doberman to the reservoir every day so he could run freely. The dog looked like a dull red greyhound as he stretched out, running full-speed down the deserted stretch of winter beach. He never got too far away from her before skidding to a stop, turning, and running back to her.

Jake thought of the postage-stamp sized yard behind Meredith's townhouse in southeast Denver. No wonder she came to the reservoir every day. He had heard her call the dog... knew his name was "Rusty."

When she reached the East Boat Ramp at the reservoir each day and took him out of the car, she looked carefully around for any sign of human life before removing the leash. Once Rusty knew the leash was gone, he began running with a joy that brought a smile to her lips. It was as if the dog knew he had fifteen minutes of total freedom each day and wanted to make the most of it.

She laughed as she watched Rusty chase a flock of Canada geese from the grassy knoll into the air and onto the lake. The geese honked angrily at the energetic dog for making them leave their comfortable spot on the grass and forcing them into the icy waters. Rusty had chased them to the lake's edge before slamming on his brakes and sliding to a halt. Even though she stood several feet away, sand flew into Meredith's shoes.

She called Rusty to her, put on his leash, and began walking back toward her yellow Cadillac.

Jake McGregor put the field glasses to his eyes and looked at the beach to the southeast. Water lay between the beach where Meredith exercised her dog and the sand on which the man stood. The short, swarthy man was busily picking up what appeared to be a camera, complete with tripod and long lens. He walked briskly toward a nondescript brown car.

Jake hoped he had been more careful than the other man observing Meredith... that the other man did not know of Jake's presence. He didn't think so. Jake didn't follow her to the park like the other guy. He got to the reservoir and inside the building that hid him before Meredith arrived.

Jake noticed that the man appeared on the beach the last three days within moments of Meredith's arrival. Had it not been for this intruder, he would have already called her to schedule an appointment. For three days, the man set up his tripod and camera equipment. The park grounds with the Rocky Mountains hovering in the background over the reservoir made photography a perfect cover. The guy was taking pictures, alright. But they weren't of the beautiful scenery. He was taking pictures of Meredith Morgan.

It was time to follow this mystery guest, Jake decided.

After Meredith drove away, he walked quickly to his minivan. He'd have to change cars tomorrow... just in case the other guy got more careful, more curious.

It would take a few moments for the man to get his camera equipment loaded in the car. If his timing was right, Jake would arrive at the only exit on the park's southeast side after Meredith, but ahead of Mr. X. There was a traffic signal giving access onto Parker Road. It was a very long light, he knew.

Jake got to the light first. As he approached it, he saw Meredith's yellow Cadillac turning left onto Parker Road. He breathed a sigh of relief that he hadn't pulled up behind her as she waited for the light.

He slowed, the light cycled to red and he stopped. Jake watched in his rear view mirror as a camper pulled into the left turn lane behind him, then smiled as he saw the brown car come around the exit curve and pull behind the camper.

Traffic was heavy on Parker Road. It always was, but at this time of day it was terrible. Jake turned left, towards Denver, pulled into the right lane and stayed well below the 45-mile per hour speed limit. The brown car passed him. Jake did not even turn his eyes toward the car in an effort to see the other man. There was time for that. The intruder was not going to get very far ahead of him in this traffic.

Jake's "spy" was easy to follow. It was particularly easy when the man pulled into the Holiday Inn at Interstate 225 and Parker Road. The guy was going into Jake's hotel. "How convenient," he said to himself.

The arrival of the newcomer could complicate things. Who did this guy represent? Was he an insurance investigator from her disability company? Government? The Council for International Financial Policy? The World Bank? The Federal Central Bank? If one spy was here, were others here, too? That was usually the way it worked.

There was a Doubletree Inn not too far from either Meredith's home or the reservoir. He didn't know enough about who might be at the Holiday Inn to feel safe... his opponents were not dumb. They were sloppy in this instance, but they were smart.

Better to move than take a chance. He quickly checked out of the Holiday Inn and returned to his minivan. He did not want to take a chance that comrades of the stranger might be camping there, too. One camera could mean ten cameras. One agent could mean ten agents. It could mean listening devices.

If anyone in the nation's capitol saw his face in the vicinity of Meredith Morgan so close to what he knew would be her disappearance – willingly or otherwise – his safety and hers could be compromised.

*****

While she was standing on the beach at the Cherry Creek Reservoir, a sense of not being alone swept over her a second time. It was such a subtle feeling and passed so quickly, Meredith was hardly aware of the sensation. If anyone came close, Rusty's obviously protective attitude offered a lot of comfort.

Meredith turned for one last look at the panorama before her. It was late September and the front range of the Rocky Mountains was snow-capped and served as a perfect backdrop for the beauty of the reservoir. It was set in the midst of the growing population of suburban southeast Denver. As she looked at the sun setting behind the mountains, shades varying from blue to purple shimmered between mountains in the diminished light. The closer the mountain was to Meredith, the darker the color; the further away, the lighter the blue color as the sun continued its descent in the western sky. A few stray rays of sunlight fought to stay behind and tumbled over the tops of the lower front-range peaks.

Meredith opened the door of the Cadillac. Rusty jumped happily in the back seat. He loved the car. He loved most things – with an exuberance she both respected and appreciated… and missed. Until health problems brought life as she had known it to an end, she had faced it with the same attitude... positive and exuberant about everything.

She lowered her body into the driver's seat, carefully lifting her left leg to ease the pain sideward movement always caused.

There was no doubt that she was despondent. She knew that. But she really didn't know how to be despondent, and that was almost more of a problem than the despondency.

She had a naturally positive attitude about life. It was difficult to begin thinking in terms of what she could not do. It would give priority consideration to that lifestyle rather than what her attitude said she wanted to try. It was an entirely different way of thinking. Her expectations of herself were much higher than her body's ability to cooperate. Only lately had she realized that time and experience would make her aware of what she could and could not do. The trick was in not giving up… to keep trying.

Meredith knew it sounded stupid to anyone who had not experienced a gradual loss of physical capabilities, but she understood equally well the number of times she had tried to do things – because she had always been able to do them – only to find she could not. Each time, she gained more knowledge of her limitations. It was not knowing her limits and constantly having to test herself to find them that frustrated her. It had given her a whole new insight into the problems faced by the disabled.

Meredith was finally beginning to understand that what she was experiencing was defined as "denial." She had closed the consulting company when travel and extensive close-up work became impossible for her. But having a life purpose had always been the basic motivator of her bubbling energy. Without it, she felt a tremendous sense of loss. She was adrift.

"I love thinking that life is good and I refuse to change my feeling about it… I just have to find a new means to appreciate what I have and stop placing so much emphasis on what I want," she said aloud and with feeling.

Rusty smiled his acceptance of her words.

Meredith knew she had to talk with someone… felt inherently it was required as a first step toward breaking out of what, to her, seemed a mental, physical and emotional prison. It was a good analogy, she thought. She felt locked into a lifestyle she hated. Her doctor had been right when he told her that because her stomach would not tolerate anti-inflammatory drugs or even aspirin, the only answer was to be totally sedentary. As long as she did nothing, she avoided inflaming the arthritis and, thus, avoided the pain. But doing nothing was killing her spirit.

Meredith had considered a hundred ways to re-establish some kind of productive life. She could not think of anything she could do for longer than a week before having to take to her bed to recuperate from the physical activity.

She had to talk with someone. Soon.

Chapter 5

From the time Jake met Aleksandr Plotnikov – from the time he learned the man planned to leave the U.S.S.R. without government permission and approval – Jake knew Alex knew too much. Alex also knew he knew too much. His government would never give him permission to leave. Alex was also aware that because of what he knew, he would never be safe. Thus, when he made his escape, he had to disappear.

The light that the fall of the Berlin Wall and later the failure of the Soviet economy shone on U.S.S.R. and Russian secrets would never disclose projects like the one that had haunted Alex and driven him from his homeland. The truth about the U.S.S.R. creating clones to replace powerful people would remain in the shadows forever. Through a grapevine Alex had kept open with one or two scientist friends internationally, he knew of the unexplained deaths of Russian scientists and realized what it meant. Many of the men who had worked for him at his laboratory on Sakhalin Island had met their fate. Had he stayed, he would have met his, too. Of that, he was sure. He was surprised that one or two of the scientists were still alive.

Jake began to plan his afternoon schedule when he awoke the next morning. He had to stop at the Hertz counter and change cars on the way to the reservoir. Just a precaution, but if he had seen the other guy, it was possible the other guy had seen him. He might remember his car. Today, Jake wore a hat and a business suit. His light brown, slightly graying hair was combed back rather than blowing freely in the wind. When he added dark glasses to his ensemble, Jake looked quite different than he had yesterday. He appeared more like the international businessman he was.

He and Alex had talked recently about the need to enlist Meredith Morgan's aid to help them with their project. Then Jake had received a letter from a friend who had once been the woman's business associate. The letter asked Jake to please make sure she was safe and gave a brief explanation why. Alex agreed with Jake that they needed to bring her to the ranch and explain why she might be in danger.

It was time to call home and Jake pulled his cell phone from his pocket. It would be routed via satellite.

"Jake!" Alex said. He was one of those people who, when he smiled, you could hear it in his voice. Jake heard it and smiled back.

"Interesting turn of events," Jake said briefly. "I'm not the only one on duty. It seems others are interested in the product."

Jake could hear the deep sigh.

"Well," Alex said, "we knew they might be suspicious. The fact that they are watching is no surprise. The question is, what do they intend to do, if anything? Do you know who it is?"

"No," Jake answered. "But there have been some extensive photo sessions at the reservoir. My guess is her phone has probably gone public. The question is, what do we intend to do? How great is the risk if we wait any longer?"

There was a long pause before Alex responded. "Do it," he said. "The plane will be at Centennial Airport in Arapahoe County in two hours."

"Okay," Jake responded. He quickly calculated the timing involved in this afternoon's schedule. Meredith would take the dog to the reservoir in about an hour, stay a half-hour or less, and then take fifteen minutes to get home. "It'll be about seven tonight before I can approach her at home. It will probably take an hour at the house and a half-hour to the airport. I should be at Centennial and ready to leave between 8:30 and 9:00 tonight. Tell Gil to file for an 8:45 departure," Jake said.

"Yes. I will. If he needs a brief delay, he'll be able to get it… the advantage of a more private airport than Denver International. Do you have all the information you require to get needed cooperation?"

Jake thought for a moment before responding. "She's smart, but she's still a woman confronting a stranger in her home. We don't know how much she knows… if she's seen the material, she'll understand. If not, she won't know what I'm talking about. In that event, what do you suggest?"

Alex paused for an even longer moment before responding to the question.

"I'd suggest using drugs, but I don't know what medications her doctors have her on so I hesitate to do that. Take that risk only if there is no other way." Jake could hear the stress in Alex's voice. Neither of them liked this part of the plan, but it was better than the alternative the other side had in mind for her.

"If necessary, use ether. She'll be sick for a day and may have a headache, but at least it won't conflict with any of the pills she might be taking. Appeal to her sense of logic, Jake. Everyone says it's her strong suit, so play to it. I'll tell Gil to file a medical pickup report. He will be there to fly a patient to St. Mary's Hospital in Grand Junction. Do you have the disguise?"

Jake told him he did and quickly reviewed everything to eliminate as many surprises as possible. "Okay," he said softly. "It's a go. See you tonight. Will you have transportation for us at the Walker Field airport?"

"It will be waiting for you," Alex said firmly. Jake knew that tone of voice. It meant Alex would have an ambulance at Walker Field to transport a potentially unconscious Meredith Morgan to safety.

"Later," Jake said.

Terms like "later" and other English slang puzzled Alex. He had been taught to speak proper English. After coming to America, he found he was one of the very few people who, in every day life, used it.

"Yes. Later," he said seriously.

*****

"It's not time yet, Rusty," Meredith said to the dog. He had gone up and down the basement steps twice, then walked around in circles at the bottom of the stairs, whined once or twice and now awaited her response. He wanted his exercise. He knew it was time.

After the last packing box from her recent move was unloaded, Meredith grabbed the leash and laughed at the dog's excitement as he heard her car keys jangle. She threw the mail from the packing box on her coffee table and walked across her patio to the garage.

They drove the usual Parker Road route to the Cherry Creek Reservoir and she attached the leash before letting Rusty out of the car. He walked happily at the heel position, ears up and looking at everything around him. He paused briefly, one front leg in the air... almost in a pointer position. Something in the air had caught his attention, she thought. Maybe there were some new ducks in town.

"Sorry, buddy," she said to Rusty. "There's some guy on the beach taking pictures. You won't be able to run here today. We'll walk down to the swimming beach."

They walked on the grass next to the sandy beach, the wind blowing Meredith's short hair away from her face. It was brisk today, she thought. It won't be long until old man winter makes his presence known. Denver seldom got through September without one snowstorm and a freeze.

Jake watched as Meredith and the dog walked further west toward the mountains. This deviated from the norm. Something was up. Why was the photographer suddenly on the beach she used rather than on the small island across from the East Boat Ramp? When Meredith disappeared around a curve about a half-mile away, he began to worry. He checked his watch. He'd give her five minutes, then start walking toward her along the top of the hill. He began checking the rest of his equipment... gun, dart gun and drugged insert, ether. Good grief, he couldn't use any of these things in a public place with a witness present!

Suddenly, Rusty appeared. He was running at water's edge on the beach at breakneck speed. Jake realized Meredith had taken the dog out of sight of the stranger so he could run free. With his usual exuberance, the dog had gotten around the curve before she called to get him back on the leash. When Rusty saw the stranger, he headed straight for him at full gallop.

The photographer soon realized that the dog was not paying attention to Meredith's calls and quickly reached into his pocket. As Rusty closed the distance, he pointed at the dog what looked to Jake like a gun, and fired. Rusty took three or four strides before taking one failing stride. Then he fell to the ground.

As she approached the unconscious dog, a loud, low moan escaped Meredith's lips. "No, no... he would never have hurt you!" she shouted at the man. Her worst nightmare was coming true. The man, trench coat blowing in the wind, approached her, one hand still clutching his weapon while the other disappeared into his coat pocket.

Jake stepped from the protective cover of the cinderblock hut and trotted down the grassy hill towards the beach. "Meredith!" he called out. "I'm sorry I'm late." His voice was loud and the southerly wind carried it to her ears... and to those of the stranger who stopped in his tracks. "What's happened? What's wrong with Rusty?"

Meredith's confusion increased exponentially. Who the hell was this? Did she know this man jogging across the grass to the beach towards her? He did not look familiar. She forgot about him and hurried as quickly as she could to Rusty where she knelt by his side. She put her hands on his side, but got no response. He was very still... but he was breathing. What had happened to him? She had seen the stranger's arm extended toward the dog, but had heard no gunshot. What had caused Rusty to fall? Could he have had a heart attack?

The stranger was hastily picking up his camera equipment and heading for his car, shouting that there were dog leash laws to prevent out-of-control dogs from attacking people.

Jake slowed his approach and knelt beside her. He pulled the drug dart from Rusty's chest and showed it to Meredith.

"I think one of these may have been meant for you, too, Mrs. Morgan." He put his arms under the dog... good God he was heavy! Jake lifted Rusty and said "Let me put him in my car... I have an SUV. I'll follow you home."

Meredith was stunned. Rusty had fallen because someone shot him with a drug dart? She was sure she did not know this man, but he knew her... knew Rusty's name. She shook her head, her jaw slack and her mouth slightly open. She had no idea what to say as she struggled to rise from the sandy beach.

"What do you mean a drug dart may have been meant for me? Do you have some insane idea that a man taking pictures on the beach was going to harm me?" Her brown eyes blazed with both disbelief and anger.

"He harmed your dog," was all Jake said in response. Regardless of her confusion, she followed him up the grassy knoll and watched him lay Rusty gently across the back of the SUV.

"I'll follow you home," he said. "My name is Jake McGregor and Jeffrey Lund was a very good friend of mine. He asked me to look in on you when I got to Denver. Please. Let's not waste time here... let's get Rusty home."

Jeffrey Lund was one of Meredith's really close friends. He had started his consulting career in her employ, then left to start his own company. Meredith specialized strictly in private banking. Jeff's interests leaned more to the international banking scene.

"You knew Jeffrey?" she asked.

"Yes, I did. And he gave me a message for you... a very important message. He said he sent you a packet of information. If you've read it, it will explain everything." After making Rusty as comfortable as possible, Jake closed the back of the SUV and headed for the driver's door. "Get in," he said. "I'll drive you to your car." Please Lord, he thought, keep her from arguing with me. I need to get her out of here! Now!

Meredith quietly got in the passenger side of the front seat.

"You seem to know a lot about me – my dog's name, where my car is – and you appeared out of nowhere. Why are you here? Something is wrong and I want to know what it is." Jake started the car and backed out of his parking place. "Tell me," she demanded. "What is this all about?"

"Believe it or not," he said, looking her directly in the eye, "I was planning on coming to your home tonight. I did follow you here... it just didn't seem the best place for a business conference.

I was going to follow you back home and then knock on your door. You never did say if you got the packet from Jeff. Did you?"

"I did get a rather large envelope from him. I just found it in a packing box today. I moved a couple of weeks ago... I haven't opened yet. Jeff died three weeks ago. He was killed by muggers outside his home in New York City," she said dully. "I wanted to read what he sent when I wouldn't be interrupted by Rusty's exercise schedule."

"What Jeffrey put in that envelope placed you in danger. It may be why the guy was on this beach today taking photos and shooting drugged darts into your dog. Who knows? Right now, we need to get you home as quickly as possible. We can talk there," Jake said as he pulled his car alongside hers. He was worried that the unidentified man might go to her house, try and find the document, and make a second effort at grabbing her. He might inform a partner to take up his botched assignment where he left off... to follow her home as she passed the hotel.

At least this way he would be with her when she entered the house. With Rusty out of the way, she had no protection.

She opened the garage door as the two cars approached her townhouse and turned in, leaving sufficient room for Jake to pull into the double garage beside her. Before going to the back of the SUV to check on Rusty, Jake quickly walked to the front of the garage and hit the garage door button, closing it.

"I want you to stay right here," he said. "Give me the keys to your house. I want to check it before you go in." He held out his hand, expectantly.

"Why would I give a complete stranger the keys to my house?" she asked. "For all I know, you're after what Jeff sent... you're going to grab it, or me, or both. Maybe the two of you are in cahoots. It's possible that you could be... working with him – the other guy, too. How do I know?" She looked at him, chin jutting out slightly. He had heard that she could dig her heels in pretty strongly when she felt the need.

"Look," he said, a bit exasperated. "If I wanted to harm you, I could have done so ten times by now. Why haven't I? Rusty isn't awake to protect you. I want you to lock yourself in the garage and not go anywhere until I come back for you. Where am I going to go without my car? If I take off with Rusty in the car, what do I do with him when he wakes up? Jeff said he doesn't particularly care for men… especially men with deep voices."

The jutting chin subsided a bit and her mouth softened. What he said about Rusty was true and not many people knew the dog's aversion to deep male voices. She handed him the keys. Jake entered the house and went through it with a fine tooth comb. It appeared that no one had been there. He went back to the garage.

"For the moment, let's leave Rusty here. He's going to be asleep for a while. I need for you to open Jeff's letter. Then we can talk. I promise, I mean you no harm. I am here to help you." Jake's blue eyes looked squarely into her brown ones. Her brows drew together briefly, but she walked towards the back entry to the house.

Without saying a word, she picked up Jeff's material and began reading. A frown that mirrored both surprise and shock came over her face as she quickly read the note that accompanied the contents of the packet. "Oh, my God!" she said quietly.

"That material is, I believe, why Jeff was killed. I don't believe he was mugged," Jake said quietly. "Because you were a close business associate of his, the people from whom he got the material are watching you… they have been watching you for several days now. That man at the beach has been taking pictures of you from the island south of the East Boat Ramp. I've been watching him. That is the truth," he told her firmly. "Jeff mailed me a note from the airport, too."

"Where did Jeff get this?" she asked, aghast. "And why were you watching me for the past three days?"

Jake paused. Because of the new developments, he needed to get her out of here now. He did not have time for a complicated explanation… and this would be a complicated explanation.

"Look," he said in the most sincere tone he could muster. "I was trying to make sure that what happened today didn't happen. I need to get you to safety… you and Rusty. I need you to put a few things in a suitcase and come with me. I need you to trust me."

"How can I trust you?" she asked. "I don't even know you. You show up, say you're saving me… you do help me with Rusty and that's in your favor. You say someone may want to kidnap me. You say you know Jeff and tell me about information he sent... maybe you're after what's in this packet."

"Okay," he said. "I understand your reluctance. I'd feel the same way. Let's do this. You put enough things in a suitcase to last for a week away from home. We'll get in the car and while we're driving, I'll explain what I can. If you don't believe me and don't think getting away from your home and usual habits for awhile is a good idea, we'll make some other plans. Rusty will be waking shortly and you'll have your protection back. I just want to get you to a safe place, Meredith. If it helps any, I'm a retired CIA agent. Unfortunately, there is no way for you to check that tonight, but you can check tomorrow." There was a long pause. "And, I have a copy of Jeffrey's letter in my briefcase."

There was a long silence.

"What was Jeff's address in New York City?" she asked him abruptly.

"I can't remember the exact address at this moment – I know it was on West 75th Street and that his zip code was 10022," Jake responded.

"It will take me a few minutes," she said.

"Thank you, Lord," he said under his breath.

Meredith reappeared in the small family room in less than a half-hour, bag and briefcase in hand. Hung across her arm was a tote bag with a lot of paper showing. "My important files," she said as she performed the routine things anyone does when leaving home... adjust the heat, turn off the lights, turn on the security system, and bolt lock the doors. He noted security bars across the patio door. She locked them as they left. Jake raised an eyebrow at her relatively cool demeanor.

"I'm ready," she said. "I want to check on Rusty first."

The big red dog still lay quietly, exactly where Jake had placed him. "Grab that bag of dog food, will you?" she asked.

"Sure," he replied. "You get in the car... I'm going to take a peak out of your gate before we leave. I just want a look at the lay of the land," Jake said.

She raised her eyebrows a bit, obviously impatient to hear the mystery he had promised to explain while they were driving, but she complied with his request.

"Well, there's nothing in the lane to your garage, but it's impossible to see around the corner at the end. We'll just have to take our chances. Please duck your head down," he said quietly.

Not knowing what to say, Meredith simply did as he asked.

As he headed slowly toward the general exit, Jake turned on the headlights. He quickly removed his jacket and hat, and put on his glasses. He ran his fingers through his hair, causing it to fall down around his head. He hoped he looked sufficiently different to the camera man so if he or any of his friends were waiting on the street, he would go unrecognized.

He rested his elbow on the driver's door and put the palm of his hand against his face, leaning his left cheek into his hand. He hoped he looked like a tired businessman going to a late evening meeting.

"There they are," he said quietly. "Stay down. It's the camera man's car and there are two men... sloppy work," he said.

Jake turned right onto Jewel Avenue and stopped briefly at the light on Havana. As quickly as traffic would allow, he turned into the right lane. He watched the rear view mirror to see if any other headlights appeared at the traffic signal, but saw none.

"It's okay for you to sit up, now."

"His car was really there?" she asked.

"It was," he answered soberly. "I didn't dare look in the car to see if it was the same guy, but it was the same car."

"Okay, Jake... what did you say your last name is?"

"McGregor," he answered quickly. "Jake McGregor."

"Okay, Jake McGregor," she said. "So you are a retired CIA agent who was contacted by our mutual friend, Jeffrey Lund and Jeffrey asked you to look in on me next time you were in Denver. Have I got it right so far?"

Jake smiled. She definitely was an A, B, C thinker.

"So far, yes," he said, "except what he asked me to do was protect you. He knew what he was sending would endanger you." Jake glanced over his right shoulder into the back seat. "Turn around and grab my briefcase. Jeffrey's letter is right on top. Read it."

She did as he directed and read the note from her former business associate. She could tell it had been hastily scribbled. When in a hurry, Jeffrey's handwriting was hard to read. She looked at Jake for a long moment before speaking.

"Why did he send the material to me? Why not send it to someone in his own consulting firm in New York?" She shook her head back and forth slowly as she spoke. "Why was someone willing to shoot a drugged dart into my dog – or, as you seem to think was going to happen, shoot one into me? You think it's because of Jeffrey's material?"

"The reason he sent the material to you rather than his company is because he knew they'd get an agent into his firm's offices to search for it," Jake responded. "You saw the material... you know whether it could pose a major threat to very powerful people. I can tell you that Jeffrey was spending a few days consulting for three different international banking groups in Brussels, Belgium. I believe he accidentally picked up the documents he sent to you, read them on the plane, realized how dangerous they were and dropped them into the mail before he left the airport. He was killed outside his apartment in New York the night he arrived home.

"I would like to take you someplace safe... with your permission, of course." He did not indicate that he planned to take her to safety whether or not she agreed to go. "Once you are safe, we can spend whatever time you want discussing what it all means."

"In truth, I'm not sure I want to know any more than I already do," she said.

"I can understand that, Meredith, but you have to accept the fact that as far as 'they' are concerned, you are already a threat to them and their plans." Jake paused. "They would not have been on that beach today ready to drug you and Rusty if they had no intentions of finding out just what you know. Even though the beach is pretty deserted this time of year and at this time of the evening, it was pretty dangerous work. This will not go away," Jake concluded.

Meredith sat quietly for a moment.

"I have a friend. His name is Alex. He has a ranch a short distance from Grand Junction. He has invited you to stay as long as you need," Jake told her, making his voice sound as casual as he could.

This was the critical moment, Jake knew. She was either going to cooperate, or she would show resistance. Her next response would determine whether or not he would have to use the ether in his jacket pocket.

Her brow furrowed and she was silent. Grand Junction was a short flight from Denver, on Colorado's West slope. A slight whimper and a soft thud from the back of the vehicle caused Meredith to turn in her seat to see Rusty trying to raise his head.

"We need to stop the car. Rusty is coming to and it looks like he needs help," she said.

"I can pull off of I-25 in a mile… onto Arapahoe Road. We can stop there," Jake responded with a slight smile. He knew that, in a way, this was a test to see if he would stop the car when she asked. He would comply.

It took about fifteen minutes for Rusty to be sufficiently revived to re-start their journey. His ears were down, but the big dog was awake.

As Jake turned right out of the well-lit car lot he had chosen as a place to stop, Meredith looked at him with a steady gaze.

"Are you taking me to your friend?" she asked.

"Yes," he said. "I am." He took a deep breath. "There is a private jet waiting for us at Centennial Airport," he explained. "It's a fast flight – just the other side of the mountains. Then, if you want to return to Denver, you can."

"Do you think I should return?" Meredith asked, still looking directly at him.

"I think if you return, you will be the victim of a mugging within days," Jake replied.

Meredith thought for a moment. "I'll go with you," she said. "I want you to know why I'm going." She took a deep breath before continuing.

"I don't trust you, Jake, because I don't know you. For all I know, you could be taking me to a den of thieves and international spies. But I know this: The note you have is from Jeffrey. And, only someone who actually heard from Jeff just before he died could have known that he mailed this material to me from the airport... from JFK in New York just before he was killed. If Jeff trusted you enough to send you a message from the airport telling you he mailed this stuff to me, that adds credibility to what you're saying... enough for me to at least listen to you." She paused again... a long pause this time. "After I listen, though, I will make up my own mind about where I go from there. Fair enough?"

Jake did not take his eyes from the road as he responded.

"That's fair enough."

Chapter 6

The private jet wended its way over and around Mounts Lincoln and Garfield in preparation for landing in Grand Junction. As the small jet turned into its final leg of descent to the Walker Field runway her ears popped, loudly. Rusty whined and she guessed he'd just had the same experience. He was fully awake now but was still groggy.

She looked nervously at her watch. It was getting close to 9:00 o'clock. She removed her reading glasses and began organizing the paperwork. When studied more closely, the material contained in Jeff's packet was more upsetting than she had initially thought. What were the governments and central banks of the world thinking?

She turned her attention to her fellow passenger who was sitting with an open briefcase on his lap, also doing paperwork. "You said your friend's name is Alex?"

Jake nodded and smiled. Her silence had given him the chance to get caught up on some past due tasks. He closed the briefcase and stowed it under his seat.

The pilot's voice on the intercom interrupted them both, telling them they were within five minutes of landing. It was a short flight and the time had gone by quickly.

Seatbelts were fastened. Jake reached into a bag he carried when they boarded the plane.

"We'll need for you to change your appearance just a bit," he told Meredith as he held out a wig, a scarf to tie around it, and a long black coat.

"The plane is bringing a patient to St. Mary's Hospital. Our objective is to keep you hidden. An ambulance is waiting. You won't have to go through the terminal. They have security cameras."

Meredith took the items from his hand, looking at the dark-brown, medium-length wig like it was from another world. He was good at his job. For the first time, she realized he had intended to bring her to Grand Junction whether or not Rusty had been shot with a drug dart. Otherwise, he would not have had this disguise waiting for her.

"You don't have to hurry," he said. "We'll be taxiing for a couple of minutes and we can sit here until you're comfortable. It'll take the ambulance some time to reach the plane."

As she was ready to deplane, Jake held out his hand and said, "And here are your glasses." They were horn-rimmed and quite large. The lenses were slightly darkened.

"Leave all of your things here. You're too sick to carry them. Gil will gather them up for you," he said.

"I want them with me," she said.

"Okay," Jake replied, smiling easily. "We'll sit here until Gil stops the plane and I'll ask him to pick everything up and follow us off the plane and hand it to you in the ambulance. Will that do?"

Meredith nodded, a bit uncertain. Every objection she raised was met with a logical, reasonable response. It was difficult to disagree with logic and reason.

After the ambulance departed the airport, it seemed only a few minutes before the ambulance stopped and Meredith's car door was opened by a shadowy figure.

"Quickly, Mrs. Morgan," the voice said. "If you'll get out here, Jake can return the ambulance to the company where we rented it. We'll be sitting on that bench under the tree, Jake," Alex said quietly and with a smile.

Meredith looked around. She found herself at the edge of a large parking lot adjacent to the hospital. "If I wasn't paranoid before this experience, I will be when it's over," she said, holding out her hand. "I understand that I am indebted to you for your hospitality," she said.

"And I understand that you've been a remarkably good sport about all of this," the man responded. He took her elbow with what Meredith could only describe as old world courtesy and walked her to the bench. He had a slight accent and probably was old world, she thought.

"Where's home, Alex? Warsaw? Moscow? I hear the accent, but it's very hard to detect." Her head was cocked to one side as she spoke.

"Very good, my dear," he laughed. His comfort with directness and honesty had never left him and he found himself instinctively liking this woman. "My home roots are Russian... but closer to Leningrad – St. Petersburg – than Moscow." He paused before continuing. "Oh, yes... I remember," he said quietly. "Your first husband was Polish, wasn't he? Your in-laws were from Poland? No wonder you recognize the accent!"

Meredith's eyes opened widely. She had done little to hide her background. It was, after all, part of her history. But her first marriage was a lifetime ago. There had since been a second husband, a new last name, and a totally different career. No one in the banking world knew of the tragedy of her first marriage and the baggage that went with it. She had done nothing wrong. She was not the one who went to prison. Why should she be defensive? But she knew she was.

"And you know this from what source?" she asked.

"I have a very thorough file on you. Jake and I have known for about two years – since the article you wrote for that international retail banking journal about the dangers of economic dependency on credit, and then the speech you gave in Toronto in 2003 about private banks and laundered drug money – we knew we needed to talk with you," he said. "We began researching you in 2003." He paused, taking time to look at her more closely. Her eyes were wide-set, clear and looked directly into his. "Then Jake got that note from Jeffrey over two weeks ago and we realized we needed to get you to safety. It moved our time schedule up and changed the way we introduced ourselves."

"What else do you know about me?" Her voice was crisp, but not brittle. The idea of someone digging up her past was more disconcerting than anything else. Meredith had lived a fairly public life and had few secrets.

"Let's save this conversation for a more private place," Alex said. "And I'll make you a promise. I will give you two files to read... yours and mine. It's only fair that you know as much about me as I know about you. Can we talk tomorrow?"

There was a long pause before she responded.

"How long have you been in the States?" she asked, curious.

"I arrived the year the wall came down," he said quietly.

For a few minutes Alex amused her with stories of the night he left East Berlin. A grey SUV pulled into a parking place close to where they sat and Meredith saw Jake behind the wheel.

Alex took her elbow and the two walked to the vehicle. He opened the back seat door for her. "I apologize," he said. "But you'll be less conspicuous back here. Besides, Rusty is looking for you and he's in the back seat."

They drove only a few moments before turning onto what signs said was I-70 East. They drove for about a half-hour before leaving the freeway. They turned right and wound around on a couple of dirt roads and Meredith lost interest. She was lost and had no idea which direction they were going... South, she thought.

Rusty put his head on her lap when she got in the back seat and Meredith contented herself with gently stroking his ears. He must be thirsty, she thought. She was always thirsty when recovering from anesthesia.

After using an automatic opener on three gates and driving over two or three cattle guards, they stopped in front of what appeared to be a quaint log cabin. Surely there was not enough room here to accommodate three people?

"Let's get Rusty some water," Jake said. "You both must be tired and hungry. We can take care of that."

"Indeed," Alex offered. "I hope you like a good steak, Mrs. Morgan. We raise our own range-fed beef here."

Rusty lapped thirstily at the bowl of water Jake placed in front of him. It reminded her momentarily of the unpleasantness at the Cherry Creek Reservoir. Was that just three hours ago? Maybe she just wanted to avoid thinking about it. If she did, she would also have to think about being out in the wilderness with two complete strangers.

"You can let him off the leash," Alex said. "He can't get into trouble here for miles and miles around. We'll go fix some food for all of us... including Rusty. You said you brought his dog food, Jake?"

"Sure did," Jake responded. "She wouldn't leave home without it," he chuckled.

He was a decisive guy, Meredith thought, used to controlling his own environment. That would likely cause some interesting interaction because so was she. For now, however, she did as he suggested and they entered the small cabin.

"Wow, talk about deceptive," Meredith said. "This is huge! How did you do this? Is it built into the side of a hill, or something?"

"Well, yes and no," Alex replied. "The cabin you see from the outside sits on top of a hill." They walked down several steps into a large living area. "This lower portion of the house is partially built under the bottom level of the cabin... under the hill. The walls and roof are made of old automobile tires, hay, steel beams, cement, and enough dirt was poured over it all for normal plant growth to take hold. It maintains a natural temperature of 70 degrees, summer and winter – though it needs a boost from our solar panels every now and then. This is a totally wireless property... no utilities, no telephone wires, no electric company." He paused. "Here, let me show you to your room."

The total quiet descended on Meredith in a strangely relaxing way. It was a lovely bedroom and certainly did not convey a feeling of being buried under a couple of feet of earth. The lighting was well done and the furnishings welcoming. A private bath with a walk-in shower completed her tour of the room. The far bedroom wall consisted of glass panes with a patio door in the center. Total darkness met her eyes as she observed what she thought must be intended as a patio area.

"And what happens if I open the patio doors?" she asked, smiling. She assumed the wall and the door were there simply for show... to give a greater sense of space. "Do I run into a dirt wall?"

"Well, open them and see for yourself," Alex responded. She gasped as the doors opened to a private patio with a small garden. A light came on automatically.

"You've thought of everything!" she said enthusiastically. "How do you get the flowers to grow with no sunlight? Do you use sunlamps?"

Alex laughed. "No. During daylight hours, there are glass ceiling panels... what are they called?"

"Skylights?"

"Yes. Skylights," Alex said as he put her suitcase on the end of the bed. "They are computerized and open at dawn." He paused. "If you need anything, just let me know. I'll be making a trip into town tomorrow and I can get whatever you need. Join us when you're ready."

With that, he left her alone, closing the door behind him.

Meredith took advantage of the free time to wash her face and hands and change her sweat suit for a pair of jeans and a shirt. She slid into the moccasins she had thrown into the suitcase... she lived in them.

Alex had been right about Rusty not going far. He was happily ensconced in a warm spot by the fireplace. He raised his head as she entered the room. He looked a bit forlorn and confused. She probably did, too, she thought.

Though it should have been a very strained environment for everyone, the remainder of the evening was quite comfortable. It surprised her. The conversation was light and focused on current social affairs, avoiding crisis topics. As she rose to excuse herself for the night, Alex accompanied her to the hallway where he removed two large files from a table and handed them to her.

"I promised you two files and here they are," he said. "I would recommend reading them tomorrow, but do as you choose." He smiled and wished her a good night.

Rusty immediately staked out a spot on the floor just inside of the bedroom door. He looked at her as if to promise that no uninvited guests would be coming into the room unannounced. She could not wait until morning for a shower and hoped the use of so much hot water wouldn't upset anyone else's plans.

She did as Alex had suggested and put off any reading for the morning. She was terribly curious, but she was also very tired and went to sleep almost immediately.

When Meredith wakened, she was looking into Rusty's eyes. His way of letting her know he needed to go outside was to walk to the bed, place his head on it, whine slightly and stare at her. It always worked and this time was no exception. The clock on the table next to her read 7:15 a.m.

She dressed quickly in last night's jeans and shirt, slid into her moccasins and opened the bedroom door. Rusty trotted eagerly ahead of her.

"Well," Jake called from the kitchen, "up bright and early are you? How do you like your eggs?"

"You mean that's not in my file?" she asked dryly.

"Actually, it is," he responded. "But you have your file. Sunny side up? Over medium? How?"

"Over medium," she said, smiling. "Rusty needs to go out... I noticed the security system and didn't want to set off any bells and whistles." She followed him back into the kitchen after he let the dog out. She was surprised to find a rather stout woman doing the cooking and was introduced to Nancy Waggoner.

"Did I hear you say over medium, Mrs. Morgan?" the woman asked.

"Yes... and please, call me Meredith. It's nice to meet you Mrs. Waggoner. Was it you who cooked that delicious steak I had last night? It was a wonderful meal."

"The name is Nancy... and I'm glad you liked the food. This'll just take a minute or two. Would you like some juice? You can choose between orange, tomato, or grapefruit," she said.

"Yes, please. Orange would be great."

"I'm leaving early in the morning," Jake said, "but have errands that will keep me busy all day. I won't be back until late tonight so probably won't see you until I return. I have an out-of-town appointment. I'll be back in a few days," he said quietly.

Jake's hair was combed back and he was dressed in blue jeans, cowboy boots and a blue work shirt. She really had not noticed before, but he was a very attractive man. He was too young for her, but very attractive. He had the kind of deep blue eyes women felt they could swim in, she thought. He picked up the car keys and a briefcase and turned to look at her.

"You've got a lot of heavy reading to do today. You might want to talk with Alex about any telephone calls you need to make. They can be arranged. Until Alex programs a cell phone for you, calling will be impossible." With that, he turned to the door letting Rusty in as he went out. "See ya... and I'm glad you're here," he said as he left.

After breakfast, Meredith went quickly to her bedroom and immediately turned her attention to reading the files Alex had provided. She was able to skim through her own file pretty quickly. It contained a lot of information, most of which she recognized. She was surprised at the amount of data that had been collected... her psychiatric evaluations when she became a vice president at the Denver bank were included.

So, having read the evaluations, the two men knew she would cooperate but would not compromise what she perceived to be truth. She would fight, not flee, if pushed into a corner. In fact, they knew a great deal about her. Her psych evaluations had been very thorough and accurate.

There were the headlines she had tried so hard to forget... her picture on the front page of the *Rocky Mountain News* as the wife of a police burglar. What a horrible time that had been! It had been the beginning of the rapid demise of her youth. Looking back, she realized that at 23 years of age, it had happened far too soon. She had become so serious... survival demanded it. There were copies of speeches she had given and most of the articles she had written over the years.

Now that she knew what they knew about her, it was time to investigate the mysterious Mr. Smith. The first thing she learned upon opening his file was that it was "Doctor," not "Mister." He withheld nothing from her, including his real last name... Aleksandr Plotnikov. He was a Soviet scientist... a bio-geneticist and physicist. Though the file did not go into detail, it did disclose that he had cloned human life.

Toward the back of the file was an overview of the childhood and educational years of Alex Smith nee Aleksandr Mikhail Plotnikov. It was better reading than any fiction story.

Meredith spent the entire morning going through the files. Reading them was a mixture of memory lane and a ghastly kind of horror at how her bio had been gathered methodically over decades. The same could have been said of Alex's bio. It was complete yet lacked any trace of emotion. Her own past, she recalled, was riddled with emotion. She wondered if Alex's was too. Time got away from her and before she realized it, her stomach was beginning to grumble. A gentle knock at the door brought a low but very quiet warning growl from Rusty's throat.

"It's okay, Rusty," she said, putting her hand on his choke chain as she called to her visitor to come in. The door swung open slowly and Alex's head appeared. Rusty rose to his feet, tail wagging.

"Well, it appears you've made a friend," Meredith said, smiling.

"And it is probably time to start working on making another," he replied, returning her smile. "How about some lunch?"

She glanced quickly at her watch. It was almost two o'clock in the afternoon!

"Oh my goodness!" she laughed. "No wonder I just heard my stomach growl. I would love some lunch."

It was a light meal, consisting of chicken noodle soup and a grilled cheese sandwich. She said nothing about the material in the files. She noted that Alex had placed them in a briefcase, locking it before they left her bedroom.

They sat on the large patio just outside of the living room. He explained where the ranch was located in relationship to Grand Junction to the west and the town of Parachute to the east. It was, altogether, a most relaxing time. Still, she thought, nothing meaningful was said. There was truly an eight-ton pink elephant sitting between them, and it was being assiduously avoided.

"Why am I here?" she asked. It was typical, straightforward Morgan-speak.

"I'm glad you asked... I was waiting for you to ask. You are a rather amazing woman to leave your home with a stranger, spend the night in another stranger's home out in the middle of nowhere, and not complain or demand anything," he said.

"Well, the reading material certainly kept me captivated," she responded. "Pardon me for asking, but how did a communist who is a bio-geneticist and physicist who, according to your file, has cloned a human being… how did you get from Sakhalin Island to the western slope of Colorado? Why is everything so secretive here? What are you doing that involves a not-so-retired CIA agent as a partner?"

He laughed. "They're fair questions," he said, becoming more serious. "Jeffrey said you were bright, but I did not know how much common sense you might possess. Let's start the discussion over a good martini, okay?"

"Too strong for me… but make it a glass of juice and I'll sign on for that idea."

Chapter 7

"For many years, the USSR swore that the red tide of communism would inundate the world... like a friendly flood," Alex began, looking steadily at Meredith. "The Marxist ideal of a communist utopia took hold in many of the world's governments. You're aware of this?"

Meredith hesitated before answering. Alex thought her brown eyes became a bit distant. She disliked the topic of socialism and communism because for years she had seen politicians and Supreme Court justices rewrite America's Constitution and Bill of Rights to make the nation more compatible with socialist and communist governments around the world. She did not know him well enough to answer the question honestly.

"I'm not a political person," she said slowly. "Do I know the Soviet Union was expansionary? Yes. I know what I read in the newspapers. How reliable is that?"

"Not very," he answered. "In fact, many of those who embraced the concept of the red tide are the very people who own America's largest newspapers and set policy for what will be published in them. Much of what is read around the world is slanted to support the cause of world government... a world government based on what people think is socialism but, in reality, is communism. Or perhaps, at the moment, fascist democracy would be more accurate. I'm not yet sure."

He explained how he knew that twelve men from senior management at major newspapers were hired to provide a list of the most influential newspapers in America to the most powerful special business interest groups in this country. "I know the list contained the names of 179 newspapers. That group of men and their companies bought controlling interest in the 179 papers. Later, they boiled the list down to 25 newspapers which, because of size and reputation, could control public opinion. I know that control of these papers was retained by these special interests. And, I know that is why, though your newspapers in America are interesting to read, they have little to do with facts," Alex finished.

"That can't be true!" Meredith said, her voice dripping disbelief.

"Go read your own Congressional Record, March 1959... Congressman Oscar Calloway, a Texas Democrat, stated that in 1910 wealthy bankers and industrialists bought controlling interest in 179 newspapers for the purpose of controlling public opinion in the United States. He said their holdings were reduced to 25 newspapers with the highest circulation in 1915."

He took a sip from his martini, and for what seemed to her to be a rather long moment looked her straight in the eyes. They sat in the living room with the patio doors open. It was warm, but the late afternoon air in September seemed to grow crisper every day. The dark wood floors with off-white Berber carpeting and dark cherry wood furniture and light tan leather couches and recliners was both formal and masculine. Meredith noticed the straight lines, almost geometric, in various areas as she broke eye contact and looked around the room. It was dominated by the large rock fireplace. The fireplace wall separated the living room from the hallway that led to the bedrooms.

"I run the risk of having you think me a conspiracy nut if I tell you the truth of what I see happening in the world... especially in your world of America. But I can't tell you why I am here, why you are here and why you are in danger if I don't take that risk," Alex continued.

"If you're asking me to keep an open mind, I'll do my best," she answered, returning his direct eye contact. "Jeffrey's death and the material he sent will help me keep an open mind," she offered.

"Do you know what motivated Jeffrey to take the precaution of mailing that material to you from the airport? Did he write you a personal note of any kind?" The look on Alex's face left no doubt as to his curiosity.

"There was a note and there was scribbling on the back of the manila envelope – it looked like he was doodling while he thought this all through," she replied. "I really could not understand it. There was no explanation of why he felt sufficiently threatened to take it to the airline counter and pay a ticket agent $50 to put it in the mail to me."

"How do you know that's what he did?" Alex asked.

"The ticket agent wrote a note and attached it to the package," she said quietly.

Alex suggested they finish discussing the background of how he got to this place at this point in time. He explained his perception of the history of communism and why the promise of utopia it offered to world governments was so enthusiastically – if not publicly – embraced.

Marx, he said, proposed that injustices could all be eliminated if the "bourgeoisie" – those who controlled the production of wealth – were eliminated, not just from their positions of power but eliminated from society. Those who create wealth, he told her – entrepreneurs – needed to disappear. According to Karl Marx, they were at fault for the painful poverty so apparent around the world.

"Using this as his excuse, he blamed all of the world's ills on capitalism," Alex said. "Keep in mind, Karl Marx's work was the result of the philosophies of Engels and Nietzsche, of Hegel and Rousseau. Many were atheists or agnostics who rejected belief in God." Alex went on talking about the history of communism and the reform efforts of Mikhail Gorbachev and how the failing Soviet Union made it appear that Marx and his philosophies were on their way to the junk heap of history.

"Are you saying that 1991 was not the dying gasp of communism in Russia?" Meredith asked, quietly.

"I'm suggesting that you remember the day Kruschev took off his shoe and banged it on the podium at the United Nations. I am suggesting you remember his words about how the Soviet Union would destroy America: From within and without firing a shot," Alex responded in a bit of a monotone. "My former countrymen are very persistent people," he said, smiling. "They do not give up easily once an objective has been set.

"And that brings us to why I left the Soviet Union and what I am doing in America," he continued. "If you would be so kind, I would appreciate your telling me about how and when you and Jeffrey Lund began talking about an economy dependent for its survival on the indebtedness of its government and its citizens."

He had surprised her. "How do you know about those discussions?" she asked.

"Jeffrey was in West Germany consulting for a client when he had a problem requiring the attention of the American Embassy. That is where Jake was stationed at the time as an in-house auditor. He was, of course, covert CIA. The two developed a friendship over the years… input from the international banking community is always helpful to the CIA, and that was how it started. Jake wanted information and used Jeffrey as a resource. But they became real friends in that process. They shared many thoughts and worries with one another," Alex said.

She thought for a moment about what he had just said before speaking.

"Jeffrey worked for my company back in the early 1980s," Meredith said slowly. "We worked through a lot of my research data together."

He had one of those ageless faces, she thought. She knew from his records that he had been born in 1947. Though he certainly did not look it, he was 59. He would reach his 60th birthday six months after she did. His dark hair was only slightly gray and was cut in a traditional style. When it fell over his forehead, it added a slightly boyish look to the otherwise very serious face. He looked like a very gentle person… a very gentle person in his late forties.

"I'll tell you what," he suggested. "Let's have dinner and talk about something – anything – besides the problems of the world and the material Jeffrey sent you."

Meredith agreed and rose as he held out his hand to help her from her chair. Nancy had been so quiet – or, their conversation so intense – she hadn't even realized the other woman had entered the house and was cooking in the kitchen.

Alex was as good as his word. Not one sentence passed his lips that required any deep thought. Instead, they chatted about music, art, the theater, and her penchant for gray horses.

She noticed that when he smiled, the left side of his mouth tilted slightly higher. "This," he told her, "is the end of harvest season and the fruits and vegetables here are as good as they get... speaking of which, now that the clouds have cleared, we should have an early hunter's moon outside tonight. Shall we?"

They rose from the table and walked up through the cabin to the front entrance. Rusty, glad for a call-to-nature break, joined them on the front porch.

The time spent away from the former intensity of the conversation was what they both needed. Each eased back into a relaxed frame of mind with more clarity than either of them had before the conversation began. He talked of college times in Moscow, she of having raised two children alone. When they re-entered the house, both were ready to talk about the reason fate had brought them together at this place and time.

Alex had read the book she had written about entrepreneurs and how poorly banks served their credit needs. She had to explain, however, that information about entrepreneurs – or, the "bourgeoisie," as Karl Marx called them – had come to light after Jeffrey left her company. He was unaware of the new findings. She had never published her final insights into the powerful personalities that created wealth.

Alex understood her research determined that there were two kinds of people in America. One she dubbed active/self investors, the other passive/market investors. Actives were wealth creators – those people Karl Marx so hated – and passives were wealth managers. The second group had become America's elitists... its corporate executives and government bureaucrats.

"You hold a much broader view of this total puzzle than I do, Alex," Meredith suggested. "I don't know if this will explain why Jeffrey sent the material to me, or if it will help you in putting your puzzle together, but I'll tell you what I learned.

"Actives truly are the capitalists of America... independent businesses employ about 80 percent of the working class. Did you know that? From the media attention, you'd think it was the big, multinational companies. It's not."

"So," he interjected, "if someone wanted to get rid of capitalism in America, one best first step would be to neutralize independent businesses... or, as you call them, active/self investors, right?"

"I've never really thought of it that way, but, yes, I suppose that's an accurate perception," she replied.

"And one good way to do that would be to pass legislation that encourages America's big companies to move portions of their businesses to other countries and do away with jobs in this country, right?"

"It's an assumption, but it makes sense," she said. "If the giants continue to leave the country, it will be a huge blow to small businesses everywhere in America. Much of their profit depends on providing products to the giants of industry and technology."

"And, if at the same time, government over-regulated independent businesses so they could not grow or made it costly enough to quash new business starts, what would that do to the economy?" He raised his eyebrows and his eyes were so intense as to be almost hypnotic.

"It would tip the balance of power that has always existed between independent business and big business growth in favor of big business, no doubt about it," she replied, eyebrows furrowed, a wrinkle appearing in her forehead.

"And you would have a nation of risk-averse passive elites in control of the nation's productivity, would you not? And risk-averse people – like these elitists – want government to shoulder risks so they do not have to manage it, right?" Alex felt like he was holding his breath, awaiting her answer.

"Yes," she said. "What became very clear as the research continued after Jeffrey's departure is that actives have the drive to manage risks because they have the need to control their own destinies. They are individualists who want a life independent of big companies and big government. Their dominant personality drive is control, not risk management, as we originally thought. When actives take risks, they want to be able to control them. What government has been doing is taking that control from their hands.

"Equally, passives are attracted to large corporations, partnerships, education, and government careers because they are motivated to gain sufficient power – or, access to it – to sustain their security needs. This group's primary motivator is power. So, in America we have one group that seeks control of self-destiny and another group looking for ways to gain power over the first group. That doesn't sound terribly important, but it is. It changes the entire equation and many of the assumptions in my first book on this subject."

Alex momentarily covered his face with his hands, elbows on his knees with eyes glimmering at her between spread fingers.

"I need to add one more thing," Meredith said thoughtfully. "Be careful when you use the words 'power' and 'control.' Control happens behind your own nose. Power occurs when one injects one's self behind the noses of others. People misuse these two words." She hesitated. This was one of the hard parts of the concept to explain. It sounded simple but it was not. "One person might say to another, 'you're trying to control me,' right?"

Alex nodded his assent.

"Well, you'd naturally think that the statement is a control issue. It isn't. When one person tries to control another, it is power – a negative force – not control, at work. If a person cannot force a person to do a thing, a person has no power over another. The other person cannot be controlled. This is a case of one person wanting to exercise power over another. It has nothing to do with control. The minute 'control' is used behind another person's nose, it becomes power."

Alex raised his eyebrows again. "I need to think about all of this," he said. "Can we talk again tomorrow? Jake won't be back for a day or two and I want him to get updated on our discussion. Think back to how our conversation tonight began, Meredith. I know there is a tie between the anti-God views of Karl Marx and the resultant philosophy of communism that seeped one deadly word at a time from his pen. How does destroying faith in God get tied into a package of world government? Any ideas?"

"Maybe… but why is this piece of the puzzle so important to you?"

"Somehow, removing God as a resource for people holds one of the keys to the total conspiracy… there, I've said the word. Do I believe there is a conspiracy to destroy capitalism? Yes, I do. Here in the year 2006, I see a somewhat new and well-directed effort to destroy Christianity in America. They are going about it in a different way than they did during the Russian Revolution, but the result will be the same. That's why it's so important."

"Wait a minute." Meredith rose and went to her bedroom.

She removed a document from her files and returned to the living room. "This is an article I just finished writing for an online news magazine. I think it holds the answer to part of your puzzle. I'm going to go take a shower and go to bed and, hopefully, turn my mind off and get some sleep. I suggest you read this while you sip your bedtime toddy."

Alex took the papers from her hand.

"Sleep well," he said. "I will be gone for awhile early in the morning, but will see you shortly after breakfast."

"Good night, Alex," she replied, smiling.

Alex turned an additional light on and began reading about a man named Professor Tytler… many people had mistakenly called him Tyler, but Meredith's research had found his correct name to be Tytler. He had been a professor of history at the University of Edinburgh over two hundred years ago. An email had circulated about him for years regarding comments he once made.

She noted in her References that the quote she was using had been attributed to Alexander Tytler, Alexander Tyler, Arnold Toynbee, and Lord Thomas Macaulay. Ronald Reagan had, in the *New Hampshire Manchester Leader*, attributed the quote to someone by the name of Fraser Tydler. A speech given by another well-known name in September of 1961 cited Alexis de Tocqueville as the author.

"I have chosen" her article said, "to attribute the quote to Alexander Fraser Tytler, Lord Woodhouselee, because of all the quoted sources, Tytler has what I believe to be the most credible roots."

Her article began…

"In 1787, a Scottish history professor at the University of Edinburgh said about the fall of the Athenian republic (about 300 B.C.), 'A democracy is always temporary in nature. It simply cannot exist as a permanent form of government.

"'A democracy will continue to exist up until the time that voters discover they can vote themselves generous gifts from the public treasury. From that moment on, the majority always votes for the candidates who promise the most benefits from the public treasury. The result is that every democracy will finally collapse over loose fiscal policy (which is) always followed by a dictatorship.'"

No wonder America's founding fathers had established the nation as a Republic, not a Democracy, Alex thought. Jake once told him that the word "democracy" was not a part of the American vocabulary until after World War II. He began reading again.

"The year 1787 was the time our forefathers and the thirteen states they represented wrote and adopted our Constitution and Bill of Rights. Perhaps they should have listened more closely to Professor Tytler.

"The good professor further said 'The average age of the world's greatest civilizations from the beginning of history, has been about 200 years. During those 200 years, these nations always progressed through... the following cycles:

"'From bondage to spiritual faith. From spiritual faith to great courage. From courage to liberty. From liberty to abundance. From abundance to complacency. From complacency to apathy. From apathy to dependence. From dependence back into bondage'."

That was it, Alex thought. To escape bondage required faith in something greater than mankind. Remove faith in God from the equation and the elite could put people in bondage permanently. He began reading again.

"No wonder so many people believe we are in the final days. The Athenians and Romans probably felt the same way as they watched their traditional civilizations crumble around them. We may well be in the final days. But are they the final days before the second coming of Christ? Or, are they just the final days of a 200 year old republic that politicians have turned into a democracy?

"There is no doubt we progressed from the courage of our fore-fathers to liberty and from that liberty came great abundance."

There was more, but the end of Meredith's article caught Alex's eye.

"The number of people who do not vote or just do not want to be bothered with the process of choosing candidates who serve the people rather than their party is evidence of the move from complacency to apathy.

"Too, people become apathetic when they experience changes they do not want imposed by a government they cannot control.

"Do average Americans want illegal aliens legalized? No. Did average Americans want NAFTA? No. There are a lot of 'but we don't want it' programs on the list.

"We only need to look at government programs and the number of people dependent on them – Social Security, welfare, Medicare, Medicaid, national health care, a government school system – to know we are dependent on government for our daily existence.

"As Tytler predicted we would in our 200 plus year old republic-turned-democracy, we have gone from apathy to dependency.

"If Professor Tytler's thesis is correct, the next stage for America is a return to bondage. Some people think we are there, already. In fact, we have gone far enough down the road to government dependency, it seems to me the only way to save ourselves from Tytler's predicted destiny is go back to square one: To spiritual faith and courage."

Alex sighed deeply. This did, indeed, help. For someone who viewed herself as non-political, his houseguest certainly had some meaningful insights, he thought.

"What a remarkable day," he said to himself.

Chapter 8

Meredith wakened, looked Rusty in the eye, tossed back the blankets and quickly got out of bed. She was not a morning person... but her dog was. She washed her hair and brushed her teeth and quickly dressed.

As she had drifted off to sleep the night before, other things had come to mind... like prescription medications she would soon need refilled. She needed to contact her elderly mother and stepfather. There were other personal things she had avoided for the past two days. It had been like living through a dream – or a nightmare, depending on your perspective.

She drank some juice and cooked a couple of eggs. Turning, she found a note from Alex on the kitchen table. He had driven to town and should return by the time she ate breakfast.

After eating, she suddenly felt very alone and went to the door to let Rusty in to keep her company. The dog was not in the place he had adopted as his place to lay while awaiting re-entry into the house. She called for him – somewhat tentatively – and got no response. She called louder and then loudly. There was no response.

More reality descended on her. A tinge of fright made its way into the light from her subconscious. She had become so interested in the mystery unfolding before her she had disregarded the ugly truth that she had a starring role in it. Meredith walked to her bedroom, kicked off the comfortable moccasins, and changed into walking shoes. She grabbed a jacket, input the security codes Jake had given her and opened the door, then walked out of the cabin.

She hadn't walked far when she called out for Rusty again. She smiled broadly when she heard him bark. She watched as first his head, then shoulders, then legs appeared over the steep hill. "You're dirty," was all she said to him. He seemed very happy with his status.

As she returned to the cabin, she could see a dust cloud ahead of her. A car was approaching. She was glad to see Alex when the SUV pulled into the carport beside the cabin. She had questions that needed answers... and she needed a key to the front door. Until she got answers, it would be impossible to plan for tomorrow, let alone next week.

"Been out for a walk, have you?" he asked, smiling. "It's a beautiful morning for it! I've picked up some things for you and some dog food for Rusty." He opened the back of the SUV and retrieved his purchases. When his arms were full, Meredith offered help.

They took the sacks into the kitchen and laid them on the counter.

"For one thing, here is a cell phone for you to use. I need to do some programming on it first, but I know you need to make some calls," he said in a businesslike tone. "We have our own tower here. It routes calls through a variety of locations so they can't be traced," he smiled. "The only thing I ask is that you make your calls as short as possible." He saw the serious look on her face and asked, "Is that okay?"

"We need to talk," she said. "I have to get some answers so I can make plans. I don't know why my situation hasn't frightened me before, but it's frightening me now."

"I apologize," he said.

"For what?"

"I should have realized that the events a couple of days ago when Rusty got shot and you got whisked away from what I believe was grave danger would cause some delayed trauma. I wasn't thinking. Your article was so much help to me in starting to grasp a problem I've been wrestling with, I let my priorities get out of order. I should have never left you alone."

He took her arm and they walked out onto a large deck along the west end of the cabin.

"Let me get you a glass of something... lemonade? Juice? Diet cola? Just sit for a minute while I get refreshments... get your thoughts together. I'll answer your questions, Meredith. You have nothing to fear here."

Without waiting for her response, he went inside. He quickly returned, handed her a glass of lemonade, and sat in a deck chair opposite her.

"Now, what has frightened you?" he asked.

"I feel uneasy... not knowing why I'm here or when I will be able to go home. I lived a large part of my life based on uncertainty and it is not my preferred lifestyle," she said.

"What's your first question – the one most important to you right here and right now?" he asked.

"Where am I? What is this place? What do I need to know to function here?" she responded. "When I closed the cabin door this morning, I didn't know if I'd be locked out. My pal over there was wandering around and I suddenly felt very alone." She wondered if he thought she was being childish.

"Let's answer those questions first. Come with me. Leave the lemonade... it's in the shade and we won't be gone that long." He grabbed the car keys as he walked.

Alex drove the SUV down the same path Meredith had walked less than a half-hour ago. He took a sharp left turn and stopped in front of a hill covered with small bushes and other greenery. He pressed a button on what looked like a garage door opener. The small hill opened and Alex drove inside a cool, dark building.

"Another underground building," she said in a tone of wonderment.

"This is the garage," he said. "It will hold six vehicles. Come with me for a moment," he said quietly. She couldn't tell if it was a command or a request.

They walked to the back of the garage and went down some stairs into what appeared to be an old fashioned corral. The stables were not underground. Well, she thought quickly, the actual building was underground. The front of the stables, however, looked out over the valley below. From overhead, all that would be visible was the corral. They entered the building. It was filled with horses and their heads appeared over the gates of individual stalls.

"I might as well throw them some hay and give them some water," Alex said. "It will only take a minute."

He finished his chores in short order and they walked back to the garage, got back in the SUV, backed out of the building and as he hit the remote, the earth began sliding smoothly back into place. When the two sides of the opening met, the gaping hole closed. Unless you were looking very closely, it was almost impossible to see a line indicating it was anything but a hill.

"I will make sure you have a garage opener and a key to the front door by tomorrow evening." His serious tone caused her to look at him. He looked at her and his eyes were very serious.

"I was a captive of my government when I worked on Sakhalin Island. I remember what it feels like to lack control over your life. I'm sorry I didn't think of making you more comfortable with your surroundings sooner," Alex said quietly. "We aren't through, yet."

He turned left, then turned left again and went down a steep hill. The road led back around to a cabin that looked a great deal like the one atop the main house except it was invisible from the main road. Alex stopped the car and tooted the horn. Nancy came out on the porch.

"I hear Joe isn't feeling well," he called to her. "Tell him I've fed and watered the horses. They can do without exercise for a day."

Nancy nodded her agreement, waved, and Alex quickly turned the car around and returned to the road. "That," he told her, "is the bunkhouse."

As they drove back to the house, he told her where the closest town was – DeBeque – and how to get there. "You can't drive or step on the cattle guards without using a remote control. It sets off an alarm. There's a remote in every car. You can find keys to any of the cars in the kitchen cupboard next to the stove. It's locked. I'll get you a key – to the cupboard and the house," he said.

Seated once again on the deck of the main house, Alex asked for her second most important question.

"What do you do here? Why all the secrecy? Why is all the security necessary?"

There was a long pause between her question and his answer.

"I am a bug about security," he admitted. At least a minute passed before an answer was forthcoming. "Tonight, I want you to tell me what happened that caused your husband to go to prison," he began.

Meredith quickly interrupted him. "That's not a time in my life I want to remember, let alone talk about," she said firmly but quietly.

"I want to know you, Meredith, really know you." It was apparent that both of them had a high regard for eye contact.

"I'll think about it," she responded. "And that was a very smooth way of getting around my questions, wasn't it?"

He sighed deeply. "I can make a start on the answers," he said. "It will mean doing what I'm asking you to do… share a painful time of life." He paused, put his elbows on his knees and cupped his chin on his hands.

"First, there is nothing illegal that takes place on this ranch… except me, of course. I'm illegal… but so are fifteen or twenty million other people in your country. It doesn't seem to bother anyone very much.

"Second," he told her, his voice quiet and serious, "the security is required because of my prior life. You read my file. You know it says I have cloned human life." His raised eyebrows turned the statement into a question.

"Yes. I read the comments… they were brief and really didn't say anything beyond the fact that it is something you have done."

Alex told her about his life on Sakhalin Island. "The old Soviet Union – now Russia – issued a kill-on-sight order on me. The U.S.S.R. placed those clones into positions of power in various parts of the world. Russia continues to support them. The clones have never been discovered. Russia has never stopped looking for me," he said, looking at the ground, "and you can imagine how worried they are that the rest of the world will find the depths of depravity to which they are willing to sink. It's a horrible thing."

Then he told her how he escaped and explained how he met Jake and how Jake had helped him, how the two of them had worked together almost ever since.

After he had talked for perhaps an hour – maybe more, she thought – he stopped and just looked at her.

"I have never told anyone this much… not even Jake," Alex said. "My little project has never been disclosed, Meredith, because some of the clones that I created are in powerful places within your government, your halls of justice, your major networks and they write stories for your major newspapers. The originals of some are living on Sakhalin Island in Russia.

"That is why there is such a high need for security and secrecy here," he said. "If the Russian government found me, I would not live long. I am responsible for a great deal of damage done to your country. Even worse, since coming to America and discovering that I believe in God, I consider myself the most egregious of sinners. I want to make right what I did wrong. That is what I am trying to achieve." He paused for a brief moment. "Perhaps I am seeking forgiveness, too," he said, smiling grimly.

"How about letting me fix you some lunch?" she asked.

Alex gave a tight-lipped smile and nodded his agreement. "I'll call Nancy to let her know she doesn't have to come to the house to cook today. I'm sure you and I can find enough food in the house to survive."

He looked at her rather intently for a moment.

"I'll fix your cell phone so it's available for use," he finally said, changing the subject in a not so subtle way. He frowned. "There is one other building on the property we did not visit," he said. "It is my laboratory. I will take you there sometime. I just didn't think today was the right time. I have some work to do if you'll be comfortable staying in the house alone. I'll let Rusty in the house on my way out."

The morning's tension had been eliminated for now. On the way out of the house, Alex showed her how to input the security code and release it. And, it helped Meredith to call her parents and her children.

Alex returned as darkness approached and they enjoyed their evening meal together. The conversation was light and no serious or intense subject was broached. After kitchen clean-up he poured himself a glass of wine and lit a fire. Meredith chose a glass of cranberry juice. They let the dog out and settled in for what both knew would be more serious talk.

Though it was difficult for Meredith to start her description of what life had been like when her husband was arrested and sent to prison, once begun the words poured out. It was not a subject she talked about and she was surprised at how much emotion and tension she felt being released as she spoke.

She explained how, when they started arresting police officers in the Denver police scandal of 1970, her husband had become very tense and nervous. Then, he bought a police radio for their car… a strain on their personal budget. He was always on duty, he said, and it would help him do his job better. News stories began appearing about crooked cops being arrested and he became tense during the summer months. There were hours in the early mornings when he was gone with no explanation. She was worried, and she was pregnant.

She went to the priest who had married them – the same priest who had given her lessons in the Catholic Catechism so she could be baptized in the faith. After listening to her concerns, he took her across the street to the church. She must confess, he told her, to be forgiven for lacking faith in her husband.

Three months later, when she was seven months pregnant, a woman drove through a stop sign and hit the car she was driving in the driver's door. It spun the car around. Both cars were doing thirty miles an hour and Meredith was hospitalized. They could take no x-rays below the breast because of the baby. She was in traction for several days. It was, she said, the cause of the arthritis that now was so persistently ruining her life.

She talked about carrying the baby full term but being in labor for three days before her daughter was born. She explained her decision to have natural childbirth rather than put any drugs in her system that might harm the baby. She regained her strength quickly and went home on the third day, feeling good.

A short time later, the various mental, emotional and physical tensions through which she was going caused a severe bout of post-partum depression. And then the secondary pain struck. She did not find out until thirty years later – when an x-ray of her left hip had to be taken – that her pubic bone had been broken in the accident and that was what caused the belated, almost unbearable pain. The doctor had no idea what was wrong with her and did nothing to find out. He appeared to have forgotten that she had been in a serious auto accident three months earlier and that no x-rays had been taken because of the pregnancy.

"They finally re-hospitalized me and after a few days of bed rest I felt better." She spoke softly. He could still hear the pain in her voice after all of these years.

"A month later – April 28th," she said quietly, "Ron was arrested for his part in the police burglary ring. Over fifty policemen went to prison. At that time, he told me he had caught cops breaking the law. He said when he reported the first incident he was warned to keep quiet. His sergeant – to whom he made the report – was involved, too. He said the next time he caught them, one of the guys pushed a fifty dollar bill into his pocket and that was the extent of his involvement. I found out later that wasn't true. He had met them in a deserted park in the wee, dark hours of the night where they pulled a safe from the back of a police car and put it in the back of our Rambler station wagon."

She talked about how they had been painting their small living room when the police came to arrest him... how her mother and stepfather had come over that first night Ron was in the city jail and finished the painting. They put up the money for Ron's bail by putting a second deed of trust on their home.

"Ron's fabulously close family in New York were more concerned that his mother not find out about what had happened than they were in helping to deal with the problems Ron had created," she said quietly. "It was okay for my mother to mortgage her home and to see her daughter's face all over the front page for something he had done, but it just wouldn't do for his mother to find out what her son had done," Meredith said. Her tone of voice indicated the disdain she felt for such behavior.

"Did he plead guilty?" Alex asked.

"Not at first," she answered. "We hired two attorneys and it created some big legal bills – which Ron's sister mostly paid. But Ron knew we couldn't afford a trial and he signed statements confessing to involvement in four burglaries. For years I believed the threat of a trial we couldn't afford was the reason he signed statements of guilt. I have no idea if he was really involved in all of the charges to which he pled guilty. I now wonder if he was involved in more. He was named by other policemen in four cases. That wasn't a reliable source. They were all talking and giving as many names to the District Attorney as they could to negotiate lighter sentences for themselves," she said. "No one, and I mean no one, really knows the whole truth about that entire mess."

"So he went to prison," Alex said.

"Yes, in February of 1971. That, in turn, started another – but different – set of problems. It was thirty-five years ago, but, when I talk about it, it still feels like yesterday. My skin crawls," she said, rubbing her arms. She continued, slowly.

She'd had to have surgery from complications caused by the pregnancy and auto accident. Meredith had managed to get a job as a legal secretary and worked for a criminal lawyer, a former judge who was defending police officers charged in the scandal. He also sat on the governor's police crime task force.

"One day, the bottom drawer of the filing cabinet was unlocked. It had all of the task force minutes in it. I made copies."

She explained how she had no sick leave from her job and when she had to have surgery it was done on a Friday. She snuck out of the hospital on Sunday night so she could return to work on Monday. She was the total support for her one- and two-year-old infants. Her parents had divorced after 32 years of marriage, and her mother had just remarried. No one had the financial resources – or the time – to help.

"I collapsed two weeks later... pneumonia. I had to go on welfare. It was only three months, but it was awful." There was a heavy sadness in her voice as she spoke.

She talked about the telephone calls in the middle of the night, the stalking by guys who called to say her husband really wasn't guilty and who would admit to his crimes in return for sexual favors.

"I cannot imagine what it must have been like for you," he said. "I did know about the two times you went on welfare. Your government keeps good records. A couple of years ago, I recall reading about you being one of the highest paid women in the country. That's certainly going from one end of the spectrum to the other."

"Yep... the second welfare experience came after I divorced Ron. I got pneumonia again. Only two months that time... the last time, fortunately."

Alex refilled her glass with more cranberry juice.

"You stayed with your husband for several years after he came home, didn't you?" Alex asked.

"Five years... until he got off of parole," she answered. "Prison destroyed him, Alex. In those days, I had no idea of what happened to cops who were sent to prison. As I said, I was pretty naïve. After five years, though, I decided the example of manhood he was setting was not what I wanted for my son or daughter.

"I divorced Ron, got a job as director of public relations for a camera company, remarried George Morgan three years later, divorced him after two years – we got along fine, but he wanted my children to live in the basement of the house and not bother him in the main living area. I decided then that I would never remarry until my kids were grown... Ron had deserted us, sent no support and, as a result, was out of our lives. My kids and I were a family."

Meredith completed her narrative by explaining how, when she divorced George Morgan, she had gone to work for Denver's largest bank, was blessed with rapid upward mobility. Ten years later, she resigned her vice-presidency to start her own consulting company.

"You started the first private bank in America," he said.

"Yes... credit-driven, wealth-creation private banking. There are two kinds of private banking: Wealth creation and wealth management."

"And that's when you got into the study of the personality traits of affluent people?"

"Yes... and right now I'm so tired if I don't go to bed I'm going to fall asleep right here on the couch," she said, yawning sleepily. "We'd better let Rusty in for the night."

Alex held out his arm, sending a signal to stay seated. "I have one more question. It won't take much time."

"Okay," she replied. "Shoot."

"What impacted you most?"

She raised her face to the ceiling, brows furrowed. "I've asked myself that question a hundred times – at least a hundred times," she said. "I'm not sure I know the answer. How raw and unjust justice is? How the church deserted me in my hour of need? But I realized my faith in God got stronger about that time. So, I lost the church and found God.

"It cost me my youth. I used to be very carefree and had a great sense of humor. Recovering from all the scars and raising two children alone took those things away," she said. "I couldn't afford them any more." She looked him directly in the eye as she spoke the words. "I had to grow up overnight to keep a family together and survive. The thing that hurt most? I think it was facing the truth about someone I loved and in whose hands I had placed my future."

Alex nodded and rose from his chair. "We're going to be good friends, Meredith," he said softly.

"Good night, friend" she said sleepily and walked slowly to her room.

Chapter 9

When Meredith left her room a half hour after rising, the house was quiet. She could hear Nancy working in the kitchen and knew she was not alone.

"Hi," she greeted Nancy. "I heard voices. Is Jake back?"

"Yes, Jake is home." Nancy grinned back at her.

Meredith sliced a banana for the oatmeal Nancy was cooking and by the time she finished her meal, Jake and Alex returned.

"My God!" she cried when she saw Jake's face. "What happened to you?"

"Good morning to you, too, Mrs. Morgan," he laughed. "Don't make me smile. It hurts. I'm fine, I'm fine. It looks worse than it really is. I just had more of an adventure than I planned," Jake said.

She looked first at one, then the other of them, obviously puzzled. A concerned frown appeared on her face.

"You need to see a doctor," Meredith told him. "And speaking of the medical profession and before I forget again, I need some prescriptions filled. How do we do that?"

"Give them to me. I'm on my way to the doctor. I'll take care of it," Jake said.

"So, what's happening? Is there anything I can do to help, Jake?" His face looked like he had run into a brick wall. "I used to be pretty good with cotton balls and iodine."

"Thanks, but it's been cleaned. The doc wants an x-ray." She could tell he was nervous and looked curiously at Alex for some kind of explanation. Eventually, Jake launched into a story that caused her breath to catch in her throat.

Even with the jagged cut and serious bruising across his left eye and cheek, Jake was so animated, his eyes so alive, it injected a positive energy into the room. He asked if she was at all familiar with Sakhalin Island.

"I know what Anton Chekov said about it," she replied.

"Chekov?" Alex asked. At one time he had been a fan of the famous Russian playwright and author. "What did he say?"

"He called Sakhalin Island 'Siberia's Siberia… inescapable.' In Chekhov's time, it was a dump for convicts. He called it 'utter hell.'"

"Well, that's where I've been," Jake told her. "I went to Alex's 'Twin Village'." He gave a half-grin. "It didn't feel like utter hell until I hit the wall…" he joked.

"Twin Village?" she echoed.

"Where they raised the older clones," Alex explained in a monotone.

"So you've been to Russia… on Sakhalin Island?" she asked Jake, somewhat aghast. "At the Twin Village… where the older clones are kept?"

"Yes," Jake replied. "The older clones and the old originals live there."

"What do you mean, 'the old originals?'"

Alex explained to her that when they had aged the clones sufficiently to replace the people from whom they were created, the person who had been cloned was kidnapped and taken to Sakhalin Island. They were taken to Alex's former laboratory at the Twin Village. The original was at first secretly observed by his clone. Then the two interacted. After a brief time the clone replaced the original who was then held prisoner.

"Frankly, I thought – feared – the originals would be killed. Evidently the government kept some of them alive for 'just in case' scenarios."

"What's a 'just in case' scenario?" Meredith asked, puzzled.

"Just in case a clone fell in love with the power that came with replacing the original and forgot his loyalty to the Motherland," Jake said. "Or, if a problem arose and they needed to get an answer from the real thing."

"Oh," she responded, feeling at a loss. "And?" she asked.

"And Jake was able to bring four original Americans home in the wee hours of the morning," Alex said, a smile spreading across his usually serious face. "Of course, he got a little chopped up in the process, but this is a major victory for our side! I'd say 'well worth the price,' but it's not my face."

"I'll say it for you, then," Jake laughed. "It was worth the price." He winced at the pain the use of facial muscles caused and they all laughed.

Alex cleared his throat, a bit nervously she thought. "The upshot of all this is that we have four new houseguests," he told her.

The house became totally quiet very suddenly.

"You mean...?"

"Yes, Meredith. I mean our guests now lodged in the bunkhouse with Joe and Nancy are the Chairman of the Federal Central Bank, Arthur Redbridge, the senator from New York, John Martinez, the very well-known radio talk show host Jerold Joseph Branchman, and His Honor the Supreme Court Justice, Avery Scott."

"You're kidding," she said. They both shook their heads in the negative. "And what are you going to do with them?" she asked, her tone reflecting her skepticism.

"We're going to put them back into the positions of power from which they were snatched, once we reeducate them," Jake said. She could feel him watching her closely for a reaction to the news.

"What do you mean, 'reeducate'?" The term gave her a bit of a chill. It sounded Orwellian.

"They have been totally out of touch with the news of the world for years now. They need to be brought up to date. We have computer disks with news stories involving each of them – rather, their clones. They need to know what decisions have been made through the years in their names by the clones who replaced them," Alex said.

"Right now," Jake interjected, "they are having their first American-cooked meal in many years. They are taking warm showers and being allowed to shave and dress in clean Fruit of the Looms, Levis, and casual shirts."

After Jake left to see the doctor, Meredith dug the truth from Alex about the dangers Jake had faced on his 'adventure.' She learned that Jake had flown to Fairbanks, Alaska, where he met three other men he had hired for the project. One was Brett Radov, Jake's former CIA partner. Radov still worked for the CIA. The second man was Bill Bryant, an ex-Seal. Bob Grosvernor was retired Special Forces, Army Intelligence. All spoke fairly fluent Russian.

Jake's "crew" flew to Sapporo, Japan, on the island of Hokkaido. From there, they caught a train for Wakkanai. It was from there the shipping container in which they hid was shipped by a ferry that plied the Pérouse Straits between Wakkanai on Hokkaido and Cape Krilon on Sakhalin. The ferry carried them across the 27 miles of international waters between Wakkanai and Cape Krilon… between Japanese and Russian territory.

Jake's captives had been forced to wear what Alex referred to as "blind glasses" to prevent them from seeing where they were being taken. The glasses looked just like those worn by people immediately after cataract surgery. However, they were designed to prevent any light from reaching the iris of the eye. Alex told her what the "blind glasses" were made of, but she forgot the name before they finished talking.

Meredith was shocked to find that Jake and his friendly mercenaries had hidden in a shipping container for several hours. She was even more shocked to hear that their powerful new houseguests had been drugged and unceremoniously thrown on the floor of that same container for almost a full day.

The shipping container had a hidden compartment with a false wall. The front of the container was loaded with computer supplies and equipment being shipped to the Oceanographic Institute on Sakhalin Island. Their container had been placed on a rail car in Wakkanai. It was then loaded onto a ferry going to Sakhalin Island. After arriving at the island, the rail car was attached to a narrow-gauge train that stopped near the Twin Village. It was then attached to a slow-moving subway that pulled the rail car through an underground tunnel to a rail yard where the cars were unloaded.

Jake's face, Alex told her, got injured as they hopped out of the slow-moving rail car into a widened area in the tunnel, about four miles from the rail yard. He'd had to run alongside the train car to re-close the container's secret entry... and that's when he literally ran into a stone wall.

Like most women, Meredith abhorred violence. She did not understand it. The details of what Jake had been through made her shudder inwardly and she asked no more questions. She would ask Jake about it later.

Meredith was, however, compelled to ask Alex about where the money came from to pay for all the expenses of waging this personal war he had obviously shouldered. The question had been on her mind since her arrival at the ranch.

"Come with me for a moment," he suggested. "It will be easier to explain to you in my laboratory."

When she hesitated, he laughed softly.

"Don't worry, Meredith. There is nothing there that will shock you... I'm out of the cloning business. Well, almost..." he said and then laughed at her raised eyebrows.

"Do you realize what a huge black market business there is for donated organs?" he asked.

She looked at him rather blankly. "You mean – like, livers and kidneys?"

"And hearts, eyes... yes, that's exactly what I mean," he replied. "I've been able to grow cloned organs since the mid-1980s. Yes... I did that, too, Meredith."

Alex continued his story as he drove her to another hidden building. He explained how he had been able to earn money on the side in the U.S.S.R. by secretly cloning organs for important people who were not approved by the government to receive them. He did not tell her many of them were organized crime figures. "It provided enough money to buy this place and get me to this country, but not enough to live like we do... private planes, security and other technology." He hesitated for a moment. "We run a few cattle; have some hogs and chickens, grow some fruit and vegetables."

He told her that when Jake retired from the CIA, he had come to stay with Alex who, at that time, had been able to afford to build only the main house. He once again admitted he was a bit psychotic regarding security.

One of Jake's closest friends, he explained, was an extremely wealthy man who had insulted his liver sufficiently to cause cirrhosis. It became life threatening. At Jake's request, Alex agreed to help. He cloned a liver for the man who lived another three years free of pain before dying of a heart attack.

"No one was more surprised than Jake and I to learn that, prior to his death, the man had liquidated most of his assets and paid the taxes on the money. He put it in a safe place only Jake would know. He sent a note telling Jake to go there when he died. The man and his wife never had children. I think Jake filled that role for them. The man's wife predeceased him – died of cancer – and he created a Trust into which his oil profits flowed. He made Jake the trustee when he became disabled or died. Jake took care of him for the last year of his life. He left me enough monthly income from the Trust to remain comfortably on the ranch whether I earn a living, or not.

"So, my money bought the place and Jake and I both pay for the upkeep and the security. Gil works for Jake and Jake pays for his airplane, trips to Russia and other places in the world. He owns businesses in several countries. Jake is a very wealthy man," Alex finished, grinning.

They arrived at another small cabin on top of a hill. It was built like the others… small structure at the front, steps down into an area built into the back of a large hill. "I want to take a sample of your blood," he said quietly.

"What?" The word exploded from her mouth.

"Put your suspicions to rest, Meredith. I merely want to analyze your blood and do a complete workup. I want to test your blood gasses, your vitamin and hormone levels. I want to see if your blood tells us why you are so sensitive to anti-inflammatory drugs, and examine your history to see if we can reverse the damage being caused by your arthritis."

Alex folded his arms – very much as her personal physician of many years would do – and awaited her reply.

"You don't intend to grow me a new liver, or anything?" she asked, suspiciously.

He laughed. "Not unless you need one!" He paused. "I've never seen you take a drink…"

"I had my day with it," she said, somewhat seriously. "I came close to the edge. It was one of the escape mechanisms I used for several years." She paused. "What about all of my other health problems?"

"In addition to the arthritis?"

She nodded.

"What are they?" Alex asked.

"Let's see…" she said, putting her index finger under her chin. "Stress-induced asthma, fibromyalgia, thyroid disease, arthritic gout, high cholesterol, high blood pressure…"

"Make me a list," he interrupted her, frowning. She laughed.

"I'm not joking," he said. "Make me a list."

She rolled up her sleeve and looked away as he drew several vials of blood from her arm.

"Hopefully," he said, "I will be able to create a vitamin and hormone program designed for your body and its needs," he said.

"Yes, doctor," she responded dryly. "Do you have any written information about this stuff?" she asked.

"As a matter of fact…" he handed her two books.

"Two books?" Meredith asked, grinning at him.

"The first is about DNA and how it can be used to improve your health. The author is so obscure, his name doesn't even appear in the book," Alex said, grinning at Meredith.

"You wrote it?" she asked.

Alex merely nodded his response. "It can't be published, but I wanted to leave what I have learned behind." There was a pause as he handed her the first book. "The second is about how medicine is practiced in America. I think you will find it… enlightening. Did you know that cancer is a trillion dollar business here?" Before she could respond, he continued. "And Jake wants to talk with you about getting everything out of your town home. You only packed for a week," he said. His direct eye contact had a way of disconcerting her when broaching topics about which she was insecure.

"We can talk tonight," she said, returning the stare.

After a long pause, he said "You have become disabled by various health problems, but I think you are in denial," he said somewhat casually.

There was a long silence.

"I don't know how to answer that because, in some ways, I agree with you. It's a newly-discovered reality for me. I haven't come to grips with it yet," she said sadly.

"Jake has had a friend watching your town home. It's been invaded," Alex said softly. "That's why he wants to get everything out. He thinks your records have been ransacked and you may have lost data from your computer."

She had heard that people whose homes were burglarized felt invaded.

"Tell Jake to do what he needs to do," Meredith said in response to his unasked question. Her voice sounded tightly controlled. "I'm not worried about what was on the computer. I put everything on flash drives while I was packing to leave, that first night. I've got everything with me… everything, that is, except a home."

"Let's go," he said. Before she could say anything, he took her arm and led her back to the SUV and drove toward the main house. When he stopped the vehicle in front of the house, he did not turn off the engine, but hopped out of the car to open her door and let her out. He saw her to the front door of the cabin where Rusty greeted them.

"I need to go over to Joe's and Nancy's and visit our guests," Alex said quietly. "Will you be okay alone?"

She nodded and smiled, closing the door behind her. It would be a good chance to make a couple of short telephone calls and do some reading.

Chapter 10

As they moved into October, days were shorter. Darkness and cold descended earlier. The days, however, were still warm.

As evening approached, the sun turned rock formations surrounding the back patio into shades of gold and pink with intermittent and dramatic slashes of black shadows.

Meredith sat, taking turns looking at the natural beauty that surrounded her and then reading one of the books Alex had given her. It contained nothing beautiful. Its ugliness almost made her ill.

The book described the giant size of the business of medicine… specifically, the business of cancer treatment.

She had never really thought about it before. Diseases and the treatment of them, however, had become a major part of the American economy… one-seventh of the economy, to be exact. It could not be eliminated from the gross domestic product without dire consequences to the economy. As Alex had said, cancer treatment was a trillion dollar "business."

When Meredith thought of the trauma and pain caused by this disease, the thought that effective treatments for cancer were being withheld from what was supposed to be a capitalist, open marketplace made her shudder.

Meredith was 60 years old. She remembered when President Richard Nixon declared a "War on Cancer" in 1971. According to this book, a century ago, one in 33 people got cancer. Today, her book said, "it is more than one in three and growing." Talk about a war lost, she thought. The book stated that when effective treatments for cancer from natural substances rather than chemically created drugs were found, it was impossible to patent them because they were natural substances. Without a patent, corporate profits went unprotected.

Expert researchers and cancer physicians had written this book. They believed that a powerful conglomerate of government agencies, international drug companies, oil companies, and major cancer treatment hospitals put profits before a cure. They did not want the public to learn about and pursue effective alternatives. The text even documented who provided the funds to start the national cancer charities, research groups and other organizations upon which people relied for progress in treating this dread disease.

Those in control of research were, it appeared, those whose profits came from the pharmaceutical industry. Those who profited from treating cancer with chemicals rather than natural substances, diet and other alternatives held the reins of power. Why had Alex given her this book to read, she wondered? She had barely asked herself the question when she heard the patio door slide back and Alex stepped onto the wooden deck.

"Learning about the integrity of our health care system, are you?" he asked, smiling.

"I think this is one of the most fascinatingly disgusting things I've ever read," she said quietly. "You're a scientist. Do you believe it?"

"I believe most of it," he responded. "Tell me, Meredith, what would happen to America's October 2006 economy if, at this moment in time, a trillion dollars from the gross domestic product was removed?"

"Removed how?" she asked, frowning a bit.

"Let's say a cure for cancer was found and expensive chemotherapy was no longer needed. What would happen?"

She closed the book before speaking. "The economy, which is sitting precipitously close to a cliff, would probably go over the edge," she said without hesitation. "But there would be a cost for the new treatment. It would replace the cost of chemotherapy."

Alex smiled. "What if the cure was a natural substance you could grow in your own garden or purchase inexpensively at your local vitamin store?"

She sighed deeply. "Then we're back to the economy sliding over a cliff," she said quietly.

"It's a money and power game," Alex said in a disgusted tone of voice. "Believe it or not, I've seen worse done in the name of political power."

They both looked at the natural beauty surrounding them for a moment. The leaves on aspen trees were just beginning to turn yellow. Soon, the valley would look like a yellow paint can in the sky had been turned upside down to cover the quaking aspen leaves.

"How can such ugliness exist in a world filled with this kind of beauty?" she asked him, sighing pensively.

He looked at her for a long moment before responding. "For every positive on earth, there is a negative of equal strength in opposition to it. It is how nature achieves balance." His voice was very quiet.

Alex walked to the redwood ledge surrounding the patio. It was a big drop into a rocky canyon from this deck. The ledge banister was supported by slats that were four feet high and sturdy. He said nothing for a full minute. "What do you think they can do about it?" he asked her quietly. "What can you do about it? Why are you allowing it to continue? You are 'the people.' I am 'the people.' Whatever the government is, we are. Whatever big business is, we are. So tell me. What are you going to do now that you know this situation exists?"

His question almost stunned her into silence, but not quite. "Me? What can a person with no medical credentials do to correct corruption resulting in a holocaust of cancer victims?"

Alex held his chin between his index finger and thumb, rubbing it slowly, bringing the two fingers together at the cleft in his chin, and then moving them apart. He was deep in thought. "But you do have banking credentials," he said softly.

"Yes," she said tightly, "but what has that got to do with the existence of cancer cures being hidden by large pharmaceutical companies and the need for someone to do something about it?"

Alex chuckled. "Sometimes," he said, "it is easier to see the mote in the other person's eye – the other industry's eye. Take a look at the mote in your own industry's eye. When the big failure comes – and, it will – are you going to wonder what you might have done about it had you thought ahead to soup kitchens, people on the streets freezing to death, and children with no food? You have read the material Jeffrey sent. You read the newspapers and see the plans in the pages Jeffrey sent being implemented."

He walked around the outside rim of the patio and her eyes tracked him. The wind blew his hair in his eyes and he quickly brushed it out of his face.

Meredith knew she had been suckered. He got her to make moralistic comments about the evils of the pharmaceutical industry. He then pointed out that her industry was no less evil.

"And what do you think I should do about it?" she asked with a frown. She was angry and it showed.

"What I think is, if we can get you healthy again, you can go to Washington with the real Arthur Redbridge and help him turn things around," Alex said quietly.

She looked at him as if he were a crazy man. Then anger flared in her eyes.

"So that's it! That's how I figure into your little plot! You brought me here to use me as a tool in your Superman fight to save my country… a country you helped destroy!"

She seethed silently for a moment. "How much danger was I really in at my Denver home, Alex?"

Meredith rose and walked as quickly as she could into the house where she almost tripped over Jake. He had a clean, white bandage covering half of his face. He was on his knees in front of the fireplace, laying wood for a night fire. He rose and put his hand gently on her arm.

"I can answer that, Meredith," he said, serious blue eyes staring directly into hers. His face was lean and angular and… honest. The bandage covering half of it added emphasis to his words. "Your packet from Jeffrey would have been found and you would have been killed," he said in a deadly serious tone of voice. "I had your things moved into storage today. Your mail and telephone messages are on your bed. Among those documents is a real estate contract to sell your townhouse. Sign it, or not… as you choose. But we need to talk first. All three of us need to talk." He slid the patio door open and told Alex to bring the discussion into the house.

She looked at the fire and was grateful not only for the warmth it projected, but for the crackling sound of the wood being burned. Its gentle noise somehow broke through the wall of anger she had allowed Alex to motivate. Was she angry at him? Or was she angry that her health made it impossible to do anything to help protect America's banks? She was unsure of the answer.

The living room was comfortably furnished with a tan leather couch with recliners at each end. Placed around it were matching recliner chairs, scattered in a semi-circle. Though it was obviously a room furnished by and for men and could use some feminine touches to soften it around the edges, it was thoroughly western and very comfortable.

"Well," Alex said as he walked rapidly from the hallway to the living room, "let's get started. We'll have to stop when Nancy comes to fix dinner."

Meredith's hands came up in front of her chest, palms facing out, fingers pointed to the ceiling and spread apart. "Wait just a minute, please. I don't want to have a conversation that ends up limiting my mobility." She looked seriously from one man to the other. "In other words, after we talk I don't want to hear the words: 'But you can't leave now… you know too much.' Am I clear?"

"I told you she was bitingly honest," Jake said to Alex without looking at him.

"You did, indeed," Alex answered, smiling. "Did you sweep the room?"

There was still tension present from the earlier conflict and all of them could feel it.

"I did… and it's clean. Would you please sit over here, Meredith?" Jake's voice was a bit monotone for him. He was staying out of the battle between the other two participants in the conversation.

"That little metal object on the coffee table scrambles anything we say in this room," Jake said quietly but with a rather wistful smile on his face.

The professionalism of the security, and the quiet way in which it was handled, never ceased to surprise her. Just when she thought she knew all about it, something new was added.

"Okay," Alex began. "First, if I insulted you by suggesting you should become part of our 'Superman plot to save your country,' I apologize." He hesitated long enough to reach for some chips and dip. Then he sipped his Scotch.

Meredith heard the underlying coolness in his tone. "No," she responded. "You caught me off guard. I don't know you well, Alex, but I know you well enough to believe you caught me off guard on purpose. I don't think you do things that are ill-considered without weighing the outcome." She paused, looking at him with a raised eyebrow. When she saw him inhale to answer her, she began speaking again before he could respond.

"It angered me and I over-reacted. I'm probably the one who owes you an apology. As Jake said, if the two of you hadn't gotten me out of Denver, I would probably have been murdered in my sleep."

Like two cats trying to decide whether they would do battle, they eyed one another for a moment.

"Can we put that to rest for now?" he asked her with a bit of a crooked grin on his face. She only nodded her response. Alex had to suppress a smile because she so accurately identified his motives. He *had* weighed the outcome of his comments and had known it would lead to further discussion. And that was what he wanted.

"Good," Alex said. He turned to his friend. "Jake?"

"Basically, what Jeffrey's material suggests," Jake began, "is that the Federal Central Bank will continue overprinting our currency, causing it to be devalued. Central banks holding America's debt internationally will drop the dollar as the international currency of trade. They will begin to trade in euros – or, some other currency or basket of currencies. We require so much credit internationally to finance our trade deficit this switch in currencies will cause investment in America's devalued dollar to diminish. The cost of basic living will inflate dramatically. I have it on good authority that a major oil service company will move its headquarters to Dubai next summer. And, I've heard that Dubai wants to back its currency, the Dirham, with gold. The lost jobs and devalued dollar Jeffrey predicted are happening. Am I right?"

Meredith took a slow sip from her cranberry juice before answering. "You could be right. Equally, you could be wrong. The Fed is reacting as it always does to hold the cost of money down. Was the resultant inflation planned… part of a conspiracy scheme to achieve some other long-term objective? Or, is it just a normal economic cycle being fought the way the Fed always fights credit crunches… by printing money? Inflation always results when too much money is created, so it was no surprise."

Alex's eyebrows furrowed as he listened. He'd had the same argument with himself and with Jake. "What do you think?"

She sighed deeply and closed her eyes for just a moment. "The lost jobs are highly indicative that Jeffrey was right. So, too, is the ongoing overprinting of our currency and the predictable devaluation of the dollar. The euro has been steadily rising in value against the U.S. dollar. Several factors make me think you may not be crazy. Something of a conspiracy could be occurring."

Meredith launched into an explanation of symptoms of something drastically wrong with normal banking practices as far back as 1990, sixteen years earlier. She quoted statistics regarding consumer home refinancing and low interest rates.

"The Fed kept lowering the cost of money and interest rates on new mortgages fell and kept falling," she said with a frown. "It motivated people to refinance their homes. While they were refinancing, they decided to increase what they owed on the old mortgage to take advantage of investment opportunities, or improve their homes, or take an international vacation – send kids to college – a lot of things. People used the equity in their homes like a personal ATM." She told them that if it had stopped there, she would have thought it was just stupidity. But, it did not stop. The reduced mortgage rates created a tremendous demand for new homes.

"Suddenly, people who couldn't afford to buy new homes could buy them. Credit standards were lowered and the 'sub-prime mortgage market' was born. The cost of real estate inflated quickly, as a result. The inflated value of resold older homes quickly followed." She paused for a moment to give Jake and Alex a chance to add to what she was saying or to ask a question if they wanted. They were quiet and so she continued.

She explained how rates were lowered again and people were once again encouraged to borrow against the ongoing inflated value of their homes. Equity lines of credit were born as a means to motivate people to borrow. At one time, she informed them, she wondered where all of the new mortgage companies that were springing up all over the country had come from and, even more significant, where they got their funding.

"I even wondered if making low-cost mortgages available was a new way to launder drug money." She stopped long enough to take a sip of her juice.

"Bear in mind, the only real value of a home is the actual equity in the property, not the estimated market value. That can drop fifty percent in one day. The inflationary result of all of the above is a real estate bubble. People argue about whether it exists, but it definitely exists. These events motivated many Americans to go into debt up to their eyeballs," she said.

Jake and Alex sat, waiting for her to continue. When she did not, Jake smiled and asked her if she was going to leave them hanging, or if she was going to tell them the end of the story.

"Look," she said. "I'm a career banker turned consultant. I'm not into plots and conspiracies. I almost hate to say where I believe the end of the story goes from here."

"Make an exception," Jake said, chuckling at her reticence. He reached for some cheese and crackers and offered some to her. She smiled, refused his offer, and continued her story.

She told them that when the real estate bubble burst, all of those inflated home values would drop by thirty or forty percent, or more. People would owe more on their homes than they were worth. Then, she told them, the Adjusted Rate Mortgages that made low-cost loans possible would be re-set. People would be unable to make the increased payments.

"Those whose property is undervalued and those who cannot afford the payments will walk away. At the same time, the value of the dollar sinks into the basement so the cost of living – and I mean necessities like rent, food, clothing and the means to stay warm or cool – inflates to high levels. So homeowners walk away from mortgages on properties that are valued at less than their loans on them. After the housing bubble bursts, you will see credit card delinquencies increase, then car loan payments will either be late – or, not made at all."

"What happens next?" Alex asked quietly.

"There would be a banking and mortgage banking crisis. There are a lot of investments that would get hit... derivatives and commercial paper are two that come to mind. Most banks do not hold onto mortgages for the term of the loan these days. They sell them. But they sell them to people who include them in derivative investments... and many banks are heavily invested in derivatives. My broker friends tell me that some assets contained in mortgage-based derivatives have been leveraged one hundred times, so only 1/100th of collateral value actually exists in some real estate-based derivatives."

She pointed to the blatant disregard for personal property rights – the taking of private property owned by real people from all walks of life. She pointed out that the law and recent Supreme Court decisions made it possible for cities or counties to take private property, sell it to a hotel chain or a developer, and make money both on the sale and increased taxes.

"That validates the idea that government does not hold the ownership of private property in high regard," she concluded.

The silence in the room once again became unbearably loud.

"That concept was not included in Jeffrey's material," Jake said.

"No," Meredith replied. "Jeffrey's material discusses the international aspects of what the economic collapse of this country will have on the rest of the world and how the collapse will be brought about. It discusses the United States, Canada and Mexico and possibly some of the Central American nations forming a single trade zone... as European nations did when they created the European Union. Some call it 'the North American Union.' It discusses something called 'the Amero,' a new currency for Canada, America and Mexico."

"And what do you think about that?" Alex asked.

"I can tell you that a member of executive management at one of my client banks in Canada told me sixteen years ago that one of their vaults held a common currency for Mexico, Canada, and America. He told me it was just a matter of time before it would come out of the vault."

The sound of the front door opening caused Jake to put his finger in front of his lips with one hand while the other hand swept the scrambling device into his palm before Nancy entered the room.

"Well, this looks cozy," she said smiling. "Do we have any preferences for dinner tonight?"

Chapter 11

After dinner, Alex threw some wood on the fire and each of them returned to the seats they had occupied before Nancy's arrival. Once again, Jake's jamming equipment appeared and Alex excused himself to switch computer and telephone connections. They awaited his return before starting the conversation again.

"Okay, Meredith," Jake said. "How does all of what you said tie in with Jeffrey's data?"

She sat thinking with her eyes closed for a moment before answering. "I'm not sure I know," she responded, brown eyes opening as she spoke. "Jeffrey understood international banking. I don't. I'm sure there's a link but I'm not sure I can find it. I've been thinking about what I said earlier. America, Canada, and Mexico merging into a single trade zone is very possible. A failed currency could open that door. Say the dollar crashes. They hold out the opportunity to join the dollar with their stronger currencies to repair the Continent economically.

"To further answer your question, Jake," Meredith said softly, "some of Jeffrey's data was projected far into the future. It dealt with the impact on the U.S. dollar and on the total economy if the euro replaces the U.S. 'petrodollar' – if oil should be traded in petroeuros rather than petrodollars," she suggested. "I don't understand the projections because they go way, way over any previously made. For Jeffrey's data to be accurate, just about everyone would have to start using euros to buy oil, or some currency other than dollars," she finished, frowning.

Jake and Alex looked quickly at one another and the silence following Meredith's proclamation extended to a full minute. Meredith could not help thinking just how quiet it was here when no one was talking. Living in a city brought with it the accompanying sounds of people and traffic.

"What if a middle-eastern nation opened an oil exchange that accepted petroeuros rather than petrodollars? If nations can pay for oil with dollars that are decreasing in value or another currency that's increasing in value, they will choose the other, right?" Jake asked, sounding almost hesitant.

"Well, Iran attempted to start an oil bourse in 2005, didn't it?" she asked. "I wish I had the expertise to answer the question, Jake. I don't." She stopped talking, waiting for comments. When none came she told them that the huge trade deficit, combined with an over-spending Congress, meant the U.S. dollar was dependent for its survival on being the international currency for trade.

"Will there be a new oil exchange? The way you asked the question…" her voice drifted off into uncertainty. Jake rose from his chair, walked to the stereo and turned it up a bit.

"Do I know anything for sure at this point?" Jake asked. "No. Have I heard something that makes the projections you got from Jeffrey sound possible? Yes. I have. I've heard that a Middle East Oil Bourse is in the works for 2008… maybe headquartered in Dubai, not Iran," he said. "Further, I hear the bourse will be supported by Russia, China, Germany and France plus a few other nations."

"I know Russia and China are talking about buying oil with something other than dollars – about mid-year 2008," Alex added. When Meredith looked at him with expectation, all he said was "Don't ask."

"Same here," Jake added. "Don't ask."

"So," she asked hesitantly, "Dubai, you say, is going to seriously visit the idea of creating an exchange to sell Middle-Eastern oil with something other than petrodollars?"

Neither Jake nor Alex answered her question which, she figured, in itself was an answer.

Another long silence followed. Alex rose and walked slowly back and forth, arms clasped behind his back, his tall frame bent somewhat forward. The fire crackled quietly.

Jake finished his glass of wine and put the empty glass on the table by the scrambling equipment. He cleared his throat. "If the currency collapses and people are hungry, there would be anarchy. Such a solution – a new currency – would be welcomed with open arms. You must admit it is a far better alternative than joblessness, homelessness, and starvation. When you boil down the information Jeffrey sent, isn't that really what it's saying?" he asked.

"When you boil Jeffrey's information down," Meredith replied, a bit sarcastically, "it is saying that for one world government to be put in place, America must be brought to third world status. That's what Jeffrey's information says."

"With the European nations already melded into one economic zone… hmmm. Once North America follows in their path, one world government is on third base waiting for a hit to get them to home plate," Alex said, shaking his head.

Jake and Alex quickly entered a discussion. They talked about America's reluctance to protect the border with Mexico and the tendency of Supreme Court justices to interpret the Constitution on the basis of international rather than sovereign American law.

"What you've said makes so much sense it's scary," Jake said. "Start with the currency," he requested, sitting down once again by his scrambler and indicating by the movement of his arm that he wanted her to re-take her seat.

"What you have said is that our currency is backed by nothing… not like it used to be with gold, right? And those who are supposed to manage our money supply are causing our currency to go down the tubes… possibly on purpose. Right?"

"Right," she responded. "Think of it this way, Jake. President Herbert Hoover once said that a gold-backed currency was the only thing protecting Americans from greedy politicians and corporations. The value of the dollar was tied to the cost of an ounce of gold – 40 percent of each dollar's value had to be backed by gold. I'm not saying the gold standard is the answer to everything. In fact, with today's big currency numbers, there might not be enough gold in the world to make it work. Some standard that defines the value of our currency is needed, though. Maybe precious metals combined with productivity and gross domestic product is the answer. We have to have a standard."

"That makes sense," he responded. "So, how does a person protect personal assets? If all of the dangers we've discussed occur and the economy slips over the edge, what do people do? Buy gold? Invest in foreign currencies? How... what does a person do?"

It was the age-old dilemma of people caught in the political struggle for power, she thought to herself. Americans had become so nonchalant about their freedom... cavalier, she realized. They assumed they would always be free people. They would never have to do much to continue waking up that way every morning. How naïve!

"I'm a banker, not an investment analyst. But the first thing I would advise is get out of debt... no mortgage, no anything you can't afford to pay immediately. I'd advise you to keep your money in several different banks. In your case, Jake, I'd have a personal bank account in every country where you own a business and in a few other places with strong currencies. Remember, when the savings and loans crashed, all most people could get out of their accounts regardless of how large the balance was $900 per month. They were insured by the FSLIC – the Federal Savings and Loan Insurance Corporation – just like banks are insured by the FDIC.

"They promise to insure your money, but they do not promise to give it to you in a lump sum, do they? Their general practice is to pay all deposit accounts immediately, but in a crisis they can take the time they need to give you what you once had deposited in a bank. It didn't matter how much money people in Ohio had in their failed savings and loan accounts. All they could get was $900 a month. In some cases, that went on for a rather long time. I'd tell you to buy some bags of silver coins from the U.S. Mint – or, a good coin dealer. And yes, foreign currency is a good way to hedge your bets. But when the housing bubble bursts and consumer spending in America goes down, it will have a negative impact on most economies in other countries because they have invested heavily in the American mortgage markets. Some of those international banks will fail. They may be the first to fail, in fact. That, in turn, can have a negative impact on their currencies. Be careful which country's currency you choose – and which banks."

"But how can a person find out which banks are heavily invested in mortgage-based derivatives?" Jake asked.

"You ask the bank's Chief Financial Officer, in writing," she told him. Her tone was sad as she told Jake she wished buying gold was the answer. "It isn't that simple. Back in the 1930s, Franklin Roosevelt insisted that people take their privately held gold, silver and gold certificates to their banks... turn it all over to the government. The banks were to deliver all of the gold coins and bullion and gold certificates the people surrendered to the Treasury.

"Roosevelt thought – or, said he thought – that if enough gold was taken from the people who owned it, the Fed's paper money could be saved," she told them in a disgusted tone of voice.

"And it was saved... wasn't it?" Alex asked, unsure of his own statement.

"Before the birth of the Federal Central Bank in 1913, the dollar was worth one-hundred cents when valued against an ounce of gold. Today that same dollar is worth four cents. If you call that 'saving the American dollar,' you could say the Fed's paper money was saved."

Alex looked at her, shook his head and then lowered his eyes. "I read your article about the cycles through which successful democracies live. I realize we are not only being attacked as a financial empire. All of the strengths that have made America a great society are being attacked... the innate sense of moral law is being destroyed. Education, law, faith, the family – everything," Alex said quietly. "The cycles quoted in your article say people begin in poverty and slavery, gain courage from faith, fight for freedom and gain it, become wealthy and spoiled, then become complacent and slide, once again, back into slavery."

"Can I read that article?" Jake asked.

Alex walked to the end table on which he kept a black folder containing a reading file. He removed the sheets of paper Meredith had given him a few days earlier and handed them to Jake.

Meredith yawned, stretching her arms high above her head.

"I'd say your yawn says precisely where we are at this point," Alex commented in a somewhat lighter tone. "I think we're all too tired to carry such heavy subjects any further. It's time for bed."

Alex looked at her for a long moment. "Can you put together an overview and do a presentation for us? We could record it so Jake and I could use it as reference material."

"That's a great idea," Jake concurred quickly.

Thinking of her earlier over-reaction to Alex's request for help, she was going to try and make a joke. She thought better of it. She smiled and nodded her head at both of them. She immediately saw an opportunity. She could get input from them, too. She was curious, and decided to make them a deal.

"I'll do a presentation if you guys will. Talk on topics involving your areas of expertise… Sure." She rose slowly. The pain in her back had returned but she walked carefully towards her bedroom. Too much time in front of the computer today, she realized. She could not see the wince on Alex's face as he watched her leave the room.

After she left, Jake shook his head. "She's going to be crippled soon if you can't help her," he told Alex. His friend merely looked at him and nodded his agreement.

*****

"I have a dog out here who wants to know where his companion is. Can he come in?" Jake's muted voice came from the hallway. She could tell he was smiling. She looked at her watch and realized she had been working for close to an hour. Meredith had risen early to start working on an outline for the presentation she had agreed to give. She quickly saved her work onto a CD and opened the bedroom door.

"Hi, Jake," she said in a business-like tone. "Come on, Rusty Man, let's see if we can find some breakfast around this place." With that she walked past Jake and headed for the kitchen.

Breakfast conversation focused on football. Meredith had Jake and Alex laughing out loud with her story about how she had started the National Football League Fans Union (NFLFU) when the players and their union decided to declare a strike in September of 1982.

"I announced the formation of the NFLFU from the end zone by the South stands at the old Mile High Stadium," she said. "I was amazed at how many members of the media showed up to cover the story. It made front-page news all over the country."

"You really referred to it as the NFLFU?" Jake asked, laughing.

"Indeed I did... and I have to admit, it was an accurate reflection of how I felt at the time. The media, however, showed better taste than I. They didn't use the reference on television. The newspapers used it, though. I even wrote a song about the NFLFU and had it recorded by an artist in London," she finished.

"What happened to this union... this NFLFU?" asked Alex.

"We had a lot of people respond with membership funds," she said. "It required time to get the word out... time I didn't have. It could have worked if a full-time person had been running and promoting it... but I had a job. I did, however, write letters to all the team owners offering to negotiate on behalf of football fans. I think it scared them a bit. I got some great letters back," she said, reminiscing.

She rose from the table and carried her dishes to the sink, rinsed them and put them in the dishwasher. She smiled at each of the men as she passed them to go back to her bedroom and the computer.

"Meredith, wait a minute," Alex called after her. She stopped and he caught up with her at the bottom of the entryway.

"I need you to come with me to the lab for a few minutes," he said, looking directly at her, his eyes serious. "I have created a DNA-based medication that will help slow the progress of your arthritis. If you're lucky, it could even stop it in its tracks – cure some of the damage already done. It could help with some of the other health problems, too," he added.

Her eyes were downcast as he spoke but Alex saw the doubt in them when she began to talk. "Medication?" she asked. "I haven't had much luck with drugs, Alex. My body just doesn't seem to react well to them. Something to do with my immune system..."

"Well, this concoction is not a pharmaceutical drug. It uses your own DNA, with some natural substances added. If I've done my job properly, your body will heal itself. Maybe you should talk with Jake."

Thoughts quickly flashed through her mind... scenes in doctors' offices where hope in a vial with a needle or from a bottle of pills was extended. After dozens of attempts and failures, she hated the thought of letting her hopes go up again.

"I... I'm not sure, Alex. Maybe I should talk with Jake," she responded.

"Trust him, Meredith," the quiet but firm tone of Jake's voice came from behind her. "I'll go with you to the lab if you want. If you can get rid of that pain with every step you take, isn't it worth an IV?"

"IV?" she asked, eyes widening. "I thought we were talking about a shot in the arm or the butt," she said.

"Meredith," Jake began, "when I came here I was bloated from the drugs they put me on to treat my osteoarthritis. They don't treat diseases anymore. They treat symptoms. I was 50 pounds over-weight, first from Cortisone, then from non-steroidal anti-inflammatory drugs. Yet, here I am today... all because I trusted this guy. Hell, anyone who can duplicate Arthur Redbridge can't be all bad!" Jake laughed and she smiled at him. "One thing is for sure. Whatever Alex has concocted won't harm you," he finished.

Meredith's head bowed and she looked at the floor for a long moment before turning towards the front door. So much of what Jake said rang a bell in her mind. She was going through many of the same symptoms and problems he had experienced.

"Okay," she said. "If we're going to do it, let's get it over with."

Alex smiled at her as he secured the IV needle with tape. He told her to relax in the recliner, to close her eyes and just think pleasant thoughts. He turned on some oldies music and she did as she was told. At the end of the procedure, she felt no differently than she had when it began.

"Am I going to have to lie down or anything when I get back to my room?" she asked as Alex slipped the needle from her arm.

"Nope... just go right back to work." He helped her rise from the chair and then turned towards the door. "I've got some work to do but will drop you off and then see you back at the house for lunch, okay?"

She nodded.

Rusty jumped from the car as they pulled in front of the cabin and Jake opened the door.

"I see you survived the ordeal," he said, reaching out an arm and placing it around her shoulders, giving her a quick hug. Alex wasn't aware of the small frown that crossed his features as he watched the closeness between the two friends.

"If you're anything like me, you will feel nothing for several days. Then you'll begin to feel a tiny bit stronger every day and your aches and pains will go away... very, very slowly, but they will go away." He gave her a broad grin as he finished the sentence.

Meredith thought about his words for a moment and then turned towards her bedroom and the computer that awaited her. No one had to knock on her door to tell her it was time to eat. She saved her data on a CD and walked to the kitchen to help Nancy make lunch.

"You're very quiet after such a perky morning," Jake said.

"Perky?" she asked, grinning widely.

"Perky is the right word," he said. Jake had changed into a dark blue shirt made from some kind of light velveteen fabric. It made his blue eyes the dominant feature of his face. He was certainly handsome, she thought, wondering how two such good-looking male specimens had stayed single for so long. She raised her eyebrows as she thought of one possibility.

"Serious work makes for serious minds, I guess," she answered, smiling back at him.

"You've been locked up all day with your computer. How are you coming along?" Alex asked as he took the final bite of his sandwich.

"I was hoping we would be able to start our presentations by Saturday afternoon, but is five days enough time for you guys? I know you're busy with other things..."

"It may be a day early for me," Alex responded.

"Sunday afternoon it is then," Jake said stoically.

"Monday," Alex said. "Sunday, we rest."

"I guess I'd better get to work, too," Jake said. "You do have a way of stirring up activity, don't you?" With that, Jake left the table and headed for his computer.

Rusty followed her down the hallway as Meredith returned to work and began inserting disks, looking for research data to fill-in her outline. By tomorrow, Jake had told her, he would have her "hooked up" and it would be possible for her to find new research resources on the Internet.

The question is, Meredith thought, how do you find this snake's head so you can chop it off?

Chapter 12

Meredith was surprised to find Arthur Redbridge seated in the room where she, Jake and Alex were to give their overviews on topics about which each had some special insight. Alex noted the slightly raised eyebrows when she first spotted Redbridge and smiled broadly at her.

"I think you'll be pleasantly surprised," Alex said quietly in her ear. His scent and the warmth of his breath in her ear raised a few hairs on the back of her neck. It startled her. Sexual desire was an emotion she thought long buried, but that was what it felt like for ever so brief a moment. She quickly took a seat at the table where lined yellow pads and pens had been made available for notes.

She looked around the office for a moment. It was a larger room than she had thought on her first visit. Jake and Alex each had a desk. The ceiling skylights had off-white curtains covering them. Because the office was in the stable, her nose was happily assaulted by the scent of horses.

"Dr. Redbridge and I have been meeting for several days," Alex began. "We have been reviewing not only what the Federal Central Bank has been up to since his kidnapping, but also the information you provided, Meredith. He asked if he could make some comments today, and I agreed. Unless either of you have objections?"

Meredith and Jake both shook their heads.

"Good," Alex commented in an enthusiastic yet businesslike tone of voice. "Then Dr. Redbridge, the floor is yours."

Redbridge rose, pulled some notes from his pocket and placed them on the table.

"In a long-ago article I wrote, you and I once discussed America's need to return to a gold standard, Mrs. Morgan," Redbridge began. "That need is even greater today than it was when we spoke of it."

Jake and Alex were surprised by the personal reference. Meredith had not mentioned that she knew the Chairman of the Federal Central Bank personally. She could feel their eyes on her for a brief time. So she knew the Chairman of the Fed. So what?

"Government," Redbridge continued, "steals from the people very subtly through inflation caused by overprinting the nation's currency. That has certainly been done by my pretender!"

Redbridge began on that note and continued speaking for over an hour. His words were properly authoritative. This was a man who had been there and done that. He knew what he was talking about and did not have to guess or estimate. He believed the only way to save the economy was to gradually put its currency back on gold and silver mediums of exchange balanced with a productivity formula. He was saying that the Federal Central Bank had to be gotten rid of or the nation would have a depression that made the 1920s and 1930s look like child's play.

"I will close by making one point very clear. I became Chairman of the Federal Central Bank during President Rory McCoy's administration. I put together a plan for the President on how to gradually do away with America's fiat currency and the fractional-reserve banking system that supports it. We need to stabilize our currency, not destabilize it. Its value must increase with productivity rather than from the decision of a group of bankers who profit from the nation's over-spending and debt. Aside from the United States Congress, no one person or group of people is constitutionally entitled to oversee our currency and its policies.

"Before I was able to present my plan to the President, I was kidnapped and replaced with a clone or twin or whatever. I am angry that my imitator's policies have taken this nation so close to bankruptcy. I am shamed that it has been done in my name. Frankly, such behavior supports not only old, but new enemies, as well." He looked directly at Alex as he made the comment. His final words

120

were said quietly but the force of a strong personality rode the waves of his voice.

"He is right about the need to make sure the Federal Central Bank is brought down in a controlled manner," Meredith said quietly after Redbridge was taken from the room. "If it happens too quickly, it will cause anarchy and tyranny. Terror will rule the day." She looked at the serious faces of Jake and Alex sitting across the table from her and knew that they, too, had a sense of concern.

She flipped the "on" button of the overhead machine and words appeared on the computer screens in front of Jake and Alex. Both looked at the bottom, right corner of each of their screens to see who was being quoted. It was Woodrow Wilson, in 1913, from his book, *The New Freedom*. The quote spoke of a power so great that it frightened the biggest men in American commerce and manufacturing. They were, Wilson said, afraid to speak "above their breath" when condemning that power.

Meredith said nothing. She merely gave them time to read the overhead, then removed it and replaced it with another. Again, Jake's and Alex's eyes looked to see who was being quoted. This time it was Franklin Delano Roosevelt in a November 21, 1933 letter to Colonel Edward Mandell House, advisor to President Woodrow Wilson.

"The real truth of the matter is, as you and I know that a financial element in the larger centers has owned the Government ever since the days of Andrew Jackson."

Again, Meredith quietly removed the overhead without making any comment.

"For today's discussion, I wanted to quote what history says are the most powerful men in America openly saying there are hidden forces, not elected legislators, running things. Perhaps my reasons seek to assure the three of us that we are neither crazy nor paranoid. Eisenhower made such comments, too… as did other presidents and vice presidents. Ike warned us of the military-industrial complex in the 1950s, but we didn't listen."

Her first handout was about five pages. "I'm not going to spend time on it, but I put together an overview of secret and other societies perceived by a lot of Americans to be 'the financial element' or the 'hidden power' about which Roosevelt and Wilson spoke." The list she handed them included the more known or suspected groups. It also included some of the lesser-known elitist groups that wanted one world government.

"I did my research and kept trying to apply what I saw in Jeffrey's material to what I found. There is no other explanation that fits the material as well as a conspiracy for one-world government."

She suggested to the men that they take a moment to scan the pages she handed them, and they did. The room was so quiet that she feared the lack of sound would make her ears hurt. Truly, she thought, silence is deafening.

"This is quite good," Jake said. "Are you sure you aren't CIA?"

She laughed. "I'm very sure."

She put a new overhead on the lighted surface and their computer screens were covered with an organizational chart. It showed the Bank of International Settlements (BIS) at the top with the International Monetary Fund (IMF) and the World Bank just under it. She briefly reminded her two listeners that Jeffrey's papers had come from the hands of someone attending a meeting sponsored by an international banking group.

"BIS is run by an elite group that represents central banks around the world. It controls most of the money transferred from one central bank to another in almost every country in the world. It's a very secretive group, and the members are almost exclusively the heads of the world's central banks – like the Federal Central Bank. One member is our own cloned Arthur Redbridge. It is the pinnacle of 'good old boys' clubs."

She gave them another handout. "This flow chart will give you an idea about each of these groups and what their organizational responsibilities are in the international banking community. There's no sense in boring you with all of the details now… it's just important that you know how the international financial world and banks that support it are structured. This gives a brief explanation of how the flow of money between all of these banks and our own Federal Central Bank – and the central banks in other countries – occurs."

Meredith briefly explained that the defined purpose of the International Monetary Fund was that of establishing currency cooperation internationally. The IMF's stated intent was to make the balance of international payments more easily managed.

"The IMF is believed by some to support the establishment of a global economy with a global government," she said. "A single world currency would no doubt make their job much easier. The organization's history is a bit colorful. The primary thing to remember about the International Monetary Fund is that the price to become a member is giving up some national monetary sovereignty. All members – which are the central banks of the world – must agree to let the IMF control certain parts of their nation's economic behavior."

When she paused, Alex asked, "What do you mean by 'colorful history'?"

"Well, according to some history books, at one point a world currency was a stated objective of the IMF. And, one of the early heads of the IMF is thought by many to have been a top Soviet spy."

"Just cannot trust those Russians," Alex said.

'I'll keep that in mind in our future financial transactions," she said, chuckling.

She then explained the meaning of the fiat currency system in place in almost all nations of the world. "Fiat currency is a piece of paper with nothing like gold or silver backing it," she said. "We've already discussed this so I won't waste time on it... in short it is dollar bills printed at the whim of bankers and politicians. Our paper currency used to be a promissory note from the government, but it no longer is. Depending on circumstances in a nation using a fiat currency, it may – or may not – be of any value at all. It is worth noting that fiat currencies have been attempted many times over hundreds of years all over the world. They have always failed."

She once again began using overheads that appeared on their computer screens. "Our founding fathers took honest weights and measures and a stable currency very seriously." She told them they might want to keep in mind that the Mint Act of 1792 said "...if any of the gold or silver coins which shall be struck or coined at the said mint shall be debased or made worse as to the proportion of fine gold or fine silver therein contained... every such officer or person who shall commit any or either of the said offences, shall be deemed guilty of felony, and shall suffer death."

"They knew just how important maintaining the value of our currency is." She handed each of them a single page. "This tells you which coins The Act authorized production of and the amount of gold or silver required for them to be legal tender."

"Wait a minute," Jake interrupted her. "Has this Mint Act of 1792 ever been amended to reflect the reduced amount of gold or silver or copper now being used in our coins?"

"I found changes, Jake, but nothing specific," Meredith responded. "The Mint Act clearly specifies the amount of silver to be used in half-dollars, quarters, dimes and nickels and that amount of silver is no longer being used. I know that."

Meredith then began explaining the history of gold... about why and how it was used. She drew a colorful picture of pre-paper money history... about how heavy gold and silver coins became when a person carried very many and how unsafe it was.

"Goldsmiths became early bankers," she said. "They had the most secure means – the strongest safes – to hold gold for people." She told them she did not want to waste time talking about history she was sure they probably knew, but wanted to make clear where the concept of fractional-reserve banking began.

"The goldsmiths of the 1600s made loans. At first, they loaned their own money. Then, they noticed that they always had better than eighty percent of the gold people gave them for safekeeping in their vaults.

"The goldsmiths began lending up to eighty percent of the gold that belonged to their depositors, charging loan interest rates while loaning other people's money. The goldsmiths knew and our bankers know that as long as from ten to thirty percent of customer deposits are available, there is always sufficient cash to give clients the money they need when they need or want it... unless there is a run on the bank. If banks miscalculate, they can go to the Fed and borrow what they need. In essence, that is how fractional-reserve banking started in modern America, today... the goldsmiths of yesteryear.

"Today, when a bank makes a loan of $100,000, of that amount $90,000 becomes newly created money – from thin air. The ninety thousand dollars increases the money supply…"

Jake interrupted her. "Is the ten percent withheld because of reserve requirements made on checking account deposits?"

"Exactly right," Meredith replied. "If not for the reserve requirement, the bank would create one hundred percent new money when it made a loan. Banks must hold their reserves as vault cash or keep them on deposit at a Federal Central Bank."

Jake laughed and shook his head. "I see… they're doing what the goldsmiths did back in the 1600s… but the goldsmiths weren't creating new money that devalued their currency every time they made a loan. You're saying that's what they do today."

"Well, Jake, that is how banks create money from thin air. That's what Arthur Redbridge meant when he referred to fractional-reserve banking. It is in place in almost every nation in the world. I want you to think about what's happening in today's America. We talked a few nights ago about how Americans are going into debt, willy-nilly. Why do you think it was made so easy for people to borrow the equity out of their homes? Because every loan made creates new money for Washington to spend – or, tax. Why were people who really did not qualify for home loans given those loans? Because every loan made created more money for the government to spend and is controlled by the banking industry… a system governed by the Federal Central Bank."

She explained that good economic theory said the supply of money controlled the cost of goods. If the supply of goods and services expanded at a three percent rate annually, that is the how much the supply of money should increase.

"Unfortunately, that has not been true in America for over a decade," she said. "The Fed has increased the money supply at twice the rate our goods and services have expanded. These policies have created a credit bubble that will, eventually, burst. Fractional-reserve banking makes it possible for central bankers to control the money supply by either raising or lowering loan interest rates. That puts them in the driver's seat when it comes to running governments around the globe."

She paused for a drink of water.

"Using international banking, an interlocking system of national banks that administer highly inflatable money systems has been created. International trade agreements such as the North America Free Trade Agreement (NAFTA) and Most Favored Nation (MFN) trading status, and the lure to foreign countries of huge profits through international trade with America has allowed the U.S. to set up a worldwide system that it administers and profits from enormously. The whole system is backed by the U.S. dollar as the world's currency of choice for conducting trade. It uses the U.S. military as the world's police force.

"It's a huge and complex system, so we don't need to describe it fully here, but the essence of the system appears to make the world a golden goose for big business. It eliminates risk by insuring the system's losses will be paid with taxpayer money. It provides job opportunities for the system's administrators by using revolving doors between multi-national corporations and the U.S. government."

Jake shook his head, finally interrupting her. "You know, the more I hear you say the words 'big business' and then think of the illegal alien problem and Washington's refusal to solve it, the more I realize that it is all about big business acquiring a cheap source of labor on this continent." He paused for a moment before adding, "It sounds like slavery re-lived, doesn't it? Instead of cotton fields, it's construction sites and factories."

Meredith just looked at him for a moment. She'd had the same thought but had never verbalized it before. It sometimes surprised her how much the two of them thought so alike.

"The offer of great riches through trade with the U.S. is the carrot of American foreign policy," she continued. "The stick is a system of sanctions, such as trade embargos, ending with the threat of military action. Gaining every nation's participation in this worldwide system of trade is crucial. After all, it is the money of the citizens of foreign nations that enables America's debt and what appear to be upscale lifestyles… I say 'appear to be' because a real upscale lifestyle does not involve borrowing one's self into bankruptcy."

She turned off the overhead and the room became quiet as the motor's hum stopped. "What I'm about to say is merely speculation.

It is not a fact." She turned her back to them for a moment. She hated speculating, but knew the time for it had come.

"Since World War II, America has used the economic wealth and productivity – especially consumer spending – of our country to lure other countries into the 'family of nations,' as it has been called.

"Hundreds of years ago, conquerors occupied the nations they defeated while stealing their wealth. When there were no more wealthy nations to conquer, armies were disbanded and those nations who achieved wealth by conquering others collapsed. They disappeared into the sandy hourglass of historic memory.

"Well, aside from the Middle East, there are few nations with sufficient wealth to risk bringing them into the family of indebted nations. I think this may be the primary problem we have today. Our consumers have just about reached the limit of their debt capacity and so the thing on which our foreign policy relies for its success is faltering. Consumer spending and borrowing is going down, not up. It seems to me that our currency is being maintained through military might."

She paused. "I have all of this material printed and a copy for each of you. If you don't mind a little reading, I can give you a brief overview and get through this more quickly," she said, smiling.

"I want to make sure I understand what you just said," Jake said, quietly. "Are you suggesting that, ultimately, the only thing keeping our currency viable in the international markets right now is our military?"

"That's not the only thing I'm saying but, generally speaking, yes," she replied. "Any country that issues a currency accepted internationally must have national wealth to justify that status. The United States is now a debtor nation, not a wealthy one. If a nation has no wealth, then it must have the military might to guarantee ongoing control over the system.

"Because at the current time we lack a currency backed by wealth, gold or productivity – it can be said that the only thing backing the U.S. dollar right now is military force… that and propaganda. If that military might is lost, the country printing the paper money with no precious metals or national wealth backing it is in great danger. At the current time, we're spending better than six percent more than our gross domestic product – GDP – every year. That is not indicative of a nation with great national wealth backing its monetary system. We are borrowing ourselves into poverty. Such a system destroys the character of a nation's people. Getting what appears to be something for nothing evidently does little to build character," she said with quiet finality.

A rather long quiet fell over the room.

"I'll be damned!" Jake said. "Amazing. What happens next?"

"There's an in-depth explanation in the printed material, but the short form is this: As long as the U.S. dollar is the preferred international currency, the guys running the dollar printing presses make the rules. If the dollar crashes internationally, social unrest will result. Anarchy is the likely result and the government will use martial law. Wealth and political stability are lost. The guys running the printing presses no longer make the rules... so there are no rules."

In closing, Meredith discussed how she could not see any way to separate the grab for the power of a world government from the history of gold being confiscated from American citizens. "President Roosevelt did it in 1933." That, she said, brought them back once again to the packet Jeffrey had sent.

"We talked about this the other day. The seizing of gold can be done again. When Roosevelt demanded that average American Joes and Janes give up their gold, those who did not want to obey faced some pretty stiff penalties for noncompliance... ten years in prison and a $10,000 fine. Even with such severe threats, FDR's plan only got about 22 percent of gold coins and a little over half of gold certificates from the American people. There were some examples made, but no basic military boot on neck while searching private homes for gold occurred." Meredith smiled grimly. "That's not to say it couldn't happen."

Jake and Alex looked at one another nervously.

"But surely they could not get away with confiscating people's gold coins and certificates today – and you said bullion, too, right? Not in the 21st century!" It was the first time Meredith had seen Alex truly nervous and she noted that his Russian accent became far more pronounced.

"Oh, but they could," she replied, to a degree playing devil's advocate. "If you don't think so, I suggest you pay closer attention to the Executive Orders that have been written in the past three years.

"I think Jeffrey may have felt it was possible that should martial law be declared because of national unrest, any asset owned by any American could be used by the government as collateral to get the world's financial institutions to bail us out of our national and international debt. What if he was telling us that when the mad days of overspending bring America to its financial knees, the cartel of central banks I explained earlier demands as collateral from our government the homes and farms and ranches and businesses owned by the American people? What if government uses the private property of its citizens to guarantee to the international banking system that our debt will be paid? What's the difference between real estate and gold?" she asked. "They are both private property – until government demands access to them. And, look at the recent decisions involving private property. These precedents suggest that if government can benefit from taking your property, it has the right to take it."

There was total silence in the room.

"Under what law can the president seize gold?" Jake asked.

She quickly wrote it on an overhead and splashed it against their computer screens: Title 12, United States Code, Section 95a (1)(A). "The law says those powers can only be exercised if we are at war and should be used in conjunction with trading with the enemy laws, but Roosevelt ignored them... I suppose any other president could, too. FDR set a precedent." She stopped and took a sip of water.

"I never knew you were so shy about expressing your opinions... you need to get over that," Jake joked, a bit grimly.

Alex was still frowning, reading from the pages she had provided. "Let's break for lunch," he finally said, looking up.

"I have one last question." The three of them were moving toward the door as Alex decided to ask about something that had bothered him earlier in the day. "What did Redbridge mean when he said '...such behavior supports not only new, but old enemies, as well?'"

"I caught that, too," Meredith responded quickly. "There wasn't time to think about it at the time, but I couldn't help but wonder if he was referring to an old enemy – the Soviet Union – and a new enemy – the Russian clone now in his place at the Federal Central Bank."

Alex stopped dead in his tracks. "In what context was the remark made? What was he talking about at the time?" he asked anxiously.

"Unless I'm mistaken," Jake said, "he was talking about the plan he and President McCoy had to put our currency back on the gold standard... something like that. You've got it on film."

"That's right," Meredith said. "He had to be making reference to the cloned Arthur Redbridge. He was trying to remind you that the Fed Chairman you cloned is a spy for the then Soviets – old enemies – and now Russians – new enemies – and the clone is the one now implementing the Redbridge-McCoy Federal Central Bank plan," she said.

How could he have missed such an obvious reference?

They drove from the stable to the main house and Meredith breathed deeply of the fresh, clear mountain air. It was definitely fall in Colorado's mountain country, she thought. The aspen were rapidly turning yellow. Rocky outcrops jutted from the hillsides and added colors that ranged from gray to red. There were few, if any, red-leaved trees here. It made the yellow aspen appear even more dramatic.

"What are those mushroom-shaped trees that still have all their leaves?" she asked Jake.

"Globe Willow trees," he said, smiling. He loved the Globe Willows. "They are also the first to get their leaves... usually about mid-March. Spring comes early here. Like you, I've done a lot of traveling, but this is the only place I've seen this particular tree. They're beautiful, aren't they?"

They were beautiful, she thought. Everything that surrounded her here was beautiful.

Chapter 13

"I don't know about you guys, but I think we should break for the day," Alex told them over lunch. It was as if he were reading her mind. "Having Redbridge here to speak put us behind schedule a bit."

"I agree," Jake replied.

After taking care of personal tasks, they had a quiet dinner, an after-dinner drink and light conversation about life in Russia or life as a CIA agent. There was a lot of laughter and it felt good.

Much of the conversation during her stay at the ranch had involved personal information about Meredith. She was, after all, the newcomer. They knew little about her and she knew less about them. She realized the necessity for them to first learn about her. Her presence had a direct impact not only on their personal and professional security, but on the project to which they had devoted so many years of their lives. They had gotten information as subtly and gently as possible, but Meredith knew their objective and understood the reasons for it.

"It was good to get all of the information you provided on video tape," Alex told her, a smile on his face. "Jake and I thank you for all of your work."

Meredith looked from Alex to Jake and told them they were welcome and that she was looking forward to sitting in the audience for the next day or two.

"Watching your presentations will be an interesting experience for me," she said, a hint of a smile tugging at the corners of her lips.

"The two of you are such opposite personality types but have such similar belief systems," she said.

"Opposite? In what way?" Jake asked.

Meredith pulled the lever on the recliner and lay back in the seat with her feet up. It felt heavenly, she thought as she sank into the pillowed comfort of the brown leather.

"Opposite like... I see you, Alex, as a bit of a brooding scientist and you, Jake, as a typical G.I. Joe action figure. You are alike in that you both value truth in a way that is unique and rare, in my experience. You are alike in that you value friendship and commitment; alike in that you both always question the answers you find to your questions."

"That's an interesting observation from an outside source," Alex said quietly and paused for a moment. "Brooding? How am I brooding?"

She laughed. "It's just a term used to describe serious minds that often end up in science labs," she said. "You are serious and quite intense. Jake, you are intense, too... but in a totally different way than Alex."

"Define intense," they both said at the same time.

Meredith shook her head. She could rest her case about them being so alike on their joint response. She ran her fingers through her short brown hair and paused for a moment.

"Well," she began, still thinking of her answer. "To be intense is to be strong, powerful, and forceful... physically, mentally, emotionally and spiritually. Hmmm... intensity is to have depth as a person. I guess it means you look at life beyond the obvious. It means you have strong beliefs and feel passionately about them," she answered.

Alex studied her for a moment before speaking. "You are getting comfortable being here? You will have no problem staying for awhile?" he asked.

"I'd say that's probably an accurate statement," she said more seriously. "I'm comfortable here. I feel safe. You two have lured my mind into your project... there are few things I love more than my country. I think we're right about a conspiracy to push the various international communities into a world government. If I can help fight that, I will."

Alex nodded, smiling at her. "What if this 'project' takes a hold on your life, like it has for Jake and me?" he asked.

"What are you saying?" Meredith asked.

"I'm saying I was born and raised in a communist country. I see very clearly the difference between those who want an environment of freedom and those who want to play like they are free while escaping the responsibilities required of free people. Elitists do not seem to understand that to be free a person must have both the right to succeed – and the right to fail. When the right to fail is removed from the equation, freedom no longer exists." He paused, smiling at her again. "I'm saying that the reason your mind has been lured into our project is because you are a risk manager... a capitalist, a free-market supporter. I'm saying once you see the actual impact you can have saving your country... you will be like Jake and I: Unable to walk away from it."

His adamancy on the subject surprised her.

"Elitists become elitists because they are risk-averse people who cannot embrace capitalism, a system that requires risk management," she responded. "Many – if not most – of them live on fortunes created and left to them by a capitalist who took risks. My research says people who inherit wealth are defensive about losing what they have. They innately know they could not reproduce their wealth or the standard of living it buys. They become a clique of risk avoiders who hate the very premise upon which the government they are forced to live with is built: Capitalism. They love the idea of world government because that takes them closer to the risk-free environment of socialism or communism." She paused. "One of America's biggest problems is its inheritance laws."

Alex raised his eyebrows, silently asking her to continue.

"People should be able to inherit the money their ancestors leave them," she began, quietly. "They should not, however, inherit the power that comes with huge fortunes. They should not be able to create foundations that fight against the very thing in which the ancestor who earned the money believed. They should not hold responsible positions on corporate boards in a capitalist economy because they do not understand capitalism."

Alex looked at her for a moment. She had surprised him with her response. He realized she was giving him personal insight into her own belief structure. He finally shrugged as he began to speak.

"There is nothing new about elitists and they are not limited to America. They come from aristocracies, theocracies, the church... whenever politics becomes involved in anything, elitists appear. Elitism is power-driven, as you have said."

The three friends discussed problems and possible solutions until Alex finally said, "This brooding scientist has to get some sleep. He has a presentation to listen to tomorrow and doesn't want to sleep through it."

They nodded in unison. It was late and they were all tired.

Alex did the usual before bed rituals. He was tired and the thought of sleep was a welcoming one. The flannel sheets he pulled around his tired body felt like food to a starving man. He was, after all, 59 years old. He sometimes had to remind himself. His DNA technology kept him looking and feeling years younger, but he could count the years and knew his body was counting them, too.

He tossed and turned in his bed, an unusual occurrence for him. Usually, he slept and wakened easily. "This is one of those nights when you are not really asleep, but not really awake, either," he thought. He hadn't had one of those nights since he left Sakhalin Island. He'd had nights of no sleep after he first disappeared into that dark alley in West Berlin. They were motivated by fear and uncertainty about the future, he realized. Why now, he wondered? And then he remembered the subtle but definite electricity that had gone through him as he bent to whisper into Meredith's ear, telling her Arthur Redbridge wanted to speak at their little gathering. The soft, sweet scent of her perfume had assailed his senses with his own masculinity.

He smiled to himself, realizing he had solved the problem. He knew sleep would not be far behind.

When morning came and breakfast was over, Alex asked Meredith to accompany him to his laboratory for another intravenous treatment. On the short drive to the lab, both of them realized that their usual sense of ease with one another had changed slightly, but neither knew the other felt that same sense of… loss?

He glanced quickly at her somewhat stoic body language: Arms crossed, face averted, her eyes covered with large sun glasses against the glare of the morning sun.

"Meredith," he began uncertainly, "something has changed, hasn't it?"

She thought for a moment before responding. The SUV pulled perpendicularly to the lab and Alex turned the engine off, silently awaiting her answer.

"Changed? Yes, I think so. Do you feel it too – this, what is it, tension?" she asked.

"Yes, I feel it, too," he answered with a gentle smile.

"Oh," she said brightly. "Then everything is okay."

Alex knew Jake would have better insight into this kind of confusing female behavior than was available in his lexicon of experience. Her response and smile had, indeed, made them comfortable with one another again, though.

The two of them returned to the main house where Rusty greeted them on the front porch of the cabin. Alex opened her car door and the two of them walked into the upper level of the residence.

"Well, it's been busy around here since you two left," Jake said. "The realtor I talked with in Denver sent an email, Meredith. He has an offer on your property if you decide to sign the listing contract. He could not take the person inside because he doesn't have one. A client described your place as something he was looking for. The two of them looked through all the windows. He liked what he saw and the price is no problem. I hope you sell the place," he said. "Even if you decided to leave here tomorrow, I wouldn't want you going back there."

"Oh, good heavens," Meredith said softly. She walked down the entryway stairs, through the living room to the glass doors and out onto the patio. She stood at the railing, taking in the beauty of the countryside.

After a few moments, both men joined her. She turned to them, an inquiring look on her face.

"You are welcome to stay here as long as you want." Alex told her. "In fact, I would prefer that you stay."

As he spoke, Meredith saw Nancy gesturing from the kitchen window. Lunch was ready.

"Nancy's waving us in to lunch." She walked slowly towards the kitchen entry. "I need to think about this until tomorrow morning, okay?"

They walked into the house for a light lunch. Alex had asked Nancy to make it light so no one would become a victim of SALS – sleep after lunch syndrome.

Gathered once again in the stable office, Jake began his presentation. It focused on the history of plotting and planning that had gone into the concept of what most people termed "the New World Order."

He provided a list of historic occurrences, beginning in the early 1900s and continuing to the present time. She was amazed at how involved in the ills of the country the Stonegal family had been since the early 1900s. Their Foundation had financed almost every destructive activity in which America had been involved for well over a hundred years.

Why had no one noticed until now, she wondered? She remembered the book about cancer she had read. The Stonegal Foundation had financed many of the cancer research facilities that focused totally on pharmaceuticals for treatment.

"I find it interesting that we both ended up going to what, to both of us, must appear to be the logical conclusion: There is a conspiracy to implement a world government without the approval of the citizens of the world in their various countries," Jake began, addressing Meredith.

He pointed out that his list of historic occurrences had less to do with the monetary system and more to do with the intelligence community. He admitted that after spending twenty years with his country's international intelligence agency, he had no idea so much material existed on the subject of one world government.

"There is little doubt in my mind that this country's movers and shakers have been planning how to achieve world government since the late 1800s... perhaps around the time of Cecil Rhodes, the guy for whom the country of Rhodesia – now Zambia and Zimbabwe – was named. He was one of the richest guys in the world because of diamonds.

"I decided to focus my remarks on two key people: Cecil Rhodes and Antonio Gramsci. There have been others... but these two will serve as good examples."

Jake gave a quick overview of Cecil John Rhodes, born 5 July 1853; died 26 March 1902. "He was," Jake said, "born in England but was a sickly child and was sent to South Africa to work on a cotton plantation his brother, Herbert, owned. He became a businessman and mining magnate... even a politician. We're all familiar with Rhodes scholarships and famous Americans who have received them," he mentioned as a point of reference as to how this man's impact was still being felt.

"The world will always remember Rhodes as the founder of the De Beers Diamond Company," Jake said. "At one time, that company controlled 90 percent of the world's diamonds... it still controls at least 60 percent, today. He also held a major ownership in the Niger Oil Company. I have a complete bio on these two people in the handout material."

An overhead projected a paragraph from Rhodes' Last Will and Testament for the establishment of a secret society. Great Britain, he said, should dominate the world. America, its one-time colony, should be brought back into the fold of the English monarchy and under its rule.

"In 1902 when he died, here is what Rhodes, one of the wealthiest men in the world, said he wanted his money to buy," Jake said. "He wanted to establish and promote the development of a Secret Society. So, to those who ask 'where do the kooks who believe there is a conspiracy for one world government think all of the money for such an endeavor comes from?' here is part of the answer. It is probably a big part. We need to keep in mind that Rhodes wrote seven Wills, not just one."

In 1902, Jake explained, the Pilgrim Society was organized in London as an Anglo-American club. Its members were both English and American. "The Waldorf Astoria Hotel hosted the founding of the American branch of the Pilgrim Society in 1903. The goal of the

Pilgrim Society is clearly the reunification of the United States with Great Britain and all of her perceived 'colonies.'"

Jake explained that Rhodes viewed his concept of secret societies as a holy quest, suggesting in one of his Wills that it be a kind of "church." In the limited amount of time available, Jake had found that in each of Rhodes' seven Wills, additional trustees were added. Toward the end, the sole trustee became Lord Rothschild... "Yes," Jake said, "the same Rothschild family of banking fame throughout Europe. The same Rothschild banking interests so well represented when powerful men took the train ride to Jekyll Island to establish the Federal Central Bank, and the same Rothschild who said 'Let me issue and control a nation's money and I care not who writes the laws,'" Jake quoted. He provided an overhead that listed the men who had gone "hunting" at Jekyll Island and came back with a plan for a central bank designed to control America's monetary policies.

"It's clear these are the men who created our Federal Central Banking System. It is equally clear that some of them were members of the Pilgrim Society. They are best known for being concerned with building and maintaining the traditional wealth housed in Europe and on the East Coast of the United States.

"And now let's move on to Mr. Gramsci.

"He was born in Ales, Italy in January of 1891. Gramsci became a founding member of the Italian Communist Party and in 1921 at age 30 traveled to Moscow as a member of Communist International.

"Gramsci thought Stalin's methods might work in Russia – Stalin murdered millions in his power quest – but those methods would never be accepted in western societies. Gramsci was right. Mussolini thought Gramsci's ideas so dangerous to Mussolini's fascist plans, he jailed him. Gramsci died in prison, but not before writing 33 books about how communism can peacefully cause a capitalist nation to collapse from within through a systematic change of capitalist ideals."

Jake gave examples of Gramsci's concepts on how to implement communism in a capitalist society, using Gramsci's new definition of "hegemony" as a key tool.

"Define hegemony," Meredith requested.

"Domination... social authority... the powers that be," he began in response. "Hegemony is generally defined as the 'ruling' or 'dominant class' of a total society," Jake said, frowning a bit. "But Gramsci created a definition of hegemony focused on individual groups within a culture. These were groups that could be recruited to support a new class within a capitalist society... a new class that would create its own hegemony having nothing to do with the total society other than finding ways to destroy it. These factions were made up of people rejected by society. They were people who could be easily turned against everything perceived to be the strengths of those who dominated society... a society that rejected them."

Jake explained that Gramsci understood that in developed industrial capitalist nations, schools and the media along with pop culture gave people hope that future generations would progress, each succeeding more than the last. In America, that is what happened. The poor who migrated to this country moved into the middle classes and each generation progressed a little further.

Gramsci, he told them, argued that there was a big difference between a "war of position" and a "war of movement." Russian Communism, for example, came about as a result of a war of movement... a Revolution. Gramsci's war begins as a war of position which, as support is gained and a foot soldier turns into a supportive army, becomes a war of movement.

"A culture war is one where anti-capitalists gain primary or majority positions in various forms of mass media – print and electronic – as well as in the school system. They use the schools to teach a form of social revolution," Jake said. "People who are not even aware that the philosophy they are espousing is communism can implement a war of movement once there are enough of them. You might say a war of position embodies a soldier or two and a war of movement embodies an army. When you have enough followers in positions of power within the media and the education system, an actual war against capitalism can begin."

There was a long pause as Jake went through some of his notes and papers.

"How can normal people from traditional homes be so easily influenced by communism in such a short time?" Meredith asked.

Jake had known one of his two listeners would ask this question. He had sought a sensitive answer to it but finally realized there was no way to answer it sensitively.

"Gramsci used those excluded from normal society or normal traditional behaviors as his foot soldiers in the war of position. He needed to get enough of them as centers of influence before beginning a war of movement," Jake answered slowly.

Meredith could tell Jake was uncomfortable answering her question but waited for him to continue.

"Gramsci plays on the emotional scars of those who perceive themselves as social rejects and victims... of racism, sexism, and others who view themselves as social outcasts. The hegemony of society rejects them. This includes homosexuals, criminals, fat people, smokers... you name it. Anyone who has for any reason been rejected by those who dominate society is a target to be recruited as Gramsci foot soldiers.

"Particularly on elite college campuses, Gramsci said to use the plight of women, minorities, gays and other victims of cultural domination established by the 'ruling class.' It has been thoroughly researched and students who have felt the sting of social bias can be indoctrinated to the point of thought and speech control," Jake responded.

"They are gathered together, group by group, and taught that capitalism and religion are responsible for their victimization. They are taught to hate capitalism and, thus, America and its government. Many of them are those inheritors of wealth you were talking about last night, Meredith..."

Jake paused, looking through the rest of the papers he had in his hands.

"Gramsci appears to have had great insights into what I term 'malignant energy,' – or evil," Alex said.

Gramsci, Jake told them, decided that to change any nation from within, the nation's entire culture had to be evaluated. A form of "divide and conquer" had to be established. An almost constant state of class warfare had to take place.

"We Americans have certainly been witness to that for many years," Jake said. "Gramsci was a believer in using the mass media

140

and recognized its usefulness in convincing the public that a lie was the truth. A supportive media is, in fact, required for Gramsci's concepts to work," Jake said in a disgusted tone of voice. "But, enough soldiers have to be in decision-making positions at numerous media outlets for the war of position to become a war of movement."

Jake sighed deeply, then explained that in western societies, Gramsci saw that one way to create class warfare was to attack the bonds that exist between citizens of all classes and those things they hold as almost sacrosanct.

"Family, church, schools, the organizations of its civil society... it didn't matter whether it was a community leader, politician, or social stalwart. In fact, during the war of position phase, a 'soldier' might rise within the ranks of a church or school. He or she might do something to disgust the public with his or her actions... causing doubt whether the church or school deserved the respect society gave it. A teacher might have a love affair with a much younger student. A minister or priest might use their position of spiritual influence to lead a young man into a homosexual relationship. As I said, those who have felt the sting of bias can become victims of thought control and make perfect martyrs. Once the deed is done, the Gramsci media makes the soldier into a martyr. The publicity strikes a blow to the dominant part of society's formerly untouchable altars. One person, a foot soldier who becomes a martyr and gets publicity, is responsible for recruiting hundreds if not thousands of like-minded individuals who have also been rejected or victimized by society.

"It's brilliant, really. And look how well it has worked. Gramsci specifically points to the importance of the schools in local communities. They have to be under the control of those seeking to undermine the existing dominance of the current society. The weapons of those who have subscribed to the Gramsci concept are propaganda and political correctness," Jake said. "This certainly explains for me why our public school system has become so dysfunctional."

"Particularly our universities," Meredith added.

He turned the overhead machine off again. The soft hum of the fan ceased and the room became totally quiet.

His audience was spellbound. How could all of this be going on when no one knew about it? Was everyone so indoctrinated as to not recognize what was happening to them every day of their lives?

"Wow," Meredith said.

Jake laughed. "In the handouts, you'll find a lot of data about the various 'secret societies' and other tyrants who have certainly helped the cause along."

Meredith frowned, looking at the table top in front of her for a moment. "Jake, is there any evidence suggesting that Rhodes' money was used to select certain people and groom them for whatever role his secret societies needed them to play to achieve their objectives?"

He chuckled. "Good question. There is reference to identifying and supporting those who have 'a malleable set of standards'... people who can be trained to do what is needed in the realms of politics and business. There is no proof of it, though. Why?"

"It's just something I've always wondered about," she replied. "Some people just seem to arrive on the big scene for no logical reason... they come by wealth easily, use money to buy access to public opinion, then work to mold it this way or that. I just wondered if it was part of the overall plan..." her voice trailed off.

Jake looked at Alex and apologized for taking so much time, but felt it necessary to present all of the information because it so strongly supported Meredith's conclusion that from a business and finance perspective, a conspiracy for one world government did, indeed, exist.

"No apology needed, my friend," Alex responded. "Like Meredith, I am a bit taken aback by all of this." He shook his head. "Fascinating! And, I think we should call it a day. I think we should finish this up tomorrow afternoon... take tonight and tomorrow morning away from it all. What do you guys think?"

"Agreed," Meredith said quickly. She was tired.

"Me, too... good idea," Jake said, picking up the materials in front of him and passing two small piles of paper to each of the others.

The three friends had a quiet dinner and were all glad to discover no one really wanted to talk much that night. Music played and the fire crackled and everyone tried not to think… and failed, of course. They were all thinking people and the last two days had given them a lot to think about.

Chapter 14

~~~⁓~~~

Alex would make the final presentation... at least for now. Who knew what the future held?

He began by saying he wanted to define some common words people use every day. In reality, he told them, the words frequently meant different things to different people. Questions from the overhead machine were awaiting Meredith and Jake as they sat down and looked at their computer screens.

1. What is Communism?
2. What is Socialism?
3. What is Fascism?

"Even though we use these terms all the time, I want to define them. Communism," he began, "is the economic system that abolishes private property. All property is jointly owned by all the people, with the state holding it in trust. I lived forty years under the communist system and found the state cannot be trusted. The system, enforced by the state, seeks to eliminate all traces of individualism. As in the case of my homeland, it is aggressive in conquering other nations to bring them into a worldwide communist system."

Alex paused, looking at his audience of two with a twinkle in his eye, before continuing. "And before you think too harshly of the Russians for their efforts at building communist nations around the globe, please keep in mind your own efforts in the Middle East. Is it more wrong to conquer a people to bring them into a communist state than it is to bring them into a capitalist system?" he asked, nodding his head as if satisfied with his own question.

"As for socialism, most people from developed nations think socialism is a more civilized form of communism. It doesn't eliminate all private property... not immediately. Socialism effectively places privately-held property at the bidding of the state when the state demands it. Initially at least, most property remains in the hands of those who earn and own it. People are comforted by the illusion of private property rights even as they are being systematically taken away by government."

Meredith could not help but think of the two articles she had recently written about private property abuses in America. Kelo came immediately to mind. There were, however, many more abuses of Americans being removed from their homes by government than most people knew.

"Marx and Engels," Alex continued, "originated the communist theory. They defined socialism as a transitional form of government – from capitalistic private ownership of the means of production and personal property to state ownership of both... to communism."

Alex cleared his throat before continuing. "In other words, communism is permanent. Socialism is temporary. Its entire purpose is to transition a capitalist country to a communist state. I have not noticed among the American people an awareness of this basic truth," he said.

"For example, I see little parental concern when competition is removed from children's grading systems and in school sporting events... clearly an example of removing a sense of individualism and competition from America's youth. It is certainly one of the early steps in teaching children to live and think as a group rather than as individuals. Parents seem to be unaware of – or, certainly unconcerned about – this." He sat on the edge of his desk for a moment, then rose and began to slowly pace from one side of the room to the other again.

"Fascism," he began, a studious and slightly worried look on his face, "is what worries me most. America appears well on its way to becoming a fascist state.

"Perhaps the best person to define fascism for us is its creator, Benito Mussolini. He said: 'Fascism should properly be called corporatism, for it is the merger of state and corporate power.'"

Alex handed them a copy of an article he had read recently. It outlined various modes of behavior that were symptomatic of a social move to fascism.

As Meredith read the material, she was struck by how many of these symptoms were, since 9-11, considered patriotism by Americans. Interestingly, the article pointed to the need by government to unify a soon-to-be fascist nation around a perceived common threat or foe. One of the categories of "foes" listed was "terrorists." Other symptoms included cronyism and corruption... Congress was filled with both. Fraudulent elections were a symptom as was giving the police almost limitless powers to enforce laws. She thought of the stories she had read recently about SWAT teams being used unnecessarily to enter people's homes... sometimes, mistakenly. The use of fear to generate support for national security... all of it sounded like America post 9-11.

"That's more than a little sobering," she said. "I hadn't even considered fascism as a part of any world government plot... but corporatism is happening and it is the thing that seems the most serious threat. Whew!"

Alex smiled at her before continuing.

"We could go on to define liberalism and conservatism... but I think it would be a waste of time," Alex continued. "Both have changed dramatically since the 1960s. 'Liberal' used to mean emphasis on the rights and freedoms of the individual... it limited the power of elitists and other power groups and kept social power in the hands of working people. Based on the voting records of liberal politicians, quite the opposite is now true.

"Since the Soviet Union came apart, I think conservatives and liberals have become politically psychotic. It's as if they needed the U.S.S.R. and the Cold War to keep political equilibrium in America. Liberals think nothing in the world can work without government involvement and control, complete with regulations and taxation – and an ever-growing government – to enforce them. Their philosophy no longer keeps social power in the hands of working people.

Now it places power in the hands of government. Surely they know that is a very simplistic definition of socialism and communism.

"The definition of 'conservative' has changed at least as much as the definition of 'Liberal,' – maybe more," Alex continued. "Politically, 'conservative' used to mean holding on to tradition... maintaining traditional order. Old-time conservatives did not want sudden change in the established social or political order. Again, what I have seen since the fall of the Soviets is that conservatives have discovered tyrannical power can wear a coat of many colors. If there is not an enemy, conservatives will find one. Both political parties have involved themselves in nation building. The Democrats got America into Korea and Viet Nam... the troops are still in Korea. Republicans got you into Afghanistan and Iraq... with talk of Iran, yet to come.

"So, Meredith, how do you define conservative?" Alex asked.

She looked at Alex, then at Jake. She drew her brows together for a moment. These were terms to which she had not given a lot of thought. A brief response was difficult to pull together so quickly.

"I... I'd have to say that conservatives I know are pro-U.S. Constitution as written, not rewritten. They don't buy the 'living document' theory. They consider it a document written in the blood of our forefathers and not open to broad interpretation by judges or justices with political axes to grind. They are upset at the imaginative interpretations of the Constitution by Appeals Courts and the Supreme Court. They believe the courts are trying to legislate from the bench." She paused, biting her lower lip for a moment. "Constitutionalist doesn't define conservative today, but it's as close as I can come," she said with a bit of frustration in her voice.

"I would say that I agree with your Cold War comments, Alex," Jake interrupted. "And Meredith, I agree with your view of conservatives, but so, too, would many libertarians. Conservative philosophy, as I understand it, does *not* include many things libertarians believe in ... like legalizing drugs, open borders, and so on. I just wanted to make that point."

Meredith smiled at him and then continued. "I don't believe those who create capitalist nations by force so corporate elitists and government bureaucrats can profit from it is conservative political behavior. It sounds like fascism at work."

Both men looked at her for a moment. She kept saying she was not a political person and had no qualifications to answer political questions. It did not sound that way to Jake and Alex.

"I would add that there are two types of liberals and conservatives, today," the former CIA agent told them. "One is traditional... they are people from both parties wandering around feeling they have no political party. On the Republican side, the second element at work is neo-conservatism... which I perceive to be liberal: big government, big spending, big business, big schools and universities, and so on. On the Democrat side, the second element is progressive secularists... people who seemingly want no societal rules. Anything goes. Change for the sake of change. They attack everything traditional Americans have always held to be sacrosanct, from faith to families."

Jake paused for a moment and took a deep breath. "Frankly," he began, "I think one of the biggest political confusions today is that 'Republican' no longer means 'conservative.' 'Democrat' no longer means 'liberal.' It accounts for why both Republicans and Democrats are losing their voter base," Jake concluded.

"Do you think the Republicans will maintain their control over the House and Senate in the 2006 elections next month?" Alex asked.

"No, no... I do not," Jake responded. "I think traditional conservative voters are fed up with a lack of anyone representing their beliefs in government... the total government, not just the Senate and the House."

"How about you?" Alex asked Meredith quietly.

"I haven't paid much attention during the past couple of weeks... but I agree with Jake. Republicans will probably lose their power base in the 2006 elections because their legislative behavior has appalled their base," she observed. "When you abuse power, you lose power. I think the Democrats will do as they usually do – promises, promises – will win the election, and people will get very little delivery on the promises."

"What is the people's greatest source of dissatisfaction with government right now?" Alex asked.

"A lot of things, but illegal aliens are at the top of the list," Jake responded immediately. "The crime rate is soaring because of illegal aliens. There is increased access to drugs smuggled into the country by illegals – who get many of the same Social Security benefits as people who have paid into the system for fifty years. Sometimes, more. And, about a third of the prisoners in our jails are illegals. It is very costly," he finished.

Before Alex called her name, Meredith supported Jake's statement. "I agree," she said firmly. "The media pushes the idea that Republican voters are deserting the GOP because of the war in Iraq, but that's not what everyone's talking about. Everyone – and I mean everyone – is madder than hell about illegal aliens and the lack of action taken to close our southern border. I would add to what Jake said. I believe what's causing conservative and liberal anger is political hypocrisy. Government tells people we are a nation of laws. Government, however, chooses which laws it obeys and enforces. That's why people are angry. The veneer of political hypocrisy has been scratched and people don't like what they see."

"Exactly right," Jake reinforced her statement.

"I think we should take a fifteen-minute break," Alex said. "I want to ask the two of you to ponder something. How could shrewd politicians who run the Republican Party make such a gigantic error in judgment about such basic things as immigration and over-spending... unless the Party wants to lose this election?"

There was a long silence.

"What do you think they want to lose?" Meredith asked.

"The Congressional majority when the elections are held next month," Alex replied softly. "I agree. The Republicans will lose."

Alex turned off the overhead machine and turned to the door. "I'm going to take a walk," he said and departed the room.

"Wait," Jake said loudly enough to stop him. Alex poked his head back inside the door. "Does your question suggest that Republicans will lose power in November 2006 because they *want* to lose power... that there is a *reason* they want to lose power?" Jake asked. He had a surprised look on his face.

"That's exactly what I'm suggesting," Alex replied and continued to exit the room. "I want to know the reason the Republicans want to lose."

Jake thought for a moment after Alex departed the room before speaking. "I guess I'll walk the opposite direction. The office and the stable are all yours," he said, grinning at Meredith.

As Alex walked toward Nancy's and Joe's house, he knew he had not planned this break or his question. It had just happened. As his two friends were talking, it had suddenly dawned on him that the answer to this question was a key.

He looked at the sky. Gray clouds swirled overhead, moving in an easterly direction. To Alex, they gave warning of a storm. Snow this early in the year was quite unusual, and when it happened, it sometimes turned into a full-fledged blizzard. He'd have to remember to call Joe and make sure everything was prepared. He quickly decided he'd walk to the bunkhouse and talk to him in person, then return to the stables. A cool wind blew his dark hair across his forehead and Alex pulled up the collar of his jean jacket.

Tomorrow he would go fishing at a small private lake on his property. A few fresh trout for dinner might just hit the spot. Jake had gotten some trout from the fish hatchery just outside the town of Rifle and stocked the lake. After five years, it was teeming with them. "I hope it won't be ice fishing," he said to himself as he continued his walk, trying to piece together an answer to his own question.

Jake walked toward the main house... about a half-mile from the stable. "What a question!" he thought. Jake had known Alex Plotnikov for almost twenty years and the man's mind never ceased to amaze him.

What Alex's question suggested made sense. The Republicans had set themselves up to lose the coming election... but why? In truth, the success or failure of elections relied more on the policies of political parties than on individual candidates. Politicians needed state and national parties for financial support. Who could get elected without money? Lobbyists supported political parties and expected legislative support in return for their money. The entire system had become immune to what the people who paid for everything wanted. By the time political candidates names appeared on a ballot, the candidates represented their political party and the lobby-ists that supported it, not the people.

They needed something during the next two years that only Democrats could accomplish. Alex was right and that must be it! But what was it? What did "they" need, who were "they" and how were "they" going to accomplish it?

Jake started walking back toward the stables, his mind awhirl with more unanswered questions. He rubbed his hands as he walked. It was getting cold, he realized.

Meredith, too, found thinking easier when she was up and moving, but a long walk was out of the question for her. She walked to the stable, went to the stall of a grey horse named "Togram," and picked up a grooming brush along the way.

"Why would the Republicans set themselves up for an intentional loss?" she asked the horse. Togram stomped her right front hoof as if to tell Meredith she was listening. She began brushing the mare's mane and tail. The question was one that took a person directly to the core of a problem, she realized. She smiled because that was the way Alex's mind worked, and she admired it… respected it.

Meredith realized she was not enough of a politician to take such twisted logic and toy with it until it became a logical thought. She walked slowly back to the office. A few minutes later, Jake and then Alex came through the stable door.

"Looks like a storm might be blowing in," Alex said. "We might get an early snow."

"And while you were figuring that out, did the answer to your question happen to slip through your mind?" Meredith asked.

He smiled and then laughed at her question. "Let's talk job descriptions. My job as a brooding scientist is to ask the right ques-tions. Your job, as a consultant, is to answer them. Get it?"

"Got it," she said.

"Good," he said. They all laughed at the old Danny Kaye comedy line.

"Did you come up with anything, Jake?" Alex asked his friend.

"Not really. The most promising thought I had is that whatever the power group behind the one world government movement wants to achieve requires liberals, progressives and secularists in control of the legislature to get it done."

Alex nodded his head several times, his brows knotted a bit and his right index finger rubbed his lower lip. "That's what I think, too. Okay," he said. "So, in the late eighties, we had a Republican President and Democrat Congress. The power base switched to Democrat in the Executive Office in 1992 with a Republican Congress in 1994. What was accomplished then that required the unique support of the liberal camp? What happened that would have caused a huge outcry from conservatives had a Republican president done it?"

The room grew silent. Meredith felt the air becoming chillier and unconsciously rubbed her upper arms with her hands as she thought. Alex noticed and walked slowly to the corner of the room where he turned on a small gas stove. The numerous windows were suddenly not allowing sufficient light into the room and he turned on the overhead lights. Clouds, he realized, were covering the sun and the cold wind was increasing in its intensity.

"Well," Jake began, "there was the North American Free Trade Agreement – NAFTA. It caused, as Ross Perot said it would, a huge sucking sound as American jobs were lost and sent to Mexico."

"What else?" Alex asked.

"Keeping the labor unions from over-reacting to NAFTA – the Democrats have the power there," Meredith added. "Then, there was the first violation of Posse Comitatus at Waco – the use of the U.S. military against American citizens."

She thought for a moment of the 74 people killed at Waco, so many of them children. It was impossible to think of Waco without remembering Ruby Ridge.

"And what strength do democrats have that the republicans do not have? What can democrats do that republicans can't? What requires a democrat rather than a republican congress to be elected in the 2006 elections next month?" Alex asked. "You get to lead off, Jake."

Jake stood and walked slowly back and forth. He is a man who looks great in blue jeans, Meredith thought to herself. With his boots and blue work shirt, his tall but muscular frame made him look like a cowboy hero about whom Zane Grey might write.

The ear-piercing sound of a siren suddenly filled the room. Jake automatically grabbed his shotgun and headed for the door. Alex quickly hit the intercom to Joe's house. "Which gate is it?" Alex asked. "Are all of our guests in their rooms?"

Joe's voice came authoritatively over the intercom in response. "All the chickens are in their coops, Boss… it's the first gate. I've hit the lock button on the second gate," he said. "I'll go see who is trying to pay us a visit."

"Probably nothing to worry about," Alex said to Meredith who knew she must appear startled because she was.

"A tourist out looking for property or a hunter looking for a place off of the beaten path… it happens every now and then."

"Oh," she said quietly as she watched him unlock a cabinet and pick out a rifle. He held out his other arm for her, indicating they would be leaving the stable. She noted that all of the skylights were being covered by earth panels that were normally only activated at night.

"Let's go. I want to get you safely back to the house," Alex said, a note of impatience in his voice at what he perceived to be her lack of immediate response. His Russian accent was more pronounced, she noticed.

They took the old Jeep from the garage, shut the covering so the building appeared as just another sandy hill with green ground cover growing around it, and drove quickly to the house.

"Where did Jake go?" she asked as they entered the front door. Alex quickly hit all of the security switches for the house, and the skylights throughout were suddenly darkened by the earth covering them.

"Joe will go see who is on the road while Jake covers him from some unseen spot," Alex said in a monotone.

"Every time this happens, you must wonder if they've found you," she said quietly.

"True enough," he responded in an equally quiet tone, "but now I have to wonder if they've found you, as well."

She realized that she was beginning to feel so comfortable and secure in her surroundings with Jake and Alex that she had put some of the danger out of her mind. Maybe she had never really believed in the danger, she thought. Maybe she was just enjoying what in her heart of hearts she thought of as an adventure.

The immediate reaction to an unknown vehicle crossing one of the cattle guards was obviously well-rehearsed. It made her realize she was going to have to rethink what she perceived to be her new reality. It worried her that if people were looking for her, she might be drawing unneeded and unwanted attention to Alex. She might be safer being here, but was he?

Chapter 15

A lex looked at his watch again. "It shouldn't be more than a few minutes," he muttered and went to the kitchen to pour her a glass of cranberry juice. As for himself, he chose a scotch and water.

They spoke of mundane things like the sudden change in the weather, what preparations would need to be dealt with in the coming days to get ready for winter, and Meredith's need to go shopping for clothes. Meredith ran her fingers over the dark wood of the end table next to her chair and noted that the room needed a good dusting.

"I guess this helps me decide about the offer for my townhouse in Denver," she said thoughtfully. "Knowing what I know now, the thought of being there alone and waking up to noises in the night holds little appeal. Besides, I'm ready to leave Denver. It's changed…"

The silence between them continued for what seemed to Meredith a very long time. She did not feel like talking. She more carefully examined the well-constructed wood flooring and suddenly realized she had no boots or winter coat with her.

The short, high-toned beeps caused when Jake punched in the security code to the front door brought both of them to their feet. Jake had only a jean jacket with him when he left the stable and he looked half-frozen. Rusty had accompanied Jake and, still wearing his summer coat, the dog looked cold, too… cold, but invigorated.

"I sent Joe home," Jake said. "I'm going to take a fast shower and put on some dry clothes before I catch pneumonia," he walked to the hall as he spoke. "I think it's a good idea to keep the security system on high alert, but go ahead and light a fire," he told Alex, smiling at Meredith.

Relieved and glad to have something to do, Alex walked out on the patio to get a load of kindling and a couple of logs. He took the oil-soaked clay apple ball from its metal container, rolled it in yesterday's ashes, lit it and put it under the wood he had just placed in the grate. He then went back outside to bring in additional logs. The fire was soon crackling and Rusty was happily ensconced in front of it.

"Why don't you give Nancy a call and tell her to stay home. It's getting on to dinner time and I can cook tonight. There's no sense in her coming out in this weather," Meredith said in an intentionally calm voice. She got up to go and see what food was in the refrigerator, saw some defrosting ground beef, put it into a pot with water and beef broth, and then put the pot on the stove to heat.

"How about some chili and tacos?" she asked. "It goes well with the weather. I don't know why I crave Mexican food when it gets cold, but I do."

"Sounds good to me," Alex said. "How do chili and tacos sound to you, Jake?" he asked the figure coming out of the hallway to join them. Jake wore plaid wool lounging pajamas, a robe, and wool slippers. He looked totally comfortable.

"Sounds good to me, too," he said, smiling at Meredith. "You've taken over the kitchen for the night?"

"Yep... it shouldn't take long."

"Can you make it extra spicy for me?" he asked. Her only response was a smile.

"A car did come across the first cattle guard," Jake said to Alex. "Joe stopped them on the road, told them they were on private property and they left. He said they looked like a family – man, woman, a couple of teenaged kids. After they left, I put a security camera down there, just in case. That's what took so long. It was snowing too hard for me to see much," Jake finished.

There was a long pause. "So, where were we?" he asked.

Alex and Meredith looked at him curiously. "Where were we?" Alex echoed, obviously at a loss to know how to respond.

"When we left the stable... we were talking about liberals and conservatives and why who was getting elected and who wasn't." Jake looked back and forth between the two of them, puzzled at their disconnection with his question. "Right?"

"Get your scramblers and turn on some music," Alex said, chuckling.

They discussed the intolerance of the liberal left and the inability of the conservative right to communicate effectively. They also discussed the over-spending and lack of attention to the nation's southern border by both groups.

The three of them sat quietly for a while. Meredith went to the kitchen occasionally to check on the progress of dinner. They chatted and listened to the crackling of the fire. It was dark now and though the patio barriers had covered the glass doors, sealing them in for the night, they knew it was snowing outside. They decided they had sufficient input about Republicans and Democrats and liberals and conservatives. They wanted to get back to Alex's question: What was on the political or social agenda that required a liberal legislature from 2006 until the next election in 2008? And, how did that agenda tie into the Jeffrey's data?

"I suggest we have a drink, eat our dinner, Jake and I will clean up while you rest, Meredith, and then we can talk some more," Alex said.

After dinner, the three friends gathered once again in front of the fireplace.

"You said something at the office I want to ask you about," Alex said, lowering his tall frame into a matching recliner chair across from her. "During a break you said you have a theory that might make for good after-dinner conversation. What's the theory?" He leaned forward and put his elbows on his knees, then rested his chin on his hands.

"Oh... I think we were talking about progressives and I was referring to my unchanging principles and changing values theory," she answered.

"Unchanging principles and changing values, huh? Wow. That sounds like light after-dinner conversation," Jake said laughing.

She thought for a moment before she began to speak. Jake and Alex knew her well enough by now to realize she was putting her thoughts into A, B, and C categories. It was the way her mind worked.

"How would you define 'values?'" she asked Jake, smiling as she saw him mentally reaching for a fast answer and unable to give one. "It takes some thinking, doesn't it?" she asked.

"Yes… yes it does. Give me a minute. You surprised me," Jake responded. He looked at her, one eyebrow raised. "I think I need a definition from you, first. The way you're using the word in conjunction with principles tells me you are not asking about a dictionary definition of values – the worth of something – how highly we esteem it or the price tag we put on it. You want me to define a system of social values reflective of the laws and rules made by humans to create a stable society, right?"

Meredith loved Jake's need for specificity and nodded her agreement, smiling broadly.

"Values are man-made laws – a social legal system – that must be obeyed or society can assess a penalty against the violator. Values are also rules that religions, clubs, and other groups determine members must observe if they want to belong to the group."

"I'll buy that… very good on-the-spot response," Meredith said, admiringly. "We need one more definition, though. How would either of you define 'principles?'"

Jake looked at Alex who lifted his chin from his hands as he spoke. "I would say a principle is a… a fundamental truth. Principles are the key element of a system of thought or a line of reasoning. God's laws are principles. Universal laws are principles." He thought for a moment longer. "As Jake said, values – or, man-made laws – are created to support a system of thought… or, principles."

"What I figured out is what you just said. Values derive from principles. Principles do not derive from values. We have God's laws – or, universal laws, as you pointed out Alex. Laws that are created by a source greater than mankind – God or the universe – are immutable. They are unchanging. Principles flow from immutable laws. Like the universal laws principles support, principles cannot be changed without changing the underlying universal law.

When universal law is misinterpreted, the principles that support the newly-understood meaning of the law will change... but that's the only time."

She paused.

"Explain," Jake said quietly. "What's an example of a misunderstood universal law?"

"Universal law as interpreted by human beings once held that the world was flat," Meredith replied quickly. "Galileo was scorned by his church and society when he suggested the world was round. The law or principle – or, Galileo – was not wrong. The human interpretation of it was." She raised her eyebrows at him as if to ask if that clarified what her statement meant.

"Good example," was all he said.

"Okay," she said, ready to continue. "Principles represent the social application of universal laws and they rarely change. We have a system of values – man-made laws – which support the principles. But here's the important part. Until God rewrites His laws or the universe stops working the way it always has and changes the laws of nature, principles are the way we identify those laws that come from a source greater than human beings. Because principles are tied to immutable laws, they do not change. Values, however, change."

She chuckled. "Now, after all of that definitional clarity, here's my theory: Changing values must be tied to unchanging principles. It is the only way positive progress can occur while maintaining a stable society."

She paused to give them a moment to think about what she had just said. "There is only one way to keep social values positive yet progressive. Changing values must be tied to unchanging principles."

The room was quiet for a few moments. She knew it was a complicated theory and wanted to make sure they were with her. She almost smiled, realizing that with Alex's physics background, he was probably ahead of her.

"Unchanging principles... like day and night, winter and summer or sunrise and sunset?" Jake asked.

"Sort of like that," she responded. "But God's laws are also supported by unchanging principles... Thou Shalt Not Murder,

Thou Shalt Not Steal, Honor Thy Father and Mother, and so on." She paused again. "If values do not have the stability of unchanging principles attached to them, they lose their social value. They become destructive."

"Yes, well, principles are supposed to make it clear to everyone – government, the people, businesses – what the universe requires of them... regardless of whether it is God or Nature that requires it. Values require behavior that achieves the objective of the principle," the scientist added. "Until a society becomes sufficiently observant of the world around it to identify universal principles, the rules of man – a system of values – cannot be created to support unrecognized universal laws. Values cannot be established until a society achieves a point of evolvement that enables it to identify laws from a source greater than mankind. Values must be established to support the principles as they are identified and defined. Right?" Alex smiled at her.

"Right," Meredith nodded. "The point is, when people start trying to change principles, they are trying to change universal laws... or God's laws. Freedom is a principle. It is granted to us by God, not by our government..."

Alex interrupted her. "Communism tried to impose itself as the ultimate absolute authority and we can all look at the twenty million dead bodies to see the human cost for such arrogance." He looked at her, shrugged and apologized for the interruption.

"My point is, for the principle of freedom to remain as our forefathers intended, the definition of freedom must stay fixed. It has not. The 'one worlders' have slowly been redefining it.

"They have taken the word 'freedom' and given it the same definition as 'license.' They have re-defined 'freedom.' Most of us do not accept their re-definition, but that is what they have done."

There was a protracted silence before she continued speaking.

"Values must change or societies do not progress. There are countries on this planet that still function as they did several hundred years ago because they tie their unchanging societal principles to unchanging values. Unchanging values results in no social progress."

Alex, always wanting to boil things down to a simple format, gave the example of transportation as a value tied to the principle of freedom. "The freedom to travel must remain the same because it is part of the principle of freedom. But the value of a horse and buggy can change to that of an automobile. Freedom is only damaged when the principle of the right to travel is changed. Right?"

Meredith laughed. "That's a great example... very clear. Principles are unchanging. Values change as societies progress – or, regress. By bonding values that change to principles that do not change, societies throughout history have maintained stability in the long-term and flexibility for positive progress in the short-term. It's a difficult, but necessary, balance. No societal stability means no unchanging principles are in place. No social progress means no changing values are supporting unchanging principles."

Jake and Alex liked the theory and the three of them discussed at some length what a positive social environment really was and how it could be defined. They all agreed that the primary function of good government was to motivate positive attitudes and behavioral preferences in the people governed.

"So," Jake proffered, "I guess we could agree that only when social values have a positive impact on society can they be called 'values.' Negative behavior has a negative social impact and is of 'no value.' Is that right?"

"I agree with that," Meredith said after thinking about his comment for a moment. "I really hadn't thought of the 'no values' part of what you said, but it makes sense... provided you define negative behavior correctly," she said, frowning just a bit.

"Correctly... like how?" he asked her.

"Well, I'm sure there were a lot of people who probably thought the Boston Tea Party and the Revolutionary War represented negative behavior," she said. "The determining factor was the principle of freedom. Those who subscribed to the principle of freedom won the argument," she said, then paused. "Those who wanted freedom were standing on the principle of a God-given right. Those who supported the Crown were standing on a changing value... the Crown is not unchanging and cannot be a principle. It is a social value."

"So," Jake laughed, "unchanging principles trump crowns."

"Yep," she chuckled in return, "especially when the crown is trying to make its edicts of more significance than those of God and the universe. In that case, the crown was trying to establish itself as an unchanging principle – and, it is not."

The three of them discussed how principles, when based on nature's laws, accurately reflect daily occurrences.

"If it happens in nature, we can be sure of it. What goes up must come down. For every action, there is an equal reaction. For every cause, there is an effect. All living things grow to maturity, level off and die. The line of least resistance creates crooked rivers – and so it probably creates crooked people, too." The room was silent for a time after Meredith spoke. "They are nature's laws and God created the universe and the laws that govern and keep it working harmoniously."

"Sounds like Physics 101 to me," Alex commented, thoughtfully. "Have you got another example?"

Meredith thought for a moment. "A principle: The sun rises in the east every day. A value: In four-season climates, in winter it rises on trees with no leaves. The sun rising in the east equates to an unchanging principle. No leaves on trees equates to changing values that allow nature to progress from winter to summer."

Alex looked at her with a different expression on his face than she had seen before. "So, hundreds of years ago, social values allowed men to have more than one wife. Today, we call that polygamy. The principle of marriage is the same; the value has changed." All three of them laughed, agreeing it was a good example.

There was a comfortable silence that exists among friends during times of thoughtful reflection. The fire crackled. It was burning down. It was getting close to bedtime, Meredith thought.

"I believe this theory explains why we had so much difficulty today defining 'liberal' and 'conservative,'" she said. I believe this theory applies to the Gramsci philosophies Jake explained yesterday. "Nothing is black and white because powerful people are removing our unchanging principles. They are re-defining freedom."

Alex cleared his throat before speaking. "You're saying the reason for all of the confusion in both political parties is caused because powerful people are removing the unchanging principles that have anchored American society for a few hundred years."

Meredith looked at Alex, then Jake, before responding. "What I'm saying is that the only way to move America from capitalism to communism is to re-define words like freedom, faith, family, education, sovereignty, independence, competition... all of the words you mentioned in your presentation, Alex. Those words represent the unchanging principles on which America was founded. Changing the meaning of these words makes it possible to ignore the Declaration of Independence and Constitution of the United States... the basis of our most important unchanging principle: Freedom."

"Yes," Jake said softly. "You're also saying that a lot of powerful people not only want to change values, they want to detach them from unchanging principles, too. That may be the reason Democrats need to be elected next month. Giving up the sovereignty of the United States requires people who think everything is relative. It requires people who believe that all change is progress – whether it is, or not – people who think of themselves as 'progressives.'"

He sat looking thoughtfully into the fire.

"It reminds me of the chief demon in C.S. Lewis' book, *The Screwtape Letters,*" Alex said, pensively. "Screwtape was the chief demon who wrote letters to a human he was recruiting to help him deliver the human race to the Devil." Alex frowned as he tried to remember the story he had read.

"Screwtape said something to the effect that change was supposed to be a means to a defined, better end, but they had to make people believe that change was an end 'unto itself.' That's what's happening, isn't it? Demons have convinced Americans that change is an end unto itself."

Again there was silence as the three friends thought about how Meredith's concept they had at first found so amusing might be more than just an interesting theory.

"Some people seem to think if there are no rules of behavior, no one can misbehave, don't they? With no rules, no one can be held responsible for what they do." Alex's voice was quiet and thoughtful.

"Dear Lord," Jake said. "There are two of them in the same house!"

They all laughed and agreed it was time to speak of nothing more serious than Rusty's need for a call to nature before bedtime.

When they opened the front door to accommodate the dog, six inches of snow covered the ground and more was falling. Rusty bounded around in the powdery snow like a puppy for a few moments.

"Well, I'm going to be housebound for a few days," Meredith commented. "No winter boots, no coat, and no winter clothes… can we drive into Grand Junction after the storm is over?"

They both looked at her and nodded at the same time. It made her laugh.

Chapter 16

A lex did not let the snow on the ground keep him from his date with trout destiny. Typical of a fall day in Colorado after a big snow, the sky was blue, clear and sunny. By noon, the snow on the roads would be melted. It would stick around on the ground for awhile, but the roads would be clear. Colorado's snow was not heavy and wet… more like dry powder.

The yellow leaves on the aspen trees were loaded with snow and some branches were bent dangerously low from the weight. Some boughs, he knew, had been broken, especially on the globe willows. He, Jake and Joe would have to take a walk around the property to prune them after the snow melted. For now, the color contrasts brought about by the rising sun, the snow, the yellow leaves, and the mountains with their different colored rocks… it was breathtakingly gorgeous. The air was so clear!

He put his fishing gear in the Jeep and drove past Nancy's and Joe's house, then his laboratory, and continued west, going uphill to the lake. Alex figured one hugely important thing had come out of the three days of meetings. He now knew the 'one worlders' were dependent for success upon monetary system failure. If the economic problems could be solved, everything else would be put on hold. The importance of getting Arthur Redbridge back into office almost overwhelmed Alex as he thought about it.

Even with his advanced scientific knowledge about helping his body stay young, he had lived a high-stress life. He probably wouldn't be around too long after it all happened. He did not want to live through another bout of communism. He realized he thought of it as a disease.

Alex knew that most of the threats popularized by the media were propaganda...but how could people be anything but anxious? One day they could look forward to death caused by bird flu, the next day by dirty bombs from Russia stolen by terrorists, the next day from global warming. If those things did not get them, terrorists on airplanes would. While their minds were being directed at one emergency after another, the people's Constitutional freedoms were being taken from them, one at a time. Very Gramscian, Alex thought. Keep class warfare going and divide and conquer.

Like most fishermen, his thoughts drifted off to more pleasant, non-serious matters when he lowered the small row boat from its hoist in the boat house. There was a foot of snow on the ground and the water was clear. There was no ice. As the full sun rose above the mountains, orange streaks filtered across the clear water. The white ground surrounding it glowed in sunlight that sent the glorious warmth of life everyone took for granted each day.

He smiled to himself. This was his home now and he truly loved it.

*****

"Where's Alex?" Meredith asked Nancy. "Sleeping in this morning, is he?"

"Went fishing," she replied simply.

Jake and Nancy both laughed.

"I just asked the same question," he said, looking up from his newspaper. "It seems Alex had a date with some trout up at the lake. Guess what we'll be having for dinner tonight? Left over chili and tacos won't be on the menu no matter how much more appealing it sounds."

When Nancy put her omelet on the table along with a rasher of well-browned bacon, Meredith told her to forget about clean-up. "Jake and I can handle it... and I know that having other guests has given you more work to do," she told the woman. "Why don't you take some of that chili home for you and Joe? You can take what you need for your guests, too."

Nancy smiled at her. "I'll take you up on that offer. I'm doing a lot of cooking, these days. I've got to get the laundry done today, so I sure appreciate it." Nancy put on her coat and left Jake and Meredith to eat their meal and clean up the kitchen.

The two ate mostly in silence. The conversation that did occur related to articles in the newspaper he was reading. Jake drove several miles to the mailbox at the main road every morning to get it.

"It's beautiful outside," Jake commented casually. "Did you say you want to go into town to do some shopping? I can take you, if you'd like."

She grinned at him appreciatively. "I'd like to visit Arthur Redbridge, but I don't have boots or a coat. I need a lot of things. My stuff is all in storage, right? When will you and Gil be flying to the Denver area? If I know that, I can figure out how many clothes I need... what to buy. Next time, maybe you can pick up a clothes box or two?"

Mouth full, Jake grunted and nodded his head in assent.

"Why don't we do this?" he asked after swallowing. "Gil's in Rifle and I'm not planning to do much today. I think we all need to recover from the last couple of days. Weather on the east slope permitting, he and I can fly to Denver today, pick up your clothes, and you can talk with Redbridge. We can be back in three or four hours. I'll give you one of my jackets to wear."

With that, he stacked all of the dishes on the table and carried them to the sink for rinsing, then began inserting them into the dishwasher.

It sounded like a good plan to Meredith. She finished tidying up and turned, bumping into Jake who was standing behind her with a jacket in his hands.

"Here," he said, placing it around her. "This should keep you warm enough." His hands lingered for just a moment on her shoulders. The leather bore his scent and it was pleasing to her. He drove the SUV as close to the house as he could. She was able to get in the car with her feet still dry. When they reached the bunkhouse and as she departed the car, she handed him the signed real estate contract for her Denver condo.

"You're sure?" he asked. "We don't want…"

"I'm sure, Jake," she interrupted him. "Just being at the ranch this past month has made me sure I don't want to be in Denver anymore." She got out of the car and turned her back to him, her arms bent upward at the elbow and her hands in the air as if to say "let it be."

He smiled as he backed the grey SUV out of the driveway.

"I told Dr. Redbridge you were coming," Nancy said as she opened the door to the bunkhouse. "Why don't I put a pot of coffee together for you to plug in and pour?" Meredith smiled at Nancy's thoughtfulness.

"Coffee sounds like a good ice-breaker," Meredith observed.

Until now, Meredith had not thought of Fed Chairman Arthur Redbridge locked up and alone at Joe's and Nancy's place. It made her glad she had waited for Nancy to put the water and coffee in the pot as she followed Nancy down the hallway.

"Your guest is here," Nancy announced to the man inside the room and waited until Meredith entered before leaving. "Just call me on your cell phone when you're ready to leave," she said as she closed and locked the door.

The room was much like her own – bed centered against the wall on the right, bathroom at the end of the wall on the left as you entered the room, patio door in the middle of the far wall – though this patio was a bit smaller than hers, she thought.

Redbridge rose to greet her and took the coffee pot from her hands. "What a nice thing for you to bring with you," he said, smiling. "And I'm certainly glad for the company. I have read so much and watched so much video tape, I'm beginning to feel over-informed… submerged in too many facts. Let's sit out on the patio. Please," he said graciously and as if he were welcoming her to his home, "have a seat." He placed the pot on the small patio table, plugged it in and it quickly made noises that let them know it was doing its work.

"I… I really do not know what to say to you, Arthur. I can't tell you how learning of your captivity saddened me. It is the most internationally disgusting political move I think I've ever heard," Meredith said quietly.

"And yet you're the guest of the man who created my clone, I believe..." his voice was neither questioning nor sarcastic. It was just a statement of fact made with no emotion.

"I know Alex well enough to know that had his government not forced him to create your clone and had he not accidentally found the technology to do so, it would've never happened. I know it took Alex and Jake fifteen years to get you home. I know they used their personal, not government, funds to buy your freedom. I know it was quite costly, and I know you are the only prisoners that have ever escaped from Sakhalin Island," she responded coolly, but with a smile. "No one can make up to you for what you've lost, Arthur... not even you. Had you or I been in his place, we would've done the same thing. The question is: Are you ready to move on and take back your life?"

He sat opposite her, watching her intently. His shaggy eyebrows drew together as she spoke. He might get sympathy here, he thought, but no redemptive help.

"How did you end up here?" he asked, almost abruptly.

She gathered her thoughts, trying to think ahead to what Jake and Alex would want him to know, and then answered him with a question. "What have you been told about my being here?"

"I know you're not a Jewish mother," he said, smiling. He put his hand to his mouth and coughed briefly as they both laughed lightly.

"I was told that you were in residence temporarily while the two men – Alex and Jake – helped you through a personal problem," he answered her at last.

"Well, that's an accurate statement," she told him honestly, her eye contact direct and even. "Do you remember Jeffrey Lund?" she asked, still looking directly at Redbridge.

"Yes, yes I do. He did some international banking work for me at the Fed. You two used to work together, didn't you?"

"We did," she answered. "Jeffrey was killed about a month ago... a mugging the New York police said." Her tone of voice was low and controlled.

"Killed!" Redbridge blurted, obviously surprised. "Killed by muggers?"

"Well, that's the official story," Meredith said calmly. "Before Jeffrey died, he sent me some papers that were obviously taken from a meeting of one of the international banking organizations... I'm not sure which one." She paused, realizing the need for caution here. "He put them in an envelope, addressed it to me and gave the package to a ticket agent at JFK in New York when his plane touched down. We think he knew someone followed him. He made sure the papers were mailed before he left the airport, so he knew he was in danger. He sent Jake a note, too, telling him what he had done, suggesting I might need protection. That's how I got here," she finished. "I've been here going on a month now."

Redbridge studied her and then looked away. He thought for a moment. The coffee pot had stopped making noise and he offered her a cup.

"Papers from an international banking group, huh?" he asked. "Can I ask what they are?"

"You can ask," Meredith responded, "but Alex and Jake will have to make the decision about your accessibility to them. They're working hard to try and straighten out the mess this country is in right now. I won't involve myself in their business without their knowledge."

Again, he was silent. He leaned forward, elbows on the table, and hunched his shoulders, a frown on his face. "How honest are these two men?" he asked her bluntly.

Again, he showed no emotion. He barely inflected his tone at the end of the question. Redbridge's voice still had the same rasping quality she remembered.

The look she gave him was equally cool. She hesitated before speaking, again trying to make sure her words were well-chosen. Her wide-set brown eyes studied him for a moment.

"Do I know them well enough to tell someone else to trust them?" Meredith took a sip of coffee before continuing. "No. I've only known them for a month. But Jeffrey knew Jake for years... and you knew Jeffrey. He was very careful in his associations. His reputation was everything to him. Do I trust them, personally?"

Again, she paused. "Yes, I do. I believe Alex is sick over the Russian government using his skill the way it did. It was not something he did willingly and he got away from the Soviet Union as quickly as he could. He has a death sentence hanging over his head. They are still looking for him... and this place is filled with so many security devices, you cannot move without someone knowing about it," she said. There, she thought. Let him chew on that.

"And, they are trying to create a plan to return you to your office as Fed Chairman... but certain things have to be in place first. How do they get rid of your clone replacement? How do you become more fit so that when you return to your office there won't be disparity in the way your clone looks and the way you look? The treatments Alex is giving you should make you look quite a bit younger within a month or two," she stated, rather flatly. "The rest needs to be your choice. You need to work out and regain your strength. You have been malnourished for years. What's your choice, Arthur?"

He blinked. He remembered hearing that she was pretty direct, but in his old life he had been surrounded by politicians where "pretty direct" translated to a lot smoother dialogue than Meredith's comments had just been. He looked away from her briefly.

"Based on the material I've studied for the past three weeks, I agree with the conclusions you came to in your presentation the other day," he said, ignoring her question. "Alex brought the tapes to me and I found them very interesting. If I had not already read the past ten years of Fed history before seeing your presentation – and Jake's – I probably would have thought you were both mad," he finished.

Meredith took a sip of coffee, waiting for him to continue. She said nothing and began studying her fingernails, intentionally avoiding eye contact with him. She was not going to lead him to any thoughts or conclusions. What he was going to decide had to rest at Arthur Redbridge's door and no one else's.

"I am feeling better," he said abruptly. "I can do more than I have been but will need some exercise equipment to help me along," he said.

She looked at him and smiled. "That can probably be arranged. I'll have to ask. Frankly, I'm not privy to Jake's and Alex's plans… at least, not beyond a certain point. I'll find out for you."

"How will they get me back in office at the Fed?" he asked.

"I don't know the answer to that, Arthur, but they have asked me if I would go with you to help."

"And?" he asked, quietly.

"I can't make that decision until I know what the plan is. I won't go if it is not with your approval. Like you, I have some physical problems that prevent me from globetrotting like I used to," she said. "Age is a bitch, isn't it?"

They both laughed. "I wonder if you would do me a favor." Redbridge took a sip of coffee, but his eyes never left her face.

"If I can," Meredith responded. "What do you need?"

"Find out for me if there is someone with good intelligence connections who Jake and Alex trust. If so, I would like to ask that person to find someone for me. If this person can be found… well, it might put me in a position to help with a workable plan to fix our sick economy."

Meredith's mind immediately went to Jake. Alex had once told her he was the best man for intelligence work he had ever met. So, Redbridge did not know of Jake's CIA connections.

"I'll see what I can find out and get back to you," she offered. "Will you let me take a picture of you, Arthur? "I want to run some comparisons with pictures of the guy who is passing for you in Washington." He agreed, amiably, and she took a digital camera from her purse.

"Will you be developing the film yourself?" he asked a bit nervously.

"Oh, my dear, we do not develop film any longer. This is a digital camera. Here… you have a computer. I'll show you." She snapped several shots of him, then pulled the connector from her purse and plugged it into a USB port and hooked the camera to the computer. After she hit a few keys, the photos she had just taken appeared on the screen.

"Oh my," he said, startled. "I really will need someone to help me with all of the technological advances if I get back, won't I?" He laughed.

She felt she had laid some necessary groundwork and that it was time to end the visit. This guy was still extremely shrewd, she knew. They both needed time to think. Meredith took her leave graciously, dialing Nancy's home phone number on her cell phone, informing her that she was ready to leave. The door was unlocked a moment later. During that time, she and Arthur Redbridge said their good-byes. They were both smiling.

Joe gave her a ride back to the main house. It was the first time she had met Nancy's husband and she enjoyed his energetic personality. His father's Native American heritage shone in his face. Meredith asked how long Joe had worked for Alex and Jake.

The rear end of the SUV slipped to the right and Joe quickly turned the steering wheel in the direction of the slide. "Whoa, Scout," he said, laughing. "These snowy roads will clear pretty fast," he added. "I've been here since the early '90s. It's a good place to be. I owe Alex a debt I can never repay, but he's given Nancy and me a good life. You're from Denver, I hear," he said as they pulled up in front of the house.

"Yes, grew up and went to school in Denver," Meredith responded.

"I hear we are having spicy chili tonight so Nan won't have to cook. You're a nice lady. Thanks for being concerned about her." With that he backed out of his parking space and drove home.

Meredith greeted Rusty with proper enthusiasm and they disappeared into the house. It would be a good time to make some telephone calls and send a couple of emails, she thought. The intensity of the work they had done to get ready for the meetings had tired her. She enjoyed being alone. It was what she was used to and there was always comfort in the familiar.

She went online to the FCB Web site and downloaded recent photos of the person the world knew as Arthur Redbridge. She wondered how far they would have to go to get the real guy back in office. The photos showed a man – a clone – who looked at least ten years younger than the man with whom she had just met. His eyes were alive with energy, not dull and tired like those of the real Redbridge.

She went to a drawing program she had on her laptop and added hair to the current Arthur Redbridge's photo. It helped a bit.

Just about the time she finished all of the small tasks she had set for herself, she heard the front door open and close. "Anybody home?" she heard Alex call and then heard the security panel click off and then back on.

Meredith turned off the computer and walked down the hall to welcome him home and ooh and ah over his dead fish. They were beautiful, she thought.

"You've already gutted them, so let's wash them, put some ice in the sink and put them to rest on it for awhile," she suggested.

"I will cook you a magical dinner tonight," he said. She could not remember ever seeing him smile so broadly. His hair fell down over his forehead and he looked like a kid who had just found a freshly-baked birthday cake on the table. She was not the only one who had needed to relax, she realized.

"Well, you have enough fish here for several meals, it looks like... so, if you cook me a magical dinner, I will fix trout almandine for your breakfast tomorrow."

"You cook trout for breakfast?" he asked, somewhat surprised. "I've never had trout for breakfast. Who eats trout for breakfast?"

"I'm a Colorado girl," she responded, as if that would answer any questions regarding the fine art of outdoor living and cooking. "And President Eisenhower used to eat trout almandine for breakfast at the Brown Palace Hotel in Denver when he came to Colorado to go fishing." She thought for a moment. "That may have contributed to his heart attack while he was fishing here in the high country, come to think of it." She laughed at the expression on Alex's face.

He took off his coat and hung it on a hook behind the front door.

"Okay, Colorado girl, I'm going to have a beer. What would you like? I'm afraid we're out of cranberry juice... Nancy needs to go to the market," Alex commented. "We have orange, grape or grapefruit juice... or would you like something stronger?"

"Grape juice is fine." She went to her recliner and sat back, enjoying the calm atmosphere. It seemed it was the first time it had been really calm since her arrival.

He told her how beautiful it was at the lake and how relaxing it had been just sitting out in the middle of all that water and snow by himself. "But it's back up into the 50s already," he concluded. "Where's Jake?" he asked.

"He and Gil flew to Denver to get me some clothes. He decided it was a better alternative than driving into town to go shopping. He should be back in about a half-hour," she told him.

"How about a fire?" he asked. Meredith concurred and Alex began preparing one. He clicked a remote and soft music filled the room.

They conversed about what is often thought to be meaningless but so often turns into the meaningful things of life... the quiet times each had enjoyed. Neither of them had very many on their list. They laughed about that.

"Do you know what I would like to do?" he asked her casually. She shook her head in the negative and he rose and held his hand out to her. "I would like to dance with you."

Meredith sat motionless for a moment. The first thing that entered her mind was that she had not danced in years and was too old to start again. The second thing was that perhaps it was not a good idea to become too close personally to anyone at this point in her life and under these circumstances. The third thing she thought was, "For heavens sake, he just asked for a dance!" She rose and they both took a few moments to recall something they had once enjoyed and been good at, but had not done in many years.

"I haven't danced since I went to school in Moscow," Alex told her, eyes laughing.

There was a magnetic pull between them, he realized... he knew he had not intentionally pulled her closer, but during the second dance he found that her body was pressed closely against his. Feelings assailed him that he had for too long ignored, he knew. Both of them were relieved when they heard the security system announce someone entering the front door. They knew it was Jake and Meredith thought about the importance of timing in life.

"Help!" The cry came from the man carrying snow-covered boxes through the entryway. His arms were loaded. They both went quickly to assist him. "Do you want these in your bedroom?" Jake asked, laughing.

"Yes. Bedroom," she responded, also laughing.

"Now that the wanderer has returned, I'll start dinner while you two finish with the box unloading," Alex called, walking to the kitchen. "We're having trout for dinner, Jake."

"Magical trout," Meredith corrected him. She started to pick up a box and carry it down the hall to her room, but Jake told her he would do it. She turned to Alex and asked "Do you need some help?"

"Help?" he asked. "With the trout, no. I might need help with potatoes and a vegetable, though."

He got the electric potato peeler out for her, took two cans of cut green beans from the cupboard, and pulled the makings for salad from the fridge.

"Electric potato peeler?" she asked in an astonished tone of voice. "You two guys really rough it here, don't you?" He showed her how to peel potatoes with it and she laughed. "I've got to get one of these!"

Meredith cut the potatoes into thin slices, diced an onion, added some cheese and evaporated milk to them and then placed them in the oven. "So you know when to start the trout, they will take about an hour," she told him. She drained the beans and dumped them into a baking dish, added some of the left-over diced onions, bacon, and butter and poured sliced almonds on top. They would soon join the potatoes in the oven. Meredith returned to her bedroom to find it full of boxes.

She began opening them and was relieved to find how easily she could determine what had to go into storage and what did not. Jake placed the boxes she needed to unpack on the far side of her bed and put the others in the hallway.

"I can't thank you enough," she said. "And I'm sorry I've inconvenienced you with such a huge load... I didn't realize – "

"After I pulled you out of your home with no warning and brought you over here," he said, interrupting her, "I owe you at least this much so say no more. I don't know about you, but I'm ready for a drink... maybe we'd better check on how Alex is progressing with dinner. As I said, I'm starving! By the way, your townhouse is sold," he finished.

"Well, I'm glad you saved the unimportant stuff for last," she said. For a moment, Jake couldn't tell from her tone if it saddened her. "Come on," she said, grabbing him by the arm. "I'm going to pour you a drink... you've earned it! What would you like?"

"Martini sounds good... two olives, please." Her energy level at this time of day surprised him. She was usually running down by late afternoon. He raised his eyebrows at her as he folded himself into his recliner and relaxed.

Later, the three of them sat down at the table to the most relaxed dinner they had shared since Meredith's arrival. Alex told them about the fish he had cooked for Colonel Yuri Malashenko and what a significant role that night had played in helping him plan his escape from Sakhalin Island.

"So, how did your meeting with Redbridge go?" Jake asked.

She noticed Alex's eyes narrow a bit. She stopped, fork halfway to her mouth. "That, my friends, is a topic for after dinner," she said, and continued eating.

Was it her imagination, or did the two of them begin eating faster? So much for a relaxing day off, she thought, smiling to herself.

Chapter 17

"So, Arthur Redbridge," she said before anyone else could bring up the topic. "I wanted to wait until all three of us were together so we would all be on the same page," she said, looking directly at Alex. "I spent about an hour with him late this morning. I need to get answers to two questions on his behalf."

She paused, waiting for some response. All she got was a nod from each of them.

"Is it possible to get him some exercise equipment?" It was a rather simple question. She expected a quick response, but there was a long silence.

"You did it, didn't you?" Alex asked with a smile that spread slowly across his face. "You got him to want to go back to Washington."

"Well," Meredith responded, "I got him to agree to workout. I got him to commit to putting more effort into preparing himself to return to Washington. He is curious about it, though. He asked how it would be accomplished. I told him the plans were in the hands of you two geniuses."

Jake looked at Alex and laughed. "I can go to the mall in Grand Junction tomorrow and get whatever he needs."

Meredith got up and went to her room to get copies of the pictures she had taken of the real Redbridge and the ones of the clone she had downloaded from the Fed's Web site. The computer drawings she had done to show him with more hair were included in the package. She handed them to Alex. He, in turn, handed them to Jake.

"I can help stimulate hair growth with some DNA additions to his IV," Alex said, looking at her admiringly for her foresightedness. "There is a specific gene portal for that."

"Oh… is that why you two still have full heads of hair?" Meredith asked. They just smiled a response. No words were needed to tell her she had uncovered a secret having to do with male egos.

"And what else did Dr. Redbridge have to say?" Alex asked.

She took a long sip of grape juice. "He wanted to know if the two of you have a good contact in the intelligence community… someone who can find a person for him. He says if this man can be found, he may be able to fix our economy," she finished.

They both just stared at her, not knowing exactly what questions to ask. Men like Arthur Redbridge did not say such things without something tangible in mind.

"He gave you no idea what kind of plan he has in mind?" Jake asked and Meredith shook her head.

"No," she replied. "He said nothing… just asked the question. He has some trust issues – I don't think anyone can blame him for that," she finished.

Alex merely looked down, saying nothing.

"He and I had a talk about you, Alex," Meredith said calmly. "I think you might find his attitude somewhat changed on the trust issue. If you think it is okay, I suggest you let him take a look at Jeffrey's papers. He and Jeffrey knew one another. If you let him see the papers, it might help pave the trust road a bit – and it will let him know just how serious things are."

They waited for her to continue and when she did not, Alex asked her about the rest of the conversation. "If it's not personal, I'd like to know."

"Some of it is personal," she told him. "He asked me if I trust you and Jake. I told him I do, but I also told him I would not tell him or anyone else who to trust."

Again, the Russian said nothing. It was a painful subject for him, she realized, and she did not expect a response. Instead, she continued with her overview of the hour she had spent with the Fed Chairman.

"And here I thought we all had a wonderfully relaxing day," Jake said, breathing deeply, then, chuckling. "I imagine that his suspicions extend to me as well as you, Alex. I was the one who drugged him and locked him in a shipping crate."

Alex was looking steadily into the fire, but heard every word Jake said. "Trust is a difficult thing," he finally said. His voice was quiet and sad. He wondered if by saving Redbridge and putting him back in power, he was dooming himself.

"I think I'll take an early shower and watch some television in my room," Meredith offered. She was an expert at feeling other people's tension levels. "It will give you guys a chance to talk."

Alex rose as she did, telling Jake he'd be right back. Rusty followed the two of them as they walked down the hallway to her room, his nails clicking on the wood floor.

She opened the door and the dog preceded her into the room. Alex took her hand and pulled her one step closer to him, bent forward and kissed her lightly on the lips. He heard her sharp intake of breath and knew he had surprised her more than he had intended.

"Thanks for the dance," he said, grinning. Meredith smiled, nodded her head and slowly pulled away from him, closing the door behind her as she entered her room. What a nice way for him to take her back to the moment before the two of them had been interrupted by Jake's return. There were no sexual overtones to his kiss, just a friendly peck on the mouth... well, maybe a bit softer than a peck. Still, it surprised her and she knew when she tried to sleep tonight she would remember feeling his hard, muscular body against hers as they danced. She smiled, thinking it was nice that he wanted to re-visit those moments alone with her before saying goodnight.

Meredith set the alarm clock so she would be out of bed, showered and dressed in time to have breakfast cooking when the two men got up. Then she turned on the television and found old re-runs of the X-Files on the Sci-Fi channel. She had loved that series and undressed while listening to Dana Scully tell Fox Mulder that he had to learn to be more scientific about things.

*****

"I've re-set the cable, cell, and satellite technology," Alex said to Jake as he re-entered the living room.

"Oh, that's where you went," Jake said in a sarcastic tone of voice indicating he knew Alex had another reason for leaving the room with Meredith. "You two looked pretty cozy when I opened the door earlier," he commented dryly.

"Yes, I know," Alex said and offered no further explanation. "Let's talk about a plan for Redbridge. What do we do?"

They should have discussed this much earlier, Alex thought, but neither he nor Jake wanted to talk beyond the point of recovering the cloned prisoners. It had been a high-risk project and needed their full attention. Too, they knew it would take months to re-educate Redbridge and the others. They would have time to plan.

"Well," Jake said, "to start with, he's a famous man. If he disappears with no explanation, the media frenzy would resemble piranhas in a pool with fresh meat. How do you handle that?"

They were both silent for a long moment. The fire crackled and Jake suddenly dropped the leg support on his recliner, sitting upright. After a moment or two, he got up, went to the door and opened it, stepped outside briefly to get another log and returned to place it on the dwindling fire. He loved this fireplace, he thought, all rock from floor to ceiling and covering most of the wall. The hall to the bedrooms was on the other side of it. It had a big opening for the fire in case they had to use it for cooking. Being unattached to utility companies had its insecurities. And, it had heating ducts to each bedroom in the house should heat be needed. No one would break into a sweat from the heat it provided, but it, combined with the earth house formula and solar panels, would keep them from freezing even in the coldest of weather.

"Maybe I should get another log?" he asked Alex.

"No," the other man responded, "I've been up since before sunrise and am going to hit the sack pretty soon. Any ideas?"

"Hit the sack?" Jake laughed. "Are you finally becoming Americanized?" he asked. "Let's say we start with an auto accident involving the clone's limousine." Jake would have normally said 'limo,' but he knew Alex hated slang. "We provide the ambulance that picks up the cloned Fed Chairman and the real Redbridge is hiding inside of it. We take the real Redbridge to a hospital where we control the environment. Don't ask how... it can be done. Let's say we put Redbridge in a heavily-guarded room at a private hospital with our own doctor and nursing staff on duty – that is doable. Brett and I can handle the medical stuff. Once the real Redbridge is in the hospital, we take the clone to the airport and fly him back here. From the moment Redbridge is not taken to a place like Bethesda or Walter Reed, the media will be hunting for his whereabouts..."

"Wildly hunting for his whereabouts," Alex interrupted.

"Right wildly hunting... so why doesn't Redbridge ask Katie or Charlie or Bill or Barbara to join him for an exclusive network interview? They have to promise that four hours after they air their exclusive they make it available to other media outlets. Brett Radov has contacts we can use in the Secret Service. Redbridge can request someone Brett knows to guard him – the President would not dare deny such a request."

Jake finished speaking and looked at Alex for a reaction. After a short silence, Alex asked how they could keep Redbridge's location secret if they took the national news media to his room.

"Redbridge tells them his terms through his security guard. That's why we need a Secret Service guy... the news network has to be able to check him out. The Redbridge security guy tells the media personality that the interview is conditional on the network not knowing Redbridge's location. He wants a written agreement to that effect. The possibility of a large law suit over a contract violated would make everyone very careful. Redbridge tells them he needs privacy to make a full recovery, but understands the people's right to know that he has survived the accident and will be back in his office within a week or two. We put Katie or Charlie or Bill or Barbara with their camera crew in a panel truck. No windows. We change trucks – from black to white – during the ride to the hospital, in case they track us from the air. The change of vehicles takes place under some kind of covered drive or in a tunnel. We'll have to look around for the right place," Jake said, pausing long enough to drain the remnants of his drink.

"We make sure the hospital's identity is not visible between the hospital's parking garage and Arthur's room. The room has to be close to the elevator. Security clears the hallway at the time the media personality arrives. Redbridge is interviewed with his face swathed in bandages, but with enough face showing to be recognizable. We have to work on his voice to make sure he sounds just like his clone. What do you think?"

Alex paced in front of the fireplace. He walked from the patio doors to the stairs leading to the cabin's upper entry several times. He was lost in thought.

"I think it could work," he finally told Jake. It amazed Alex how his partner could create complex plans involving physical action and secrecy and do it so quickly. Maybe Meredith was right about him... he was a G.I. Joe action figure. Alex paused for a moment, then added, "Isn't it funny how much more tired you get on a relaxing day than one when you work your butt off? I'm going to bed. We'll talk more about this tomorrow... it's a good start, though."

Jake sat watching the log in the fireplace burn down. He went to get a beer and sat back down to drink it. He reached for the remote and turned on the music. "Unforgettable" by Nat King Cole was playing. Was that what they'd been dancing to when he walked in, he wondered? Jake had a natural sense of protectiveness towards Meredith. He had practically abducted her and brought her here, after all. But he also had a brotherly kind of love for Alex Plotnikov. He could not read Meredith's feelings well, but he could read what Alex had on his mind and it bothered him. Right now was not the time for any of them to have their minds on anything but what they needed to accomplish. He thought about it for awhile, clicked the music off, put the Coors Beer can in the sack for recycling, and placed the fire screen protectively tight against the stone wall. He then walked slowly down the hall wondering if a protective attitude was all he bore towards her. It would have to be, he thought conclusively.

When he walked back down the hallway the next morning, Jake could hear laughter coming from the kitchen.

"Is that the promised trout almandine I smell?" he asked, making a point to ask the question before rounding the corner at the end of the hallway. "Isn't that what Ike ate for breakfast when he used to fish in Colorado?" he asked.

They laughed in response to the question and Jake guessed this was ground they had already covered.

"It is the promised trout almandine," Meredith said, laughter still in her voice. Either Alex's IV was working overtime on her, or she was glowing for some other reason, Jake realized. Maybe it was both.

"So tell me. What's in this Presidential dish? Trout and...?"

Instead of Meredith's voice, Alex chimed in, repeating the ingredients he had seen her use. "Butter, lemon juice, parsley, finely-sliced almonds, and just a touch of garlic," he said. "Of course, the trout was dipped in egg and corn meal first," he added.

"Of course," Jake said knowingly.

Meredith removed the trout from the skillet, placed them on a serving dish, raised them up an inch or so by the tail and with a fork quickly de-boned them.

"She's a Colorado girl," Alex told him in response to the look on Jake's face.

"If you will toast each of us half of an English muffin, we can eat," she told Alex.

She had mashed the leftover cheesy potatoes from last night's dinner, fashioned them into small cakes, dipped them in egg, then corn meal and fried them in butter. "Gentlemen, your breakfast is served." The words came out lightly. She was enjoying this, Jake could tell. How did someone who obviously got so much pleasure from something as simple as cooking end up in all those bank boardrooms?

"The coffee pot is on the table," Alex commented. Jake automatically turned to the table and poured three cups while Alex buttered muffins. "What a team!" Jake said softly. He was surprised to see the newspaper lying on the table by his place setting. "Well, who do I have to thank for making the trip to the mailbox for me?" he asked.

"Both of us," Alex said putting a hand on the other man's shoulder. "Meredith is not yet ready to admit it, but the IV has kicked in," he laughed. "She appears to have her doubts about the brooding scientist's skills."

"Not true," she answered. "I do feel better," she admitted, "but my banker's skeptical mind tells me to wait for firmer ground before declaring this experiment a success." She nodded her head definitively at both of them.

The three ate breakfast quietly. The only comment made was when Alex told Jake he could certainly understand why a President of the United States had chosen to eat trout with his eggs for breakfast. He looked briefly towards the heavens and closed his eyes. Meredith considered it the ultimate compliment that Jake did not open the newspaper until he finished eating.

She shooed them out of the kitchen, telling them she would handle the clean-up.

Alex made sure she knew one of the SUVs was parked in front of the house and the keys were on the kitchen countertop. On the way to the mailbox, he had shown her how to click the button to open and de-secure the security gates when she crossed over them and then re-secure the gates once past them. He was making sure she knew she had free rein.

Meredith picked up her cell phone and dialed Nancy's number, asking if she and Joe would like some trout almandine for dinner. "If either one of you has a problem with blocked arteries, I would definitely not recommend it," she warned. When the other woman laughed and said no one at her house had such a problem and she would be right down to pick the food up, Meredith told her not to bother. She would drive it to their house.

She put Rusty out while she put on boots and a jacket and combed her hair. She looked at herself a little more closely in the mirror and saw the change of which Jake had spoken earlier. She was getting better... but it was too soon to get her hopes up just because she was losing a little weight and had fewer gray hairs today than she did yesterday. Looking more closely at her image, she knew it was more than that. She just looked...younger. She'd never had many wrinkles in her face, so that wasn't it. There was a difference in her eyes and in her complexion. And, she knew she felt better. Was it because of the medication? Or was it because she was, for the first time in a very long time, happy?

"Oh, no, Scarlet," she said to her mirror image. "You are just going to have to wait and worry about that tomorrow." She almost joyously drove the short distance to her neighbor's house. It felt good to be free, she thought.

Meredith had been back at the main house for about two hours when she heard the car drive by. If it was Jake and Alex, they were probably taking the exercise equipment to Arthur Redbridge, she thought. Maybe she should be more security conscious and she picked up the telephone to call Nancy. Before she could complete the call, she heard the car engine again. That was strange, she thought. With the number dialed but the cell phone "Talk" button not pushed, Meredith went quickly to the front door to look out the glass panel.

"Oh, my God!" she said out loud. Rusty's ears perked up. She quickly turned to the security system, hitting the security button to close the divider wall across the back of the upper cabin entryway. The closed divider hid completely the larger downstairs area. She called Rusty to follow her. She ran down the hall to the bedroom, shut and locked her bedroom door and hit the talk button on her phone almost all in one motion. "Nancy, we have unwanted guests. I know they are unwanted guests. They are the same people who tried to kidnap me in Denver. Tell Joe to get here quick!" She hung up the phone immediately.

She spent five nervous minutes waiting, not knowing what else to do. Then she heard the security system emit the sound of someone entering and held her breath until she was sure the alarm had been properly key-coded to shut it off. She heard a knock on her door and shut her eyes. "It's me, Meredith," Joe said. She was so glad she had met him yesterday and recognized his voice. She opened the door cautiously. Rusty stood by her side.

"Oh, Joe, I'm so glad to see you!" she said. "When I saw that brown car, it scared me to death!"

"It was the car from the other day," he said in a soft but serious tone. "They stopped and looked in the window panel of the door. I saw them but they didn't see me... I don't think they did, anyway. You had a cool head to remember to hit the room divider button. All they saw was the one room – the back wall of the entry – and an old looking cabin. Are you okay?" he asked, noticing her reddened face and rapid breathing.

"Yeah," she replied. "I just need to sit for a minute. Did you close the divider wall when you came down the hall?" she asked.

"Sure did," he said smiling. "I'll go take a look and see where they are. Nancy is standing on the road down by our place, so if they went back that way, she'll see them and call me. Be cool. Everything is okay." He felt torn... Meredith was obviously upset and he hated to leave her.

He moved towards the stairway and she followed behind him. She wanted that divider closed, just in case they somehow found their way back.

A few moments after she sank back down in the chair, the security system buzzed again and was quickly encoded by whoever was on the other side of the divider wall. It, too, opened, and she was overwhelmingly relieved to see Jake and Alex hurry down the stairs towards her.

"We can't leave you alone for a minute, can we?" Jake asked. "You just have a penchant for attracting danger." He could still see the remnants of her red face. Joe had met them at the first gate and told them what had happened and the upset it had caused her. He pulled some cartridges from his jacket pocket and looked at Alex. "I'll go check these," he said. "I'll be right back."

"It upset you that much, did it?" Alex asked. Her reaction puzzled him. She had been so calm after the first crisis in Denver. "I'm sorry it happened, Meredith, but you handled it so well... it may be the best possible thing that could have happened."

She looked at him as if he had lost his mind. "What did you say?" she asked him. "Best possible thing?"

He looked at the closed patio cover and smiled. "You're a rather amazing person. You have only been here a short time. You hear a car engine, look out the window to check and when you see the car that tried to kidnap you have the presence of mind to hit security switches and room divider switches, go to your bedroom and lock yourself in, call Joe. You let those jerks look in the front window to see an old cabin with one or two rooms. They decided you wouldn't be in a small, run-down shack. They were checking things out, Meredith, and we passed the test. We're off of their list."

She thought over what he was saying and was about to respond when Jake entered the room carrying photographs.

He handed them to Meredith. The security camera Jake had left at the first entry when the intruders came two days ago had clearly photographed the man on the beach at the Cherry Creek Reservoir. It was the same car he had been driving that day. If she'd ever had any doubts, they were gone. They wanted the material Jeffrey sent to her. They wanted her. She shivered and gave brief thanks to God for giving her the good sense to let Jake bring her here.

"How did they get past the security system?" she asked. "How did they get across the cattle guards without setting off the alarm?"

Jake said nothing, just looked at her for a moment. She was truly upset. "They must have gotten suspicious about something day-before-yesterday. They had to guess there was a security system in place... they got such a fast response from Joe to their entry. People usually aren't out walking up and down a country road in a snow storm. Maybe that was it. They obviously have some sophisticated equipment. We'll have to keep the gates locked for awhile."

They all sat quietly for a few moments and then Jake offered to reheat the chili and taco mix for dinner. Alex poured himself a drink and lit a fire, then sat down across from Meredith.

He held out his right hand to her. "Come on," he said, standing. "Let's sit on the couch." She did not look at him, but took his hand and rose slowly, following him to the couch. She needed to be close to someone right now. He sat beside her, took her free hand in his and just looked at her, sadly.

After putting the remaining chili into a pot and turning it on medium-low, Jake looked around the corner of the dining room to see them sitting on the couch, Alex's arm around her and her head on his shoulder. He didn't know quite what to do... he couldn't spend the night in the kitchen. Instead, he walked quietly past his two friends without casting a glance in their direction. He entered the hallway and turned towards his bedroom. It was an uncomfortable situation and it bothered him.

"Okay," Alex said softly to her. "Tell me what you're feeling. I don't know you well, but I know this is an overreaction. I know your tension level had to be terribly high and I'd expect you to have an initial reaction of fear. But this is more than that, isn't it? You're dealing with a scar, aren't you?" Fear was one thing, but unreasonable fear once a threat had passed was something else.

She raised her head and looked at him rather strangely. "How did you get so smart?" she asked. "How could you know that? Ah, I know. You have your own scars, right?"

No words were spoken, but he nodded his head once and looked down. She saw gentle concern in his eyes when he raised his head to speak to her.

"When did it happen... the thing that left this scar?" His voice was very gentle and yet totally reasoned.

She was quiet for a long time before answering. "I never got over the fear I had of the prowlers who bothered me while Ron was in prison," she said quietly. "I have never really felt secure since then when staying alone. I thought I was over it – until today. It all came sweeping back over me," she declared, obviously feeling her emotions very strongly.

The arm he had placed around her shoulders bent at the elbow as he stroked her hair and then let his hand rest on the side of her head as if he were holding it in place on his shoulder. "Tell me about the prowlers," he said softly.

"I don't want to talk about it. I appreciate your thoughtfulness, but your specialty is physics, not psychiatry." He waited a moment, but she said nothing more.

"Let go of it, Meredith. It will help, I promise," he argued gently. "Tell me about the prowlers."

She wiped her eyes on the back of her hand. He reached into his pocket and provided a handkerchief. She stood and moved back to her own chair. "Don't you think I've tried to let go of it?" He heard the underlying tremble in her throat. "There must be something I'm supposed to learn from that whole nightmare that I haven't yet learned. Talking about it won't help."

Alex moved to his chair so that he could look directly at her. "Who, other than yourself, have you ever really told about the prowlers – and whatever else happened that caused such deep hurt?"

She knew he was right. She had never talked with a counselor, her kids, or anyone else about the true terror she had felt during that time. "Alright," she said. She smiled at him. She raised the recliner's foot rest and let herself sink back into the cushions.

"At first, I had no idea who was doing the prowling. I'd call the police, they came... no one was ever there. Then one night I was sitting in my dark living room late at night. I heard a noise outside the dining room window. I looked out and saw a shadow bending over, under the window. That was where our telephone connection came into the house. I screamed out the window to my neighbor to call the police and, thank God, her bedroom window was open. The guy ran. She told me the next day that the figure bending over the telephone line was a police officer. That's it," she said and the finality in her tone let him know she was through talking about it.

"So, there you were," he went on as if she had not uttered the last comment, "at – what, twenty-one years of age?"

"No, I was twenty-four."

"A twenty-four year old young woman with two babies to protect who were lying asleep in their bedroom, a husband in prison, and those who are supposed to be protecting you are trying to break into your house. They were trying to frighten you, weren't they? They wanted to keep you off balance and make sure your husband kept his mouth shut. I guess I can understand how that might leave a scar." He leaned forward, elbows on his knees, as he asked the question, hands gesticulating as he spoke.

"I know, I know," she said. "I'm being unreasonable with myself. I understand the problem. I just don't seem to be able to fix it."

"What else happened?" he asked. His tone was businesslike.

"What do you mean 'what else happened'?" she asked, somewhat surprised.

"Did something else happen to you?" he repeated.

"There were the telephone calls in the middle of the night," she offered. "Someone would call about one in the morning. They would just breathe into the telephone. The caller even found me on a Saturday in the law office where I worked. That told me he had to be following me. I was in a huge, almost deserted building... that scared me, too."

"What happened? Did it end?" Alex continued the questioning.

She sighed deeply before continuing. "My mother and stepfather came to my house in the wee hours one morning because of a prowler incident. The phone rang, my stepfather answered. When he heard the breathing he threatened to meet the guy and beat the crap out of him. I never got another call after that," Meredith concluded.

"What else happened during that time?"

"You can be a ruthless bastard, can't you?" Her voice wasn't angry, but it was strained he noted.

"What other kind of person could walk through a nursery every week and look at babies being grown in fake wombs that he had created?" he asked. "Only a ruthless bastard could do that."

"Stop it, Alex!" she demanded. "Stop demeaning yourself!" she said.

"I would ask the same of you," he replied in a sarcastic tone.

There was a long silence as they looked at one another. She finally closed her eyes and whispered, "And I committed adultery."

Alex shook his head back and forth slowly. "And now we know what the anchor is that keeps you tied to the past, don't we? It's guilt. I want you to tell me about it." He took a slow, deep breath.

She shook her head hard and fast. "No," she responded. "I have never talked about it. I do not want to think about it, let alone talk about it."

"Well, you're going to have to talk about it... and as I said, it's much easier to talk to me than it is to yourself. I know because I've tried it, too. It doesn't work, does it?" he demanded. On this subject, he was an expert, he thought to himself. "Would it help you know that I am incapable of judging you if I told you about the whores the government used to send to my residence on Sakhalin Island to take care of my needs because they would not risk letting me socialize?" he asked. "Don't feel lonely in your guilt," he said.

After a long pause, she began. "When I went on welfare while Ron was in prison, I was barely getting enough to survive. Food, rent, utilities, telephone, doctors, and gasoline... driving three hundred miles roundtrip for Saturday visits with Ron was costly. "My mother and stepfather invited me to go out dancing with them and a woman friend of theirs one night. I really didn't want to go," she said, sounding as if the memories were very vague in her head. "They talked me into it and we were all sitting at a table having a drink and a really nice-looking man asked me to dance. I danced with him... more than once. He asked me if he could take me home and I told him no, that I was married and just out for an evening of fun with my parents." After a long pause, she asked for some more water.

Alex rose, walked to the kitchen, and refilled her glass.

"Go on," he said.

"He – his name was Dick – asked the other woman with us to dance and later joined us for breakfast at an all night restaurant. They began seeing one another. Within a week or two, they both began calling me from her house. They stopped by once or twice. He called one night to say he was going to swing by. I thought he meant the two of them, as usual, but he showed up on my doorstep alone, carrying a couple of large steaks, some milk and some baby formula and food... some other groceries, too. It felt so good to eat until I was full. I barely drank in those days. He brought some liquor and I had a couple of drinks. I wasn't drunk... but I slept with him that night and kept sleeping with him for the next month, until shortly before Ron was released from prison. He never spent the night, but as long as his car was parked in the driveway, I had no more prowlers. I felt safe for the first time in a very long time," she said. "I don't know which was more appealing. Him, the food, the sense of security, the lack of feeling so alone... I don't know. I do know that during that time I found out that there was nothing wrong with me sexually and that my husband was a lousy lover," she finished.

All Alex could think of was how long she had lived with this in her head. "You were a virgin when you got married, weren't you?" he asked suddenly. He knew it was one of his "I've identified a core problem" moments. She merely nodded in response.

"An innocent young woman – child, really – gets married and starts having babies right away as a good Catholic should," he said. "Her husband makes some stupid mistakes and suddenly everything she thought she could rely on for food, protection, support, justice, and faith cave in on her. And someone else came along and held out his arms to you and you went into them. How terrible! Please! What tremendous pressure you were under at the time," he said, his voice filled with empathy. "Where was your husband's family? How did they help? What did they do to make life bearable for you?"

"His sister helped financially... with lawyer bills," Meredith responded, dully. "They didn't want his mother to know about it... I told you that last time we talked about this. Other than that, his family did nothing. They lived in New York and I lived in Denver."

After a brief pause, he said "As I recall, you told me the IRS filed suit against you both because you had filed joint tax returns. You had to pay taxes on money he was supposed to have received from burglaries in which he was named, right?" Again, she nodded. "And even though you – not him, you – were making payments to the IRS as agreed for taxes on money you never saw, the IRS still came out in the middle of the night and took the car you were using to get to and from work to support you and the kids, didn't they?"

"What are you trying to prove with all of this?" she asked, angrily.

"Good! Get angry! Shout at me! It's about damned time you did!" he said in a raised voice. "That son of a bitch decided to play cops and robbers, failed, let you pay the price while he sat in prison, came home, let you support him for over five years before you divorced him, then blamed you for the divorce when, during that entire time, he never supported you and the kids once, did he?" Alex demanded.

"No, he didn't," she said. She was looking at him and the indifferent gaze was gone, he realized. "He tried... or, he said he tried. All I know is, I was very tired of working all day to support everyone and working all night to take care of hearth, home and kids," she said weakly.

"And when you divorced him, he declared bankruptcy and left you with all of his bills, didn't he? And you paid them, didn't you?" He was being unrelenting, he realized, but she needed to come to grips with this, get over it and move on with her life.

"Yes. I paid them," she said, remembering the three years she went without clothes, car or any of the other necessities to pay his bills.

"Meredith, for God's sake! Look at what you've done with your life! Look where you started and look where you ended up! So you had sex with some other man while your husband was in prison and you feel guilty about it. Any moral person would feel guilt. A Christian like you would feel even greater guilt... but a repentant Christian also knows that the sins for which she asks forgiveness are forgiven. That's what the Cross is all about, isn't it? I'm going to tell you something I had to learn while I was trying to recover from my misbegotten life. It's all about forgiveness. The most important thing you have to do now is to forgive yourself for the mistakes you have made – or, if you prefer, the sins you've committed. Deep inside yourself, you fear God has not forgiven you... because you have not forgiven you. You have forgiven everyone but you. That just doesn't make good sense, does it?"

She just stared at him. It was as if he could see inside her head, places she had been too frightened to look.

"I think it's time we let Jake come out of his room and have something for dinner, don't you?" he asked, smiling and hoping to break the tension in the room.

She sighed deeply. "I'm glad I taught you guys how to put your own tacos together the other night, because I'm going to bed. I just don't feel like eating tonight."

He started to stop her, but knew she needed time to think it all over. He waited until he heard her door close, then walked to Jake's room and told him to come and have some dinner.

Chapter 18

She felt like a wet washrag that had been wrung out and hung up to dry, but as tired as she was, sleep evaded her. She was not hungry. She had no appetite for food or for life at this moment. Somewhere deep inside, she knew Alex was right. She had not forgiven herself for violating her personal beliefs.

He had made her realize something – perhaps something important. It was not the lost safety and security that had left the scars she hid so well and that frightened her so deeply. It was the way in which she had sought – or accepted – security when it was offered. She understood better than anyone the weight of the burden she had carried at the time, but burdens were no excuse. Neither was tenderness of age. She would have to think about that… but she had done enough thinking for one day. Instead, she got down on her knees and prayed to the God she worshipped. This time, however, rather than asking God to forgive her, she carefully asked for His blessing and the gift of His grace to help her forgive herself. She did not have to tell Him the depth of her sorrow. He knew.

Alex had lived through his own nightmares with conscience and understood how weak the battle left its participants. When he had first moved to the ranch, he could not be seen in public. He spent his days and nights alone. It gave him time to figure out many things he'd never had time to think of before. Alex had never been inside a church. He was raised in a political system where government imposed itself on people as the ultimate God-like authority.

He was amazed at the number of churches listed in his local telephone book's Yellow Pages. This was just a small city. What must the list be like in big cities like New York or Chicago? He had been puzzled when his satellite dish was hooked up and he turned on the television. How could a nation so fixated on churches run the hundreds of depraved forms of what they termed entertainment twenty-four hours a day? If it wasn't violent, it was vile. How could all of these Christians who went to all of these churches watch this stuff? Someone had to be watching it or no one would pay for and sponsor it, he thought.

On one of his shopping excursions to the mall in Grand Junction, Alex picked up several books, including the Holy Bible. Reading it directed his feet to a road that finally led to an epiphany. As he read the words of Christ, he equated being born again to a process. Christ told Nicodemus, a member of the Sanhedrin and an elder of Judaism, that a man must be born again to enter the Kingdom of Heaven. As it had not at first made sense to Nicodemus, it at first did not make sense to Alex.

Then he read one of the other books he had purchased. It was *People of the Lie*, by contemporary author M. Scott Peck. He began to understand that being born in sin meant being born a creature of the earth... as all animals are creatures of the earth. To find spiritual life, people, he realized, had to go through the same kind of transformation a butterfly must make... a process of metamorphosis. In his book, Peck had referred to evil as "malignant energy." Alex liked the term because it clearly defined the meaning of evil. It was a malignancy, he thought. Left to its own devices, evil would grow and kill healthy tissue as physical malignancies did. Then he came to realize that as darkness was merely the absence of light, evil was the absence of God.

Perhaps because he was a physicist who thought in terms of equals and opposites, he kept pouring through words in his mind to think of what the opposite of malignant energy might be. He finally decided his definition for the opposite of evil would be "metamorphic energy." He figured out that he had been born in sin – an animal in a world of animals – and had the opportunity to use metamorphic energy to become closer to his Creator... to be born again, as a butterfly was when it went through metamorphosis. Being born again, he decided, was the primary purpose of his life.

He also read books written by his countrywoman, Ayn Rand. In *The New Intellectual*, Alex found her description of the differences between human beings and animals fascinating. She said animals and humans shared two ingrained traits: Perception and sensation. All animal life had the gift of sensation... of being sated by food or sex or winning a competition. All had the gift of perception and could innately sense danger or safety or hatred or love. Though her explanations went much deeper, Alex agreed and took from her words the basics: Humans and animals shared those two traits. Alex also realized that if a human being wanted to live life at a level higher than four-legged animals, he had to tap into a different capacity than sensation or perception... a different capacity than other animal life possessed.

Man, according to Ms. Rand, had a third capacity that was beyond anything non-human animals could achieve. It was the capacity for conceptual thought and it belonged exclusively to humans. No one could force people to use it and no one could prevent them from doing so. That was how freedom came to be. It was conceptualized. Conceptual thought, Alex realized, was the base from which all creative expression came. And, as a physicist he understood that for every positive in nature there was a negative of equal strength – and vice-versa. He realized that creative expression could result from either malignant *or* metamorphic energy. Creative energy could be good or it could be evil. People could conceptualize positively, or negatively. It was their choice.

It was on these realizations that his faith in God and appreciation for truth had been born. Like anything newborn, the truth he sought about his Creator continued to grow. It was still growing. At first, Alex's philosophies about God tended to parallel the concept of Dualism explained by C. S. Lewis in *Mere Christianity*. Because God had created Nature and the Laws of Nature, he found those ideas easiest to adapt to his physics background and lack of any religious training. Prior to this discovery, he had viewed things like gravity as "universal laws" or "laws of physics." He soon realized that the process of metamorphosis – of each individual being born again to find God – had to be based on people of free will choosing good over evil. Sin and the forgiveness of it was one thing. Evil was something entirely different. Mostly, Alex figured, sin became evil when people rationalized sinful behavior into positive intentions. God forgave sins. Alex was unsure if He forgave evil.

In his own mind, he designed the way he would exercise his metamorphic muscles to grow them stronger. That was when he discovered the necessity and value of forgiveness… of self and of others. As Christ had said, forgiveness was the key to everything.

It was his own experience that had given him insight into Meredith's pain. Also because of his physics background, he knew the energy of the mind – his thoughts – was an energy form. It was sent into the universe as surely as any prayer. He realized that mouthing positive prayers at night after a day of negative thoughts was hypocritical. Faith, he realized, was a growth process.

He hoped he had not used his discovery too harshly with Meredith as he showered and went to bed. She was a person who innately understood what it had taken him years to work out for himself. She, however, had not yet formalized the means by which to implement self forgiveness. She had mastered the forgiveness of others, but not self.

The next morning, Meredith was in sweats cooking bacon and eggs when Jake and Alex walked into the kitchen. "There's coffee made," she said, smiling at them.

"Are you okay?" Alex asked, concern echoing deeply in his voice.

"Not yet," she replied quietly. "But I will be."

The relaxed environment of three friends enjoying one another's company had suffered a blow. There was tension in the air and she could feel it.

"How about a game of chess?" she asked Alex after breakfast. Her voice sounded a bit strained and nervous. It was a request out of the blue and it surprised him.

"Let me get this straight," he said, trying to be responsive to her efforts to introduce a sense of normalcy. "You, an American, are challenging me, a Russian, to a game of chess?"

"You got it, Ivan," she said, laughing. It sounded a little forced, but it would take time before her natural humor returned. She knew he realized that and was holding out a hand of redemption to her when, with eyebrows raised, he reached for the chess board.

Jake completed his kitchen duties and watched them study and make their moves for a few minutes. Then he announced that he was going to the lab to do some exercising. He was smiling when he left.

As they sat studiously over the chess board, there was no mention of the past few days, no soft music, no active concern was expressed. It was just a game of chess between two acquaintances.

"You're scheduled for another IV today," he said after check-mating her king. "Starting next week, we only have to do them once a week." Alex thought for a moment. "Why don't you stop by today and exercise with Redbridge on the treadmill we got him?"

She nodded, agreeably. He was right. It would be easier to exercise with someone around her.

The exercise tired her. When they went to the lab, he inserted the IV into her arm and turned on the soft music. No words were exchanged between them. They returned to the house and Meredith told him she was tired and was going to lie down for awhile. She did not wait for his answer. Rather, she turned down the hallway, called Rusty in after her, and closed the bedroom door. It was not an abrupt action... just a definite one.

He knew she was inwardly afraid that if the camel put its nose under the tent, it would soon reside in it. He was the camel, she was the tent. He had gotten too close to her last night – the nose under the tent. She was going to try and make sure he got no closer. It would have to work itself out.

The next few days were spent pretty much as those that preceded the "invasion of the brown car," as Meredith had come to think of that day. Jake and Alex worked on plans for getting Arthur Redbridge back into the driver's seat at the Fed. Meredith continued to research people and policies at the Federal Central Bank. The two men also started spending more time with the other three returned captives. She had no idea what the plans were for them. She could add nothing to their areas of expertise... law, politics, and talk radio.

If she was going back to Washington with Redbridge, she needed to be able to place as many names and faces as possible. As she searched online pages, she found the cloned Fed chief had surrounded himself with his own personal clique.

It was while reading various articles from online news sources that she came across two pieces that caught her interest. One had to do with the Department of Defense admitting that they had, at some time during the past ten years, lost the financial records for trillions of dollars of defense spending. She probably wouldn't have thought too much about the significance of this announcement had she not stumbled upon another article immediately afterwards about a man alleging he had been given trillions of dollars over an extended period of time by President Rory McCoy's administration. He was to invest the money on behalf of the American people, he said.

Meredith immediately sought confirmation of the story at other Internet Web sites and found numerous stories saying a variety of things about this man, Leonard Williams. Had she not read the story about the Defense Department's lost financial records before reading this one, she would have marked the guy off as a loon and forgotten it. The two stories taken in context, however, had similarities that raised her natural curiosity.

McCoy had been president through 1988, and she calculated the defense budget for those years. She had to go well into the 1990s for the total amount of the entire defense budget to reach into the trillions.

Leonard Williams claimed that when he consulted for President Rory McCoy, he had been given a huge amount of money to invest on behalf of the American people. Meredith couldn't help but wonder if "huge amount of money" translated to "trillions of dollars." He was to invest it in such a way as to help the Soviet ruble crumble… which had apparently been achieved in 1991. President McCoy, Leonard Williams said, figured the cost with no American casualties would be far smaller than continuing the cold war or having it turn suddenly hot.

The guy in the article was, among other things, a currency trader. Between 1988 and 1991, he invested heavily in Russian rubles. In some way she did not yet understand, he had caused the failure of the ruble and that, in turn, caused the failure of the Soviet Union. What he had done struck a familiar chord in Meredith's memory bank. Much of what this guy said was the kind of manipulation that was now being used to destroy the U.S. dollar.

In January and February of 1991, it was rumored this Leonard Williams had taken possession of 2,000 metric tonnes of Russian gold at a time when just that amount of gold went missing from Russia's Central Bank. Was it a coincidence? She didn't think so.

She checked back to find that the average cost per ounce of gold from 1991 until 9-11 in 2001 had averaged about $325 an ounce. Just prior to 9-11, it was $271.04 an ounce… that was the same year the Department of Defense lost all those financial records. Then, after 9-11, the cost of gold went steadily up. It had averaged over $600 an ounce throughout 2006. The experts said it was heading for $800 plus by year-end 2007. If the government had "borrowed" trillions of dollars from the people to get 2,000 metric tonnes of Russian gold, silver, and a bunch of foreign currencies, the gold alone had more than doubled in value… and, it was gold. It was not paper dollars, decreasing in value. Silver had tripled in value.

Meredith printed copies of each article. She was going to share this information with Jake and Alex, but first she would take it to Arthur Redbridge. He would have a lot more insight into what it might mean than she could calculate. International banking and foreign central banks were enigmas zipped up in conundrums to her. She could recognize a scam when she saw one, but knowing what it meant was another matter altogether.

The next morning when she went to exercise with Redbridge, she took a pot of coffee down the hall with her. He smiled and plugged the coffee pot in as she handed him the articles.

"So, we're going to do some paper work?" he asked. He sat across from her and began reading the articles. "Oh, my…" he whispered at one point about the lost Defense Department invoices. When reading through the second article he said "Good heavens! I can't believe it!" He looked at her with a stunned expression on his face. "This is the man I wanted an intelligence resource to find. His name is William Leonard… well, that's the name by which I knew him. They call him Leonard Williams in this article."

She thought for a moment before proceeding. There were several trails to be followed here and she was not sure precisely which one to track. "The first day I saw you here – at the meeting in the stables – you said you had put together a plan for President McCoy to start eliminating the FCB on a slow but steady basis. Does this have anything to do with that plan?" she asked, cautiously.

He quickly covered the nervousness showing in his eyes, she thought, and answered almost reluctantly, "Well… this man *was* the plan," he said, averting his gaze. "I always wondered if the President found my plan – it looks like he did. The man in this article is using a different name, but so much of the information about where he lived, where his office was located, what he did for a living… it's all the same. I'm sure it's the same guy. With the information provided here, a good investigator should be able to find him, right?"

She was silent for a long moment. She reached for the coffee pot and poured them each a cup. "Cream?" she asked calmly. She waited until he had swallowed his first sip of the hot liquid before continuing. "I have his address," she said quietly.

Redbridge dropped his cup and jumped out of the way of the spill. "Good grief! I couldn't have moved that fast a month ago," he said. "You have his address? Are you sure?" Redbridge asked her to wait a minute while he changed his sweat pants and disappeared into the bathroom. Some of the hot liquid had landed on his leg. Or, she wondered, did he just need time to think?

"The plan," he started speaking as he exited the bathroom, "was for Leonard to buy up to a hundred billion rubles at a time. It was an arbitrage scheme to bring the Soviet economy to its knees. Evidently, it worked. He was to establish bank accounts all over the world – in Russia, France, Italy, Belgium, Lichtenstein, Luxembourg, South America, and the United States – everywhere. He was to invest in gold, silver, and foreign currencies. We knew the value of the dollar was headed south which meant gold was headed up. Because of our national debt, the Fed would have to have Treasury print a lot of dollars. That would cause inflation, but in a controlled way. By over-printing dollars, the value of gold was bound to rise… that's a no-brainer. If he invested in gold as planned, with the cost at what it is today – combined with the decrease of the dollar in value against foreign currencies – the amount of money earned on that investment over fifteen years— well, I cannot begin to imagine its worth."

She just looked at him for a moment. "And he got the money for what appears to be a money-laundering endeavor... where?" she asked.

"From the government... it was planned for 1990 and 1991," he said. "The money began to be taken from the Treasury before that time. As you know, President McCoy left office in 1988, but the money was paid out of the Defense Department budget before then. It took awhile to set up this arbitrage scheme of Leonard's, you know. I'm not sure the president who came into office after McCoy was even aware of the scheme." He lowered his eyes. It was almost as if he did not want her to see the excitement in them, she thought.

"Let's get started on the exercises while I think about this," she suggested.

"You said you have his address?" Redbridge asked her, a bit of anxiety showing in his voice.

"I have an address for him, but it's on my computer. I had no idea this was the guy you wanted to find," she responded. "It's an old address... the article listed where he was imprisoned."

"He's in prison somewhere? In America?" Redbridge asked, not even trying at this point to hide his anxiety. "I need to see the other information you have on this man, Meredith. It is of critical importance," he said. His tone of voice was almost conspiratorial.

"Well, the address was in Illinois. I think he was initially arrested in Europe, but he ended up in prison in Illinois... for tax evasion. I think he owed $18,000?"

"Really!" he said. "He was put in prison over $18,000 in IRS debt? The fact that this is all so unbelievable makes me think it's true," he uttered, quietly.

Meredith stepped onto the treadmill and turned it on to three miles per hour. She would walk a mile in twenty minutes, then sit down and use the bike peddle machine for fifteen minutes. She decided to forego the hand barbell exercises today. She needed to talk with Jake and Alex about this. She smiled because she was no longer limping when she walked.

Nancy had baked a ham for everyone, the three of them included, and Meredith thought it a good time to suggest an after-dinner discussion. They had not had many lately. Jake had without explanation gone out of town a couple of times and Alex kept himself busy between his four guests and working out formulas for them at his laboratory. When she made the suggestion, both men seemed surprised.

"Has Arthur figured out what Jeffrey's papers mean?" Alex asked, curiously.

"No," she said slowly, dragging out the last part of the word. "It's something even more interesting. Do we have some cranberry juice?" She went to the refrigerator and poured herself some juice. The two men reached into the cupboard for an after dinner brandy. They easily slid into their pre-brown car day agenda, Alex re-setting all of the electronic and technical equipment while Jake set up scramblers. Each claimed their usual seat and the two men looked at her expectantly. Wordlessly, Meredith handed each of them a copy of the two articles she had shown Arthur Redbridge. As they read the material, their reaction was very like Redbridge's had been. Meredith reviewed the conversation she'd had with Arthur. Both men remained totally silent for at least a minute after she completed her overview.

"So this loony who was locked up in Illinois is the guy Redbridge wanted my intelligence contact to find?" Jake finally asked, breaking the silence.

"That's what he says," Meredith responded. Her demeanor was quite serious.

"Redbridge thinks the President found his plan and continued with it after his disappearance, right?" Alex asked.

"That was what he said," she replied, "but he was shaken, Alex. When I told him I had the man's address, he literally dropped his coffee cup... had to change sweat pants. He had to have been thinking the same thing I was: What if the person who found the plan was his clone? What if he was the one who presented the plan to the President... with the Soviet Union being informed and making changes to the plan so the U.S.S.R. – later Russia – came out the winner? What if the plan was changed to meet the needs of the

U.S.S.R. in the long rather than the short-term?" She then handed them the remainder of the material which had not been shown to Arthur Redbridge.

"The long-term meaning...?" Alex asked.

"A good chess move... a sacrifice of the queen if it lets you checkmate your opponent. The Soviet Union is gone in the short-term, but what if it has a plan which, if the right moves are made, makes Russia the long-term victor? You must admit, there is a lot of similarity in the way the Russian ruble was destroyed and the way the dollar is being destroyed..." She sighed deeply as she finished talking. This was intelligence stuff and it was not her bailiwick. She realized the sigh was probably one of relief at handing the problem over to Jake. He would know what to do with all of this to find an answer. She did not.

"There's too much documented stuff here for this to be phony," was Jake's initial reaction. "Good grief, they have the address of the prison where he was held until ten years ago, they have passport numbers under different names, and his Social Security number. There have been court cases involving the Internal Revenue Service claims to past-due taxes. There have been court decisions regarding who owns the contents of the various accounts he has... and I'm sure he has not disclosed them all – and the courts say he owns them. Court decisions can be checked to verify all of this really did happen," he concluded.

He busily re-read the material. Alex and Meredith sat quietly, each lost in their own thoughts about this mystery man. "Unbelievable," Jake said quietly. "They let him out of prison on $250,000 bail for an $18,000 IRS debt? He has evidently been arrested in several different countries, but no one has been able to hold onto him or make anything stick. Now, it looks like he's starting to fight back." Jake re-read the material and found it as amazing the second time as it had been the first. "What did Redbridge say his real name is, Meredith?"

"Leonard, William Leonard," she replied.

Jake sat, shaking his head. "I cannot tell you how far up the political ladder this thing goes if what these papers say is true... and I guess that's the first thing we need to find out, isn't it?"

Jake and Alex both read the documents yet again. Meredith sat quietly, waiting for them to finish.

"Meredith," Jake started, "I need to talk with Brett about this right away – and it's not something I want to do on the telephone. I need to go to Washington. I was going to take you to Salt Lake tomorrow to open a bank account. Before we do anything though, I need to get you a driving license in another name... and a Passport. I should have thought of that." He paused briefly, and glanced once at Alex. He hated stepping on anyone's toes in a territorial sense. Since Meredith had mentioned buying a house here in the Valley after her Denver home closed. Alex had said nothing more about her plans. In fact, his friend had been pretty tight-lipped about their houseguest since the day of the brown car.

"I promise that while I'm in Washington I will get the Passport and driving license. I need a photo, name, and some ID." He looked at her expectantly.

"Use the name Mary J. McIntosh. I have a miniaturized copy of my birth certificate in my purse in the name of Meredith J. McIntosh. My Dad changed the spelling of the name from McIntosh to MacIntosh when I was a baby... no legal change was ever made from Mc to Mac. Will that do?"

"Give me the birth certificate. It will help Brett get the other documents issued," Jake said, smiling. "Oh," he said after a moment. "I see what you're doing. If anyone looks for you under the name MacIntosh they won't find you because you're spelling it 'McIntosh.' Clever..."

*****

Arthur Redbridge heard a car door slam and the doorbell ring and realized he had not yet gotten ready for his workout. He hastily donned a sweat suit and combed his hair, then sat in his chair and grabbed a newspaper. He didn't notice that the paper was upside down, but Meredith did when she entered his room.

"Good morning," she said, cheerily. "Ready to have a go at something a bit more difficult than a treadmill and bike pedals?" she asked.

"Meaning...?" he asked.

"Meaning Alex and Jake think we need to spend some time using the exercise equipment at the lab. They say it's tougher." She tried to sound carefree and as if she was looking forward to harder workouts.

"If you're willing to try, so am I," he responded, but his tone was anything but upbeat. She just looked at him, hoping he would give her an explanation without her having to ask for one. "Sorry, Meredith... your news yesterday has put me into a mood I'm unable to shake." He refused to look at her as he spoke.

"Well, I'm heading for the gym at the Lab. If you'd like to come with me, you're welcome." She was no shrink, but she could feel the man's frustration. It filled the room. She certainly understood it. She'd been feeling the same way. Inwardly, she smiled when she realized she was using the same technique on Redbridge that Alex had been using on her... let her figure things out for herself.

"I'm coming," he said quickly. "You're driving?"

"I am," she said. "We have the Jeep at our disposal, today... and it is a beautiful day. Typical of this area," she said. Based on his comments, she was baiting him, she knew.

"What area are we in?" he asked, trying to sound casual.

"Well, you are probably never going to find that out, Arthur. Let's face it. You're going back into the power-driven world of politics where the exchange of information regarding people wanted by other governments is a valuable asset. Alex is still wanted by the Russian government for what they perceive to be his treasonous disappearance. It's been seventeen years and they're still looking, but they know he has a secret that can undo all of the progress of their cloned replacements. They won't give up looking for him," she concluded.

"He thinks I would tell someone where he is if I found out?" Redbridge asked. His tone was incredulous.

"And I think the same thing, Arthur," she said, looking directly into his eyes. "In your world, people are pawns. Let's not play that game. We both know it's true. Once you're returned to power, what if the Russians offered you a deal that would benefit the nation in a huge way – $50-a-barrel oil – and all you had to sacrifice to get the deal was one man: Alex. The only way Alex can protect himself is to keep where he is a secret. If you knew where this place was located… well, I'm sure you can see why you will not be told where we are."

She started the car and remained silent until they pulled up in front of the lab. She noticed Arthur trying to look at the license plates on the Jeep and on Alex's car parked in front. It was to no avail. Jake had made magnetized pads out of a grey fabric that covered them. They were used when the vehicles were driven on ranch property.

The two of them were good for only a half-hour of exercise on the heavier equipment. Meredith was amazed at how her pain levels had receded and was grateful for it, but she tired so easily!

Redbridge hesitated, but could not contain his curiosity. He asked the question she was waiting for. "Did you bring the other material on William Leonard? You said you'd bring it today."

"No, I didn't, Arthur." Meredith's voice was steady and rather expressionless. "It was old information… almost ten years old – from 1997. Jake took off for D.C. this morning to get a friend at the CIA to investigate all of the points made in that material. When he returns, you can be sure what you are reading is accurate. Fair enough?"

"Fair enough," he echoed.

"I have a question for you. What if President McCoy didn't get your papers regarding William Leonard? What if your clone got them? What if he involved Russian intelligence in that plan and they are playing the same game with the dollar that Leonard played with the ruble?" Meredith pulled the Jeep up in front of the bunkhouse, but left the engine running. She looked at him expectantly.

He hesitated. He was relieved that she had asked the question.

"Hmmm… you're saying glasnost was a Gorbachev ploy?" He paused long enough to consider the possibility. "You might be right. A similar thought kept me awake most of the night. It's altogether possible."

She turned off the car engine and opened her door. "Come on, Arthur, I'll see you back to your room."

Chapter 19

Jake returned home two days later. He brought with him a new driving license and a United States Passport in the name of Mary J. McIntosh. She had two photo IDs. In America, it meant she could do just about anything she wanted as long as it was legal.

"Gil and I flew into the Rifle airport and he can fly us to Salt Lake City tomorrow to open your bank account," Jake said. "And, you said you wanted to buy a car. It would probably be a good idea to buy it and get it registered in Utah... while we're there, tomorrow. Then you fly back into Grand Junction tomorrow afternoon with Gil. I'll drive your car home."

They left late the next morning arriving in Salt Lake City shortly after noon. It was a busy time. They opened the checking account using cash Jake brought with him. They then moved on to rent a post office box where the car's Registration could be sent.

They asked the postal clerk about a good place to buy a used car in the immediate area and it took only an hour for Meredith to find what she wanted. It was a 2004 blue Cadillac Seville four-door sedan with tinted windows. They returned to the bank and got a Cashier's Check for the car. It took only moments to get the paperwork completed and a temporary Utah license on the back window of the car. Meredith used the name and address of a relative in Salt Lake City for the Registration, but used the post office box as her mailing address.

"Okay," he said. "You drive the Cadillac, I'll drive the rental. Follow me to Hertz. I'll return the car and drop you off at the airport where Gil will meet you."

When she returned home, Alex was waiting for her at the Rifle airport and they were back at the ranch by dinner time… but only barely. Salt Lake City was a busy airport and it had taken time for air traffic control to give Gil a runway for departure. Jake was driving the Cadillac home from Salt Lake City. He would arrive later that night.

It had been a very busy day for her and she was tired. Alex seemed a bit on edge. As soon as they left the kitchen, he reached for the television remote and began watching a show she knew didn't interest him. It was his way of providing an environment where she didn't feel obligated to converse with him if she preferred silence.

"We can still talk, Alex," she said quietly.

He hit the off button on the remote. Silence filled the room. It surrounded her with a sense of peace.

"I'm sorry you want to leave… buy your own house, Meredith," he finally responded. "You have lived your life and faced the problems you had to face. Jake and I have done the same. At our ages – I'll be 60 in August, you'll be sixty in February, and Jake is fifty-eight – no one has a clean slate. I understand your desire to have your own space. I'd prefer you stay here… would feel better about your safety. But you are a grown woman. You have lived most of your life alone. Being picked up and thrown into the midst of two grown men who also lived most of their lives alone had to be pretty stressful for you."

His comment stunned her. She had felt no discomfort being around Alex and Jake. They were friends. And then she and Alex had become more than friends and she had innocently begun talking about buying her own home "here on the West Slope."

"Is that what you think?" she asked. "That I want to get away from you and Jake? Oh, Alex, nothing could be further from the truth," she offered in an apologetic tone. He just looked at her and took another sip of brandy. "I've been very happy here… maybe happier than I've been in years," she finished.

"But you need your own space?" he asked, shaking his head a bit as if to clear it. "If my actions offended you, Meredith, I'm the one who owes you an apology. I haven't had a lot of experience in establishing relationships. I won't lie to you. I've known a lot of women... but I never had the chance to establish a real relationship before. Since leaving the island, I've pretty much lived in isolation. If expressing my interest in you was done badly, mark it up to inexperience... at my age! Can you imagine?" He laughed, but there were brittle tinges on the edge of his expressed humor.

There was a long pause before she responded. She closed her eyes for a moment and then spoke in a clear, non-accusatory voice.

"Have you stopped to think that the reason I might suddenly start thinking about buying my own place is so I can avoid repeating history? That I might avoid turning to a man for security when I'm in need because it reminds me that I've done it before and am just finding how deep the scar it caused is?"

She paused for a long time as they looked at one another.

"Do you not recognize the similarities to my situation of over thirty years ago and the problem I face now? Can you see that I might want whatever relationship you and I may have in the future to be right – to be free of any reminders to me of a long ago, very unpleasant experience?"

Her voice trembled a bit towards the end of her monologue.

It was his turn to be stunned.

"You mean..." he began, but she reached for the sound system remote and clicked the on button. "I mean... do you suppose we might finish that dance we started about two weeks ago?" she asked, smiling.

The two of them just stood in the middle of the room with their arms around one another, swaying in rhythm to the music. Being close was not only enough, it was one of the most intimate moments either of them had ever experienced. Both were old enough to know there is intimacy... and there is *intimacy*. The former is a sensate experience of the body. The latter involved making contact with one's soul.

The level of satisfaction Alex felt just holding her close to him was not just enough... it was everything.

The song ended and another began. They leaned back and looked at one another. Each face searched the other as if answers to life's mysteries might be found in the other's eyes.

"Though standing here with you makes me wonderfully happy, I'm exhausted. I hope you will understand that I need to lie down?" she asked. "I'm going to give Rusty a moment outside and then go to bed. It's been a huge day for me." She pulled away, gave a small laugh and turned back toward him. "So there are no misunderstandings, my brooding scientist, the IVs are working. I could not have done what I did today a month ago. The arthritis pain is greatly reduced and, well… things just seem to be getting back in order inside of me. My energy's coming back. It's hard to explain," she finished.

"Jake said almost exactly those same words," he chuckled. "I don't know if you've noticed, but you look about ten years younger. It's very subtle, and I'm glad you're feeling positive changes." He did not want her to leave him just yet, but he could see the tiredness.

Meredith let the dog out the front door and saw her new Cadillac drive slowly by. Jake was driving it to the garage. He had made good time, she thought. "Jake's home," she called to Alex as she passed the living room on the way to her bedroom.

As Jake entered the house, Rusty came inside with him. Alex was sitting in his chair finishing the brandy he had poured for himself after dinner. The music was still playing and Jake was surprised to find him alone.

"Where's Meredith?" he asked, suddenly worried that something might have gone wrong.

"She just went to her bedroom for the night," Alex answered, smiling at his friend. "Have you eaten?" Alex asked. "There's leftover ham in the fridge."

"I grabbed a Burger King on the way home," his friend replied. "So she got home okay and her new car is here. You got to the airport to pick her up… everything is calm on the home front."

"Indeed it is." Alex was calmer than Jake had seen him in days.

"Do you have time to talk about our plans? Or would you rather wait until morning?"

"Morning is soon enough," Alex replied. "I think I'm going to bed, too. It was a long day."

Jake took his usual seat and put his feet up as he reclined. He was tired, too, but he was not yet ready for bed. There was nothing worthwhile on television. His eyes were too tired from driving to read very long. It did not take him long to get sleepy.

Over breakfast, they decided the information Jake had gathered about William Leonard on his Washington trip needed to be shared with Arthur Redbridge as soon as possible. Jake offered to pick the Fed Chairman up and deliver him to the stable office for a meeting.

The four of them sat in a semi-circle and Alex began the discussion by informing Redbridge that he and Meredith would be hearing the information Jake had gotten about William Leonard for the first time, too.

Jake gave an overview of Leonard's background that showed a clear picture of a scam artist who started small and ended up buying and selling billions of Russian rubles, doing huge trade deals with Russia involving food and oil for money after the collapse of the Soviet Union. He had been arrested and convicted for money laundering at foreign banks, twice. There was no doubt in Jake's mind that because of the size of the deals Leonard had put together and because the deals involved people at the very top of the communist party in Moscow, he either worked with the backing of the CIA or the Russian Mafia – or, both.

"When I retired from the CIA in the early 90s," Jake said, looking directly at Arthur Redbridge, "one of the reasons was the total loss of control over the purpose of the organization."

Redbridge broke eye contact with Jake as he spoke. So, Jake was retired CIA, he thought.

Jake went on, giving an overview of the deals in which William Leonard had been involved. He had started small, but traded in just about everything and anything... black market computer technology, cigarettes, food, oil, multiple foreign currencies, and precious metals.

"He and four other scam artists did what you suggested as part of your plan to pressure the Soviet ruble almost out of existence,"

Jake said, disdainfully. "In just a few months, these guys cut the price of the ruble in half."

It would have been, Jake explained, impossible for the CIA not to know what was occurring while Leonard was sending faxes worldwide selling rubles and gold.

"What I want to know, Arthur, is how you found out about Leonard… who put you in touch with him? What was your plan? How much of that plan was in writing – if your clone found it, what did he find?"

The room was silent for a long time. Meredith was seeing a new side of Jake's personality. For the first time, she saw him as an intelligence operative and a hard man who was disgusted with the entire concept of what that represented. The man in front of her today was harsh, concise, and there was no gentleness – or gentlemanliness – about him. His tone while questioning Arthur Redbridge was demanding.

"Yes," Redbridge finally said. "I can feel your disgust, Jake. If it makes you feel any better, I used to go home and shower immediately after meeting with this guy. Then I found out Leonard was a black ops agent working under the direction of the President of the United States. I found out that his con artist background had been created to make him a believable operative. In answer to your question, our President at the time, Rory McCoy, was the person who put Leonard in touch with me. This guy was a specialist par excellence and knew how to launder billions of rubles – hundreds of billions – being sent out of a failing country by the elites who wanted gold for their rubles. He knew how to take advantage of fear and greed… and he did! And we won the Cold War!" Redbridge's voice was a bit confrontational and he gave Jake a look of disgust before lowering his eyes.

Redbridge paused, took a drink from the water glass in front of him, cleared his throat and continued. "My plan was kept in a safe in my office. Only I had the combination to it. With someone who looked just like me taking my place, it would have been no trick to crack that safe and remove the plan. They had all the time in the world to do it. I'm sure you know there are rogue operations within the Agency," he said, looking directly at Jake. "This sounds like one of them."

Jake thought about that for a moment. "Yes, it does," he responded, curtly. His blue eyes still held a hint of anger, but he fought to maintain an open mind.

"This is an important question," Redbridge said, sounding somewhat unsure. "Part one of the plan was the destruction of the Russian ruble, true. Part two was to use the funds gained from those trades to access large amounts of gold from Russia's Central Bank. The gold was to be used as security – collateral, if you will – on a 140 billion ruble contract. Did that deal occur? If it did, it means Leonard did get the two thousand metric tonnes of gold from the Russian Central Bank." Redbridge was anxious and it showed.

"That deal appears to have occurred... at least, two thousand metric tonnes of gold disappeared from the Russian Central Bank about that time," Jake answered quietly. "Why is that important?" he asked.

"As Meredith's numbers pointed out the other day, between 1991 and 2001, the price per ounce of gold hovered between $275 and $325. It is now selling for almost $700 an ounce. Where is that gold? What happened to it? Here we are in November 2006 and it has more than doubled in value if it's still in safekeeping for the people of America!"

No one knew what to say. Everyone in the room was stunned. Each was trying to calculate the same thing: To how many dollars did that translate?

"Was it metric tonnes?" Meredith asked.

"They were metric tonnes... I was taken to Sakhalin Island before it happened, so I can't say for sure," Redbridge responded.

"So, each metric ton holds 32,150.7466 troy ounces... I can recall that much. Times two thousand tonnes – do you have a calculator in your purse?" he asked Meredith. "It's going to be somewhere around 65 million ounces of gold, I'd guess."

Meredith quickly reached in her purse for her calculator, unsure if it was big enough to hold enough numbers to complete the calculation. "It is 64.3 million ounces," she said. "Times $675 an ounce... it totals $43,402,500,000. At $275 an ounce, Leonard would have paid $17.7 billion… a nice profit for the country. I can't even fathom that much money… that much gold," she concluded, sounding a bit breathless.

Redbridge smiled. "That was part of the money President McCoy wanted to use to buy America out of debt. Leonard did a lot of other deals, too." He paused, nervously looking down at his hands. "The money from the entire venture should have been enough to pay our foreign debt at the time. That was the plan," he said almost sadly. "Then, once back on some form of gold standard, we planned the gradual elimination of the Fed. I can't help but wonder if the American banking system has been using the value of Leonard's gold as a means to gain access to credit internationally… and that was what motivated Leonard to begin fighting for the right to those assets – for declaring they were his, not the government's. If so, a banking crisis will soon be looming…"

Jake looked at Redbridge, opened his briefcase, and took out of it a 30-page report. "Don't give up on him yet, Arthur," Jake smiled. "Here's a report of Leonard's actions as of last week… last week, can you believe it? According to this, Leonard is making big trouble for the U.S. government." He tossed the report to Redbridge and handed a copy to Meredith and Alex. The room was so quiet, all Jake could hear was the four of them breathing and pages turning.

"I'll be damned!" Redbridge said. Could he believe what his eyes saw? "William Leonard still has all that money and is fighting to keep the U.S. government from stealing it. This was just a week ago, for heaven's sake!" he cried. "He's in Europe! He's using the courts in Europe against this country! I have to get to him before this gets side-tracked! Look at all these documented court cases that have been filed!" Redbridge quickly scanned the pages Jake had handed him. "He has been adjudicated the official owner of all these accounts which appear to total eleven trillion dollars! The government's trying to take the money and Leonard is telling them it belongs to the American people, not the government! This is unbelievably good news!" he almost shouted.

Jake paced nervously, running his right hand through his hair. "Why haven't they just iced the guy?" he asked. "What's to keep them from killing him when he appears for one of his court cases?"

Arthur Redbridge was almost giggling. "They don't know where all of the money is," he said, gasping a bit for air in between laughs. "He has let them see large amounts of it, but only he knows where the rest of it is. If that weren't true, he'd already be dead!"

Jake shook his head and then saw the humor in what the Fed Chairman said. "And he probably has heirs or a will or a family trust hidden someplace... that could keep the government in court for a long time!" Jake began to laugh too. "He's got them in a corner!"

Meredith just shook her head. "I need to think about this," she said, stretching her arms over her head. "One thing seems pretty apparent. These big numbers – we couldn't figure out what they meant in Jeffrey's packet. Think about it, guys. This must be what was on the agenda at whatever meeting Jeffrey was attending when he picked those papers up by mistake. And if they were discussing the liquidation of all that gold and foreign currencies, their plans for doing so can't be too far away, can they? It's been close to two months since Jeffrey was killed," she reminded them.

"We're dealing with a time issue, aren't we?" Alex asked Redbridge.

"Indeed we are," he replied. "Someone will figure out something to do... even if it's the wrong thing." His brow furrowed as he spoke. "There has got to be some kind of exchange in the making," Redbridge finished, stroking his right jaw bone with the fingers of his left hand, thumb under his chin. "We need to figure out where and when."

"My God, it's all going to come to a head at the same time," Alex said, barely above a whisper.

Jake provided Redbridge with copies of all the William Leonard documents and then escorted him back to his room. During the drive, Jake explained that there would be no time for exercise today. There was just too much to do.

"It doesn't surprise me you were CIA, Jake. You think like a well-trained agent. But today you proved you're a friend," Redbridge said. His voice was even and strong. "I've learned a lot about power and its abuses during the past fifteen years. I will never endanger either you or Alex... I will never mention your names when I return to Washington," he vowed.

Jake was driving and did not take his eyes off of the road, but he could feel the man's eyes burning into the side of his head. "Oh, you'll be saying my name, Arthur. I'm going to be on your new security detail when you go back. Meredith is going to be your newest and highest ranking assistant."

Arthur Redbridge felt his stomach tighten. So, plans to restore him to office were moving ahead. Was he ready for it? God! He prayed he was! Would the Russians find out and try to kill him? What difference did it make, he asked himself? Had they left him on that damnable island, he might already be dead. He had been going steadily downhill the six months before his rescue. Still, when the car stopped in front of the bunkhouse and before Jake could exit, Redbridge stretched his arm and an open hand across the seat and Jake accepted the strong handshake.

It was moving too fast, Jake knew. Haste makes waste... and causes errors, he thought, driving back to the main house. He realized they could not afford mistakes. There would be one chance and one chance only. When he got to the house, Alex and Meredith were sitting in their chairs re-reading the material he had brought home with him from Washington.

"I hate to interrupt your study group," Jake said, "but we need to have a meeting – a planning meeting. We are now dealing with a time element that wasn't part of this project until today."

Alex and Meredith put the papers down. "What kind of planning meeting?" she asked.

"You are about to hear the total plan," Jake began. "Alex will be hearing this for the first time, too – there have been some changes since we last discussed this," he told his friend. "Brett will be leaving the Agency around Thanksgiving. We'll have his help. He had some excellent ideas, Alex. I've added them to the list of things we need to get done." With that, he departed the room. Alex and Meredith looked at one another a bit surprised but waited patiently.

When Jake returned, he carried three sets of papers with him. "I'm going to light a fire before we start," he said. "As we go through each of these pages, your copy of that page will be burned. My copy with any comments added tonight will go in a special place for security matters."

It sounded a bit sci-fi to Meredith, but during the past weeks she had learned to take Jake at his word. He had a reason for everything he was and would be doing.

"I can't take notes, then…" Meredith said, knowing it was more of a statement than a question.

"You can take them, but I'll be burning them as we finish with that page," Jake corroborated. "Commit what we are talking about to memory," he suggested.

"That would have been a lot easier ten years ago," she said, sarcastically. All three of them laughed.

"You'll be fine," Alex said. "It's not going to happen tomorrow and we'll have several of these discussions. Believe me. It will be engraved in stone in your head before we're through."

Jake went through the details of the plan to return Arthur Redbridge to office. It had been expanded and even more details had been added.

One interesting change Brett and Jake had made to the plan was using Redbridge's accident recovery time for facial plastic surgery. They could make Redbridge appear more like his younger clone. Brett had the right hospital and medical connections. He would have to coordinate things before he left the Agency, though. The surgery could be performed and his head wrapped, appearing as scars from the accident when Charlie or Bill or Katie or Barbara was invited to do the television interview.

Jake, posing as an Emergency Medical Technician, would drug the clone. The real Redbridge would be unloaded on a gurney and taken into the hospital. The clone would be hidden in the ambulance while it was in the underground parking area of the hospital. The clone would be taken immediately to the airport where the Lear jet, with Alex on board, would be waiting to fly him home and drive him to the ranch. The real Arthur Redbridge would place a personal call from the hospital to the President of the United States and explain that he had lost confidence in his security detail. Jake and Alex both agreed that the clone's security detail consisted of Russian handlers.

The remainder of the conversation dealt with the need to gather information on behalf of Redbridge before he ever entered his office.

Brett had been able to provide a great deal of data on the clone's personal life. They needed a dental model, fingerprints and a dozen other things for which Jake would have to enlist Brett's help.

Meredith would have to precede the genuine Redbridge into his office to learn everything from computer codes to people's names. They needed access to his calendar.

"And what happens when my face shows up on the front page of the *Washington Post* as the new assistant to Arthur Redbridge?" she asked quietly. "Am I going to be visited by brown cars and kidnappers? Am I going to be mugged?" she asked them.

"You will be protected every step of the way, Meredith," Alex told her solemnly.

"If it's possible for us to kidnap the Fed Chairman in an auto accident, what will prevent them from creating an auto accident for me?" she asked.

"Remember, Meredith," Jake said slowly, "the Redbridge clone is involved in whatever plans the international banking groups have underway. He's in on the plans contained in Jeffrey's data. The real Redbridge will tell them that you came to him with Jeffrey's package because you trust him. He will say he has gotten the packet back and will be returning it via one of his security guards. In short, you will be totally off the hook and of no interest to them. He can tell them that the reason he's hiring you as his personal assistant is to keep an eye on you... keep you under his control."

He smiled, pleased with himself. She blinked a few times before returning the smile.

"Okay," Alex said. "This is a start and it's a good start. We need some dinner... we skipped lunch today and I'm starving."

Meredith looked at her watch. "Good grief! How did it get so late?" She looked outside and the sky was beginning to turn dark. "I have one last thing to say."

The two men were on their way to the kitchen to implement their plans for a night of leftovers for dinner. Both stopped in their tracks at her utterance.

"I believe we should get a good teeth whitener at the nearest pharmacy because Arthur will need it for his media interview, within a day of his hospital admittance. I don't think the Russians kept him in Crest and good toothbrushes," she said, sounding indignant.

"My kind of girl," Alex said. "She likes details." He winked at Jake and waved for her to join them in the kitchen.

He waited for her and put his arm around her shoulders as they walked into the kitchen. Any questions Jake had as to where things stood between the two of them were answered when he saw her dip her head into Alex's shoulder for a brief second. He was surprised that in his immediate sense of happiness for these two people, he also felt a twinge of sadness. In a way, he was glad he would be leaving town again for a couple of days. It would give him a chance to digest these changes and how they impacted him.

Chapter 20

"Jake won't be home until about two in the morning," Alex told her over dinner. They were having a tossed green salad and vegetable soup which, to Alex, resembled stew more than it looked like soup. Meredith had cooked it that day.

"I... I think I'm going to drive into Grand Junction to get my hair done and do some shopping. I was thinking of going tomorrow." She hesitated. "Is there anything I need to do before I go? And can I borrow some cash?"

Alex handed her his billfold and told her to take it with her. He thought for a moment before telling her tomorrow was probably a good day. He would be up late, driving to the Rifle airport to pick Jake up during the wee hours of the morning.

She explained that getting a permanent and haircut took from two to three hours and she needed to do some shopping. With the drive time she would probably be gone most of the day.

"How about a game of chess?" he asked.

"Let me get this straight," she said, smiling. "You, a Russian, are asking me, an American, to play chess?"

They both laughed and he reached out and took her hand.

"I don't know what to say to you, Meredith," he began, putting her hand to his lips. When he became very serious, a small line appeared on his forehead, between his dark eyes. "Now is not the time for either of us to talk of commitments or a serious relationship. The future is just too damned uncertain. And so I talk about chess games and you get your hair fixed."

She could feel his frustration. She knew he wanted to move their relationship forward from friendship to romance. She knew it because she felt the same way… and she felt his same frustrations. All of the what-ifs started running through her mind. What if the Russians found him and took him back to Russia? What if Redbridge was killed? What if she was killed? These were not uncertainties on which to build a relationship! Yet, circumstances had placed them under the same roof and a relationship was staring them in the face, like it or not.

"I know," was all she could say. It came out as a whisper, she realized, a bit surprised.

They rose almost simultaneously to begin taking dishes to the kitchen and Alex moved to her side of the table. As she reached to retrieve his soup bowl, he put his arm around her waist and turned her slowly toward him. She moved easily into his arms. They held one another tightly, as if each was afraid the other might disappear.

"Experience tells me these dishes will be here later," he whispered in her ear. What was it about his breath in her ear that made her tingle inside, she wondered? It was electrifying. He nibbled on her ear lobe and the tingle turned into a slight ache. It had been so long, she barely recognized it as yearning to meld her body with his to seek a sense of completion.

He could feel her rapid heart beat against his chest. He tilted his head away from her and, putting his index finger under her chin raised her face, and then slowly lowered his head to hers. It was, he realized, a kiss he had always wanted and never had. He knew this woman was his perfect opposite – her yin and his yang, his balance in life – nature's provision of an opposite of equal strength. Alex had never found it… until now.

"I never felt incomplete before," he said, trying to laugh slightly as he spoke. "I did not realize I was not a whole being until this very moment," it came out as a ragged whisper and he bent to kiss her again.

It was a gentle kiss, this time. She took his hand and the two of them made the long walk down the hallway to her bedroom. As the door closed, Rusty stood in the hallway cocking his head from side to side, his ears attentive. The look on his face clearly said that some mistake had been made. He lay down in the hallway and waited to be admitted into his sleeping quarters.

This, she realized, was making love. It was not just having sex. Alex treated her body as if it were a temple at which he wanted to worship and she felt the same about his. There were moments when his hands felt as light as a piece of silk floating across her skin. And there were other moments when they demanded that she join him in deep passion. Dear Lord, she wondered as she cried out his name, how could she have lived for sixty years and not known this kind of fulfillment?

Later, he asked her softly, "Do you remember what I said just before we made love?"

She had to think for a moment. "You said you never before realized you were incomplete. It was a beautiful thing to say," she said, snuggling against his naked body.

"Well, until now, I've never been complete, either." He held her closer, kissing the top of her head.

They fell asleep in each other's arms, but not before Alex set his cell phone to ring and waken him at 1:00 a.m. He had to go to Rifle to pick up Jake. It pained him to get up and leave her, but he did. Rusty was finally admitted into his bedroom for the night.

Meredith was awake early the next morning. As she stepped into the shower she felt so gloriously alive she could hardly believe it. She was in love; totally and completely in love with this Russian scientist. She donned a blue sweater and jeans and put Rusty out while she made toast and coffee. The house was quiet.

She let the dog back in, re-set the security system and as she went outside was surprised to see her Cadillac in front of the door. Alex must have remembered she wanted to go to town this morning and had driven it from the garage to the house for her. He had also put the cattle guard remotes in the front passenger seat for her. She had forgotten about them. She probably would have remembered about the time she approached the first cattle guard, she thought, smiling.

It was a pleasant drive into town. The skies were blue, the weather mild and the highway clear. It was at least fifty miles to the

Mall. She knew there were several beauty shops. Surely one of them would have time for a walk-in?

Three hours later she was an ash blonde with a circular hair cut she loved. It was short, but curly and, as Jake would say, "Perky."

She did some shopping before heading home. She found a twenty-two karat gold Kokopelli men's necklace in a jewelry story and decided it would make a wonderful Christmas present for Alex. Kokopelli was a fertility deity. She laughed, knowing when Alex looked the deity up on the Internet – as he was bound to do – he would find Kokopelli was an unrealistically endowed male figure in the spirit world of some Native Americans.

She left the shopping mall shortly after two in the afternoon, figuring she would be home within an hour. It was funny how she now thought of the ranch as "home." She had lived there less than three months, but it felt like home. It had the most important part of what represents home to all people: Love, stability, and hope. Meredith knew she had not gone into Alex's arms seeking security or escape. She had willingly entered his embrace seeking his love and wanting to give him hers. She thought – hoped – she had found it. At least, she thought more soberly and putting romantic notions behind her for a moment, she had found something very special that resembled the love she had always wanted but never found. Really deep and lasting love, she knew, took time. The thought all older people have flitted through her mind as she wondered how much time the two of them would have together.

As she exited the shopping center, she made a momentary decision to turn right and take the main drag through Grand Junction. Now that she was actually in town, she was fairly familiar with her location. She was on the far West end of town. She had, over the years, driven East on Patterson Road to a connection with I-70. It would take her back to the ranch turn-off. She missed the days when she used to drive through Grand Junction on her way to spend the winter in Palm Springs.

As she neared the I-70 Business Loop in the town of Clifton, a traffic signal turned red. She stopped, glad for a chance to look around a bit. As she looked at the West side of the Grand Mesa that stretched across the car's front window, her breath stuck in her throat. There, right in front of her, was an exact duplicate of the figure on Jeffrey's envelope... a giant white swan. She sat and stared at it. A horn sounded behind her and she realized the light had turned green. She waved, thanking the driver who had honked.

There was a small shopping center on the southeast side of the traffic signal. She quickly pulled into the right lane and turned into it. There had to be some kind of store where she could buy a small digital camera. She found a used one in a pawn shop, purchased batteries for it and then drove a little further down the road where she stopped and began snapping pictures.

The rest of her trip back to the ranch seemed to take forever. When she re-entered the house, she could not wait to get to her computer. No one was in the living room... Alex must be at his lab, and who knew where Jake was?

She connected the camera to a USB port and pulled up the dozen pictures she had taken of a snowy, giant white swan. She quickly pulled out Jeffrey's envelope. Interestingly, both showed the swan with its head pointing to her left. Could this be it? Had Jeffrey been to the ranch? She had never asked. This did not explain the two lines he had drawn through the bottom of the swan's neck, but the figures surely did match.

She logged onto the Internet and went to the Grand Junction Chamber of Commerce site. There was no information about the mysterious swan. Was it a landmark of some kind, she wondered? She found the Chamber telephone number and quickly picked up her cell phone and dialed.

"I'm not quite sure how to ask this question," she told the young woman who answered her call. "I just saw a large white swan on the Grand Mesa as I was driving east on Patterson, going to Palisade. Can you tell me what it is?" Meredith held her breath.

The voice at the other end laughed briefly. "That's our barometer for spring planting," the woman told Meredith. "This is an agricultural area. Even though we are at the East end of the Nevada desert and our winters are pretty mild, we do get freezes... sometimes into late spring." She paused for a moment to clear her throat. "It is rumored that no one can be sure spring has arrived until the swan's neck breaks," she said, casually. Meredith's quick intake of breath must have startled the other woman. She immediately launched into an explanation about the swan being made of snow. Tradition, she said, had it that once the snow at the base of the bird's neck had melted, "the swan's neck is broken, spring is here, and it's safe to plant."

Meredith quickly thanked the woman and hung up.

Was that what the two lines at the base of the swan's neck meant in Jeffrey's drawing, she wondered? "Was he trying to tell me that something would happen when the swan's neck breaks?"

She grabbed her camera and the USB connector, left the house and drove to Alex's lab. His car was in front of the building. She pulled in next to him and rushed inside. A strange man was lying on the recliner with an IV dripping into his arm. She startled him when she greeted him by name. "How are you, Justice Scott?"

Alex heard her voice and looked up, immediately rising and walking from his office to join her. He introduced the Justice and his house guest and led her into his office, closing the door behind them.

"What a nice surprise," he said, a broad smile accompanying his words. "You've been on my mind all day," he said, reaching out to touch her shoulder. "I think blue is your color."

"We need to use your computer," she said anxiously. "Now, please."

He looked a bit surprised at her response. Had he imagined her passion of the previous night? He remembered she had said no words of love to him...

"Well, I... Sure. Hold on a minute," he said, saving the data on his screen to a CD and then clicking an icon on his desktop.

She hooked the camera to the computer and hit a few keys. The pictures of the snow swan on the west side of the Grand Mesa appeared on the screen. "There," she said, smiling. She looked at him triumphantly.

"It's the swan on the Grand Mesa," Alex said, rather blankly. "Why did you become a blonde?" He reached out and ran his fingers through her hair. She took his hand, walked up to him and gave him a quick peck on the cheek.

"You know about the swan?" she asked.

"Everyone who lives in this valley knows about the swan," he said.

"Well, then why did you and Jake not recognize the drawing Jeffrey made on the manila envelope he sent me?" she asked, somewhat sarcastically.

"I don't think either one of us has ever seen the manila envelope," Alex responded. He realized she was very serious about something.

"Oh," she shook her head as she spoke. "I never gave you the envelope, did I? I just gave you the pages in it." Meredith paused for a moment. "When will you be ready to go back to the house?"

Alex glanced at his watch then went to his office window to look at the IV bottle that was draining into Justice Scott's arm. "About fifteen minutes," he answered.

"May I wait for you?" she asked. "That way, we can drop the Cadillac off at the garage and you can give me a ride home. By the way, thanks for bringing it to the house this morning. It was a thoughtful thing to do. Did Jake get home safely?"

"Yes," he laughed, "you can wait for me and yes, Jake got home just fine. He's next door buying a ranch as we speak," he said. "And I like your hair… you're going to look like a teenager if you don't stop." He ran his fingers down the side of her face. The way he looked at her told her everything she wanted – needed – to know.

"I like your hair, too," she said. She walked into his arms as they opened and they just held one another for a moment. "I think the guy that comes with the hair is exceptional, too. I think I'll wait in the car… I'm sorry I interrupted your schedule," she finished.

He kept her hand in his as she tried to remove it and walked with her, giving her a kiss on the cheek as he opened the car door. "You could never interrupt me, my love," he said softly in her ear. Almost as if he were afraid to see her reaction to the word, he turned quickly and reentered his lab.

Meredith turned on the radio looking for some good music to wait by and wondered if she had ever been this happy in her life.

When they arrived back at the main house, Jake's car was parked in front and Rusty was lying patiently at the door. He rose to greet them, wagging what he had of a tail.

Alex let Meredith descend the stairs from the entryway to the living room ahead of him and closed the back wall to the entry. "And are you now a happy home owner?" he asked Jake.

"I am," Jake said, smiling broadly. Meredith was startled. His hair was short and he had a two-day growth of beard on his face. He could definitely be the Marlboro Man, she thought – if there still was such a thing. "I see I'm not the only one to change my hair style – but I did manage to keep the same color. What a difference!" he said, smiling at them both.

Jake had known about Alex and Meredith from the moment he joined Alex in the car at the Rifle Airport early that morning. There was something very different about his friend and he surmised it had to do with their houseguest. Alex had just looked at him with a rather silly half-smile on his face. "So it's serious, is it?" was all Jake said.

"I think I love her more than my own life," was all Alex could say. It was the truth and he wanted no subterfuge or hidden feelings or emotions between the three of them. "I think she may love me, too." He paused. "I hope she does!"

They were quiet for most of the ride to DeBeque. When they turned off of the highway, Jake finally said, "I don't quite know what to say. What are your plans? Have you thought this thing through at all?" he asked.

"I tried," was all Alex could say. That was all that was said during the entire ride. Those few words and his reaction to them was all Jake needed to know to understand his own recent moods. He realized then that he cared for her, too.

"Well, I am a happy homeowner," Jake told them over club sandwiches and vegetable soup. "This is delicious, by the way," he said... his way of thanking Meredith for making dinner.

Jake and Alex cleaned up as she prepared copies of her photos and the manila envelope from Jeffrey. She put them in Jake's chair and waited. She had a half-smile on her face. She felt like she had made the discovery of the year and no one realized it.

Alex did his ritual thing with technology while Jake picked up the envelope and accompanying photo copies.

"What's this?" he asked.

"Look at the back of the envelope," Meredith said quietly.

"It's a swan... a swan with a break in its neck!" he said, a little more forcefully. "Jeffrey was here in April last year. He saw the swan with and without the break in its neck. It fascinated him. I told him the story..."

"And then he sent me a package with a drawing of it on the envelope. He contacted you and told you to come and rescue me in Denver, knowing I would show you the material. I did show you the material – I just never thought about showing you the envelope! So, the swan's neck is breaking in his drawing. What does it mean? Is this a clue? Something he thought of after he'd sealed the envelope, maybe?" She watched both of them expectantly.

Jake quickly rose and got the scramblers. After a few moments, they were ready to proceed.

"The swan's neck breaking is a local harbinger of spring, I guess," Alex said. "On what day does spring fall in 2007?"

"I looked it up," Meredith said. "It will be spring at seven minutes after midnight on March 21st of 2007."

All three were silent for some time. They knew they might have a clue, but had no idea how it applied to their puzzle.

Jake reviewed his meeting with Brett Radov. Then he told them he was planning on moving into his new home by Christmas. "Hopefully, we will have no November snow. We usually don't get our first snow until just before Christmas, Meredith," he said. "The one we had in early October was an aberration."

"You're moving away?" she asked, her emotions confused.

"Only fifteen minutes away," Jake responded, laughing. "I made the decision while I was still in Virginia, talking with Brett and his wife, Dani," he said trying to subtly let them know their romantic involvement was not the cause for his move. He wished he really believed that, he thought. "We need to take the swan story to Arthur tomorrow and see if the March 21st date has any meaning to him."

Alex was being very quiet, she realized. He nodded his agreement to the suggestion and went to the kitchen to refill his drink. Change was hard, Alex knew. Though Jake had always maintained a home in Rifle, for all practical purposes the two men had lived together at the ranch for almost ten years. Their friendship had been forged first by the building project, then by the plans to free Redbridge and the others. Jake was away from the ranch on business often enough that Alex was able to continue his research and his work and the arrangement had been compatible for both of them.

Alex re-entered the living room, asking the other two if he could bring them anything. When they answered in the negative, he sat back down in his chair. He smiled at Jake. "Do you need to make many changes or repairs to the property?" he asked.

Jake laughed. "Are you kidding? I've already walked around the place to find a hill under which I can build an earth home. I'll move into the house, but will start building right away. How long did it take us to complete this place? Two – three years?"

"At least that," Alex responded, also laughing. "But now we'll know what we're doing. That should shorten it by half." He hoped Jake heard his willingness to help him build his new home.

Meredith watched the interaction between the two men with some understanding of what was happening. She felt sorrow that her presence had caused a breach in the lifestyles of friends for whom she cared so much.

"You know," Alex offered, "we have three other men to get back into office about the same time Redbridge returns. If we're successful, we'll have a Supreme Court with sufficient votes to correct many of the Constitutional errors committed in the name of 'harmonizing' this country's laws with those of the European Union. We'll have a United States Senator back in office on the democrat side of the aisle and he has a truly conservative, anti-socialist view of the world. And we'll have a voice on talk radio… a voice listened to by more people each week than any other. Has anyone given any thought to that?"

The silence in the room was a sure sign that no one had thought about it.

"You think they should all be replaced at the same time?" Jake asked in a somewhat astonished tone.

"Not at the same time," Alex replied. "The others should be replaced just – I mean within a day or two – before Redbridge has his accident."

Alex launched into an explanation about how, once Redbridge was returned to office, the three remaining clones would be in danger. If they were not replaced, the Russians might kill them so they could not be replaced. They needed to inform the Russians that all four clones were in captivity and the real things returned to office. At the same time, they needed to threaten the Russians with disclosure of their clone program if any of the originals were hurt. The demand that any and all personnel put in place to support the clones be removed would also be made.

"You sure don't give a guy a lot of time to prepare for all of this, do you?" Jake asked. "How did I get from happy home owner to clone replacement expert?"

"War is hell, Jake," Alex leaned forward to slap him gently on the shoulder as he spoke. He was smiling. Meredith was overwhelmed at the size of the project Alex had planned.

"Are they ready to go back into their previous lives?" she asked.

"The radio jockey is," Alex answered slowly. "I was able to subscribe to the computer-televised elements of his clone's radio show. I've been downloading them on my computer and making CDs for him. He has the clone's style down perfectly... which wasn't hard since the clone was imitating him to begin with. Justice Scott will be ready in another month."

Jake just looked at his friend. The Redbridge switch was the most complex, he agreed, but the others might not be as easy as Alex seemed to think. On the other hand, Alex was right. If they did not get all four clones replaced before the Russians became aware that any one of the clones had been re-taken, the other three clones would not be long for this earth. They would have convenient accidents or heart attacks or strokes, or be exposed to radio active poisoning. Whatever it was it would then be impossible to put the real men back into the lives from which they had been so unceremoniously snatched. The public would think them ill or dead. They would be dead as far as their careers were concerned.

Meredith offered to go on the Internet the next day to gather whatever personal data was available about Justice Scott, Senator Martinez and J. J. Branchman. She wondered out loud how the

Supreme Court Justice and the Senator would return to households with wives and children and pets.

"That is a problem," Jake said. "Add to that the professional contacts and friends the clones have made. Meredith will be tied up with Redbridge. She won't be able to get the skinny on these other guys…"

"No," Alex interrupted. "Instead, I want you to bring Bill Bryant and Bob Grosvenor to the ranch. We'll need their help when we replace the clones with the Real Things. Between now and then, they can gather personal information we need about the clones."

The room grew quiet. Jake and Meredith were just beginning to realize the size of the total project. Alex had known how each act would be played out. He had known ever since Jake had successfully retrieved the four men. He had been part of the entire dirty story from the beginning and his roots were Russian. He understood his foes and knew how they played their political games – like chess matches: seriously and for keeps.

"Well," Meredith began, "I'm going to say goodnight. I can't wait to go and look at your new home, Jake. When can we see it?"

Jake noticed the term "we," and almost winced. He smiled instead and rose, removing the digital camera from his jacket pocket, handing it to her. "Here… you can look at the photos I took at the Fed yesterday and there are pictures of the house on the camera, too."

"Never off duty, are you?" she asked, a bit seriously.

"Wouldn't have it any other way," he said. "My life's purpose, I guess."

"Well, we'll have to do something about that, won't we?" she asked as she walked towards the hallway. "I'm going to put Rusty out. Will you let him in, Alex?"

"Yes," he laughed. "I'm always on duty, too. This house is full of dutiful people!"

Ten minutes later, her bedroom door opened and Rusty came in the room and Alex walked in behind him.

"I will miss you tonight," he said quietly, pulling her from her chair in front of the computer and into his arms. The two of them just stood close to one another for a few seconds before Meredith stepped away from him.

"Well," she said, "I think it's important for you to rejoin Jake right away, don't you? But, now that Rusty is in his room for the night, I might be convinced to walk down the hall in a few minutes – while you and Jake are still talking. I can wait for you in your room. We could at least whisper a few warm good nights to one another."

"You are a woman of good ideas. I'll see you in about an hour," he said. The gloom he had been feeling through the night lifted. Meredith worked on the computer for short time, took a shower and dressed in jeans, a flannel shirt, and moccasins. She walked quietly down the hall to Alex's bedroom, opened the door and slipped inside, re-closing the door. It was not long before he joined her. He had left Jake in the living room, reading a book. He saw her lying on his bed and quietly turned the bolt lock on his door.

"It seems so natural to see you in my bed," he said quietly as he turned on the television and found the late night news station. He turned the bed lamp off and took the book from her hands. He reached out as he sat beside her.

"Lie here beside me," she whispered. "I want to talk with you for a moment..." she had to restrain a giggle. A giggle she thought? At her age? What was there about meeting someone surreptitiously that made assignations so much more interesting?

Alex arranged a pillow so he could lie with his head raised, as hers was. "This sounds like news I may not want to hear," he whispered back at her.

"I could feel the tension in the room tonight when you realized Jake was moving away," she began. "It upset you, I know... and I'm sure it upsets him, too. He must feel uncomfortable. Because you and I have become..."

"Lovers?" he interrupted her.

"Yes, lovers... friends – and, from where Jake sits, a couple, too," she finished.

"From where I sit, too," he added. "Surely you know I'm in love with you."

His words brought a smile to her serious face. "And I with you," she responded. "But…" she could not finish the sentence because he suddenly kissed her.

"You love me?" he asked, his voice just above a whisper. "Say it. I want to hear you say it."

"I love you, Alex Plotnikov," she whispered, staring deeply into his eyes. "But we are not going to let what we feel interfere with your friendship with Jake or with a project you have been planning for many years, are we? We are not going to let it make any one of us uncomfortable, are we?"

He closed his eyes. She was right, he knew. They had to be sensitive to the entire situation and not just to their own feelings and personal discoveries. And they were not children who couldn't wait for a future life together.

"That will take some planning," he finally responded.

"We'll find time for us," she said, smiling gently at his distressed facial expression. "We'll always find time for us. We just need to put our passion on the back burner for awhile. If I know we are making Jake uncomfortable, I'll be uncomfortable – and I know you will be, too."

"The back burner?" he questioned her. "The back burner is turned off, right?"

"Well, it can be turned to simmer," she said. "Off would probably be best, but I'm not sure either one of us can manage that at this point."

"I think I've been simmering ever since I saw you get out of that ambulance," he said. It surprised her… pleased her, too. "But I know you're right. Jake is like a brother to me and I don't want to make him uncomfortable." He paused. "What's your plan?"

"The back burner can be defined as keeping our hands off of one another when Jake is in residence… not just away from the house, but in residence. We'll have time for each other when he goes on his trips. Can we manage that?"

Alex sighed deeply. "It is like asking a blind man who has seen light if he would mind staying in the dark for another month or two… but yes, we can manage that."

He stretched out beside her and pulled her into his arms and they held one another for a moment. "Say it again," he whispered. She tilted her head back, placed one hand on each side of his face and kissed him softly and sweetly. "I love you," she whispered, kissing him again.

She rose from the bed, walked to the bathroom, and turned on the shower.

"I think you're going to need that," she said, smiling, wondering how she would ever get back to her room without being seen or heard. She turned the television down, opened the door a crack and heard music coming from the living room. She opened it a bit further and saw lights burning in the living room. She waved at Alex and quickly scooted soundlessly down the hall to her own room.

She was not going to sleep very well that night, she knew. "Damn!" she thought. "And I've already taken a shower!"

Chapter 21

Jake and Alex decided they needed to spend more time with Senator Martinez, Justice Scott and J.J. Branchman before getting everyone together to design final clone replacement plans. They wanted the men to watch the video tapes of the presentations done over two months ago by Meredith, Jake and Alex at the stable office. Redbridge had already seen them. The other three men needed to know what fiscal, societal and intelligence research led Meredith, Jake and Alex to believe world government, with the Russians at the forefront, was the objective behind the ludicrous political scenario being played out in Washington, D.C. since the late 1980s.

Just before lunch, Jake walked into Meredith's bedroom with a pile of papers in his hand. He asked if, in addition to seeking personal and professional information about the three men, she would also look for various treaties and Executive Orders signed by the President and find what was on the Congressional menu at the current time. They needed a copy of the SPP – Security and Prosperity Partnership – signed by the President on March 25, 2005, creating the basis for a North American Union between the United States, Canada and Mexico. They also needed information about data supporting the introduction of the Amero... the rumored currency for the new trade zone.

"Include NAFTA, CAFTA and the impact they've had on American productivity, jobs, and workers," Jake said, handing her a list of possible topics for which she might look.

"Do I get time off for good behavior?" she asked. It was a long list

Things were moving more quickly now. Everyone was busy gathering data or planning clone exchanges or helping get the men ready to re-enter their worlds. It was a stream of unending tasks that kept all three of them busy.

"It looks like we will be doing the replacements sometime during the middle of February," Alex said at dinner that night.

"And the reason for that timing is… what?" Jake asked.

Alex took a sip of coffee before answering. "I guess it comes down to the March 21st – the swan's neck thing." He paused before asking, "How is the search for William Leonard going?"

The room was very quiet and Meredith and Alex awaited his answer. Jake poured some coffee for him and Alex before speaking and then took a bite of the cherry pie dessert Nancy had baked that day. A broad smile suddenly appeared on his face and Meredith was sure she felt her heart start beating again. "I found him," was all Jake said. He took another bite of pie.

"I went to my Rifle house today," he continued. "I got a lot of information from Brett about the Redbridge clone… his finger-prints, medical and dental records, his driving record and pictures and names of people close to him." Jake's tone was businesslike and informative.

Alex and Meredith just looked at him. This was a major step forward and he had not said anything to anyone.

He paused for another bite of cherry pie and a sip of coffee. "I talked with Brett about our need to see if the clones are implanted with radio signals. He says he can get the equipment to identify any electronic signals for us. Any of us can be quickly trained to use it." He paused. "And, if you are wondering why I haven't told you all of this, I just got the mail before dinner and was hoping we might have a meeting tonight to discuss it." He looked at Meredith and smiled a bit slyly. "It's not a good dinner topic."

Jake recognized the look that came over Alex's face. His mind was in a deep and focused state of thought.

"You know," Alex began, "getting equipment to identify possible signals coming from the clones' bodies is an excellent idea. But, if the transmitters are removed, the Russians will immediately know it when the first clone is taken. That puts the remaining Real Things in danger since we can't exchange them all at once."

The room grew quiet for a moment before Alex continued. "If we can remove them at the time we return the Real Things, we could re-implant them in the Real Things. It would solve the problem. We need to take your friend, Dr. Dean, with us, Jake. He can do the minor surgery. Then, the Russians won't know we've stolen their clones. After we've told the Russians we'll expose what they've done if anything happens to the Real Things, the tracking devices can be removed."

"So we take the doc with us to remove the implants, he re-implants them in the Real Things, and the Russians keep getting signals that everything's cool, right?" He thought about it for a moment longer. "Great idea," Jake said. Meredith quickly concurred. Her greatest concern was that the Russians would get a signal from a clone and it would lead them to Alex.

"Don't forget. Brett will be here soon... he'll stay until the Tuesday before Thanksgiving. He'll be a lot of help... I know I buried Meredith with work today. She needs some help."

Jake spent a moment going through details of what needed to be done before abruptly turning to Meredith.

"What time do you want to drive to Salt Lake on Friday?" Jake asked her. "Remember... your Denver house is closing? We need to remove funds from your checking account in Salt Lake and skip town before anyone can track the wire transfer and pay the bank a visit?"

"Oh, that's right," she said, somewhat distantly. She seemed pensive. The two men had no way of knowing she got that way when she was inundated with work. "Well, the closing is scheduled for two in the afternoon. They should be through by three... I need to be at the bank no later than that. I won't call the Denver bank with the account number and the wire transfer codes until the last minute. They should be able to get the wire transfer there within an hour."

It amazed her how many plans were just falling into place.

"We should leave Friday morning, then. That stretch of highway after turning off of I-70 towards Salt Lake City can get pretty tied up. I assume you'd still rather drive than fly?" Jake asked.

The room grew quiet. Alex got up and put another log on the fire.

"You don't need to go with me, Jake," she said, smiling. "I can make the drive. You're too busy to be hauled away from here. I need to check the post office box to see if my license plates have arrived. My temporary sticker is about to expire."

Jake looked at Alex, not really sure what to do. He had promised his friend he would accompany her. "Well, we'll talk about it again," he said. He glanced at his watch. "As for me, I'm going to make it an early night. I'll see you two in the morning – early in the morning."

Neither Meredith nor Alex said anything for at least a minute after Jake left the room. Meredith reached for the remote and found some music she thought they would both like.

"Unforgettable," – their song – began to play and Alex rose, holding out his hand to her. She recognized the "let's dance" stance and rose from her chair to move into his arms.

"It's important for you to take more time to exercise," he said softly in her ear. "You tend to get too focused on things that need to be done and forget your other priorities. Stress will eat you up alive without exercise."

"Yes, doctor," she replied in his ear. She grabbed his ear lobe between her teeth and pulled it into her mouth. His arms tightened about her. "Simmer, remember?" she said softly.

"Well, then, turn down the heat," he smiled.

"You're right, though," Meredith said. She sighed deeply. "We need to talk about a lot of things that don't involve the project or any of the topics involving it. We think we know one another. Do we, really?"

Alex stopped dancing in mid-step and she stepped on his toes.

"Don't you have a signal light or something to warn of sudden stops?" she laughed.

He led her to her seat and then turned to his own chair.

"What would you like to talk about?" he asked in a congenial tone. He ran his right hand through his dark hair and leaned forward, elbows on his knees and hands under his chin. It was his "I'm ready to chat" pose.

"How about... what are the most important lessons you've learned in your 59 years on this planet?" she asked. As she asked the question, she moved from her chair to sit on the floor between his feet and put her head on his thigh. He gently stroked her hair, and then rubbed her shoulders.

"Your muscles are tight," he commented. "Too much time in front of that computer. I'm serious about the exercise thing."

"Yes sir," Meredith responded. "Now, stop stalling and tell me the most important lessons you've learned." She laughed as she said it, lightly poking his knee with her fist. "And that feels wonderful. Please don't stop."

There was a long silence. "You know," he said, "your question is a good one." Again there was an extended silence. "This will require some thinking."

Meredith's eyes closed as his fingers worked magic on her tight shoulder muscles.

"The topic is too broad," she said, her eyes opening. "Let's put it into categories. What's the most important thing you've learned about..." she thought for a moment, "success?"

Again there was a long silence, but as long as his strong fingers massaged her tight muscles, waiting for him to answer was unimportant.

"Hmmm... Success makes me think about balance. Nature is balance in motion. Success is, too. Successful people are balanced ... mentally, physically, and spiritually."

Meredith nodded her head. "I like that," she said thoughtfully. "Success is finding balance in all of the elements that make up the human experience!" She thought for a moment before continuing. "Do you think balance must occur at the highest level possible for each individual to achieve before it is termed 'success?'"

He mussed her hair... it was short enough now that it just fell back into its curly place. "You Americans, as the French would say!" he laughed. "You are so competitive – must everything be the best of which one is capable? Can't people be successful achieving only half of their potential?"

"How can an over-achiever like you ask that?" Meredith queried. "I have a theory about achieving full potential." She rose and re-took her seat across from him.

"We shouldn't talk about your theories without Jake. It will ruin his day if he misses one," Alex said, laughing at her. "He gets a great kick out of them. They make him think."

She was silent until he relented and encouraged her to continue.

"How about starting with this?" she asked. "As you said, nothing stands still in nature. If we don't move forward, we move backwards, right?"

Alex nodded his agreement. It was a logical truth.

"Well, when we don't achieve what we are really capable of, we're never really happy. We always feel like there is something we left undone. When we stop achieving… when we stop pushing ourselves to our limits of knowledge and try to go beyond that point to learn more, we start moving backwards because nothing in nature stands still."

He couldn't argue with her logic because what she said was true, so he agreed and recanted his statement regarding what the French thought of Americans.

"What about compatibility?" she asked.

"What about it?" She sometimes changed mental gears so quickly it was difficult to figure out where she was going.

"What have you learned about it?" she asked in a very quiet voice.

"I have a theory about it," he said. They both laughed.

"Shall I wake Jake up?" Meredith asked.

"No, I think Jake has heard this one… though maybe not. You have a talent for pulling information from me that no one else can get," he said, looking at her very intently.

"About personal compatibility, let's see: When I was in graduate school, I started looking at people as if they were containers. That made it easy to draw an analogy between the person in the present and the person each might grow into one day. That's the trick to long-term compatibility … not just knowing who is compatible with you today, but knowing if they'll be compatible with you as you grow. Each person has a different capacity to work, live, love, and be creative."

He paused, realizing how long it had been since he had first thought of these kinds of things. "So, if people were containers, some would look like small juice glasses, holding four ounces because that's what their growth capacity is. Others would look like eight-ounce water glasses. A few might look like sixteen-ounce iced-tea glasses or resemble half-gallon jugs.

"The person born with the potential to hold eight ounces is compatible with other people who hold eight ounces. To achieve fulfillment in life, each must fill his or her eight ounces. The cost of fulfillment is to reach full potential for productivity in life.

"Regarding long-term compatibility, say two eight ounce people meet and fall in love. To remain compatible, both must develop equal amounts of their eight ounce potential. The size of each person's potential is not nearly as important as how much of it they develop. A person with a four ounce potential who develops all four ounces will be much happier, much more successful and fulfilled, than someone with a sixteen ounce potential who develops only half of it."

She thought about his words for a moment. "So, in your 'containers' analogy, do people have different potentials for the mental, physical and spiritual? Or, are they all the same?"

He chuckled. "Trust you to find the difficult questions," he said. "They all have the same potential. A sixteen ounce mental person is also a sixteen ounce physical and spiritual person – though people usually have a talent for developing one of the three categories more easily."

"Wait, wait, wait!" she said, putting straight fingers and the lower part of her right arm perpendicular to her left hand... a typical football sign for a time out. "Then you agree with me that balance should occur at the highest possible level each person can attain to achieve success."

He grinned at her. "It certainly sounds that way, doesn't it?"

"Oh, you!" she said, reaching behind her for the small pillow he had put there for her and throwing it at him. "But you realize, my dear scientist, that you have introduced a piece of non-logic into the fray?"

"Not me," he said. "Impossible. I couldn't do that. I've tried hard to think illogically and have never found a way to do it. If there is a lack of logic in something we've said, it must be coming from your side of the room." It delighted him to have her contradict him.

"No," Meredith responded, head turned upward just a bit, "this is definitely a lack of logic that can only be conceived in the Russian language – I have a theory about language, too."

They both laughed.

"Okay," Alex said. "Tell me the illogical error so we can correct it and go on."

"Well," Meredith began slowly, "you said to be successful, balance must be achieved at the physical, mental, and spiritual levels. Unless a person develops all three things with equal vigor, it's impossible to achieve balance. The mental will run ahead of the physical, or both will grow beyond the spiritual. To achieve balance among the three, they must unite at the same level. If a person pays too much attention to the mental and the physical and ignores the spiritual, balance has to occur at the lowest, not the highest, level – in this case, the spiritual level. Right?"

Alex just shook his head in disbelief and said, "And that brings us full circle – that you must give your physical self more exercise than you do on days when you sit in front of that computer for so long."

"Good grief!" she laughed. "It does bring us back to that point, doesn't it? Did you do that on purpose?" she asked with a skeptical grin.

"Would I do something like that to you?"

"Yes, to prove a point, I believe you would," she frowned at him as she spoke. "I'd ask you for more of that shoulder massage, but I'm afraid my back burner might get too warm – so, I'd better say goodnight." Meredith rose and took her empty glass to the kitchen, rinsed it and placed it in the dishwasher to be done with the morning dishes.

"You know," he said, following her into the kitchen, "one reason we are drawn to one another involves the concepts we've discussed tonight."

She walked up to him and put her arms around him. "Are you saying we're both four ounce containers?" she whispered softly.

He held her tightly for a moment and then leaned the upper part of his body away from her. "You are a gallon container if I ever met one, dorogoi" he said, kissing her neck gently.

"Dorogoi?" she asked.

"Darling," he informed her with a stone face showing no expression.

"Oh," Meredith smiled at him, "I like that."

"Good, because I think you're stuck with it. Now go turn off that computer, take a shower, go to bed, and I'll see you in the morning." He bent his head and gently kissed her goodnight.

After she left, Alex turned his recliner 180 degrees to face the fireplace. It was still two hours before midnight. He was not yet ready for sleep.

His conversation with Meredith had brought back memories of his homeland and the concepts of success and compatibility he had once held. Russian citizens had wanted to live compatibly in peace. They were peaceful people. Twenty million of them were killed so the communist philosophies of Marx and Engels could be tested. Peaceful people just did not matter, he thought.

The Chinese communists had killed seventy million people. The people of that huge nation were peaceful, just as the Russians had been. The problem was with the government, not the people. Chairman Mao had a political agenda. Again, Alex realized, those who subscribed to peace were viewed as unimportant and insignificant.

What we should have learned, he thought, is that when a majority of people allow the fanatics of the world to dominate because it is more convenient to live peaceful lives, history says to expect extremists to take total control... and extremists are seldom kind – or, peaceful.

It was one thing to believe in a philosophy of peace. It was something else to create an environment where conflict from those who did not believe in peace could be kept from destroying it. Those who loved peace, he realized, could only maintain their peaceful lives when they were willing to fight for peace. He feared America was in for a rude awakening. He had heard the stories from his father, again and again. He had talked with survivors of the German attack against Russia, again and again. The moment peaceful people became complacent – the moment they no longer realized that government is an enemy to be kept containable and controllable – their peaceful existences came to an abrupt end.

Alex worked for about an hour and then yawned. He placed the fireplace screen close to the stone wall, covering the opening so no sparks could escape. Much of the wood they used was pine. It had a bad habit of popping long after a fire appeared dead. He headed to his bedroom and heard the shower as he passed Meredith's door. He realized that as he had been working on his outline, she had been in front of the computer, researching all of the information he and Jake had given her that day.

He couldn't help but wonder what their lives would have been like had they met in their twenties. What would children they might have had look like? What kind of father would he have been? What kind of mother would she have been if she'd had the support of a husband and father in the home? How much healthier would she be today without the stresses that single parenthood brings to those who work hard at making a good job of it?

They were, he found, pleasing thoughts. In consideration for the hot water heater, he decided to put his shower off until the morning. He noted that clean flannel sheets had been put on the bed that day. He had to get some help for Nancy. His life purpose, he could see, was having a negative impact on those about whom he cared. He would have to think about that and find a way to correct the problem. Still, he thought, the sheets felt wonderful… warm, clean and comfortable.

It made him think of Meredith.

Chapter 22

⁓⁓

"I burned your note," Jake said.

After Jake had gone to bed the night before, giving Alex and Meredith some time together, Alex realized he had not asked where Jake had found William Leonard. He wrote a note and pasted it to his bedroom door.

"I found him in Austria. He's not in prison, but he is under surveillance... ours, theirs, the Russians – everyone."

"Where in Austria?" Alex asked.

"Salzburg," Jake answered.

Alex suggested they walk to the office at the stable. They were having their first meeting with all four Real Things. It was the first time since coming to the ranch that the four men, usually confined to their individual rooms, would mingle with one another. Jake and Alex continued their discussion as they walked. They needed to get a message from Arthur Redbridge to William Leonard. The content would be critical. What should the message from the Fed Chairman say to a guy who was probably the richest man in the world? Jake would deliver the message.

Justice Scott entered the stable office first. Scott was 58 years old, the smallest of the four men at five feet, eight inches. Balding, he wore glasses and looked like he took himself pretty seriously. Nancy said that wasn't true. She smiled when she told Alex he had the best sense of humor of them all.

Redbridge, the oldest and the tallest, was rather lanky even with the weight gain he had enjoyed since arriving at the ranch. He wore beige slacks with a pale blue dress shirt and black wingtip shoes. He was one of those people who was just angular everywhere… even in his face. As usual, he was hard to read.

Martinez, 48, was medium-sized and round-faced. He had a dark complexion and a healthy head of dark brown hair. He and J.J. Branchman were dressed in jeans. The yellow sweater Martinez wore brought out the color in his face. Branchman was about five-feet, ten-inches tall and of stocky build. He had black hair with a natural gray streak through the middle, from front to back. He had one of those faces that was, from certain angles, so handsome it made you want to stare. It was hard to tell his age, but Alex knew he was 45.

Aside from making initial comments and giving the men a chance to socialize over coffee and doughnuts, Jake and Alex turned the meeting over to the four attendees. Alex smiled as he worked at his desk and overheard comments from the group.

"I have a suggestion," Arthur Redbridge offered, his tone congenial. The other men stopped talking and turned their heads toward him. "I think before we begin, we might want to complete the questionnaire we've been given. Am I right, Alex? You and your team will use this material to help coordinate the most effective ways we can work together to achieve various objectives after our return to office?"

Alex looked up from his reading material, smiled and nodded. "That's right, Arthur. We have provided each of you with a mountain of information, but it covered only your areas of expertise. You've all been away from world events since you were taken to Sakhalin Island. We hope we can help you determine key issues and let you four guys find ways to create action plans. If we have the power of the Federal Central Bank, the Supreme Court, the United States Senate, and of public opinion garnered from talk radio all working together, what can we achieve?" He paused and looked at Jake. "Would you add anything?"

Jake, attired in jeans, a dark blue sweater and boots, looked at the floor for a moment. "Only that if anyone wants input on what a question means or why it's being asked to not be shy. That's why we're here," Jake responded. "I think Arthur's idea about completing the questionnaire before your discussions is a good one. If we've done our job right, your answers to the questions will keep you focused on key issues."

The room became quiet as the four men began writing. Both Alex and Jake were surprised at the amount of time spent in this effort. After two hours, the first pen was laid on the table at which the four men sat. A half-hour after that, all of the questionnaires were complete.

About ten minutes later, the door opened and Joe and Nancy walked in with a large pot filled with Meredith's home made vegetable soup and a variety of sandwich fillings. Lettuce, tomatoes, cheese and everything required to make a killer sandwich were provided. Jake pulled beer, soda, and milk from the refrigerator. The four men had been living in an upscale prison, for all practical purposes. Being able to interact with one another over lunch and talk freely about their views of what was happening generated a very lively atmosphere.

"You know, Alex," began J.J. Branchman, "this probably isn't the right place or time to say this, but that never stops me." He paused long enough to look at the three men who shared his imprisonment, looked down, then directly at Alex. "When we were first brought here, I was terrified." His trained radio voice was as compelling in person as it was on the radio, Jake thought. "I knew you were the Russian scientist who created the clone that replaced me. Life in captivity on Sakhalin Island was not good and it was not easy. I just want to publicly thank you for caring enough to rescue us. You didn't have to do that."

The other three men quickly added their own thoughts to those of the famed radio talk show host. All of them understood that Alex could have left them in their Sakhalin Island prison and gone on about his own life. Each in some way mentioned how their appreciation of freedom and rejection of communism had grown as a result of their experience.

Until that moment, Alex really had no insight into how these men felt about his role in their destinies. He feared they might hate him. Jake quietly watched.

"Your words bring peace to my heart," Alex began slowly. He stood behind his desk, head somewhat bowed. Then he looked each of the men in the eye, one at a time. "I thank you for what you've said. I do want you to know that what I was doing for the Soviet Union made me ill – literally, but that does not change what was done to you. No one – no government – had or has the right to take years of anyone's life. I may have been an unwilling participant in the horrors you suffered, but I was, indeed, a participant. I thank you for your forgiveness. I commit to you that I'll do anything I can to return you to the lives that were stolen from you. And that is why we're here today, gentlemen. Jake?" Alex quickly sat behind his desk and looked at his friend.

It was a powerful moment. Jake recognized it as such and briefly thought how few really powerful moments any person has in a lifetime. "We have some video tapes that were taken at a meeting we had here in the stables over a month ago. Arthur has already seen them – Arthur, if you want to spend the next couple of hours talking with Meredith, I'll be glad to give you a ride to the main house." Jake paused for a moment as Arthur said he would like to do just that. "Then, we will break for today. We'd like to invite all of you to the main house for dinner tomorrow night. We will do an after dinner review of the plan to take you home to your families and careers. We want your input and approval… it's your lives on the line when the switch with your clones is made. You need to realize that. If it's a chance you'd rather not take, you can opt out. We'll talk about what your alternatives are. Are there any questions?"

Jake waited and none were forthcoming. Rather, he had a group of four very serious faces looking at him, waiting for the promised videos. Jake turned on the VCR, touched Redbridge's shoulder and the two of them left. Alex stayed behind. The room was very quiet.

Both Alex and Jake were nervous about the greater freedoms these men would begin demanding once they started feeling free again. Attitude and getting caught up with the world had kept them under control for almost three months. That scale was about to tip as a free attitude would be encouraged. It was bound to bring problems. They expected it.

Meredith was glad for the interruption when Jake stuck his head in the room and told her Arthur Redbridge was in the living room wanting to talk with her.

"I thought you'd be glad for a break," he told her, smiling. "I know you're trying to get twice as much work done today for your Salt Lake City trip tomorrow. Are you sure you don't want me to drive you, Meredith?"

She shook her head and put her hand on his arm. "I'll be fine, Jake. There's too much going on here for you to take time away." With that, she walked to the living room to find Arthur Redbridge. She suggested that since it was such a nice day, they could talk on the patio.

"First," she said quietly, putting her hand on his arm before they sat, "I know you'll want to visit the cemetery where your wife is buried. I have the information," she said, handing him a downloaded photo of the gravesite. He took it from her hands and just stared at it. The tombstone indicated his wife had died ten years ago, at age 55. Meredith was surprised when his shoulders began to shake. Tears come from under closed eyelids. "I'm sorry, Arthur," she said. "There is no kind way to take care of this task. I'm sorry I had to be the one to do it." She walked to him and put her arms around him. He returned the embrace and sobbed quietly for two or three minutes before regaining control and taking a step away from her.

"Did they do this to Helen?" he asked, his voice shaking.

"She died of a heart attack, Arthur," Meredith responded. "Did she have heart problems?"

"No," was his abrupt reply. "She did not. Helen was as healthy as a horse."

"Well, we'll probably never know the answer to that question. Is it possible she found out the man she was living with wasn't you? Is it possible they killed her to keep their secret? Jake can tell you more about that than I."

She went into the kitchen and poured him a straight Scotch. He sat and slowly sipped the liquor. "I loved her so much," he said quietly. "She made my life worthwhile... she made everyone's life worthwhile. She was gentle and generous. How can I do this without Helen to welcome me home each night and turn the insanity of Washington's politics into something that borders on intelligent life?" he asked.

"Would you rather put off the rest of data gathering I've done?" Meredith asked. She reached out and put her hand on his shoulder.

He thought about it for a moment. "No," he finally said. "In truth, her death gives me even more of a reason to return to office." His jaw clenched as he said it and he exuded a sense of determination she had not seen before. It was nothing obvious, but she could feel it.

He was impressed with the quality and the amount of information she had been able to get from the Internet. She gave him copies of the brochures Jake had procured on his tour of the Fed two days ago. She showed him copies of the pictures she had downloaded from Jake's digital camera.

"New carpeting," he murmured, smiling at her through his grief.

They continued their conversation until Redbridge suggested it would be a good idea for him to return to the stable office for any conversation that might take place after the videos were completed.

They decided to walk to the stables. Fifteen minutes later, they joined the others. Alex quickly rose from his desk and walked to her side. He took her elbow in his hand and escorted her to a seat.

"A rose among the thorns," commented J.J. Branchman.

"Indeed she is," Alex said, putting his arm around her waist as if claiming his territory. He introduced her to the two men she had not met. "You'll find a brief bio for Ms. Morgan in your folders," he paused and then looked at her.

"We were just beginning to discuss reactions to the videos."

"Well, Arthur wanted to be here for that," she responded, smiling.

"To answer any questions you might have as to my reaction about the financial elements of the video," Redbridge quickly interposed, "I have seen it and will tell you that Ms. Morgan's facts are accurate and I mostly agree with her conclusions. Those things with which I do not agree are minor interpretations of the facts she presented." He took his seat and picked up the pen, looking at the yellow-lined pad in front of him. "I guess I would add that I never totally agree with anyone," he said, smiling at her.

"Nervy bastards, aren't they?" Branchman offered. "They seem to have little insight that from the beginning of time no one has been able to achieve what they believe is their rightful inheritance... this world government. I cannot believe the arrogance!"

The others looked down. They were from worlds not used to facing problems quite so directly. Branchman heard the quiet that followed his remarks.

"Come on, guys!" he scoffed. "Your lives were turned upside down because jerks just like these who happen to live half-a-world away and run a different government made similar decisions involving you. There is no room for anything called political correctness here." He turned from them to Alex and Jake, now standing together at the front of the room. "It seems apparent to me that the former U.S.S.R. is using the clones that replaced us – and who knows how many others – to lead this country over the same cliff from which they jumped. Am I wrong, Alex?"

Alex walked two or three steps to his right, then back before answering.

"Actually, I think that question is best answered by Arthur," he replied.

It was an offering of trust, Redbridge realized, and it surprised him.

"You're not wrong, Mr. Branchman..."

"J.J., please," the other man interrupted.

"Yes, okay... J.J." Redbridge looked at Meredith for a few seconds... as if he were trying to remember something. Then he turned to look directly at Branchman.

"You're right, J.J.," Arthur said with a new firmness in his voice. "The Russian government is using our clones and, as we know from having seen them on the Island, the clones of others, to manipulate the U.S. currency. They intend to cause the fall of the dollar and from the chaos that results, establish martial law and impose a new trade zone involving America, Mexico and Canada. That will usher in a new currency; rumor has labeled it the 'Amero'."

He paused again. Jake and Alex were unsure if he had finished his comments, but neither said anything, waiting.

"And you are also right, J.J., in saying that there is no room for political correctness. If we stand a chance to beat this ogre from our door we must face facts. We must find the truth." He looked intently at the other two men, each in turn. "If you harbor any thoughts that you can return to your sweet, powerful lives – go back to the way it used to be – get over it. Whether it is our Creator or some other force, we are going to be given a chance to save this country from destruction. It will be difficult and it will be dangerous… but it needs to be done. I don't know about the others, Alex, but I intend to make good use of this life you saved from Sakhalin Island."

Again, he paused. His voice was strong and he appeared every inch the most powerful man in the free world.

"I would suggest this might be a good time to break for the day," Redbridge said. "I think we all need to think about who we are and the reason our lives were saved and the purpose each of us is intended to fulfill."

"I agree," Branchman said quietly, looking at Redbridge with a new respect in his eyes. "And I thank you for your honesty, Mr. Chairman."

Redbridge smiled at him. "Call me Arthur, J.J.," he replied.

Meredith exhaled fully for what she thought was probably the first time in at least two minutes. She, too, smiled at Redbridge. She was proud of him. Alex noted the exchanged glances between them and quietly wondered what conversation had transpired at the house to turn Arthur into a man ready to lead troops into combat.

Jake, Alex and Meredith returned the four men to the bunkhouse. Not one word was said in the car Alex drove. She suspected Jake was having the same experience in the Jeep.

"I need to tell Nancy to come to the house and pick up some prime rib and baked potatoes," Meredith said. "I'll be right back."

Alex just shook his head as he watched her accompany Redbridge and Branchman back into the bunkhouse. He raised his eyebrows as he noticed that Redbridge walked with his hand on her shoulder.

She was able to get so many things done without even realizing what she was accomplishing, Alex thought. When she returned to the car, he said nothing.

When they got to the main house she went directly to the kitchen. "Rare, medium, or well done?" she asked Alex and Jake as she sliced the prime rib roast.

Alex and Jake just looked at one another for a brief second before replying "Rare, please." Meredith cut the meat from the center of the roast and then cut herself a serving that was medium-well. She had already placed the baked potatoes and asparagus on the table.

The meal was eaten quickly and with a minimum of talk. Both men wanted to ask her what she had injected Arthur Redbridge with to get him so emotional – he was the most non-emotional person either had ever met.

Jake lit the after dinner fire while Alex changed the electronics equipment. Meredith had no idea they were so curious about the Fed Chairman and was surprised by their immediate questions about him as they took to their chairs in the living room.

"So?" Jake asked. "What did you do to Arthur Redbridge that caused him to come back to the meeting breathing smoke and fire?"

Meredith just looked at him for a moment, then at Alex. "He was pretty emotional in that meeting, wasn't he?" she asked.

"You really didn't do anything? Didn't say anything?" Alex asked, rubbing the palms of his hands together, his elbows resting on his knees as he spoke. He leaned back, reclined his chair, raised his feet and put his hands behind his head, puzzled.

"Well," she began, "he did become very upset when I showed him the picture of his wife's grave... I downloaded it from the Internet." She paused, not really knowing what to say. "I knew he'd want to visit the cemetery upon his return to Washington," she finished.

"Oh, my," Jake said. He put the fingers of both hands across his eyes. "I hate to be the one to tell you this, Meredith. Arthur didn't know Helen Redbridge was dead."

Meredith turned as pale as a sheet and just stared at Jake, then at Alex.

"Why didn't either of you tell me he didn't know?" she asked in a very quiet, controlled voice. "How could you let me do this to that poor man? He sobbed like a baby." The picture of Arthur Redbridge, his shoulders shaking as she held him flitted through her mind like a movie. It kept replaying itself. "I owe him an apology. I'm going to give it to him right now," she said, rising from her chair and heading for the front door.

"I'll drive you," Alex insisted.

Silence dominated the ride as he drove the Jeep to the bunkhouse. She was thinking about the words she had spoken to Redbridge earlier. To just come out like that and tell him his wife was dead and buried – even showing him a picture of her grave! It made her shudder. She had assumed that either Jake or Alex had told him his wife was dead. It was her fault for assuming Redbridge had been told, not theirs. This is what happens when one involves one's self in the personal lives of other people, she thought.

When the Jeep parked outside the bunkhouse, Meredith had the door open almost before it stopped. Alex got out and walked behind her.

"I can do this on my own," she said in a totally emotionless tone.

"I'm quite sure you can," he answered, "but it was not all your mistake. Jake or I should have told you he didn't know about his wife's death. It was just one detail too many. I, too, owe him an apology."

Jake had evidently called Nancy and Joe because they were awaiting them with an open door. No words were spoken as Nancy walked down the hall ahead of Meredith and Alex to open the door.

"Arthur, I..."

"You didn't know I didn't know, did you?" He put his arm around her shoulder and gave her a hug. "I had that figured out about two minutes after you told me," he said as he looked down at the tears slipping from under her closed eyes. "Please don't cry over this or feel badly, Meredith. There's no good way to tell someone a loved one has died... no right way. It would have hurt just as badly had you or Jake or Alex been properly prepared and gave me the news more gently." He paused. "I wondered why no one ever said anything about Helen. I was probably avoiding asking the question for fear of the answer..."

"The fault was probably mine, Arthur," Alex interrupted. "There were so many details on our minds, Jake and I just kept putting off an unpleasant task. You're right to know Meredith would never intentionally say anything unkind to you."

"Regardless of whose fault it was, I cannot tell you how terribly sorry I am for being so insensitive in how I told you that Helen is gone."

Alex handed her his handkerchief and she wiped her face and eyes.

"As I told Meredith," Redbridge said, "it's a good reason to put this country back on the path of a republic like our founding fathers intended. Finding out about Helen's death just makes me more determined to stop these people. And Meredith was right," he said. "I will want to visit her grave when I return."

Now that her eyes were adjusted to the light, Meredith could see that his eyes were reddened and puffy. He had been crying, she thought.

The three of them talked for two or three minutes more before Meredith and Alex took their leave. Arthur Redbridge's confidence in his "team," as he viewed them, increased. So they missed a personal detail. It was not what they missed that got his attention in this instance. It was what they did about it after they realized they had missed it.

"You know, Meredith," Alex began as they drove back to the house, "sometimes God just figures the best way for things to happen. Arthur was right when he said there's no right or wrong way to tell someone a loved one has died. The way this happened has put a bit in Arthur's mouth. It has made him want to run a race that can positively impact the lives of hundreds of millions of people. Can you think of a better tribute to Helen Redbridge?"

She said nothing, but reached over and took his hand.

Jake opened the door for them. He took one look at their stoic faces and decided not to ask if everything was okay. He wanted to know, but he would just have to wait and find out what happened. This was the kind of mistake that happened when too many details were being processed at one time. It was the thing that worried him most about such a huge undertaking.

"It's Monday, right?" Meredith asked. "Can we watch 24?"

Alex smiled at Jake to tell him everything was okay and reached for the television remote. At the end of the program, he turned the set off and turned towards them.

"Let me start," Jake said. "I cannot tell you how sorry I am that I didn't tell you that Redbridge didn't know about his wife," he told Meredith.

"I know you are," she responded, smiling at him. "I know you wouldn't do anything intentionally cruel to me, Jake – or to Arthur. It's not your nature. And I think we need to figure out how we can use this experience to make sure similar errors don't occur."

Jake glanced at Alex and understood the look of admiration on his face as he looked at her. It was precisely what Alex would have said had she not beaten him to it, Jake thought.

"You're right," Jake answered.

"Well," Alex interjected, "it's already had one positive result. Arthur is very upset, but learning of Helen Redbridge's death has convinced him that he can give meaning to her death by returning to Washington with the purpose of cleaning it up."

Jake nodded his head, now understanding why Redbridge had come back to the meeting ready to take on the others in the room.

Meredith retired for the evening. She had to leave for Salt Lake City the next morning. She needed to prepare for a day away.

The two men turned on Monday Night Football after she let Rusty back in and went to her room.

"She must have felt terrible about whatever was said," Jake said quietly to his friend.

Alex didn't reply until what looked like an impossible pass was caught by a running back. He had slipped through the front line of the Kansas City Chiefs to catch the ball for a twenty yard gain. All of the zone coverage had been on outside pass receivers.

"I don't think she was angry, Jake. She was hurt that she had been insensitive in telling someone about the death of a loved one. That's all. She and Arthur are becoming friends, and that's good." He was staring at the television set, awaiting a replay of the pass.

Jake looked at him, rose from his chair and asked Alex what he would like to drink. Some good things never changed, he thought. Monday Night Football was one of them.

Chapter 23

After Meredith left for her bank appointment in Salt Lake City, Alex and Jake headed for their meeting with Arthur Redbridge. Jake would be leaving the next day for Austria. He would carry Redbridge's message to William Leonard alias Leonard Williams alias Roger Marchman. Brett assured Jake that Marchman was the alias under which the man was living in Salzburg. A pot of coffee awaited them when they arrived at the Fed Chairman's room. After each was seated at the table on the small patio, Jake handed the information he had about Leonard's location to Redbridge who carefully read through it. He put the pages back down on the table and folded his arms. Jake noticed that he frowned a lot as he read the documents.

"I realize what a strange and possibly dangerous task you're undertaking, Jake. Leonard is being watched by a lot of known and probably unknown sources. Let me think for a moment or two." He rose and walked across his bedroom, his face pensive.

"I'm going to have to trust the two of you with secrets that I did not even share with the President of the United States when I was in office," he murmured. "I dislike doing it for a lot of reasons, some of which include your safety. Certain information should only be shared on a NTK basis. I would say that we have reached that point," Redbridge stated.

"NTK?" Alex asked.

"Need to know," Jake said quietly.

Alex studied Redbridge for a moment, unsure of how to motivate him to continue. Suddenly he said, "You're in Colorado, Arthur."

Redbridge turned and looked intently at the Russian and suddenly smiled. "I won't tell the others," he said.

"Good thinking," Jake replied in a firm tone. Alex was motivating Redbridge by gambling with his security.

"Yes. Well..." Redbridge began, once again taking his seat at the table and picking up his coffee, sipping from it and clearing his throat. "The sentence used when I needed to see William Leonard was: 'I hear the castle at Neuschwanstein was built by King Ludwig the Second.' His response is 'Yes, he built it in the 19th century.' William Leonard is a German history buff. It doesn't surprise me that he is living in Austria. He'd probably rather be in the Bavarian Alps, but the Germans are not as accommodating as the Austrians when it comes to giant-sized money problems like Leonard has," he finished.

"Neuschwanstein?" Alex asked, his eyebrows drawn together. "That translates to 'New Swan Castle' in German."

"Oh!" Redbridge said, startled. "It certainly does. Before Ludwig rebuilt it, the Castle was Hohenschangau... or, 'high swan country.' You're thinking of Jeffrey's drawing on the manila envelope, of course."

"Maybe just a coincidence," Jake said. "Maybe not. He may have overheard something in the meeting that wasn't in writing. Maybe he thought to give Meredith a clue. Jeffrey told me she and her daughter visited there a long time ago. They say it's the model used for the Disney Castle..." his voice trailed off.

Alex scowled, for a moment looking every bit the brooding scientist Meredith had called him. "For now, we need to get a message written to William Leonard... one that will get the proper response from him. What action do you want him to take, Arthur? He's being carefully watched though is evidently not under arrest of any kind. Jake has to be able to deliver a simple message quickly. What do we want him to do?"

Jake had written the words Redbridge said earlier. He repeated them. "Have I got it right?"

Redbridge nodded. "Why don't you shake his hand and pass him a message as you say the words... that way, they won't be on paper."

"No, but if his room is bugged – as it probably is – everyone will know both the words and his response," Jake replied.

"You're right," Redbridge said. He thought for a few moments, pacing. His hands were nervously touching his face and mouth. No one spoke. "Leonard was raised in Arizona. His mother was Navajo and he speaks the language... the code Navajo Indians used during World War Two – what did they call them? Code Speakers? The enemy was never able to break that code, as I recall. We need to find someone who can teach you how to say this sentence in Navajo."

"By tomorrow?" Jake asked, aghast.

"Yes," was all Redbridge said. "Do you have a better idea? I'm sorry... I wish we'd thought of it sooner," he added, frowning. "But we didn't. It's the perfect solution."

Jake grabbed his cell phone to get the number for a Navajo-Apache Information Center he knew of in Show Low, Arizona. After confirming the Center would be staffed until five o'clock that afternoon and "yes, there is someone here who can translate from English into Navajo," he called Gil.

"We need to go to Show Low, Arizona," he told his pilot. Jake had been to Show Low in the mid-90s and had to fly into Holbrook. It was how he knew about the joint information center. "How do we get there?"

"They have an airport in Show Low, boss," Gil told him. "Since 1999."

"Will the runways accommodate the Lear jet?"

Gil asked Jake to wait a moment as he flipped through a listing all of the airports in the country. He always carried it. This wasn't the first time Jake needed to fly someplace and back quickly.

"Runway 6-24 is 7,200 feet long. Lear jets are easily accommodated," Gil informed him. Jake smiled.

"Now, for the note you will hand Leonard," Redbridge continued. He was focused on the project, Jake had to give him that. He sat down and wrote a brief message. "He's in Salzburg, right?" he asked Jake.

"Right," was the response.

"I'm telling him to meet you at Salzburg's Hellbrunn Zoo at three in the afternoon, two days after tomorrow. It contains a variety of animals from all over the world. One of the main free attractions is the wild vultures. That will be meaningful to Leonard because he always called me a vulture and a tightwad. I always complained about his expense account," Redbridge said, smiling at his own humor.

Jake realized this man had more originality than he had thought. "I'll need to find out if he's wired for sound."

"Just ask him and then wink your right eye," Redbridge said. "If he says 'yes' and winks his right eye, it means 'no.' If he says anything and doesn't wink, it means 'yes'."

Jake smiled at Redbridge. "Okay..." he said.

Redbridge handed him the note he had written and Jake read it, smiled, and asked Redbridge if he needed anything special to write a final copy. "Should I get this translated too?" he asked.

"I used to write my notes to him on my secretary's lined steno pad," he responded. "It might be a good idea for me to use one. I think it's more important that the note be in my handwriting than in code. He'll recognize it, I think..."

"Alex can find a steno pad in his office. I've got to run." Jake looked at the items he held in his hands to make sure he had everything. "I'll take a pocket recorder. That way I'll be able to listen to the sentence and practice it while I'm flying to Austria. If I flunk Navajo 101, I'll just play the tape for Leonard." He paused again, thinking of each thing that needed to be done before his departure for Munich early the next morning. "You've got until tonight to rethink or edit your note," Jake added. "I'm leaving at the crack of dawn in the morning."

Redbridge nodded his understanding. "I'll give it more thought, but I think this is it" he said.

After a quick flight to Show Low and a fast drive home from the Rifle airport, Jake got to the ranch in time to help Alex get their catered dinner ready. Alex had spent the day writing key data on a flip chart and removing any location identifiers from public areas like the living room and bathrooms. Nothing had the word "Colorado" on it. All newspapers and magazines were removed. He locked the doors to non-public rooms.

"Did you get it?" he asked as Jake entered the kitchen.

Jake held up his tape recorder and hit play. It was an interesting language, Alex thought. No wonder no one had been able to break the Navajo tongue when it was used as a code. He could barely understand the various nuances of sound that came from the recorder.

"Are you going to be able to say that?" he asked, a bit skeptically.

"I have all day tomorrow to learn... I have until about two in the afternoon of day after tomorrow to learn, in fact. The important thing is, I found someone who could do the translation for me and am ready for wheels up early tomorrow morning," Jake replied.

At about 5:30 that evening, Jake drove to the bunkhouse and picked up their dinner guests. Alex remained behind doing final preparations. They would start with a cocktail and move quickly to the dinner table. He wanted to have dinner over by 7:30 so they would have two hours for planning talks.

Alex began looking at his watch at about 5:00 p.m. and wondered where on the highway Meredith was. It was comforting that she was leaving a past behind and would be able to start a new life with him. That the permanency of a relationship with her had entered his thoughts so subtly startled him. A life together...

Alex was putting the last pan in the oven to re-heat their catered meal when Jake led their four guests into the house. Their reactions to the earth home and its security measures ranged from overt admiration to quiet surprise. The four men watched as the retainer wall covered the front entrance. The men walked to the patio, drinks in hand. It was getting dark and Jake lit the fire he had laid earlier.

The conversation centered on weather and the beauty of the locale and how nice it was to be out of the bunkhouse feeling like free men again. The latter was the closest thing said that referenced this get together as anything other than a group of friends enjoying one another's company for the evening.

Their appetites were hardy. There was some discussion of the news of the day but it was mostly quiet as the men ate. A subtle nervousness could be heard in throats cleared and short coughs as the meal neared its conclusion. Everyone must be able to feel it, Alex thought.

Jake noticed Alex looking at his wrist watch again and he, too, began wondering where Meredith was and if she was okay.

"Who is the chef to whom we owe our thanks for this feast?" asked Justice Scott. "I haven't tasted anything this good since... well, since the 1990s." He paused before continuing. "The prime rib last night was wonderful, but I love pork," he said, smiling.

Senator Martinez laughed and told Scott "I'm the one who is supposed to be the expert on pork, Avery!" They all laughed. It was good they were laughing, Alex thought.

"As for the chef," Alex said, smiling, "she owns a catering company in town."

"And what town would that be?" asked J.J. Branchman. The room was silent for a long moment.

"It would be the town that has a chef that knows how to cook crown pork roast fit for a king, J.J.," Jake replied, a bit of a scowl on his face. "Why don't we retire to the living room and enjoy the fire and some good brandy? Then, we'll talk."

Jake started the meeting by thanking the men for joining them.

"I want to go back to two comments that were made earlier," he said, a serious look on his face. "One comment was about feeling like free men again. The second was when J.J. asked where the chef who provided our dinner lives."

"Oh, I didn't mean..." J.J. started.

"Don't worry about it, J.J.," Jake quickly replied, his tone a little hard to read. Was it sarcasm? Disrespect? Chastisement? Or, was it humor? "You expressed what we would all term a normal curiosity. Based on the number of times I've heard that question asked, all of you wonder where you are. You'd be crazy not to wonder."

Jake stopped talking long enough to put a flip chart and stand into place. He turned back to face them and looked each man in the eye, one at a time.

"There are some things you need to know," he continued. Jake explained that Alex knew too much about the Russian government. He told them about the kill-on-sight order that had been issued. "They are still looking for him," he said, grimly. He told them how this Russian scientist had plotted for six years to get out of the Soviet Union and how, on a black night when the Berlin Wall fell, he stepped into freedom and found his way to America, to this ranch. Jake told them about his own connection with the CIA and why he retired when he did. He told them how he and Alex met and how he had run into him years later in Wal-Mart. When he paused, the room was engulfed in total silence.

"And that," he said conclusively, "is why you will never know where this ranch is located. It is why once you are gone from here you will never find your way back."

Though not asked for their agreement, three of the four very serious faces were nodding their heads in understanding. It was merely a quiet statement. Only Redbridge remained stoically quiet and unmoving. He leaned forward in his chair, arms on his thighs, and he was looking at the floor.

Jake then went through a list of options available to each man if he wanted to opt out of being returned to home and office. If they wanted out of the return plan, they would be taken to a city or town of their choice, a small home would be purchased for them, false ID and credentials in their professional areas of expertise would be provided.

"Understand that if you opt out – if you decide you want us to drop you off in the middle of the country and wish you well – your clone will, in all likelihood, disappear. As soon as the Russians learn that one of you has been returned, the other three will be in grave danger. And that's why three of you need to be returned on the same day without the Russians learning of your return. Arthur will be returned the following day.

"Arthur is going to be in the hospital for about two weeks. You will need to be away from your offices during that time. The Russian government cannot allow one of the four clones they know we have recaptured to live once they find out we are putting the originals – you – back in power. Let that sink in for just a moment," he said and took a seat.

The only sound in the room was the crackling wood in the fireplace.

"You certainly know how to hit a guy over the head with facts, Jake," J.J. Branchman offered quietly to break the silence. "How do we prevent the Russians from finding out one of us has been exchanged? Why is it dangerous to the rest of us if the Russians decide to kill one or more of their own clones?"

The quiet in the room dominated once again. "Let's say we replace you on Monday, J.J.," Jake began. "Let's say the Russians find out about it Monday night. "The three other clones of the men stolen by us from Sakhalin Island will either disappear or be killed. It will be made public. That means Arthur, Avery and John cannot return home. Everyone thinks they are dead... or have run off somewhere. How crazy would the public think Arthur, Avery and John are if they told the truth? How believable is it to say they were cloned?"

J.J. nodded. "It's complicated," he said quietly.

Jake nodded. "Any other comments?" he asked.

"If they would kill our clones, why won't they kill us once they know we're back?" Avery Scott asked. "How will they know we are back?"

Alex rose and walked to the flip chart. He turned over the first page. "You asked just the right question to start the discussion, Avery. Thank you." He smiled.

"They will know you are back because we are going to tell them." He watched a guarded look of shock come over their faces. "Now, as Jake said, we want you to take a few minutes to let this sink in. Jake and I are going to do some after-dinner kitchen cleaning while you do. Then we'll tell you how we plan to get you home safely."

The two men left the room so the others could be alone for a few moments. For a short time, there was no sound of voices from the room. Then there was a low murmur. By the time Jake and Alex were through putting dishes in the dishwasher, the room was quiet again.

The two of them sat across from their four guests.

"This is going to be difficult, isn't it?" Senator Martinez asked, "difficult and dangerous – for us and for all of you."

"Yes," Alex responded softly. "It will. But it is probably better than dying a dreary death on an island that is your prison. It is probably better than not seeing your loved ones again. When Arthur said the other day that you should eliminate any thought of going back to the soft life you once had, he wasn't joking. What we are about to attempt is very serious business."

Jake cleared his throat and asked who would like another glass of brandy. Four glasses went into the air. "I'll get the bottle," he said, chuckling.

"Now," Alex began again, "for the good news." He handed out all of the personal data that had been gathered on each man to date along with pictures of his clone. There were photos of family members, staff members with close access to the clones, a list of all employees and dates of hire, and photos of homes and churches. Between Jake, Meredith and Brett, they had done a marvelous piece of intelligence gathering. He explained to them that this was only partial data and that more information would be gathered over the next few weeks.

"You will be glad to know that so much attention is being paid to detail, we have ordered a tanning machine. Each of you looks like a ghost compared to your clone. Bear in mind, this person who replaced you is, in reality, very, very young. They are young and dynamic people. They are extremely well trained to act and behave as you. Each of you has a sheet listing what we know about your clone… height, weight, shoe, suit, and shirt size. We have documented their daily schedules to the degree possible. You have from one to two months to either trim down or eat up. Because their real ages are so much less than yours, you will need to exercise as hard as you can to get rid of your flab and turn it into muscle."

It was time to let the men ask some questions and Jake and Alex patiently answered all of them. Many of the answers were "We will be discussing that in a few minutes. We will give you an overview of all the plans."

The security buzzer went off and Jake and Alex both reacted simultaneously, heading for the stairs. Four startled faces looked towards the front entryway wall. The alarm was turned off and the security wall was electronically pulled into its storage unit as Rusty came running down the stairs to see who the strangers were that had invaded his home. The men sat very still. No one offered to pet him.

The dog was not aggressive, but he moved from one to the other, sniffing hands and feet, ears at the alert. Meredith called him to her and put him outside for a time. He'd been in the car most of the day and could stand the exercise, anyway.

"Sorry about that," she said, looking at each of them. "He's my protector. I'm intruding, so I'll go on to my room and answer some phone calls and… let you guys get back to what you were doing."

Alex excused himself to follow her down the hallway into her room. He had to unlock the bedroom door for her. Once inside he merely held out his arms and she walked into them. He held her very gently.

"Everything went well?" he asked.

"Just as expected," she responded. "I have a few hundred thousand dollars to give Jake so he can take care of it for me. I can pay you guys back what I've been borrowing." She paused. "Are there any leftovers from dinner? I'm starved!" She leaned forward to kiss him softly. "I missed you, my love," she said, clasping him closer for a brief moment.

"There are leftovers… and I missed you, too. I've been looking at my watch. I know it's been driving Jake crazy," he said. "I couldn't help myself." He kissed her back and stepped away from her. "The meeting…" he said.

"I'm going to take a shower and put on some jeans and a sweater. Go on back. I'll just walk through the room on my way to get some dinner, if that's okay?" She threw her purse and car keys onto the bed and took off her shoes.

"I kind of like it when you have on those heels and we're the same height," he said. "Everything just… just fits, so nicely."

"Out," she said, smiling, pointing at the door.

As he walked back into the living room, Alex could sense their eyes on him. "So where were we?" he asked in the most casual tone he could muster. Jake smiled. He had rarely seen Alex look embarrassed or discomfited by his own actions.

"I think you were telling us we might die," Branchman offered, smiling. For some reason, the idea of a romance between the scientist and the woman he had seen on the video made him feel better. It brought things back to a more pleasant level of reality than the one they were dealing with this night.

"Oh, whether you live or die! I remember that..." Alex said. "Just a detail," he laughed. It felt good. "I believe the plan we have created will dissuade that possibility," he added. "Jake... why don't you start?" His demeanor had changed ever so slightly and everyone noticed it. He suddenly appeared to be more certain than he had five minutes earlier... or, maybe just more focused. "Love," thought Justice Scott as he raised his eyebrows and sighed. It made him wonder about his wife and family... as if they were ever off of his mind.

Jake used the information Alex had noted on the flip chart that day to go through each detail listed in the plan to take them home again. They agreed that everyone would hold their questions until the entire plan had been disclosed. They would then go back through the flip chart that listed each detail. Questions could then be asked. Notes to be included in the final plan would be made on Jake's yellow lined pad.

When Jake completed his part of the presentation, Alex told them how the Russians would be notified... how they would be told that if anything happened to the Real Things, extensive evidence would be provided the media about what the U.S.S.R. and, later, Russia had done. He explained how the clones would be brought back to the ranch and "re-aged" to the normal growth cycle for each of them. "They will look exactly like you did at whatever age they really are," he told them. The four men were fascinated by the disclosures.

The questions were good and added detail to an already detailed plan. Jake then went through the flip chart a second time and each sheet was torn from it and placed in the fire as they finished all of the questions dealing with that page. The level of security surrounding the entire affair was clear to everyone. It gave them confidence.

Alex walked to the door to let Rusty in, took his choke chain in hand and walked him down the hall to Meredith's room. She might be starving, Alex thought, but she was sound asleep on her bed.

As he returned to the living room, Jake was telling their guests that Alex would be in touch with them individually the next day. "I'm leaving town for a couple of days," he said, "but want to talk with each of you when I get back. I'd appreciate it if you would make mental notes of any specific personal information you think might be helpful. Nothing in writing, please," he finished.

With that, Jake and Alex went around the room shaking hands and thanking the men for coming. Alex offered to drive them home and Jake let him. He was worn out. He headed for the shower and an early night's sleep. Five a.m. would come fast.

When Alex returned, he found the safety screen carefully placed flat against the fireplace and realized Jake had retired. He knew what he had promised Meredith, but he needed to be with her right now. He went to his bedroom, showered and put on a pair of clean pajama bottoms, then padded quietly down the hall to her room in his bare feet.

He opened the door and slipped quietly inside. She was still sleeping on top of the covers, wearing the terry cloth robe she always put on after taking a shower.

He wakened her and handed her a nightgown, holding a finger across his lips. He handed her the sandwich and glass of milk he had prepared before showering, and turned down the covers on both sides of the bed. She went into the bathroom and put on the gown, turned out the light and returned. She sat on her side of the bed and ate the sandwich and drank the milk. No words were exchanged.

Each of them got under the covers. Meredith turned on her side and Alex pulled her back close to his front, his arm around her.

"Jake will be leaving at five in the morning," he whispered. "Good night, my love."

"Good night, dorogoi," she whispered back at him. He smiled contentedly.

Alex's arm around her waist startled her momentarily when she awoke to Rusty's head on her hip the next morning. The house was totally quiet and Meredith walked to the front door in her nightgown to let the dog outside. Alex was propped up on one arm when she returned.

"It's rise and shine time," she said, smiling at him. She had not realized until this very moment just how handsome he was. His face and body made him look like he was in his mid-forties, not nearing 60. She liked his dark countenance... and he had just the

278

right amount of hair on his chest. The time he spent exercising was very apparent in the muscular appearance of his upper body.

"It is *not* rise and shine time," he said. "Jake is out of town and we are back on the front burner." His eyebrows raised in question as he held the blankets up... an invitation to return to bed. Meredith looked at his tousled hair falling across his forehead, smiled and slowly walked to him.

"There is something you need to know about making love in the daylight to old broads who have had children," she said in a light but slightly uncertain tone.

He rose from her bed, walked to the patio and turned a manual switch on the wall. The sunlight disappeared as the skylights were covered. The room darkened.

"Oh," she said. "You've already learned that lesson."

"Which lesson?" he asked, breathing softly into her ear.

"You learned the lesson about stretch marks and scars and things... how sensitive we old ladies are about them."

"My love, if you had stretch marks on your face rather than your belly and hips, it would not bother me." He paused and continued in a more businesslike tone, "I admit, I'd probably try and find a cure for it, but..."

She hit him with a pillow just before he pushed her head and shoulders onto the bed and kissed her passionately, both of them laughing. "I have been waiting for two weeks to do that," Alex said with great satisfaction.

"I feel like I have been waiting for two weeks to eat," Meredith said as her stomach growled.

"Hungry for food, are you?" Alex asked. He gently turned her onto her stomach and began to massage her neck, shoulders and back. She moaned her pleasure. His fingers dug deeply into her flesh, working on the tight spots created by the hours spent driving the day before.

"I'm going to make you some breakfast," he said, kissing her on the neck. "Stay in bed and relax a bit. I'll let Rusty in and call Nancy and tell her not to come today. We have all day, dorogoi. Nothing needs to be rushed... not for three entire days!"

She did as he asked and he returned carrying breakfast for both of them on a serving tray.

"I think we need some light," Meredith said.

"You are hard to please today, Meredith Morgan. First you do not want light, then you want light." Alex chuckled, returned to the patio and light flooded the room.

Meredith was silent as she ate the bacon, eggs and toast with zest. She had not eaten a full meal since breakfast, the day before.

"So," she began between bites, "how did your meeting go?"

Alex took a bite of toast and a sip of coffee before answering, but nodded his head in a positive motion. "I think it went well. I'll know more this afternoon when I go and talk with each man, but I think we achieved the initial objective."

"And that was?" she asked, curious.

"To let them know this is not going to be – what is it called – a 'cakewalk?' To let them understand the dangers and decide for themselves if they want to return. And, to show them great pains are going to be taken to keep each one of them safe," he responded.

"If you achieved that with one meeting, I'd call it a success," Meredith said thoughtfully. "Is there anything I can do to help you today? Or, do you want me to keep on keeping on?"

"I'd like for us both to stay in bed all day." He frowned, briefly. "You know, just because we're in bed doesn't mean sex becomes an automatic part of the day's schedule." He looked at her seriously. "I can't tell you how much pleasure it gave me just to sleep by your side with my arm around you. I think both of us old people are a bit tired today… yesterday was hard for everyone. It will make what comes – whenever it comes – just that much more enjoyable."

She smiled at his innate understanding of the dynamics that were in play between them. She listened attentively as Alex told her about Jake's trip to Show Low, Arizona, and the purpose for it. Though she thought it was a great idea, she couldn't help but laugh at the idea of Jake chasing down a Navajo Indian so he could get a sentence translated.

"Jake had a pretty hard day too, didn't he? And then he had to leave in the dark this morning to fly halfway around the world," she said. "No wonder everyone is tired. I'll bet he was worn out this morning when his alarm went off!" She took her final swallow of coffee.

They spent a casual morning in front of the fireplace. Alex lit a fire as the two of them sat in their chairs enjoying the warmth the flames provided. They drank another two cups of coffee. Later in the day, Meredith would think back on this time... how much they needed to talk about something other than clones and Real Things and plans involving them. It helped push the aching tiredness she felt back into its cage.

They were dressing as the grandfather clock in the entryway struck noon. Meredith settled in at the computer as Alex departed for the bunkhouse to spend an hour with each man who attended last night's meeting.

After over four hours of talks with the Real Things, he returned to the house and looked in on Meredith. She was sitting at the computer leaning her head on her left hand. Her elbow was propped on the left side of the desk. He knew her back was bothering her.

"Come on, love, it's time to give it up for the day," he suggested, though his tone left no doubt he would not brook a disagreement on the subject.

"Hi," she said and began saving data and started the process to turn off the computer. "How did your meetings go?"

"They were good," he said, a lilt in his voice. She could tell from his voice that he wore his slightly crooked smile.

Alex re-lit the morning fire, poured himself a drink and brought her a glass of cranberry juice. There was such a sense of relaxation between the two of them it provided an aura of comfort that seemed to spread throughout the room. He reached for the remote and selected a Frank Sinatra album. One full song played before either of them spoke.

"What would you like for dinner?" she asked.

"Why is it every time you talk to me today you talk about food?" he asked, jokingly.

She laughed. "I have no vested interest," she said. "I ate a sandwich about two o'clock. I won't be hungry for another hour. I thought you might be. Can I fix you anything?"

"I'm not very hungry right now, either," he said, rising and holding out his hand to her. They danced slowly for a few moments. Meredith estimated they got about halfway through one song before both of them realized their hunger for one another was greater than anything that might tempt them in the refrigerator.

Chapter 24

The Lufthansa flight Jake boarded in Salt Lake City landed in Munich a few minutes early. It would give him time for lunch at one of his favorite haunts, the Penta Hotel. He had two hours before catching a train for Salzburg.

Jake was dismayed to find the Penta was now the Holiday Inn Munich Centre. The old Penta dripped with Bavarian charm and Jake had many happy remembrances of it. It made him realize how much of his adult life had been spent in Europe. Why, he wondered, was he dwelling on the past so much lately? He shook the thought from his mind as a familiar and somewhat unpleasant melancholy began to settle over him. Change, he thought. The older he got, the less he liked it … and the more of it there was.

He had not stayed at the Salzburg Sheraton before. The accommodations were first rate, as was the price. It had an outdoor dining facility done in a tasteful manner. It was an ambiance only Europeans seemed able to create for outdoor dining, Jake thought.

He noted that the hotel was close to Mirabell Park and Garden. He took out the map of Salzburg and found William Leonard's address. For now, he couldn't wait to get to the hotel gym for exercise. It would drain what energy he had left and give him a good night's sleep, jet lag or not… melancholy, or not.

His cell phone alarm wakened him. He quickly got out of bed and took a shower. Room service delivered his soft-boiled eggs, toast and coffee at 7:30 and when they were eaten, he put on the headphones and turned the recorder to play. He began saying the code in Navajo as he listened to it. After an hour, he smiled. The old Navajo who had helped him would be proud, he thought.

When the time came to find Leonard's residence, he donned sunglasses and a hat. With his beard and shorter hair, he doubted anyone in the intelligence community, American or Russian, would recognize him. He assumed there would be security cameras. He walked up the few stairs to the building. The front door was locked. He would need to ring for admittance. He was glad Arthur had told him to use one long and two short buzzes should a locked entry stand between him and Leonard... another signal the two had devised.

There was a long pause after his first ring. Jake was getting ready to ring again when the familiar buzz came telling him to enter. It was a well-lit foyer and he saw two apartments on the first floor marked #1 and #2. He needed #4 and walked up only three stairs before a man appeared on the landing above and told him to halt and state his business.

In German, Jake told him he had a message from an old friend who had lost touch with Mr. Marchman. The man told him to state his message. Jake repeated the words Redbridge had given him in what he hoped was passable Navajo. The man said nothing, but looked at him curiously. Suddenly, a second figure appeared behind him and said back to Jake in Navajo, "Yes. He built it in the 19th century." Jake was glad he'd had the Navajo man also record the response to his code phrase so he could recognize it. Leonard was quite bald, as Redbridge said he likely would be. He looked to be physically fit – a man just slightly smaller than Jake and about the same age. He wore small round glasses rimmed with gold metal frames.

Jake reached into his pocket and pulled the piece of steno paper from it. Fragmented pieces from where it was torn from the steno pad ran along the top of the page. He saw the man's eyes widen just slightly and he walked down the stairs until he could reach it. Jake offered the piece of steno pad paper with its message to the man who stood about three steps above him.

Leonard quickly read the message, looked Jake over very thoroughly and then he read the note again. "Ja," was the only word that came out of his mouth. He handed the note back to Jake, turned, and walked back up the stairs, disappearing from sight as he turned left across the landing on which he had so suddenly appeared.

Jake could not believe it had been so easy. All of the crazy preparation and guess work had paid off. He ordered a large lunch when he returned to the hotel and once again headed for the gym. Jake let himself sleep an extra hour the next morning. The hotel had a car rental counter. He leased a grey Mercedes and had them park it in the hotel's underground lot. This way, after his meeting, he could go straight to the Munich airport for his flight home rather than wait for a train.

Jake realized he needed a week away from everyone, a chance to evaluate his life, to determine what direction he wanted it to go. He had no doubt about completing the project. He couldn't give up on it now. Not after all the years and the successes they were beginning to enjoy. He believed in it. But it would culminate either in success or failure within two months. Meredith had recently asked what he planned to do when it was over. It had made him think. He could travel. He could do whatever he wanted. Money was never going to be a problem. If it was, it would be because he had too much and didn't know what to do with it. Purpose, not resources, was his problem. He began to think of his new ranch.

After checking out of the hotel, Jake asked the Concierge to have his luggage put in the trunk of the car while it sat in the garage. He tipped him well for the extra trouble. He checked to make sure his recorder was in his jacket pocket before driving from the historic City Center. Across the street, on the Left Bank of the Salzach River, Roman soldiers had once marched.

Jake sat in the zoo's parking lot, watching the entrance. It was times like these that he missed smoking, he thought, grimacing. He and Alex had quit together while they were working on the house. They ran out of cigarettes one day and just decided they would quit.

About an hour before his scheduled appointment, Jake bought an *International Herald Tribune* and walked to the Hellbrunn Zoo entrance. He asked for directions to the wild vulture exhibit and found a bench near the birds. He sat, appearing to scrutinize the day's news. He saw Leonard and noted two men following about fifty feet behind him.

"One of them is mine, the other is Austrian Security," he said in German as he approached Jake on the gravel path. "The Austrian tried to follow you yesterday but said you disappeared like someone trained by the CIA," he said in English.

"Because that's where I got my training many years ago," Jake replied, smiling tightly. He pulled his recorder from his pocket so Leonard could see it and pressed the record button in plain view of the other man. "I need to ask if you are wired for sound," he said, winking his right eye.

Leonard paused for a moment, looking as if Jake had surprised him. "Yes," Leonard replied, winking back at him and smiling. That meant no, Jake recalled.

"So, you are CIA?"

"No," Jake said. "I was for twenty years but retired when friends of mine began getting killed... I'm sure you read about our mole." He used a raised eyebrow as his question mark.

"Indeed," Leonard replied. "Sticky stuff. Covert ops is dangerous business."

"A mutual friend of ours says you are the real McCoy when it comes to black ops," Jake offered, removing his sun glasses by pushing them on top of his head so Leonard could see his eyes. The reference to former President Rory McCoy was intentional.

"This mutual friend... he wouldn't be someone who walked out on his job unexpectedly, would he?"

"Not willingly, but yes. The same guy," Jake answered. "He said you would appreciate the vulture exhibit... and the fact that it was free." Jake knew it was difficult to differentiate between someone who was shrewd and someone who was smart. There were not a lot of people who were both. He got the feeling he may have just met one of them.

Leonard looked at him hard and then smiled. Jake could feel that the man wanted to believe him but might not be able. Leonard had been involved in so many scams himself there was probably no trust in him.

"Look, we could talk all day and you aren't going to believe me and I'm probably not going to believe you. So, let's cut to the chase," Jake said, sounding a bit frustrated. "Our friend wants to know if you can put off your current legal actions involving accounts of mutual interest until after April. By that time, he will be back at work. The two of you can work to achieve the original objectives you set a long time ago." Jake knew he should say more, but stopped. Something just told him to stop talking.

A long silence ensued. "I only have another minute," Leonard said quietly. "By that time, no further words will be safe… a communications van will be here and everything we say will be recorded." He looked at Jake intently.

"You have all of the right messages and information." Leonard reached into his pocket for a small, portable radio. He turned it on, too loud for an Austrian public place Jake realized as heads turned to look at them. Jake knew it would play hob with his recording. "I don't think I can delay until May, but I need to see the real man. And before I delay legal actions or take the risk of seeing him – or ask him to take the risk – I want to talk with him. Can that be arranged?"

Jake quickly nodded, and pulled his sun glasses down from his head as he did. He knew the meeting was over. "It will only be for ninety seconds. We can't chance a call being traced. Tell me when and where you can be reached."

Leonard rose, picked up his radio and said just before turning it off, "Get up and shake my hand. Tell our friend, if indeed it is him, to remember the good old days in Georgetown and to mention them first when we talk on the phone."

As they shook hands, Leonard put his left hand on Jake's right shoulder and his hand ran quickly down the front of the jacket, pausing only slightly as it passed his pocket. To anyone watching, it looked like he was brushing off Jake's jacket. He told Jake to turn around so he could get the back. Jake's almost resisted, but did as requested.

"If I were you, my friend, I would walk out of the zoo in the direction you're facing. About a block down this gravel path, you can take a sharp right through a missing bush in the hedge and it will put you out of here, close to your car. Good bye, for now."

Without saying a word, Jake walked briskly ahead. The opening in the hedge was hard to see but when it appeared, he darted quickly through it. As Leonard said, he found himself very close to his car. So, Leonard had been watching him, too. No wonder he'd stayed alive so long.

When Jake boarded the Lufthansa flight back to the States, he sank gratefully into his seat. He normally did not partake of the champagne offered, but today he did. He was never more relieved to feel the wheels of an airplane leave a runway, and never did the Rocky Mountains look as good as they did when he landed.

As he entered the house, he turned off the security system and immediately re-coded it to "on." He walked down the stairs where Meredith and Alex were sitting in their recliners. Rusty, wagging his stub of a tail, rose from his spot in front of the fireplace to welcome him. Jake scratched the dog's ears and could not believe how comforting it was to come home. He waved at them, and wordlessly walked down the hallway to his room. He immediately undressed and took a shower. God, it felt good!

Meredith looked questioningly at Alex. "Was that a little strange?" she asked him.

"He must be sorely tired," Alex responded. "I'll pour him a brandy and put it on his dresser so when he gets out of the shower it'll be there for him."

A half-hour later, Jake wandered into the living room, empty glass in hand. He poured himself a refill. He did look beat, Meredith thought. "I think I'm just getting too damned old for this kind of tension," he said emphatically. "I can't believe I lived almost a third of my life like this."

"That sounds like a retirement comment to me," Alex retorted, smiling at his friend.

Jake smiled, looking at Alex. "I don't want to talk about the trip until tomorrow, but I think it went as well as possible." He took the recorder from his robe pocket and played his conversation with Leonard. It was only a few minutes long. They all winced as the loud music came on. Fortunately the voices could still be heard over the noise. Digital equipment was hot, Jake thought. He turned the machine off, paused, and rising turned towards the hallway. He took his refilled brandy glass with him.

Meredith and Alex looked at one another for a long moment. Even with a schedule that would tire someone twenty years his junior, it was strange behavior for Jake.

They closed the house down for the night and walked down the hallway to their individual bedrooms. She stopped at her door and watched his back disappear. He walked into his bedroom and closed the door without looking back. Rusty whined, trying to tell her that she needed to close the door so he could lie down in his spot. Meredith put her hand on his head and stepped into her room, closing the door. He circled around his "spot" three times and then plopped heavily onto the floor. It was a dog ritual.

Alex was surprised by the emptiness he felt entering his bedroom alone. He had known that even though they only shared three days, he would miss her. It was an ache that penetrated his body and went into his soul. He had never experienced such a sense of loneliness – aloneness, yes, but never loneliness. Or, was it loss?

It was a long night for three people trying to sleep under the same roof.

Jake was gone when they got up in the morning. Nancy was in the kitchen cooking breakfast and told Meredith and Alex that Jake had already eaten, met with Arthur Redbridge, made a telephone call and had gone to Grand Junction to meet two friends who would be visiting. "Will they be staying here?" Nancy asked.

"Yes, they will," Alex answered. "And because you will have two more bodies to feed at your house, you don't need to come here until all these people are gone, Nancy. We'll work out a schedule to handle it ourselves." He thought for a moment before continuing. "And those guys at the bunkhouse can change their own sheets and clean their own rooms. From now on, your only responsibility to them is cooking and laundry. You might want to take them some furniture polish, rags, and scrubbing bubbles – a toilet brush – on the day you give them their sheets. They're smart. They'll figure it out." He smiled at her. "Will that make things a little easier?"

A smile of relief lit Nancy's face. "Indeed it will," she said happily. "Oh," she added, "Joe told me to tell you we need to slaughter a steer or there won't be enough meat."

"Tell him it's done," Alex replied. He and Meredith sat at the kitchen table eating until Nancy left. As the front door closed and the security system beeped, he reached across the table to take her hand.

"I never want to spend another night like last night," he said. He was serious and his tone of voice sounded almost hurt.

"Nor I," she echoed, squeezing his hand. "The night lasted forever... it went on and on. What have you done to me, Scientist?" She shook her head as she sipped her juice.

Alex cleared his throat. "I've been thinking about something," he began.

She waited for him to go on but he seemed distracted. She squeezed his hand and said "You've been thinking?"

He took a deep breath and gave her the intense look he got on his face when he was deep into problem resolution. "Look," he began again, "this is not the right time or the right way or the right anything, but it has to be now. God only knows when we'll be alone again."

Again there was a long pause until she asked him what was not the right time or way to do... what?

"I... I'm not sure how to say what's on my mind. It's about commitment. It's about having a relationship, not just a romance," Alex said, haltingly. "I need to know what your feelings are for me... if you feel the same about me as I feel about you."

"You know I love you," she said softly.

"I want more," he said. His eyes pierced hers with their intensity.

"More... how? More what?" she asked, puzzled.

"I want you to want to marry me," he said. "I want commitment and I want you to say that after all of this madness is over, you'll marry me. I know I have no right, the future is so uncertain..." he began, but she interrupted him.

"And am I to keep our intentions secret?" she asked.

"What does that mean? What are you saying? 'Our intentions?' What does that mean?" he repeated.

"It means I intend to marry you when all of this madness is over, my brooding scientist. You'll have to teach me how to spell 'Plotnikov,' though. Or do I write 'Smith' on all the checks I intend to sign?" She rose from the table and held out her hand to him. "Do I get a hug for saying 'yes?'" she asked.

Alex rose and grabbed her with such strength, her feet left the floor. It also caused the breath to whish out of her lungs.

"Honey," she said quietly, "you need to put me down so I can breathe."

Alex put her down, stepped back and looked at her. "I never thought I could love someone like I love you. I thought I was too old to even consider getting married... I am the luckiest man alive!" This time he drew her into his arms with great tenderness. He put his hands on the back of her head and stroked her hair with first one hand, then the other.

Their kiss began just as the security system beeped. They both knew Jake had returned with Bill Bryant and Bob Grosvenor.

"We were just going to clean up from breakfast," Meredith said to the three men, "but if you're hungry, I'll be glad to fry some bacon and eggs."

Jake introduced everyone and asked Bill and Bob if they would like something to eat or drink.

"We took a red eye from the East coast, so I would appreciate something," Bob Grosvenor told Meredith. He had a very deep voice but spoke very softly. She liked his smile and firm handshake. So many men were afraid to put pressure into a handshake when a woman was at the other end of the extended arm. Bill Bryant appeared shy, but nodded his head and drawled, "Thank you, ma'am."

Meredith put the food on the table and rapidly headed for her bedroom to begin the computer chores for the day.

She didn't know how long she had been working when a soft knock on her bedroom door interrupted her concentration. She sighed deeply and said "yes," without turning around.

"Mrs. Morgan," came the soft, shy voice, "Jake said I might be able to help you do some research," Bill Bryant drawled from the door. "I'm a computer programmer when I'm not being a soldier of fortune," he said, smiling. He was almost angelic, she thought.

She couldn't imagine this large but very gentle man with a gun in his hand, breaking things and killing people. "Jake told me to get a list from you of the items you're researching, talk with you for awhile about the specifics of what you're looking for, and see if I can reduce your workload a little bit," Bryant said. He smiled at her, showing a row of even, white teeth.

The two of them put there heads together and talked for over an hour. His questions were pertinent and straight to the point. He was going to be heaven sent, Meredith knew.

She heard the security beep, the input and signal cut-off and knew that Alex and Jake were home. "Oh, my God!" she said, mostly to herself. "I didn't start anything for dinner!" She looked at Bill and said, "I cannot tell you how glad I am that you are here."

Alex followed Meredith into the kitchen and walked up behind her, putting his arms around her. "Am I to gather from your quiet disappearance into the kitchen that you forgot to cook something for dinner?"

She turned to face him, his arms still around her.

"I'm sorry, Alex. What can I say?" she asked. "Time just got away from me."

The problem resolved itself when Alex suggested to Jake that they drive into Parachute for dinner. That way, Bob and Bill would have some idea where they could go to eat when they wanted to get away from the ranch for an evening. Rather than eating in Parachute, close to the interstate highway, Jake drove them up a hill to the South of town – a restaurant in Battlement Mesa. Unless a person lived there, it was not a place someone passing through would find or visit by accident.

Upon their return home, Meredith excused herself for the night. She was tired.

"So," Alex said, as he turned to face Jake, "you and Arthur made a call today. Care to share the news?"

"Yeah... things are so busy around here you and I never get a chance to talk anymore. Maybe we need to set time aside each day," Jake said, tiredly.

Alex ran his right hand through his dark hair. "I repeat... care to share the news?"

Jake hesitated but when he began to speak, the words came rapidly. "I've gotta tell you, this Leonard and Redbridge thing makes me nervous," he said. "As you heard on the tape last night, Leonard wanted Redbridge to call him. I programmed a cell phone this morning and took it to Arthur. He called and we limited it to 90 seconds. They scheduled a meeting for New Year's Eve at Neuschwanstein... I think Leonard is so damned smart, he borders on being insane. One thing is for sure. He's in love with that castle in Bavaria!"

"And you were going to tell me about this when?" Alex asked.

"Actually," Jake replied, "I tape recorded the entire conversation so we could both listen to it after Meredith went to bed tonight. You got time now?"

"Go," was all Alex said.

For the first thirty seconds, Redbridge talked about an airline ticket that had once been stolen from Leonard's room at the Georgetown Inn. The remaining minute was a confusing exchange of coded words that only the two participants in the conversation understood.

"And from that you were able to determine they want to meet at Neuschwanstein on New Year's Eve?" Alex asked. He hadn't been able to decipher one intelligent sentence.

"Hey... I'm a trained intelligence operative," Jake said, smiling. "And, Arthur was kind enough to decode it for me."

They both laughed.

Chapter 25

From the day Bob and Bill arrived, the workload for Jake, Alex and Meredith was lightened. The speed with which things were getting done picked up. Bill Bryant saved two hours at the end of each day to give computer lessons to the four men who would be returning to a world that had advanced beyond anything they could imagine in computer technology.

Meredith, Alex and Jake could take a deep breath without feeling guilty for deserting "the project." Thanksgiving was less than a week away and Meredith was busily preparing for the holiday.

On the Sunday before Thanksgiving, Alex asked Jake for an after dinner meeting. Meredith knew Jake had to be told about their engagement.

Preparations were quickly made and after Jake took his seat, he looked expectantly from Alex to Meredith. He knew this get together had nothing to do with the clone exchange… those meetings were now held at the stable so everyone involved could be accommodated. A long silence ensued and Jake finally asked about the meeting topic.

Alex sighed deeply. Meredith just looked at him. "Meredith has agreed to marry me after the project is completed. We think it's best to keep it among the three of us," he said. "No one at the bunkhouse needs to know, but you need to know. We've never had secrets, Jake. I don't want there to be any now… especially now."

"Wow," was all Jake could say. He felt like he'd been hit in the stomach but knew he had to smile and wish them well and he did. "This isn't a group meeting," he said, trying to sound happy for them. "This is a press conference! I'm sure you both know it already, but I have never seen two people more perfectly suited for one another." He rose and insisted that they drink a toast. He walked to the kitchen and noisily took some ice from the freezer. Meredith started to follow him, but Alex held onto her hand.

"Give him a moment," he said softly. Alex then turned to follow his friend into the kitchen.

As he entered the room, Alex saw Jake standing over two ice trays, leaning with both hands on the counter top, his eyes closed.

"Be happy for me, Jake... be happy for me," Alex said softly. "I know you care for her, too. It's why I had to tell you."

Jake turned to Alex, stepped toward him and gave him a bear hug. "I am happy for you, Alex... God knows you deserve happiness. It's just so much change, so suddenly..." he said. "I told you the other night, I'm getting too damned old for so much change... tension," he said, slapping his friend on the back as he spoke. "I'm just stunned into silence, that's all."

The two men stepped apart. Alex looked at his friend and told him he knew that wasn't all and that he and Meredith would always be there for him. "You're part of our family."

"You know what I think?" Jake asked, suddenly. "I think you should have Justice Scott marry you here at the ranch... sign all the papers and perform the ceremony, but wait until the project is completed to file them." He poured water into his glass and drank it quickly down. Jake had no idea where the idea had come from, but if he was looking for a diversion from his own feelings, it was a good one. He went on to explain how it could be accomplished with no paper trail.

"Look at it this way, Alex. What other time will you have the Chairman of the Federal Central Bank, a United States Senator and a national radio personality as an audience while a Supreme Court Justice marries you? How many illegals can pull that one off?"

Actually, Jake thought, he could feel relief landing on the fringes of his sorrow. Alex was right. It was better to know than to wonder.

The Russian re-entered the living room and told Meredith Jake's idea about having Justice Scott marry them with all of the ranch residents in attendance on Thanksgiving Day. When he saw the questioning look on her face, he quickly added the part about waiting until spring to file the papers and make the marriage an official, state-accepted document. "Until the papers are signed by all the parties and filed, there is no paper trail," he said. "The State would not see us as legally married, but we would be."

"It would be a great way to celebrate Thanksgiving. I think it's a great idea!" she told him, laughing.

"What about your kids?" Alex asked.

She hesitated for a long moment and then said "My kids are grown with families of their own. They haven't been interested in anything their mother does for years now. I'll write them a note in the aftermath. When the project is over and everyone is safe, we'll bring them to the ranch to meet you."

Jake told Meredith that he felt like taking a walk. He asked if she minded if he took Rusty with him. She knew the dog would enjoy time outside with his friend and readily agreed.

"Come and sit on the floor... let me rub your shoulders," Alex suggested after Jake left the house with Rusty.

"What did I do to deserve this?" she asked, smiling. "You missed your calling, Scientist. You should have opened a massage parlor."

He smiled and began slowly rubbing the tightness out of her shoulders.

"I love you," she whispered quietly and after a few moments of silence. "I think I should give you and Jake some time to talk... would you put Rusty in my room?"

They rose and he put his arms around her and pulled her close for a moment, giving her a gentle kiss. "I love you, too... and yes, I will put Rusty in your room," he said, leaning away from her, smiling.

When Meredith awoke the next morning, the house was empty. There was a note on the kitchen counter telling her that Jake and Alex had gone to Grand Junction to take care of some business. She decided to skip breakfast. She dressed hurriedly and walked to the garage. She didn't have enough time to go to Grand Junction and so turned the car towards Parachute. There was a Native American gift shop there. She thought they would have what she needed and they did.

Things, she thought to herself, were as ready for Thanksgiving as they could be. She put on a light jacket and walked out to the patio where she sat and relaxed for a few moments before Jake and Alex returned. The two men were surprised to find her there. They usually had to pry her away from the computer. They joined her on the patio for a short time and then left for a final planning meeting at the stables. Beyond this point, she knew, time would be spent implementing the plans, not creating them.

The time passed quickly and before she knew it, tomorrow was here. Over Jake's strong objections, Meredith had invited her best friend to have dinner with them on Thanksgiving Day. She wanted a female friend to serve as her matron of honor and to be with her during what she knew would be a tense time. Neither Jake nor Alex had been through a wedding before, but she had. Meredith knew how many emotional ogres could wait in the wings of perceived happiness to insert fear and doubt into the most romantic of plans.

Jake had finally agreed to the visit of Sue Hendricks from Cincinnati with three provisions. First, he would meet Sue's Delta Airlines flight in Salt Lake City and fly her to Rifle. Second, he and Alex would rent a helicopter to fly her to the ranch and Sue would not be told where the ranch was located. And, third, Sue would not be told the Real Things, who would be attending the wedding, were anyone other than who they appeared to be. Sue would not be informed of the project, the clones, or their planned return, he told Meredith firmly. She finally agreed to his conditions. If that was what it took to keep peace in the family, she would accede to his wishes.

Her numerous trips through the house as she awaited Jake's and Sue's arrival were making Alex dizzy. "I have never seen you like this... nervous, anxious and impatient. What's going on in that head of yours?" he asked. "Come and sit down." He paused. There was no response from her. After a few moments, he once again tried to start a conversation. "You look lovely," he said. Getting no response beyond a smile, he decided to try something else. "Why don't you turn on some music so when Sue enters it sounds like a pleasant place to be?" he suggested. Actually, he was half joking, but she thought it a great idea and turned on a Hooked on Classics album. Just as the London Symphony Orchestra was singing and playing its way into the "Halleluiah Chorus" introduction, the security code buzzed and Meredith was out of her seat, heading for the entryway stairs. The dividing wall pulled back and Sue stood at the top of the stairs with the same kind of expression on her face Meredith must have had the first time she had seen the wall pull back and viewed the mansion beneath her feet.

Sue looked tired, but she had that smile only she could give. It beamed, Meredith thought. Her smile and her laugh were two things a person who got close to this woman would never forget. She radiated warmth.

Jake took her suitcase to Meredith's bedroom and re-entered the living room. "I have learned many things about you between Salt Lake and here, Meredith," he said in a smiling but threatening tone.

"Yes," Sue said smiling and with a laugh in her voice. "He learned that you were not just my best friend, but my mentor."

Alex took her coat and introduced himself. Meredith noticed that he used his real last name and not "Smith" and was glad he had performed the introduction even though she should have. She would have said "Smith." Meredith led Sue to the couch on which no one ever sat. "I cannot tell you how glad I am that you are here," Meredith said, studying her friend's face as she spoke. "Now, a ham just finished cooking in the oven and dinner is ready, but if you are too tired to eat, you can take a nap and eat later. Just tell me your choice and we'll get on with it."

"You will never change, will you?" Sue asked, laughing. "You're always prepared for any eventuality! I slept on the plane, but you're right. I am tired. However, I think I'm hungrier than I am tired... airline food these days is not edible. So, why don't we eat? What can I do to help?"

Meredith smiled at her friend. Sue would never change, either. She would always want to do her part in any endeavor, even helping with dinner when she was out on her feet.

"You will stay in the living room with Jake while Alex and I get things on the table. It won't take five minutes." She and Alex started for the kitchen when Meredith abruptly stopped and turned back. "Would you like a drink and a minute to relax before we eat?"

Sue declined the drink and the plans for dinner moved forward.

The dinner conversation had so many sentences beginning with "Do you remember…" that Jake lost count. The stories were wonderfully funny, though, and made everyone laugh. He could see how close the two women were.

"We are probably boring your friends to death with all of these remembrances," Sue finally said.

"Not at all," Alex interjected. "I have learned more about my bride-to-be at this dinner table tonight than I have in the months she has been staying with us at the ranch," he said happily. "She can be pretty tight-lipped about her past life, you know."

Meredith had not told Sue about the wedding nor had she asked her to be her matron of honor. She had merely called and told Sue she needed her and Sue had agreed to come.

Sue blinked once, then twice. She looked at Meredith. "You're getting married?" she asked, more than a little surprised.

Meredith looked down for a moment, not knowing exactly what to say. She glanced at Alex who was grinning.

"Well," she finally began, "it's still a bit of a secret. At least until Thanksgiving," she said, looking uncertainly at Alex, then Jake.

Jake broke in. "I'm trying to convince them to get married Thanksgiving Day while you're here to be Meredith's matron of honor and I'm here to be Alex's best man."

Sue smiled broadly. "You should have told me!" she said, chastising Meredith. "I only brought one dress with me – and it's not formal wedding attire!"

"I didn't know until night-before-last," Meredith replied. "It's Jake's brainstorm and Alex and I both like the idea."

"Will it be a small wedding… the four of us and a minister?" Sue asked. "Will you be married here at the ranch? Or, will the ceremony take place in church?"

"We will be married here, in front of the fireplace, on Thanksgiving Day," Alex interjected. Meredith's eyebrows went up at the enlightening announcement. "There will be about a dozen people here," he continued. "Justice Avery Scott will perform the ceremony which will also be attended by Fed Chairman Arthur Redbridge – who wants to give the bride away, Meredith – and Senator John Martinez, and radio talk show host J.J. Branchman. They will all be in attendance along with some friends here at the ranch," he concluded.

Looking at the two women, Jake could not tell who was more surprised, Sue or Meredith. He laughed. "We've had a busy day, Ms. Morgan," he said. "We have a Marriage License from the friendly State of Colorado, for one thing."

"And for another," Alex interjected, "I have an engagement ring for your third finger, left hand…" His Russian accent was stronger and Meredith decided he must be nervous. "Now, even though you have already said 'yes' once, I ask you again, in front of witnesses," he chuckled, "to marry me… on Thanksgiving Day."

Alex did not wait for an answer, but took her hand and slid a beautiful diamond ring onto her ring finger. A tear slowly made its way down her cheek as Meredith reached out with her right hand to touch his face.

"Should I say 'yes' again, Dr. Plotnikov?" she asked, smiling.

He stood and helped her to her feet, pulling her into his arms for a kiss worthy of being given in front of witnesses.

"I feel like I've walked through Alice's looking glass," Sue said, shaking her head and wiping her own eyes. "You were joking about the guest list, weren't you? I just saw Arthur Redbridge being grilled by a Senate Investigative Committee while I was waiting to board my flight in Cincinnati. If he's coming, when will he be arriving?"

There was a long silence. Meredith sat down and reached across the table to take her friend's hand. "He'll be here tomorrow, Sue," she said to her friend, wanting to bite off her tongue for the lie she was telling.

Sue smiled, trying to figure out how to be a good sport about the confusion. She was happy for her friend, but something was not right. She could sense it but did not understand it. Sue turned to Alex. "Meredith referred to you as 'doctor,'" she said. "What kind of doctor are you?"

"He's a bio-physicist," Meredith told her before Alex could answer.

"Ah," Sue said. "That probably explains the secrecy surrounding this place. "Jake has already told me I can't make telephone calls from here and he wouldn't tell me if we are in Utah, Colorado, or Wyoming. You must be working on some secret government program and that's why you're stuck way out here in the wilderness." There was a long pause before Sue asked, "How did you two meet?"

Meredith told Sue the story about Jeffrey Lund sending her top secret papers that had put her in danger and explained how Jake had brought her to the ranch. She left out many of the details of why she needed protection... needed to be brought to the ranch, but the story she told was mostly true. Sue had known Jeffrey, too, and was saddened to learn of his untimely and violent death. He had a wife and children he had absolutely adored. Her heart went out to them.

"So, you've had a whirlwind romance," Sue laughed, eyes sparkling.

"Indeed I have," Meredith responded happily. "We can talk about it in the morning. I'm sure you need some sleep. It's a long trip. I hope you won't mind sharing a room with me for a couple of nights. With all of our guests, we have a full house."

Sue was in bed and appeared to be sleeping when Meredith finished taking a shower. She quietly turned off the light on the nightstand by her side of the bed. Meredith was engulfed by tiredness the moment her head hit the pillow.

When she awoke the next morning, Rusty had been put outside and Sue was dressed, sitting on the patio with the sunshine flowing into the room. "You're still on Eastern time, aren't you?" she asked.

"This is quite a place," Sue responded. "I can't wait to see it in the daylight from the outside."

"There's not much to see," Meredith responded, stretching. "It's an earth home and most of it is underground. There are five buildings... all of them are built into hillsides. Let me get dressed, cook some breakfast, and I'll take you on a tour." She yawned. "Boy! Did I sleep?"

Meredith grabbed a pair of jeans, a sweater and her moccasins and took them into the bathroom where she dressed, wetted her hair and combed it, then brushed her teeth.

"There," she said, coming back into the bedroom. "I think I'm awake. How about letting me fix you some breakfast?"

In answer to Sue's question to Alex about where he worked, a tour of his Lab was given. Sue couldn't help herself. She wanted in the worst way to ask one question... just one question: "Who are you... really? Who are you, Dr. Alex Plotnikov?"

She did not ask the question aloud, but it echoed in her mind as she tried to push the thought from her. He was obviously a nice man, a gentle man... but there was some kind of secret surrounding the mysterious Dr. Plotnikov.

Should she ask Meredith about it, she wondered? Did she have an obligation to her friend to ask? Did being Meredith's matron of honor bring with it the responsibility of having a mother-daughter talk with her? Did she know what she was getting into, Sue wondered?

Chapter 26

The dinner conversation that night was mostly dominated by Jake and Alex. They talked about their first meeting at the East Berlin Russian Embassy and the next meeting at the Waldorf Astoria in Manhattan. Alex talked about the months he spent at Jake's safe house in West Berlin when he was able to walk to freedom on that dark night so long ago.

"How did you get into America?" Sue asked, her infectious smile captivating Jake's attention.

"The same way everyone else does," he said laughing. "I came across the Rio Grande." He then told her how horrified he had been to run into Jake at Wal-Mart, of all places.

Meredith led her friend into the living room as the men did kitchen detail. Sue commented on what a good job Meredith had done training the men of the house.

"I wish I could take credit, but they trained themselves," Meredith told her friend.

"So… he's an illegal alien." Sue said quietly. "Are you sure you know what you're getting into, Meredith?" she asked her friend, a look of concern on her face.

"Listen," Jake said, interrupting their quiet conversation, "I'm going to go home tonight. I've changed the sheets on my bed, Sue, and you are welcome to use my bedroom. After the wedding, you'll have Meredith's room all to yourself for your last couple of nights here," he said, smiling.

After a short time, Sue decided to take him up on his offer. "As you said this morning, Meredith, I'm still on Eastern time. Every time I travel, I wonder how you could spend so many years on airplanes, every night in a different time zone," she laughed. Sue rose and Meredith directed her to Jake's room which was directly across from hers.

A short time later, Alex walked Meredith to her bedroom door and stopped outside. He kissed her goodnight. It was a gentle kiss, yet filled with a yearning for more.

Thanksgiving dawned a bright, sunny day. By the time Alex and Sue came into the kitchen, Meredith had already mixed up oyster dressing and was stuffing the turkey. "Got to have old Tom here in the oven by ten if he's going to be ready by three," she said, smiling. Meredith loved holidays and enjoyed cooking for them. By the time they were serving breakfast, the turkey was ready to put in the oven.

"You've always been the most organized person I've ever known," Sue said, hugging her friend. "But you are going to take the rest of the day off. I can baste the turkey and Alex said he was going to make shrimp cocktails. Aside from setting the table after we've cleaned the breakfast dishes, what else is there to do? I saw the pies all cooked and the green bean casserole in the fridge, ready to go in the oven. The cranberries are made… do we need mashed potatoes?"

"Potatoes, yes… and yams. Oh," Meredith responded casually, "I need to look through all of the clothes Jake put in storage for me someplace around here. Maybe I have a dress I can wear for the wedding this afternoon." She looked at Alex who had no idea where Jake had put all of her clothes. They had magically disappeared from the hallway the night he brought them from Denver, as Alex recalled.

"Do we have a time set for our wedding, Alex?" she asked him.

Alex looked from one woman to the other, wishing Jake would arrive. He had not realized he would be so nervous. In his mind he saw their friends arriving for dinner and kind of a "by the way, let's do the ceremony before dinner" routine.

"Well," he began slowly, "do you want a before or after dinner wedding?"

Meredith and Sue looked at one another and laughed.

"I'll make this decision," Meredith chuckled. "We will marry at two o'clock. That way, Nancy can be here for the wedding and her turkey will be done right on time at three… someone can go with her to pick up the food after the ceremony. Everyone will have time for an after ceremony drink of champagne – you do have champagne, Alex?" He nodded, smiling.

"Sounds like a schedule to me," Alex smiled his response.

As Meredith and Sue were about to begin the search for Meredith's stored clothes, Jake arrived. He had found a florist working late in Rifle the night before and purchased every flower in the place. The two men carried vase after vase of flowers down the stairs. Sue began filling each vase with fresh water and placing them everywhere around the living and dining rooms.

"What a wonderful wedding gift, Jake!" Meredith sounded a bit breathless.

"Oh," Jake laughed, returning her hug. "The flowers aren't a present. They're just a gesture. My present is your flight to San Diego for one night and half-day at the La Jolla Inn by the Sea. I've reserved a suite overlooking the ocean for you." He saw Alex's furrowed brow and hastily said, "I know you can't take much time away right now." He clapped Alex on both shoulders with his hands. "But if I have anything to do with it, you two are going to spend your wedding night away from this place!"

Jake directed Meredith to where her clothes had been stored. She found a one piece floor-length pant outfit with a white silk blouse and silver full-flaring, pleated lame pants. It had a long, sleeveless, heavily-beaded matching vest. The beading on the vest was done in various shades of gray, black and silver, matching the silver pants nicely. It was several years old… back in her good weight days. It didn't hang on her like everything else did lately. Sue helped her with jewelry and makeup, then finally fingernail polish.

"Well, my dear, it is coming upon two o'clock and unless my ears are playing tricks on me, your guests are arriving. You won't fly away somewhere if I leave to find out where we go from here, will you?" Sue patted her friend's shoulder. Rusty just looked at her.

Within moments, there was a soft knock on the door. Meredith was expecting Alex or Sue and was surprised when Arthur Redbridge, dressed in a blue suit, red tie and looking smashing, entered. Sue was behind him. In her hands she held two bouquets.

"I am ready to walk you down the aisle," Arthur said, smiling. "No one should go through this alone, should they?" He reached out and took her hand.

"Follow me, you two..." Sue handed Meredith a bouquet and then led the way down the hall. Sue was wearing a light green knit skirt with a matching sweater that came down almost to her hips. It made her hazel eyes look green. Sue, Meredith knew, was a woman men of her generation called "stacked." She had no idea what today's word was. "Hot?" Her blonde hair fell in loose curls that had been pulled from her face. Her generous mouth was curved in a happy smile as she led the trio from the hallway into the living room.

Just as Meredith and Arthur left the bedroom, a recording of the wedding march began to play. It was a total surprise to Meredith and her pace faltered. She looked quickly at Arthur who patted her hand and said what a beautiful wedding it was going to be. She had never seen Jake or Alex in dress suits and they looked... magnificent!

Arthur led her to the man she loved and placed her hand in his, then bent and kissed her cheek and Justice Scott began the ceremony.

"Dearly beloved..." the Justice began. He added words to personalize the usual legal ceremony and while repeating the vows he gave her, Meredith changed the word "obey" to "respect." Scott's eyebrows rose for a brief moment, but he nodded understandingly. He had not performed a marriage ceremony in many years, he realized, and things had changed. Alex just smiled.

When they came to the "With this ring" part of the ceremony, Alex reached out to remove her engagement ring and placed a plain gold wedding band on her ring finger, then replaced the engagement ring. Justice Scott asked Meredith if she had a ring to give the groom and she nodded. It surprised both Jake and Alex. Meredith took from the ring finger of her right hand a gold band made with linked Kokopelli figures that matched the necklace she had bought for Alex as a Christmas present. She placed the ring on her groom's left hand.

"Ladies and gentlemen, I present to you Dr. and Mrs. Aleksandr Plotnikov," said Justice Scott, ending the ceremony. Everyone clapped and Alex pulled his bride to him for a long but proper public kiss. "You look gorgeous!" he whispered in her ear. She clung to him for a brief moment.

Jake started pouring champagne and everyone shook Alex's hand and hugged Meredith. As they sat at the dinner table, Jake clanged his fork against the crystal glass at his place setting and everyone quieted for his toast. "I had planned on having the theme song from 'Dr. Zhivago' playing in the background for this toast, but we don't have it in the house. The lyrics for *Lara's Theme* were written by Paul Francis Webster and I will never listen to that song again without wondering if he knew the two of you."

Meredith smiled, deciding she would buy a copy of the recording. She had always loved the song.

"The last two verses of that song portray well how you and Meredith met, and probably tell much of your immediate future... 'You'll come to me, out of the long ago, warm as the wind, soft as the kiss of snow. Till then, my sweet, think of me now and then. God speed my love, till you are mine, again.' I think each of you always knew in your souls that the other was somewhere in this world looking for you. From all of us, we are happy that you finally found one another and will not walk alone through life again. To Alex and Meredith Plotnikov..."

Everyone called out their names and drank of their champagne and then began doing serious damage to the dinner Meredith and Nancy had prepared. Meredith could not believe the tremendous sensitivity Jake had shown in his toast. She looked at him with a kind of awe. His toast displayed a creative streak she did not know he had.

After Alex and Meredith had eaten half of their dinner, Jake and Sue never let up in their encouragement for the newly weds to go pack a bag, take some mince meat and pumpkin pie in an empty pie tin to eat on the plane, and head for their honeymoon suite in

California. Once Gil got them ensconced in the back of Meredith's Cadillac, Alex said quietly "It was an unbelievable day. There for awhile, I thought you might change your mind. Are you okay?"

She snuggled under the protection of his arm and nodded. "Yes, Alex, I am better than okay. How about you?"

"I... I couldn't be better!" He held up their two left hands and just looked at her. "Where and when did you get this beautiful ring?"

"I'd tell you... but then I'd have to kill you. It's a secret... one that is still unfolding," she replied, laughing. "You'll see," she said her comment elicited a questioning frown.

They were surprised to find that the Inn was a newlywed bed and breakfast and their deluxe room had a marvelous view of the ocean. Meredith could see Jake's busy mind looking on the Internet for just the right place, one where they could be comfortable without feeling nervous. He had certainly found it, she thought.

They were exhausted when they arrived. Jake and Sue had seen to it that a large fruit basket and flowers awaited them.

"What do you say to a walk on the beach?" Alex asked. They walked, hand-in-hand, for a long time with no words between them. He told her about the nights he had walked along the beaches of Sakhalin Island and how it had saved his sanity.

"In one way – the sound of the ocean, the breeze, and the salt water smell – this reminds me of those walks," he said quietly. "But then I was alone... I walked without any hope for the future. Here I walk with the woman I love – the wife with whom I'll share my life, who is my future." He smiled and put his arm around her shoulders.

They returned to their room and began preparations for bed. They slept late the next morning. Their love making through the night was different than before. It was slow and unhurried and totally uninhibited. They both realized that they had been feeling their way in the darkness, functioning on emotion with little reason to look deeply within the other person. They had been seeking ways to express a love neither had experienced before. Now there was a sense of permanence... of time to know one another. There was a sense of togetherness that had been missing in their earlier encounters. There was... commitment to the two of them as a unit.

When Gil came to pick them up for the trip home, they were waiting. It had been a night he would never forget, Alex realized. Jake had been right to demand they leave the ranch for the night.

The flight home was fast and smooth. As Gil drove them home the newlyweds pondered the beauty of La Jolla and their first night together as husband and wife.

"So," Alex said as the car pulled in front of the ranch, "you do not intend to obey me?"

"It took twenty-four hours for you to face me with that one?" she asked, laughing. "Did you expect me to swear to God I would obey you? You know how I feel about truth!"

"No," he laughed. "Respect. I get respect... I think I'd rather have that, anyway."

Jake and Sue walked from the house to greet them. They must have been listening for the security beeps as they crossed the cattle guards.

"Well, if it isn't Dr. and Mrs. Plotnikov come to visit, Jake. Come in, come in, make yourself at home," Sue said, laughing as she hugged both of them.

Jake gave both of them 'welcome home' hugs, too. "You're just in time for left over turkey, dressing, green beans, potatoes, gravy, yams... you know, all of it. Since you didn't get to eat a complete meal yesterday afternoon, we thought we'd do a re-play for you."

After eating a large left-over holiday meal, Alex wanted to take a brief walk. Meredith was too tired and Sue volunteered to accompany him. She needed some exercise too, she said.

Meredith told Jake how beautiful the Inn and La Jolla had been and just how perfect.

"When you get on the computer at your place in Rifle again, will you order me a copy of 'Lara's Theme'? It was such a beautiful toast. I want the CD to remember it by." She paused. "And, I want to thank you for your kindness to Sue. I know you don't like anyone to know about the ranch. I needed to have her here with me for the wedding, Jake."

Jake took a deep breath. "She's a delight... we had a great conversation last night. Bright gal," he said, smiling.

"While you were gone, Sue told me the two of you were like sisters – like you once said you thought of Alex and me as brothers. You are very different, just as you once said Alex and I are, but you are also very much alike." He smiled warmly at her. It would take him awhile to get over a melancholy feeling that came over him when he saw his two friends together as husband and wife, but get over it he would. He knew that.

She smiled at him. "How are we different?"

He paused, thinking for a moment, smiled and said, "You are both intense… but you are a bit of a brooding banker and Sue is a bit of a G.I. Jane action doll." They were both still laughing as Alex and Sue came in the front door.

"What's so funny?" Sue asked, her natural curiosity brimming over.

"I have to ask you a question," Jake answered. "Are you familiar with Meredith's theories? Have you been exposed to them?"

"Well… yes, I think so. But I get the feeling that banking theories are not what you're talking about?" Sue responded.

Alex and Jake both laughed and Meredith enjoyed their fun at her expense.

"They just don't know how to deal with my theories about things like unchanging principles and changing values," Meredith said.

"Yes," Alex jumped in, "or her theory about compatibility."

"That was your theory, not mine, Alex," she said laughing. "My theory was about balance, yours was about compatibility and how people and their potential fit into little containers, remember?"

"She's right," he admitted to Jake. "Is she showing me the respect she promised yesterday?"

Jake and Sue both laughed out loud, remembering how Meredith had changed the vow Justice Scott had offered.

"Do you guys always laugh this much?" Sue asked the other three.

"I guess we do," Meredith responded. "Okay, you two," she said. "We need a theory. Then Sue can go to bed and sleep the sleep of someone who has been to the Oracle at Delphi." She paused for a moment.

Sue watched the three of them and thought she had never seen people enjoy one another's company more than they did. "Okay," she offered, deciding to enter this competitive event, "how about... how about this. If I asked each of you 'Who are you?' how would you answer the question?" She paused for a moment. "Jake?" She turned her head to look at him expectantly.

He was a little discomfited by a question that should be easy to answer but which, he immediately saw, was not.

"I'm... I'm a child of God. I'm a man," he began. "I'm an American. I'm my parents' son. I'm a bachelor. I'm a retired CIA agent... I'm not sure I know how to answer the question," he finished, looking a bit confused.

"Alex?"

"I... I guess I'd pretty much agree with what Jake just said... except I'm no longer a bachelor and I never worked for the CIA – though I may have run from them," he responded with a gleam in his eyes. "What would I add? I'm a Russian? I'm a scientist? What?" He looked at Sue, eyebrows raised in question.

"Meredith?"

"I can only think of one answer," she told her friend. "I am me."

"Ah," Sue said. "The correct answer."

"Wait a minute," Jake said animatedly. "How is 'I am me' more correct than 'I am a man' or 'I am a Russian?'" he asked Sue.

She chuckled, feeling good that she had gotten two such intelligent men to walk into the same trap most people did when asked that question. "Because the words 'Russian' and 'man' are both answers to the question 'What are you?' not 'Who are you?' Jake. They can be shared with anyone... a countryman, other men, a brother or sister. The 'who' of you is shared with no one," she replied. "The word 'me' is a 'who' word, not a 'what' word. There is only one 'me'."

The three of them just looked somewhat blankly at Sue for a moment. Even Meredith, who had answered the question correctly, wasn't sure she understood the distinction.

"You're saying that I think of myself as a 'what,' not a 'who?'" Jake asked. He thought about it for another moment. "You know, she may be right," he said, pausing again. The room was silent. "It's a very fine distinction, isn't it?"

Sue laughed again. "It was one of the first questions posed to me by a professor of religious philosophy at the Bible College where I got my undergraduate degree," she told them. "And you're right, Jake. We do tend to think of ourselves as a 'what' rather than a 'who'."

Alex loved mental puzzles and sat looking pensively into the distance as he absorbed these words of wisdom... at least that's what they sounded like to him. He couldn't help but ask himself why understanding this concept was important. If, indeed, a person could really say they knew him or herself, a person had to understand this question, he realized.

"So," he began softly, "when a person answers 'I am me,' that person must know who 'me' is, right? Otherwise, it would be a pseudo – a phony – answer."

Meredith studied her husband for a moment then smiled as a light came on in her mind. "I think I see some of what you're saying, Sue... not all of it, I'm sure." She paused for a moment. "To understand the 'what' parts of yourself, you have to start with the 'who' part. I mean," she paused, biting her lower lip, "if I say 'I am a woman,' I must have a thorough understanding of how '*woman*' is defined... by *me*. Do I define 'woman' as a lady worthy of respect... as a loving mother? Do I define 'woman' as a sex object? Hmmm..."

Alex smiled at his new wife. "So, if a person recognizes the importance of defining the things listed under the 'what' category and does so, that person is actually defining his or her character, right? Character – or, the 'who' – is determined by the definitions a person uses to identify his or her 'what' characteristics."

Sue was tempted to laugh because they had unwound the puzzle so quickly. The few other people to whom she had explained the concept either didn't get it, or thought they did... but never saw the subtleties involved or their significance. She did not laugh, though. A great sense of peace came over her as she looked into Alex's eyes. Sue saw rank honesty in them and it almost brought her to tears. Raw truth was beautiful to behold, she knew. It made her happy her friend had found such a man.

"That's right," Sue said quietly with grave seriousness in her voice. "And that is what will, one day, be judged. It will determine where we spend eternity." She paused for a moment. "We must seek our 'what' characteristics so we know 'who' we are. I believe it's how we find our souls," she concluded.

"So, if I don't know who I am but give you a list of words defining what I am," Jake said slowly, "I really don't know myself at all. I get a big fat zero on the scoreboard of life."

Sue giggled quietly. "How can someone who quotes *Lara's Theme* in one of the most beautiful wedding toasts I've ever heard use the words 'a big fat zero on the scoreboard of life?'" It doesn't compute."

They all laughed, including Jake who quickly said "I have a broad perspective on life, Sue... and I'm flexible."

Alex rose and held out his hand to his new wife. He wanted to give Jake and Sue some time to talk and he knew any exit from the room on their first night home would be awkward. "My new wife and I will leave you now..."

"And it's about time," Sue said. "You've only been married one day. I thought you'd be in bed long ago."

Alex flushed and both Meredith and Jake laughed.

"Well, as you suggest, Sue, we are now going to bed," Meredith said, as she joined her new husband for their first walk as husband and wife down the hall to his bedroom.

Chapter 27

The next few days were hectic. Sue returned to Cincinnati and Jake and Alex started giving practice sessions to each of their soon-to-be-free guests. The lessons included how to have a conversation with someone who knows your clone but doesn't know you –someone the clone may have just talked with last week. They did dry runs of likely scenarios that would occur at the point of kidnapping the clones. What would they do if the kidnapping was interrupted by a security guard, for example?

Before leaving, Sue swore to her friend that she would keep secret the wedding and its attendees. Sue thought the need for secrecy was because Alex was an illegal alien. Meredith did nothing to dissuade her from that belief. It was, after all, true. She suggested to Sue that the reputations of the four famous men who attended the wedding might be damaged if they were personally associated with an illegal Russian scientist... brilliant, or not. Sue was concerned for her friend, but respected her privacy. Too, she was glad Meredith had found so much happiness with Alex. Legal or illegal, he was a delightful, intelligent man. The two made a good pair.

The Christmas holidays would be upon them shortly and everyone knew the captives who were looking forward to their freedom would be emotional and moody. It was not the best time to teach anyone anything. They wanted the implementation sessions done as quickly as possible with final rehearsals completed just before the big return day... a date, as yet, undetermined.

Brett Radov completed his twenty-five years of CIA service and would be joining them the next day for a week. He had worked on the project until his last day at the CIA and still talked with Jake daily.

"So," Jake said calmly at a meeting the night Brett arrived, "the men we're returning to their prior lives want to know when it's going to happen." There was a long pause and he finally said the words everyone avoided: "I guess we would all like a firm date."

Brett cleared his throat before speaking and then asked, "Why was mid-February chosen as the replacement time?"

Alex shrugged. "It was random… we were trying to guess how long it would take to get everyone ready for the switch. And there is the thing about the swan's neck – the clue Jeffrey Lund sketched on the back of the manila envelope he sent Meredith."

Brett explained that he had been thinking about that clue and wondered if it had anything to do with the spring session of the Supreme Court. "There are going to be some important cases coming up for decisions. If Justice Scott returns and suddenly starts voting conservatively, it will sway the balance of some very important court decisions. Justice Scott will need time to prepare, time to study the case law involved."

The room was quiet as everyone thought about his words.

Alex sighed deeply. "You're saying we need to make the change sooner than the middle of February, aren't you?" he asked quietly.

"I suppose I am," Brett responded in an equally quiet tone. "And I guess I would add – from an outsider's perspective, Alex – based on what I've seen and the input Jake has given me about the level of your preparation, it's time to move. The trick is to find a single date when the security of the three men you need to replace within twenty-four hours will be most vulnerable. That should determine your return date." Brett paused for a moment, looking from one to the other of them. "You know what they say about keeping people from moving when they're ready because you're committed to a date for no particular reason?"

"Yes," Alex sighed. "It's a bad idea. People become lethargic, they forget, they lose their edge. They get nervous." He frowned, looking pensive.

Grosvenor and Bryant took the floor to discuss the results of their latest fact-finding mission. They had for the past two weeks dug as deeply and followed as closely as they could the clones of Martinez, Scott and Branchman. It became apparent that the first two weeks of January was the best window of opportunity for clone replacement. The Martinez clone would be skiing alone at Sugarbush, in Vermont. Justice Scott's clone would be vacationing alone at his home in Maine. J.J. Branchman's clone would be taking in some rays on the beach at the Lago Mar Resort Hotel in Fort Lauderdale. They would have security, they always did. But like most famous people, they did not want security guards hovering over them during vacation times.

Jake made a new list of details that did not yet have a firm solution. He insisted they carefully coordinate and assign someone to make sure each was taken care of before moving forward. There was, for example, getting the equipment necessary to check each clone for a tracking device. Brett quickly informed Jake that he had what was needed and could train any of them to use the equipment in fifteen minutes.

If tracking devices existed, they had to have a doctor to move them into the bodies of the Real Thing at the point of each clone's kidnapping. "And I need to talk with Gil to see how we are going to coordinate flying the Real Things plus all of us to the East coast, and then fly the clones back to the ranch," Jake said, trying to ponder solutions as he identified problems.

Based on their discussions, Alex and Jake were ready for the Real Things who had requested a meeting at the stable office the next morning. He introduced Brett to the men as a recently-retired CIA agent who would be coordinating security for Arthur Redbridge when he returned to Washington.

"The thing is," J.J. Branchman began, "we don't want to wait until the middle of February to take back our lives if it's possible to do it sooner." He hesitated but none of the other men spoke. Jake and Alex remained wordless, waiting for him to finish. "We appreciate what you've done and are doing," he said. "But you don't know what it's like to be locked up in a room with your life being lived by someone else... somewhere out there." He gestured with his arms, trying to indicate a place unknown.

"And we're not trying to tell you what to do," Senator Martinez said, interrupting Branchman. "We'd like to discuss the possibility of moving up the return date."

"That's why we asked for the meeting," Justice Scott said. "We'd like to know what we can do to make it easier for you. Maybe we can get it done more quickly."

There was a long silence. The four men looked hopefully at those who could give them back their lives.

"You all need to understand a few things," Jake said. His tone of voice was neutral and non-accusatory, but firm. "The people on this side of the room and one person at the main house are risking their lives to give you back what was wrongly taken from you... to put you back where you belong. They're doing it because it's the right thing to do." He walked in front of the men and established eye contact with each before continuing to the next. "Are you suggesting their risk level should increase so you can be home to watch Bing Crosby and Rosemary Clooney in an old re-run of 'Holiday Inn?' Risk levels can't be increased because you'd rather sing with Bing than send Valentines in February!" Jake paused for a moment as he walked the length of the room.

Arthur Redbridge cleared his throat before speaking. "I understand how the men feel," he said, "we're all anxious to get our lives back. If you have a firm time schedule, we have to have confidence in your plans and in your judgment. If the middle of February is when it has to be, then that is when it has to be."

The others quickly nodded their agreement.

"I'll tell you how you can help move things along," Jake responded. "You, Arthur, can put on another ten pounds and lift enough weights to get the muscle tone back in your arms and back so your clone's suits won't sag on you! You, J.J., can do the exercises recommended to get rid of those love handles. Your clone is only half your age and he doesn't have them." He gave similar messages to Avery Scott and John Martinez.

Jake took a seat as Alex stood. "We met last night to determine if we can move the targeted date up. There is a dangerous way for you to replace your clones and there is a safer way. We have focused on the latter… and I think perhaps you need to do the same. However, if it will make the holidays a little more bearable, we are working to see if we can make our move in January rather than February." He paused and began pacing, his brows drawn together in concentration.

"We have something to work out with a third party, Arthur," he said casually. "We need to know the outcome of those negotiations before that decision can be made."

Redbridge nodded. Alex was telling him that they needed to know the outcome of his meeting with William Leonard. The fortune Leonard had collected in banks around the world was going to be used by Redbridge on behalf of the people of America, not to promote Washington's plan to implement one-world government.

"But you are thinking about returning us sooner than February?" Branchman asked hopefully.

"We are," Alex responded. "Do you realize how much you cost us each month?" He chuckled and sat on the edge of the desk as he spoke. "There are details that need to be worked out, J.J. – so keep your own words in mind: 'We are thinking about it.' For example, we have to know how to find the tracking devices we are sure have been implanted in the clones. If you go back to your life without those devices being removed from them and put into your body, the Russians will immediately know something is wrong. Their tracking signals will stop. Your lives won't be worth two rubles, as I used to say. To remove a device from each of them and put it into you guys, we need a doctor at the point of the change. We're working on that. So," Alex paused, "does this make you feel better?"

Branchman, the non-politician of the group, rose and walked to Alex and shook his hand, thanking him for the straight talk. "You can be a hard-nosed son of a bitch," he told Jake, grinning.

"I don't know about you guys, but it makes me feel better," Branchman said to the others. "Like Arthur said, if it has to be February, that's too bad – but okay. It's good to know Jake and Alex are open to an ongoing review."

Brett left the meeting ahead of the others and was waiting for Redbridge in his room when he returned. The Fed Chairman was startled by his presence and turned to leave. He ran into Jake. "As I mentioned in the meeting, Arthur, Brett is your new security manager."

"I thought you were going to be my security guy," Redbridge said. Like most people, he was more comfortable with those he knew than with strangers.

"I'll be there, working with Brett. But my primary responsibility is to protect Meredith. This guy just retired from the agency a couple of weeks ago. He has better contacts there than I do. I've been gone for over ten years." He put his hand on his former partner's shoulder and said "Brett was a twenty-five year man... worked with me some of those years. He's going to be here with you for the next week. He and his wife still live in the Washington area and that will be helpful – important – to you. He has the medical contacts used by the Agency that gets our hospital scenario arranged."

Brett remained quietly affable.

"I've briefed Brett," Jake continued. "He knows the plan, but you need to tell him your view of what's going to happen, Arthur. It's a good way to make sure you both understand things the same way."

Jake paused, scratching his head. "Any questions?"

"I... I don't think so," Arthur said. His voice sounded insecure and unconvinced.

"Come on, Arthur," Jake said. "You and the other guys want to move things ahead. If you need a security blanket with every change that comes along, what the hell makes you think you're ready to re-enter the world of business and finance?"

"Point taken," Redbridge replied, smiling. "You're telling me I can trust this guy – I recognize him from Sakhalin Island and the airplane," he said. "But you're right, Jake. We'll talk. Actually, it's good that Brett will just have me to worry about. The other guys each have their own security guard... now I'll have mine."

Jake held out his hand and Redbridge stood and shook it. "I'm leaving you in good hands." And with that, Jake walked to the door, telling Brett to stop by the main house on his way back to town. The two of them needed to discuss the Munich trip. He looked at

Redbridge and said, "And no, Arthur, he's not going to tell you which town." He laughed and left.

Later that night and after dinner, Alex asked Meredith if she would like to take a short walk. Brett and Jake were talking and he wanted some private time. It was an unusual request and she put on her walking shoes and joined him.

"I don't want to walk far," he said. "I just wanted to get outside for a minute."

"Something is worrying you, Alex... what is it?" she asked, snuggling her head against his shoulder and he leaned down to kiss her hair.

"You know me too well," he said. "And I'm glad," he added quickly. There was a long pause. He slowed the pace so they were barely moving forward. "It looks like we'll be moving up the return date," he said softly, biting his lips almost as soon as the words left his mouth. Dear Lord, how he wanted to put this entire thing behind them and get on with their lives!

"Do you have a date yet?" she asked, and stopped walking.

"If everything works as planned, it will probably be early January." Alex paused and pulled her into his arms for a moment. "I want you to think of everything you need to do to get ready... from clothes and hair and jewelry to shoes and handbags. And, of course, your strategy once back in the nation's capitol."

She squeezed him harder, then stepped back and took both of his hands in hers. "Alex, I'll be fine. Once that envelope is returned, which Arthur will do before I set foot publicly in Washington, I'll be safe."

He put his hands on both of her shoulders as she looked into his face. It was very serious. "I want you to hear what I'm saying," he told her and it was a firm, no nonsense tone he seldom used. "You need to stop working on the total project and concentrate only on your role. It is important."

He moved his hands gently up and down her arms as he spoke.

Meredith turned, pulling her jacket more tightly around her body. It was cold tonight, she thought. She turned back towards the house and started walking, holding out her left hand.

323

"Come on, darling, I'm getting cold," she said, encouraging him to join her. "And please don't worry. I heard what you said." She cleared her throat. "In this instance, I'll obey."

The plans continued to move ahead. Brett went home, scheduled to return to the ranch the day after Christmas. From that point on, he would stay with Redbridge until he was once again the legitimate Federal Central Bank Chairman. The two men liked one another. That was half the battle, Jake thought.

Jake had the trip to Bavaria scheduled and needed to go over the details of it with Brett. Gil was studying the air traffic regulations in Munich. The idea of meeting at a castle that looked like something out of a Disney movie still bothered Jake, Alex knew. Had Leonard really held onto his fortune? They would soon know. Once they figured a way to ensure Redbridge would follow through on his promise to use that fortune on behalf of the American people, they could set a firm date for the kidnapping of the clones and the return of the Real Things.

It was a direct and simple plan. It had a huge number of small complexities, but they were being solved at a rapid pace now they were into the countdown.

Everyone, it seemed, had waited until the last few days before Christmas to begin wrapping presents. Jake and Alex asked Meredith if she would find and buy some meaningful gifts for their soon-to-be-freed captives and she spent the afternoon of the 21st at Jake's on the computer having things sent overnight delivery to his Rifle address. Jake asked his neighbors to help him out... to accept packages when he wasn't home. When they agreed, Jake put a note on his door for the overnight delivery services. The packages arrived all at once, on the 23rd.

After lunch on Christmas Eve, Jake convinced Meredith to accompany him to Rifle so the presents delivered there could be wrapped and put under the tree.

"Just a fast trip," Jake said, "we won't be gone long."

Meredith was anxious to get back by three o'clock. She had to cook dinner. All she had to do was heat things, but with a holiday meal to be cooked and served the next day, she did not want a late night in the kitchen. She wanted the evening to be free for the three of them to sit around the fire and talk.

It seemed Jake found one thing after another to delay their return to the ranch. Darkness was rapidly overtaking the final pink rays of the sun and a light snow was falling as they neared the house. It suddenly became clear to Meredith why Jake had shanghaied her for the afternoon. Outside of the cabin, a lighted Christmas tree stood, raising its royal head to the skies. It was, she thought, praising the birth of a newborn baby. It shone through the oncoming darkness and they could see it from a long distance. Jake just laughed when she uttered her surprised comments, accusing him of using spy tactics on her.

That, however, was the least of the surprises to come. As they entered the house and Jake keyed in the security code, the divider wall moved back and another large tree appeared. Covered with decorations, it filled the corner between the fireplace and the patio doors. Except for the packages they carried in their arms, all of the Christmas presents they had been wrapping the past days were carefully placed under the tree. Standing around the tree were all of the men from the bunkhouse. As they took a step down the stairs to enter the living room, the men joined together and began singing "We Wish You a Merry Christmas."

"When did you have time to do all of this?" Meredith asked. She sounded as astonished as she looked. Her eyes glowed like those of a child awaiting Santa Claus.

"We cut down the trees two days ago. Alex and I went crazy buying decorations… but they look good, don't they? See what nine busy men can accomplish in a short time?" Jake was animated and his glee was infectious.

Meredith shook her head, her pleasure reflected in her smile. "It's beautiful!" she said enthusiastically. Alex smiled at the sheer pleasure he saw on his wife's face. That was what he had wanted to achieve.

Alex took her hand and led her to the kitchen where a large dinner was laid out.

"The caterer," he said, smiling. "I didn't want you working on your first Christmas Eve in our home. I hope you don't mind." He really never knew how she was going to react to certain things... surprises of this kind. "And I wanted all of our friends to share Christmas Eve with us... again, I hope you don't mind." He paused. "I thought it might help make up to you for spending Christmas away from your family."

Meredith walked into his arms and he could feel her trembling. "You're my family, Alex." She fought to control her emotions. "The reason I do not get emotional very often is because I have a hard time containing them once they get over the walls I built," she said. "Please don't let me cry like a baby and spoil this."

He kissed her instead.

She smiled as she realized Jake and Alex had gotten four moody men involved in celebrating what was making them moody: Christmas. It had worked, she thought.

"And guess what we have for entertainment, everyone?" Jake asked after dinner. He poured brandy for those who wanted it. "We're going to watch a DVD – the movie... J.J., can you guess?"

"You son of a..." he looked at Meredith and Nancy and stopped. "It's 'Holiday Inn' with Bing Crosby and Rosemary Clooney, isn't it?"

Everyone laughed as Jake hit 'play' and the old movie began.

Chapter 28

On Christmas morning, everyone gathered at the main house again. The presents under the tree were open amidst much laughter and thoughtful remembrance. There were so many people and so many gifts, the pile of wrapping paper went beyond the fireplace's ability to safely burn it... Jake's job.

Meredith had gotten each of the Real Things something pertaining to their soon-to-be-realized freedom. There was a 22-karat gold money clip in the shape of a dollar sign for Redbridge, a sterling silver piggy bank for John Martinez, a small gold microphone for J.J. Branchman, and silver scales of justice for Avery Scott. There was also a package for each of the men containing the usual Christmas tie, socks and cashmere sweater. The gift that got the most comment was the gold tie clip that said "Freedom." Each of the Real Things received one.

Avery Scott made a comment that told the story for all of the Real Things. "This is the first time in eleven years I even knew Christmas morning was here," he said in a hoarse voice, smiling. "Freedom..." he whispered softly as he attached his tie clip to his shirt.

"Fifteen years for me," Redbridge said, looking serious... actually it was almost a haunted look. Following Scott's lead, he, too, attached his tie clip to his tie-less shirt.

"Nine years for me," Martinez intoned.

"And seven for me," J.J. finished the litany.

Meredith and Alex were totally surprised when J.J. Branchman gave them a large charcoal portrait of the two of them at their wedding. It was, he told them, hard to keep hidden in his room. And, he said, Nancy and Joe had taken care of getting it framed for them. No one had any idea the famed radio talk show host was also a gifted artist. It was truly beautiful and was signed by all four of their guests. J.J. informed Jake he would have a similar gift by the end of the week. "You've kept us so busy the past few days, I didn't have time to finish it," he told everyone.

Meredith captured Alex for a moment, had him sit in his chair and she handed him the last gift she had for him. He removed a pine cone decoration she had attached to the ribbon of the package and everyone, it seemed, stopped talking as he opened his final Christmas gift from his new wife. "What in the world…" he began. He was speechless as he read through the first page of Meredith's gift. "How… when… where…" was all he could say. He looked as stunned as his inability to speak indicated he was.

"My friends," he was finally able to say. "This gift is for all of us. This is what we need to inform the Russians that each of you has been returned. It lists each piece of evidence that will be presented to the media and Internet blogs if anything happens to any one of you or to me. Meredith has listed the names of all the other known clones we sat down and identified two weeks ago. This tells the Russians that the clones created from the DNA of people other than you four – the ones we identified – need to retire from the careers they stole." His voice literally broke. There were tears in Alex's eyes as he stood and hugged her. "I was dreading doing this next week," he whispered in her ear. "I cannot thank you enough."

As if on cue, Nancy entered from the kitchen informing everyone that a big breakfast was awaiting them. Everyone got a plate and walked through a serving line. After breakfast, they turned on the big screen television to watch football. Beer and popcorn was plentiful. Meredith and Nancy served dinner at four o'clock and the men were back in their rooms by six.

Jake was spending the night in Rifle. Alex started a small fire so he and his wife could enjoy its warmth.

"The present you gave me," Alex said slowly as they sat, listening to seasonal music and enjoying the fire. "Where did you get all of the information? How were you able to link so many pieces of information – photos and other evidence that I have – to the statements made in your essay? How did you know the names of the other clones Arthur, Avery, J.J., John and I sat down and identified?"

"Jake," was her simple answer. "He's been so busy running around, I was afraid he wouldn't have the time to help me finish it. He made time, though." She looked at Alex and smiled.

There was a long silence as they enjoyed the music of the season. "Our first Christmas together, Dorogoi. I hope you enjoyed it as much as I did... there will never be another one like it."

"Next year, I'll cook borscht," she said, a serious look on her face.

Alex chuckled. "No, my dear, next year I hope you will cook exactly what you did today. I hope your children and grandchildren and Jake and Nancy and Joe will be with us... a real family affair."

His comment reminded her that she needed to check her cell phone for messages. Luke and Mary had probably called... they usually did on holidays. So, too, did her mother and stepfather. She frowned at her own negligence, but dialed for voice mail and held the telephone between them so Alex could hear the messages.

"See?" she said. "I really do have a family."

"I have one more Christmas present for you," he said quietly. "Do you want it now? Or would you rather wait until morning?"

"I'd like it in about five minutes... my shoulders should feel wonderful by then."

Alex complied with her request, patting her softly on the shoulder when he was done. She would let him massage her shoulders all night, he knew, but there was one more item he wanted to get behind him before the Christmas spirit began to recede. He rose from his chair, telling her he would be right back. He returned carrying a file folder and handed it to her.

"No wrappings on this one, Mrs. Plotnikov," he said. He pushed her upper body away from his chair with his knee so he could get his left leg behind her and retake his seat.

Meredith opened the file and found the Deed of Trust to the ranch inside. He had transferred ownership to the M.J. McIntosh Family Trust for which she was the Trustee. She looked at him and the pain in her eyes struck a blow to his heart.

"Wait," he said. "Before you create a drama around this, I need to remind you that the Deed to the ranch is in the name of the Smith Family Trust. This change must be done. First, our marriage certificate says 'Plotnikov.' If anything happened to either one of us for any reason, it creates problems of ownership. Second, within a month or two, I hope to be able to use my real name. That creates ownership difficulties for both of us if the Deed is registered to the Smith Family Trust," he said. "If the Deed to the ranch is in the name of your family trust, it creates no problems of ownership." He knew appealing to her logical mind would work, and it did. Her pained look receded and she looked at the papers once again.

A Christmas song began to play that she first heard fifteen years ago when her kids joined the U.S. Navy. Both were sent to San Diego to report for duty on December 20th. Robert Goulet's voice filled the room.

Meredith picked up the remote and restarted the CD. "Listen to the words of this song, Alex. It's one of my favorites and, I swear, it was written for our first Christmas together." He listened to the words of *This Christmas I Spend With You.*

One day she would tell him about the trip to California she had made years ago to spend a last Christmas with her children as a family, but not now. She had driven alone through a blizzard in New Mexico on her way back to Denver, listening to this song. Now, Alex was the one with whom she wanted to spend Christmas. He was her present, he was her future.

*****

The days between Christmas and December 30th sped quickly by and more project problems on Jake's list were solved. They were ready. Later, Jake would think back on the trip to Munich as the longest lucky streak for air travel he had ever experienced. They flew, with intermittent stops, for almost eleven hours. They stayed ahead of, above or between snow storms all the way across the Atlantic.

They would land at Munich's Franz Josef Strauss Airport in about thirty minutes, Gil said over the intercom. It was cloudy and overcast, but the ground was clear... so far.

It did not take long for the lucky weather streak to end. When Jake awoke the next morning and opened the drapes at his hotel room window, it was snowing... hard. He was glad for his early wake-up call. It was only 97 kilometers to Füssen, but the weather would slow them down. Germany's autobahns provided some of the best highways in the world, but Jake wondered at the wisdom of driving through the Bavarian Alps in these conditions. It would likely be foggy, too. Before leaving home, he had checked the train schedule and made reservations as an alternate source of transportation, just in case. "Just in case" had happened. The train would leave for Füssen at 11:30 that morning. If there was a problem with the bus in Füssen, it was only 3 kilometers to Neuschwanstein. If there was no bus, they could get a taxi. Hell, Jake thought, they could walk if they had to... even in a blizzard. He did not want to repeat this trip a week from now.

Though the train was slightly late, they arrived in Füssen at 1:30 p.m. and took a cab to the bus station. Once there, they asked for directions to the Hohenschwangau Village bus. They were directed to a vehicle, its motor running, sitting three aisles from the terminal. As they approached, the driver opened the door. They boarded, handing him their tickets.

The driver thanked them. He was an overweight man with a healthy auburn beard and moustache. He walked heavily down the stairs of the bus, took a long-handled brush to the outside windows, then re-entered, sat back down, and put the bus in gear.

Jake, Brett and Arthur were surprised they were the only passengers. Jake told the driver they were sorry to inconvenience him in such bad weather and on a holiday.

"That's okay, Jake," came the reply from the driver in English. "Arthur, we have some business to discuss. And for heavens sake, take off those ridiculous horned-rim glasses and unwrap all of those neck scarves from around your head. I need to see you. I've already been to the castle and no one is visiting there today... just you three. And me, of course."

"Oh, my God," Redbridge breathed. He quickly remembered himself and almost breathlessly said, "I hear the castle at Neuschwanstein was built by King Ludwig the Second."

William Leonard laughed. "You're not going to give it to me in my native tongue this time? Shortly after Jake butchered the sentence in Navajo over a month ago, I knew it was you, Arthur. You're the only one who knows I speak Navajo. It took me awhile to figure it out, but I finally got it." For the record, however, Leonard gave the expected response. "Yes, he built it in the 19th century." He gulped... it sounded like he was trying to hide his laughter.

"Jake, I want you to hear what I have to say." Leonard surprised Jake with the comment. He and Brett walked slowly to the front of the bus, stopping a few steps short of Arthur Redbridge.

"They know I love Bavarian castles so I can get away with coming to Neuschwanstein to celebrate the New Year. I've done it before. I give public tours of the castle sometimes on holidays when tour guides don't want to work. I volunteer my time. As I said, the castle is open, but only because I scheduled this tour. They dropped me off there earlier today. I paid the bus driver to let me take his last bus trip back to Füssen... I put on my overweight disguise, pasted on a moustache and beard, and walked right past my handlers." He paused for a moment as the driving conditions required more of his attention than he was giving it. "I usually spend the entire day at the castle, so all of the people who saw me go there this morning are expecting me to stay for another hour or two." Leonard paused for a moment. "We'll be at the Müller Hotel parking area in a few minutes. That's where I turn the bus around to make its return to Füssen. I will go with you in the horse-drawn vehicle that's waiting for you at the hotel." He turned the bus to the left, and said, "Okay, Arthur, we're almost there so put your scarves and glasses back on."

Redbridge re-took his seat. This time he put on horn-rimmed sunglasses. Jake had warned him of eye scan identification technology. With a large wool-knit cap pulled down over much of his face, the long, heavy winter coat, the scarf across his mouth and neck, and the sunglasses, no one would recognize the Fed Chairman even if the CIA had a man trailing William Leonard.

Jake and Brett, both dressed casually and wearing colorful ski jackets, caps and sunglasses, walked on either side of Redbridge. They looked like two sons escorting their elderly father. Leonard walked in front of the three men, clearing a path for them and showing the way. Jake was once again grateful for his beard. He had been gone from the Agency for over ten years. No one would recognize him. Brett, however, was a recent retiree. That concerned him. Before they departed the bus, Jake zipped Brett's coat all the way to the top, pulled his hat down and the hood up, and pushed Brett's chin down far enough into his jacket so that, with the sunglasses, very little of his face could be seen.

The five minute horse-drawn ride was truly a scene from a winter wonderland, Jake thought. Neuschwanstein did resemble the Disney castle of movie fame. In the snow and light fog, the scene took on a magical ambiance... even eerie. It made Jake think of *Alice Through the Looking Glass* Sue had mentioned when she visited the ranch.

They had to walk a short distance as Leonard showed them to the main entrance of the castle. When they entered, he locked the door behind them, put his index finger to his lips and began giving them an information tour. He introduced himself to them as Roger Marchman and told them he would be doing their tour of the castle, today. All the while, he held his fingers over his lips. "The swan was the heraldic animal of the Counts of Schwangau. When a king was named, he considered himself to be the ruler of Schwangau, which is why you will see so many swans exhibited here. As you all may know, the swan is the Christian symbol of purity – Ludwig wanted to be pure... though a lot of people thought he was insane," Leonard finished.

At the conclusion of his introductory remarks, Leonard put his fingers to his lips again and from a peg on the wall where his coat was hanging, he pointed to the microphone in the lapel. He coughed as he turned on a tape recorder which began reciting the history of Neuschwanstein. His handlers, as he called them, would think he was wearing his coat while giving the tour to these new visitors.

"Neuschwanstein exemplifies the true feelings and wishes of Ludwig the Second... more than any of his other castles," the tape continued. Jake smiled because he could hear footsteps that had been recorded onto the tape, as if Leonard and the tourists were moving through the building. He knew this guy was slick, but Jake's admiration for him as a spy grew every time they met. "This particular castle, Neuschwanstein, was never intended by Ludwig to represent Bavarian royalty. Rather, it was designed as a place where Ludwig the Second could spend time relaxing..." the tape with William Leonard's voice kept going as the four men quietly walked up a flight of stairs and into a large public room.

"Okay, Jake," Leonard said quietly, "Arthur and I will walk to the other end of the room. We are in the servants' rooms and there is no exit other than this door, so he is safe... even with me."

Jake smiled at Leonard... it was an easy-going smile that belied the tension he felt floating in the pit of his stomach. They had come too far with this scheme to fail because he overlooked a detail involving security as Leonard was suggesting he do.

"My friend will stay at the door, I will stay far enough away to allow you and Arthur a private conversation, but I will be closer than the door. I will put this scrambler on the chair between where you and Arthur sit." Jake paused.

"Unless I'm mistaken, those are your clothes folded on the chair at the end of the room... where you're heading. You can change clothes while you talk, hand me the bus driver's clothes and whatever you have on under them for padding. I'll give them to Brett so he can begin dressing in them. Clear?"

Leonard returned the smile and, looking at him with growing respect, followed the directions Jake had given him. It was a contest in ego, Jake realized. He knew he would have to give some control to the other man because he obviously had control issues. Jake didn't blame him. His own life had been bad enough when it came to the need to control his destiny, but if he'd lived the kind of life Leonard had, he would have latent control issues, too.

Redbridge and Leonard talked in hushed tones. About ten minutes into their discussion, the spy for former President Rory McCoy walked to Jake and handed him the bus driver's disguise: Clothes, beard, mustache, and padding. After another twenty minutes, Leonard began looking at his watch and took Redbridge's arm and began walking towards Jake. Brett had changed clothes, stuffing his own attire under the bus driver's jacket. He was close to Leonard's size – about an inch shorter than Jake – and now looked like the bus driver that had entered the castle with them. Leonard looked like himself, gold-rimmed glasses, and all. They stopped in the entryway and waited for Leonard to put on his coat, all of them aware he was wired for sound. The recorder was still giving a tour to those listening in and when it got to a point where it could be turned off, Leonard coughed again and did just that, removing the tape.

"I'm terribly sorry I need to leave early... the weather, you know. You did get to see most of the castle. I do hope you're not disappointed." He looked at Brett and said, "And, to answer your question Mr. Hornsby, it's okay for you to wait here in the entryway for your friend. You won't be able to get into the castle, but technically Neuschwanstein does not close for another hour. I'm sorry your friend didn't get here in time for the guided tour... this weather changed many plans today, I'm sure. Too bad you missed one another at the bus station after coming such a long way. I'll tell the hotel you'll be spending the night." With that, Leonard opened the door of Neuschwanstein and led the three of them out.

The comment to a Mr. Hornsby, Jake realized, was Leonard's way of explaining to those listening why only four men, not five, were exiting the castle. He smiled, realizing Leonard must have recorded a comment from a Mr. Hornsby onto the tape being heard by the men who were tailing him.

Three tourists and a bus driver had entered the castle for the tour directed by Leonard. Now that Leonard had joined them, five should be leaving. Fortunately, his handlers were watching Leonard, not the tourists with him. They saw Leonard departing, and that was who they were monitoring. Leonard waved to a car with two men inside as they passed. It was his way of telling them he knew they were watching and he was now leaving Neuschwanstein.

Leonard walked with the group of men to the bus where he shook their hands, said goodbye and departed for the Müller Hotel. That, he had told his security detail, was where he was spending the night. Brett climbed behind the wheel of the bus and quickly figured out how to start it up. After letting it warm up for a moment or two, he slipped it into gear and began the drive back to Füssen.

Jake and Arthur departed the bus while Brett changed his clothes. He rejoined them at a phone booth in time to hear Jake's closing comments. He was purchasing a sitting room for three on the late train back to Munich. They had to wait two hours, but it would give them a chance to eat something in a small, out-of-the-way café. Even though Redbridge's face was not known here, Jake put the knit cap back on Arthur's head and pulled it low, telling him to leave it on while they ate. Brett stood outside the café door for ten minutes to make sure they had not been followed. The three men would get back to Munich just in time to ring in the New Year.

In Munich, the sun rose at 8:04 a.m. on Sunday, New Year's Day 2007. The storm had abated overnight. Getting out of the airport was going to be difficult, however. Cancelled flights had piled up from the day before and got first priority for departures. Once they got people delayed by the storm out of the airport, very few others were traveling. It was the usual confusion... tired people who suffered long weather delays in airports all over the world.

Brett had stayed at the airport Sheraton, keeping Redbridge under lock and key until they got a firm departure time. A lot of flights had been backed up because of yesterday's blizzard. Gil had called the airport early that morning to find that the delay would be several hours. Normally, a pilot was given an EDCT or "Expect Departure Clearance Time" by Flow Control. Then, when he filed his flight plan, he would be given a firm estimated time of departure. Aircraft experiencing departure delays due to weather problems at the point of departure rather than the arrival airport were not issued departure slots so they could depart in the order they arrived at the runway, first come, first served. Once the backed-up air traffic from yesterday was in the air, they would be able to get in line and leave as quickly as air traffic allowed. Jake and Gil went into the airport for breakfast. They called Brett from the restaurant and told him when to come to the airport and where to meet them. Redbridge arrived, wearing his "blind" glasses and carrying the red-tipped white cane. There would be no eye scans. They were all immensely relieved to feel the wheels of the Lear jet leave the ground. They were on their way home.

A half-hour after take-off, Jake heard a thump, thump, thump coming from the restroom. Thinking something must have come loose and fallen, he opened the door. What he saw literally stunned him. He took two steps backwards. There, sitting on the toilet in all his glory, was William Leonard. He was smiling at Jake. "Are we out of European airspace yet?" he asked.

"How the hell…?"

"Don't ask, Jake. I won't tell you. But my presence puts you into a bit of a pickle, doesn't it?" Leonard rose from his throne and slapped Jake on the shoulder. "You can't take me back to Munich without tying this plane and everyone on it to me. The media would arrive and pictures would be taken and Arthur would be seen. We can't have that, can we?"

"Brett!" Jake called loudly. "I hope you have something to restrain this bastard because if you don't, I'm going to have Gil drop a little closer to the Atlantic Ocean and toss him in!"

Like Jake, Brett was shocked to see Leonard. He put his head in the cockpit to ask Gil where he could find some duct tape. William Leonard looked skeptically at Brett and watched Jake walk purposefully towards Arthur Redbridge.

"Alright, alright," he said, "but Jake needs to know I have an American Passport in my pocket. I also have a different flight plan showing a pilot and four, not three, passengers on this plane," he told Brett caustically. "It replaced Gil's flight plan when it was filed at the Munich airport before we left."

Jake quickly walked to Arthur Redbridge and pulled him from his seat. "Did you know about this?" he demanded.

"No, Jake. No, I did not. He said nothing to me, I swear!" The man's voice was steady and sounded truthful. Arthur did not lie well and he maintained steady eye contact with Jake for a long moment. "Here… sit down."

Jake sat and stewed. Leonard was right. He had put them in a fine pickle. Everything he had said would happen if they took him back was true. They couldn't go back. So, Jake thought, the question is, how do I go forward? As he sat and quietly thought, a plan began to form in his mind.

When they landed in New Jersey, to clear Customs and refuel, Gil found they could not fly into any airport within a reasonable distance of the ranch. The western United States had suffered blizzard conditions overnight and the airports in Grand Junction, Rifle, Eagle, Montrose, Delta and Aspen were all closed. Jake, Brett and Gil conferred and decided to land in Needles, California... just up the Colorado River from Phoenix. It would be easy to maintain anonymity in the small, California desert city. Jake needed to talk with Alex.

One question after the other flew through the telephone into Jake's ear. He had no answers. That, in fact, was all he could tell Alex: "I have no answers. I'll tell you about Customs when I get home. My head is working overtime trying to figure out what to do with him... we need to keep him under our thumb – at least until the clones have been replaced by the Real Things. He could upset the whole apple cart! Look, Alex, I'm functioning on insulin and hormones right now, so back off. We did everything by the damned book... the problem is, Leonard knows the book backwards and forwards." There was a long pause.

Alex sounded tired, too. Dear Lord, Jake wondered, are we going to live through this mess we've created?

"Do me a favor," Jake said quietly. Go to my new house and open it up. Make sure two beds are made and the heat and hot water heater are turned up. Take some food, too. I think that's where I'm going to plant Leonard for the time being... away from Redbridge. I'm going to wrap something around his eyes tomorrow morning when we land in Grand Junction." Jake told Alex he needed to have Bill Bryant bring a pair of blind glasses and a cane for Leonard to the airport when they picked Redbridge up in Grand Junction the next morning. Jake's voice was filled with fatigue and frustration.

"Call me from the plane tomorrow. If you can't land in Rifle where you have a car, I'll pick you up... wherever," Alex responded. His voice sounded more controlled now as he told Jake the snow had stopped and they were pretty sure Walker Field would be open by morning.

Jake rented a car and drove to the flight line to pick up his plane mates, then checked the four of them into a nondescript Needles motel. He grabbed the phone book for a pizza delivery place. Leonard had not eaten since the day before and, it seemed, could do nothing but complain about hunger pains.

By the time they landed in Grand Junction the next morning and Redbridge was removed from the plane, the Rifle airport had cleared and they would be able to fly Leonard around the country long enough to make him think he was far away from the Fed Chairman, then land in Rifle where Jake's SUV was parked. After they landed and before leaving his parking spot, Jake taped Leonard's hands together under his legs. It would keep him from removing his glasses. With that done, Jake started the drive home.

Leonard tried to initiate conversation several times. Jake simply tuned him out. He had heard all he wanted to hear from this man. As he neared his new home, he saw the Jeep parked in front. He turned on a music CD already in the player. He pulled the car to a slow stop but left the engine running. Alex and Bob Grosvenor stood in front of his vehicle. Jake put his index finger over his lips.

With a comment to Leonard that he would be back as soon as he checked things out, Jake exited the SUV and motioned the two men to follow him inside the house.

"So, that's William Leonard," Alex said. "Arthur is home safely and has told us some of what happened. After listening to his story, I was really sorry I blew up at you on the telephone. He obviously snuck onto the airplane while you and Gil went inside the airport to have breakfast. Who would have thought it could happen?" He reached out to his friend and gave him a slap on the back to welcome him home.

"And," Alex continued, "we brought food… steaks, hamburger, leftovers, frozen dinners, soup – anything we could find that we didn't absolutely need. There are dishes and cups and glasses and flatware in the box in the kitchen."

"Bob," Jake said turning to the other man. "Can you take the first night's watch with this guy? I'm too tired and don't trust myself to stay awake. Someone will relieve you first thing in the morning."

Grosvenor nodded his agreement. "Sure. I got a good night's sleep." He gave his quiet but confident smile as he spoke.

"Good," Jake responded. "He has done nothing but complain all day. You cannot trust one thing this guy does or says. If you turn your back for one minute, he could be gone."

The big man nodded his understanding. "Alex and I put a bolt lock on the outside of one of the bedroom doors and nailed a heavy sheet of wood over the window. There aren't any tools in his room... he can't get out without making a lot of noise."

"Don't count on it, Bob. I'm not too sure he's working alone. Well... I'll get Leonard out of the car and introduce him to you. You'll be leaving, Alex?"

The Russian nodded his agreement. It was best not to be seen.

"Okay, William," Jake said, opening the car door and using a hunting knife to sever the tape from the man's hands, "welcome to your temporary home."

Leonard got slowly out of the car. Jake helped him walk through the snow. The glasses would stay on until they were inside the house. The afternoon sun was hitting Leonard in the face as he stepped out of the car. He tried to calculate the time of day from it. They walked to the house and Grosvenor pulled the car out of sight.

"You can take the glasses off now," Jake said in a disgusted tone.

"Well, you certainly found a forsaken spot to hide me Jake... it's perfect," Leonard said, looking outside the window.

"Hid the car, huh?" He chuckled. "Good move."

After listening to Leonard's litany of complaints all day, his agreeable tone surprised Jake.

Grosvenor shook hands with Leonard when Jake introduced them and asked if he'd like something to eat.

Jake pointed out the blizzard conditions and the isolation of the place. He told Leonard if he tried to escape, he would die before he found a highway or civilization. Jake took Leonard's arm and escorted him to the room that had been prepared for him.

"Why do you think I want to go anyplace, Jake?" He looked at his captor as if he, Jake, were the crazy man. "This place is absolutely perfect." He turned his head to Bob who was walking behind him down the hallway to the bedroom. "You'll have no trouble from me, Bob. I promise."

Jake paused, taking Leonard's coat from him, telling him he was taking it with him. He took Bob's coat for good measure, too. "Take your clothes off, William."

"Really, Jake, I didn't know you cared… and if we are going to have an intimate relationship, I insist you call me Bill." Leonard removed his pants and shirt. He was in surprisingly good physical condition Jake noted.

"And," Jake added as an afterthought, "I'm taking all of the shoes with me, too." He looked at Bob and told him that he would drop someone off to relieve him the next morning.

Jake could not believe the relief that swept over him as he exited the room, locked the door, and walked to his car to go home for a shower, a good meal, and some sleep.

Alex stood at the bottom of the stairs waiting for him when Jake arrived home. It was the first time since September that the two men sat alone in the living room for a long conversation. Meredith had gone to Montrose the day before to deliver final plans to Dr. Dean and had been caught in the blizzard, unable to drive home. No wonder Alex was so jumpy, Jake thought.

Jake gave Alex a blow-by-blow description of what had happened since his departure. Alex sat, elbows on his knees, hands under his chin, listening intently. It was hard to believe it had all happened.

"And Customs?" he asked, when Jake paused for a moment.

Jake gave such an animated description of how Leonard had gotten back into the country when they went through Customs in New Jersey, Alex laughed. After a moment, Jake did, too.

"Nothing illegal… American Passport with an exit stamp from the U.S. on December 30th, same date as ours. He had an exit stamp from Munich showing he legitimately left Germany on the 1st." Jake looked at Alex for a moment. There was a long pause.

"He's not working alone," he said softly. "It worries me."

Chapter 29

The drive back to the ranch took two hours, but they were home by noon. Alex was just returning from his lab and stopped at the front door, waiting for the two cars to join him. As Meredith's car neared the house, he picked up the snow shovel and made sure there was a path from the porch to her car door.

"He never does that for me," Jake quipped as he exited the SUV.

Meredith stepped into her husband's waiting arms and they did what all lovers who have been separated do: They patted one another's backs as they hugged and, with eyes closed, smiled over each other's shoulders. It was obvious how good it was to be home, Jake thought. He, too, smiled.

"I've got to go to my place and take care of William Leonard," Jake said.

"Thanks, Jake," Alex called to him.

Jake had gotten up early to drive to Montrose so he could follow Meredith home on the icy highways. Alex had been worried about her. Before meeting her at the motel, Jake stopped by the hardware store in Montrose and purchased three twenty foot segments of small-link but relatively sturdy chains. He got several combination locks that would fit through two links when they were pulled together. He had to find a reliable way to restrain Leonard.

It was a dire solution for a dire circumstance and would be necessary for only a short time. He hated to do it, but could see no alternative. Jake had thought about it most of the night. He would be gone for weeks. Alex would be gone the first two days after they retrieved the clones and would then be busy reconditioning them. Bill Bryant and Bob Grosvenor and Brett would be providing security for the Real Things… gone. There would be no one to baby sit Leonard. They only had three days before their departure. There was not enough time to hire and train another special guard for William Leonard. Leonard knew about the clones. He knew about their plans to replace them. Quite simply, they could not risk his escape.

As Jake parked in front of his new home, he zipped his jacket against the cold and tucked the casual clothes he had borrowed from J.J. Branchman under his arm. The two men were approximately the same size, he thought.

He removed his sun glasses as he entered the house and was startled to see William Leonard, in his shorts and tee-shirt, feeding Bill Bryant a bowl of vegetable soup. Bryant had relieved Grosvenor that morning. He sat in a kitchen chair, hands secured behind him with duct tape Jake had left behind.

"Hi, Jake," Leonard called out, jovially. "We need to talk, you and I."

Jake checked out the area around Leonard and noted nothing that could be construed as a weapon was within his reach. He walked across the room, took a knife from his pocket, and removed the duct tape from Bryant's hands.

"Sorry, Jake… he caught me off guard!" Bryant apologized.

"Don't worry about it, Bill. Learn from it." He paused and then moved close to Leonard, looking directly into his eyes at an almost nose-to-nose distance. "You want to try your fast moves on me, my intimate friend Bill?"

"I'm serious, Jake," Leonard said quietly. "We need to talk. Can we just sit down and do that… like civilized people?"

"When did you become civilized, Leonard?" Jake whispered. "You sit! Now!" The other man did as commanded and Jake turned his attention to Bill Bryant. "Are you okay?"

Bryant's feelings were hurt and he was embarrassed, but otherwise, he was fine.

"You stand right here, behind this son of a bitch, with your hands on his shoulders. If you feel so much as a muscle in his body twitch, slam him against the nearest wall," Jake directed Bryant. "If you wait to see what caused the twitch, it will be too late. I've got to get some things out of the car."

When Jake walked back into the room carrying the heavy box filled with chains and locks, William Leonard paled.

"For God's sake, Jake, you have my clothes and my shoes and it's freezing outside. How the hell can I escape? If I wanted to escape, I could have… it's why I overcame this fine young man… to prove to you I don't intend to go anywhere. You don't need to do this. Really you don't!"

Jake just looked at him disdainfully. "When you tied up Mr. Bryant, you sent me a message, loud and clear. There's an unchanging principle involved here, Bill… as a good friend once told me. For every action, there is a reaction."

He threw a pair of blue jeans and a flannel shirt at him and told him to get dressed. When that was done, he tossed a pair of fleece-lined slippers at Leonard and told him he hoped they fit. "These will keep your feet warm indoors. Now," he directed the man, "sit!"

"Do you want me to roll over? Speak? Or do a sit-stay?" Leonard asked, sarcastically. "You're giving me commands people give dogs!"

"Whatever flicks your flint," Jake replied softly. He had Bryant resume his position behind Leonard, hands on his shoulders. "If he moves, slam his ass on the floor."

Jake bent down and fastened the chain around Leonard's ankle, then locked it in place. It was not too tight, but sufficiently snug that he couldn't wiggle his foot through it. He got his electric drill and attached a round iron tether pin to the floor so he could fasten the other end of the chain to it. "The way I calculate it, Bill, you will be able to get to the stove and refrigerator, the bathroom next to the kitchen, the kitchen table, and a chair I'll place nearby. That means, when no one else is here, you will be able to survive nicely… I would advise you to be very careful with fire, however."

He told Bryant he could let go of Leonard's shoulders. Jake smiled at him. He asked if he wanted to finish his soup before returning home.

Bryant hesitated a moment, then shook his head and thanked Jake with the look he gave him and a hand to his shoulder. He picked up his jacket and walked to the door.

"Now, Mr. Leonard," he said amiably, "what was it you wanted to discuss with me?"

Leonard just looked at Jake, shaking his head. "I've been detained by Americans, by the Swiss, the Russians, the Panamanians, the Germans, and a couple of others. You're brutal, by comparison," he said in a tone designed to make Jake feel badly about his methods.

"So," Jake replied, casually, "you want to discuss my brutality?"

"No, no, of course not," Leonard answered impatiently. He needed to tell this man his story and try to gain his help. "I want to tell you why I imposed myself on you to get back into the country and why I was behaving so erratically yesterday and the day before."

Jake just looked at him. "I'm listening."

"Last item first... I'm bi-polar. I had one dose of medication with me and wanted to save it for the day after you took me wherever you were going to take me so I'd be in the right frame of mind to tell you what I need to tell you. I took the medication this morning." Leonard paused and waited for a reaction. "I don't know if you're familiar with the disease, but it can take you to imaginative highs and then crush you on the rocks of despair in the deepest valley."

Jake removed a piece of paper from his pocket and gave Leonard a ballpoint pen. "Write down the name of your medication and the dosage you take," he told him. "I'll make sure you have what you need." He paused while Leonard wrote. "Why did you have only one does of medicine?" he asked.

"It was the way they controlled my movements in Austria," he replied quietly. "Thank you for offering to get my medication. I'll need it by tomorrow or I'll be off on another flight of fancy."

"What else?"

Leonard heaved a big sigh before continuing. "Thanks for the clothes, too. I really did contain that nice young man to show you I have no intention of leaving," he said. "I'm safe here and would not be, anywhere else. I didn't hurt Bryant... I could have, but I didn't. Does that count for anything?"

"All that tells me, Bill, is that you were smart enough to know you would freeze your butt before you got to civilization. You have a need to control your own environment. That's okay, unless you force yourself on someone else in *their* environment. When you do, the invaded party gets to set the rules. You know that." Jake never broke eye contact with Leonard as he spoke. The other man nodded.

"I'll bet you were a damned good agent in your day," Leonard commented.

The two men looked at each other for what to Jake seemed a very long time before Leonard broke the silence.

"Let me tell you what I know," he said somewhat hesitantly. "And I promise you that for the next ten minutes every word I tell you will be the truth."

Jake smiled and shook his head. This guy was inimitable... and when in a reasonable mood, had a certain charm.

William Leonard began a story that raised even Jake's eyebrows. What he knew about how the socialist democracies of the world planned to force one world government on sovereign nations went far beyond the assumptions and estimations he, Alex, and Meredith had made. It was the strangest tale Jake had ever heard. Leonard documented everything he said to such a degree, it was impossible not to believe him. "That comes from all of the research I did on this subject for President McCoy before he left office and that one-worlder wimp replaced him," Leonard finished.

"How did you find out about all of this – about the things that go beyond what would be considered Presidential research?" Jake asked. Leonard's ten minutes of truth extended to a half-hour before he stopped talking. He was awaiting a response and Jake was not yet ready to give him one. "Your ten minutes of sworn truth ended twenty minutes ago," he told Leonard.

"You can extend my oath of truth to the duration of this conversation," Leonard said without blinking. "I have a network... an underground network of guys like you and Brett – and, me," he said. "Intelligence operatives who joined MI-5 or the CIA or the old KGB with good intentions and who, like you and like me, became disgusted with political corruption. You know it and I know it. Organized crime is running things... that southern border of ours has to stay open to accommodate the transportation of illegal drugs. It has to stay open to provide slave labor for major corporations. I can tell you about you, Aleksandr Plotnikov, and the clones stolen from Sakhalin Island last September, if you'd like to hear it," William Leonard told him in a casual tone of voice.

He did not trust himself to let Leonard see his reaction. Jake rose from his seat, rubbing his beard. "Is that how you found out my real name? From your underground spy network?" He walked to the stove and turned the burner on under the pot of soup. "Would you like some soup, Bill?"

"Yeah," Leonard's one-word response was said softly.

"Yeah, you want soup? Or, yeah that's how you got my name?"

Jake looked in the refrigerator to see what was there and pulled out two cans of Coors Light. He handed one to William Leonard.

"Thanks for the beer, but don't give me the buddy treatment, Jake... I know you don't like or trust me. What you and Alex are planning to do when you return the four men you stole from Sakhalin to their jobs is... it's marvelous! It equates to replacing lies with truth. And don't pretend you aren't dying to know how I know all this stuff. It doesn't fly." After a brief moment he added, "And yeah, that's how I got your real name."

Jake turned to look directly at William Leonard. He leaned against the refrigerator, sipping his beer for a moment, staring at the other man, before he spoke. "What do you know about the clones?"

"Good question," the response came. "I can tell you where each one of them has a tracking device planted, if it will help your replacement effort," he said, grinning.

"Of course it would help," Jake responded. "But how can I trust what you tell me? You strike me as someone who periodically has trouble with truth-telling, William."

Leonard laughed and it sounded harsh. "You're right," he offered in return. "My lifestyle has left me with the need to lie as a matter of protection. I know you've been away from it for a long time, but you know what I'm talking about, Jake. I'll make you a deal. When we talk about this subject, I swear I'll be totally truthful with you. If I don't want to answer a question you ask, though, I won't respond and you won't push me. Deal?" He held out his hand. Jake was almost hesitant to shake the man's hand but he finally did.

"What do you know about Aleksandr Plotnikov?" Jake asked slowly.

Leonard thought for a moment before responding. "I don't know a lot about your history with him... where you met or how or if you were involved in his departure from the Soviet Union," he began, "but I know it was you who got four men from Sakhalin Island – probably with Bob and Bill and Brett helping you. They match the description given by a guard who was overcome the night of your raid on the camp. I know the only person who could have provided the information you needed to pull that off is Aleksandr Plotnikov. A guy by the name of Malashenko – Yuri Malashenko, who used to work with Plotnikov on Sakhalin Island – knows it, too. He has stepped up the search for him, Jake. It won't take them much longer to tie Plotnikov to you. So far, they've run into a blank wall."

Jake sat, tipped his chair back and raised his arms, placed his hands on his head and rubbed his scalp with both hands. "William Leonard, I swear to God I do not know what to do with you. Let me ask you one question... and if you cannot answer truthfully, Bill, don't answer. It's important. Okay?"

Leonard nodded slowly, watching Jake intently.

"Do you know where you are?" Jake asked.

Leonard answered without hesitation. "No. No, I do not. I've figured out that we are somewhere in the Western United States just based on the flying time it took us to get here. I will tell you that I don't think you've taken me very far from where you first dropped Arthur off... though the hour in the air was a genius idea – something I would have done. But I don't know if we're in Wyoming, Utah, Colorado, or New Mexico... we can't be in Oregon, Montana or Washington because the flight time from Arizona wasn't long enough..."

"That's the God's truth?" Jake asked, trying not to sound skeptical.

"It is," Leonard replied in a serious tone.

Jake took his cell phone from his pocket and called Alex. When his friend answered, Jake told him he needed to get in the

Jeep and join him and their guest. To say Alex was shocked was an understatement.

Fifteen minutes later, Jake heard the Jeep pull into his driveway. He walked to the door and waited for his friend to join them.

"Alex, this is William Leonard… and he knows all about you. He knows things you need to know… about Yuri Malashenko and how he has stepped up his search for you since we visited Sakhalin Island." Jake paused, watching the two men. "He doesn't know where he is and, for now, we're not going to tell him. You two need to talk."

Jake turned to Leonard and asked, "Truth time again?"

"Yes," Leonard replied. Jake was surprised by the look of absolute respect on Leonard's face as he shook hands with Alex.

The three men sat at the table and Jake began the conversation by giving Alex an overview of what Leonard had told him thus far. Alex sat with elbows on the table, arms bent and his right hand covering his mouth. He stared at the table as Jake spoke. When he finished talking, Alex looked directly at Leonard.

"Is there anything you would add to what Jake just said? Anything you'd change?" Alex asked the man.

"No," Leonard said speaking in a soft, low tone. "Jake got it right." He paused. "Is there anything you would like to ask me? I hold you and what you've done in very high regard, Dr. Plotnikov. I'd like to help you, if I can." He got up to walk to the sink and the sound of the chain attached to Leonard's leg caused Alex to raise his eyebrows.

"What in the world…" he began.

"Alex, what else can I do with this guy? When I got here, he had Bill Bryant tied up," Jake said and then followed quickly with a request for Alex to keep it to himself because Bryant was embarrassed by his lapse.

Leonard turned towards Jake, smiling. "I told you what you are doing is abusive," he said and then chuckled.

"Let me get this issue on the table and settled," Jake began in an exasperated tone. "In fact, Bill, my intimate friend, I want your input on this issue, too."

Leonard returned to his seat. Jake knew he had gone to the sink for water to make sure Alex saw his chains.

He turned to Alex and described their problem. Jake explained the danger Leonard posed if he escaped before the clones were kidnapped and the Real Things were returned. They had no way of knowing whose side he was on.

"Who is going to be here to guard him, Alex? With one phone call, he could put Meredith in grave danger. Do you want to take that risk?"

Alex shook his head. "No, no I do not," he answered. He smiled at Jake and then looked directly at William Leonard.

"Do you see our problem?" he asked their prisoner. "What would you do in our place?"

Jake marveled at how quickly Alex could read people. He had asked William Leonard precisely the right question. He was giving Leonard an opportunity to advise them on how they should control his future... which, in essence, put a control freak in charge of establishing guidelines to control his future. Some of the same thoughts must have been going through Leonard's mind. He looked admiringly at Alex.

"Good question," he responded. "If I were you and faced with me as a problem, I would go to Arthur Redbridge and ask him to give you as much in-depth information about me as he can. Redbridge is very high on you two and you can trust what he tells you. Just so you know, Jake, he told me nothing about you or Alex. All he told me was that he is going to return to Washington and needs access to the money I have so the trade deficit and national debt can be handled.

"Second, I would calculate how to use what I know to your benefit without risking my escape." He paused. "Jake is right. From your perspective, you must consider me a danger to your project and there isn't sufficient time for me to gain your trust. I understand that will take time. If I were you, I would give me all of the information about your plans to return these guys to office and I would ask me to give you a one-day review of it." Again, Leonard paused. His demeanor and tone was totally focused and quite serious. His hand gestures were studied and added to his perceived sincerity.

"Third, I would make sure that Arthur Redbridge and I got to spend as much time together as possible before he leaves. He cannot gain access to the funds he needs without me and we need to formulate an in-depth plan. Fourth, Jake is right. You need to keep me totally contained until the clones are returned... but you need to do it in a place where Redbridge and I have close communication as events unfold, Alex. It would be a mistake not to utilize the knowledge I am putting at your disposal."

Jake and Alex looked at one another. "You always said there'd be a problem we wouldn't exactly know how to deal with before this was over," Alex said to Jake. His voice sounded almost sad. Was this a surprise that could burst the bubble of all their plans and work? Alex couldn't help but wonder as he looked across the room.

"I can tell you where we are going to start," Jake told Leonard. "First, I'm going to call a friend of mine who is a physician. I'll get your medication so you won't have any more down time. I'll have it here by morning," he assured him. "Second, I'm going to bring you a variety of video tapes we have... of planning sessions, training sessions, interviews, and a lot of other data, so you can spend tonight and tomorrow morning studying it." He rose from his seat at the table and turned to Leonard, pointing at him as he spoke. "And, third, I'm going to figure out the most humane way I can ensure you remain in captivity for the next two weeks. By then, it won't matter if you get loose. Alex, his wife, and I will have a long talk about you tonight."

Leonard looked at him, a curious expression on his face. "His wife?" he asked.

"You'll see her on the video tapes," Alex told him. Then, looking at Jake, he continued. "We need to get a television set, a VCR, and any other information Mr. Leonard needs to do his work. We might as well get started... will you mind if we leave you here alone, Mr. Leonard?"

Leonard enjoyed the show of respect from Alex and the pleased expression on his face showed it. "I promise" he said, "I'll be here when you get back. And, no I do not mind. Thank you for asking."

With that, the two friends left what they both considered a giant-sized question mark sitting chained to the floor of Jake's new house.

They hastened to the ranch so they could get back to make sure he was still there. Brett would be watching Leonard within a half-hour. William Leonard rose from his chair, stretched, and served himself another bowl of soup. He was smiling.

It took two hours for Jake and Alex to gather the videos and documents and the technology to support them and get them loaded into the SUV. They were relieved to see Brett sitting at the table talking with William Leonard, still wearing his chain, when they returned.

"I'm going to put this stuff in your bedroom, Bill," Jake told him. "There is room in there for a computer table and I'll get that hooked up before we leave, too. You won't be able to get any entertainment television, but you will be able to watch the videos on it. Frankly, if you get through everything by tomorrow afternoon, I'll be surprised."

The next hour was a flurry of activity as Alex, Jake and Brett unloaded all of the equipment they had brought with them and got everything set up. Leonard told them he would be glad to help, but his restraints prevented it. He laughed. Brett still did not know what to make of the man.

Jake placed another round metal tether in the bedroom floor and unlocked the chain between the living room and kitchen, moving Leonard into his bedroom. When he and Alex left, the man was sitting studiously in front of his television watching video tapes.

Meredith had dinner ready when the two tired men returned to the ranch. As she listened to the whole William Leonard story, she could feel the strength of the personality of this man Leonard whom she had never met.

"So," she asked at the end of their monologues, "what are you going to do with him?"

"What do you think we should do?" Alex asked.

"Based on what you just said, I have to agree with Leonard. The first thing we need to do is talk with Arthur." She paused for a moment, biting her lip as she thought. "And, I think we should do that right now."

"We're all in agreement, then," Jake said. He got up and put on his jacket. When he returned, a curious Arthur Redbridge was with him.

"Hi," Meredith greeted him with a hug at the bottom of the entryway stairs. She took his arm and led him to his chair. He noticed the scramblers on the large, solid mahogany coffee table.

Jake explained Leonard's bi-polar condition and why he had medication for only one day with him and why he had waited to use it. "I'll have the medicine delivered to him by morning… we don't want any more episodes."

Redbridge just nodded. "And you wanted to get together for an evening chat because…"

"Because," Alex interjected "William Leonard suggested we ask you about him."

"Yep," Jake agreed. "He knows a lot about the four men that were stolen from Sakhalin Island last September. He believes the two of you should spend tomorrow together working on your plans to implement the pay-back of America's national and foreign debt. Alex and I would like to know how you feel about that. We'd like to know anything you can tell us about him. There are times he seems to be truthful and forthright, and there are times he appears to have never met a word called truth." Jake's raised eyebrows asked the question for him.

Redbridge frowned. His elbows were on his knees, his hands clasped in front of them, as he leaned forward to offer an opinion. "You know almost as much about Leonard's background as I do," he began. "The reports you got were pretty thorough. So, I assume you mean what do I know about him personally?" Everyone nodded. "Well, he's a strange duck, no doubt about it. He's probably the most intelligent person I've ever met. As you know, his background is business, finance, and investments. The intelligence connections he has are rather phenomenal – and I think he made them on his own hook, Jake. He met a few people from the CIA while working for President McCoy. Most of his contacts were made on his own, though."

"His contacts seem to be excellent," Jake interjected. "He says they are mostly intelligence operatives who are disgusted with the governments around the world they served. Do you know anything about that?"

Redbridge shook his head. "Not specifically," he answered. "But I can tell you that he generally knew more about what was going on in the covert world than anyone employed by the government's intelligence services." Again, he paused. "He has a strange thing about truth, I agree. He lied to me, many times... but I always got the feeling that it was done to cover something up – to protect himself. Whenever he swore he was telling the truth, I never caught him in a lie. He draws a very distinct line between truth and untruth. He seems to lie because he has to, and tells the truth only when he is volunteering something. Does that help?" he asked.

Again, three heads nodded. "What do you think of spending some time with him?" Meredith asked.

"When I return to office, there are things I can do to stop the velocity of the movement to establish a North American Union with Canada, the United States, and Mexico. I can complain to the other two governments about the currency values of the three countries. I can cause a delay. I can change a few policies and slow inflation down and cause the rate of savings to go up... borrowing rates will go up too, by the way. Business growth will slow as a result, making a temporary downturn economically almost a sure thing. But the only thing that is going to destroy America and result in an absolute *need* for us to join with Mexico and Canada is the number of American dollars being held by foreign governments, the over-printing of our currency by the Federal Central Bank, and inflation. The only solution to that problem is William Leonard and the money he has stashed around the world. There is no doubt his input will be required to get this done. He's the guy with all the aces in his hand... he has the money." Redbridge paused for a long moment. "Do I need to spend time talking with him? Hell yes, I do."

As Redbridge stopped speaking, it was almost as if a collective sigh went around the room.

"So," Alex offered, "it sounds like it would be a good idea to move Bill Bryant and Bob Grosvenor to Jake's new place and bring William Leonard to the bunkhouse. Jake, you'd better explain the circumstances to Arthur."

Jake put his hand to his mouth and coughed, then cleared his throat. "Well, you see, uh... at the moment William Leonard is wearing chains."

Meredith and Arthur both exclaimed "What?" For the third time that day, Jake launched into an explanation of why Leonard was in chains.

"He could upset the entire party we're planning," Jake commented warily. "Can we trust him? We won't know that for some time. If he told the Russians what we are up to before we have a chance to throw our welcome home party, it could endanger everyone's life. If anyone has a better suggestion, please tell me."

"Can't we just lock him up in Bryant's and Grosvenor's old room?" Meredith asked.

Again, Jake sighed. "Meredith, when I went to the house this morning, Leonard had Bill Bryant tied up and was feeding him some of your vegetable beef soup." Both Arthur and Meredith audibly gasped. "How hard do you think it would be for one of the best covert operatives I've ever met to overcome Nancy when she takes him his evening meal?"

"I see the problem," she said, thoughtfully. Redbridge nodded his agreement.

"Okay, Arthur," Jake said, rising. "I'll give you a ride home. If I were you, I'd get the best night's sleep you've ever had because it may be the last one you have for awhile." He paused briefly. "William Leonard will be moving into the bunkhouse tomorrow."

Chapter 30

The morning of January 5, 2007 dawned grey and threatening. It took until noon to get the bedroom at the bunkhouse ready for William Leonard's occupancy.

Leonard was amused. So he had to use the blind glasses again for the ride between Jake's cabin and the ranch, he thought. What did it matter? He was moving to where the action of a critical intelligence ploy was occurring. He willingly complied.

After Jake and Alex led Leonard down the hall to his new room, the dark glasses were removed.

"Well," Leonard said smiling at everyone, "this is certainly pleasant... an improvement for me over Salzburg and the two days I spent at Jake's house... no ingratitude intended, Jake," he chuckled.

Redbridge introduced the new tenant to Nancy and Joe. Jake explained where everything was. There was a computer ready and waiting on the patio table and Leonard walked to the patio, looking up at the skylight. "Are we in an underground shelter?" he asked, looking up at the earthen slabs that surrounded the window.

Jake cleared his throat and told him the bunkhouse was on Alex's and Meredith's ranch. "It's an earth home." Leonard pursed his mouth and nodded his head admiringly.

"To what are you going to hook my chain, Jake?" he asked in an amused tone of voice.

"Well, Bill, do you remember that I told you Bill Bryant – the guy you manhandled yesterday – was a computer genius?" Leonard looked at him, puzzled, and nodded.

"Well, Mr. Bryant put together a computer program which, once I input a code as I am going to do in a moment, will only allow the room door to open if you are on the patio, holding down a key on the computer. Isn't that ingenious?"

Jake chuckled at the look of admiration that came over Leonard's face. "One added feature is that the program only works when the bedroom patio door is closed and locked. So, there is no way you can be anywhere but locked up in your underground patio when someone else enters or leaves your room. I know you'll enjoy it more than your chains, right?"

Leonard actually laughed and it surprised everyone. "This is marvelous! I love creative solutions to complicated problems! No chains but all of the security you need. Beautiful!"

Jake asked Arthur if he was ready to spend the rest of the afternoon with the latest addition to their team. Leonard tried to hide the small smile. He failed.

Jake got everyone but himself, Leonard and Redbridge out of the room and closed the door. He entered the patio and keyed in a code. He walked quickly from the room, closing the door behind him. The room's occupants heard two locks click: The room door locking behind Jake and the patio door unlocking. Leonard raised his eyebrows, smiling. Jake had not said another word to either man when he departed the room. As he exited, Jake looked at Alex and just shook his head.

"Okay," Alex said in a quiet tone. "Let's read the review he wrote."

Leonard's report was not long, but was extremely insightful. For one thing, he recommended that Jake use a plane other than the Lear jet to transport the Real Things home from Vermont, Maine and Fort Lauderdale. He also suggested when transporting the clones back to the ranch, Gil use a small city airport close – but not too close – to the ranch. The drive home would not be too risky, but far enough away to provide any clues about where the ranch was located. That meant not using Rifle, Grand Junction or any of the other mountain airports.

The reason Leonard gave for his suggestion was that his own disappearance from Munich occurred at the same time the Lear jet departed that city. There were, he assumed, records at other airports when the plane had been used – things that could be cross-referenced. Jake thought about using the Lear when the Real Things were removed from Sakhalin Island, and when Meredith moved to the ranch from Denver. It could easily show up on a computer model. It could be tracked too close to home. It was a good point.

He further recommended that Gil should be at the airport where the clones would be brought after being kidnapped. He should take off with an empty Lear jet shortly after they arrived and fly to Oregon or California. They should, he said, use the plane as a dupe in the likely case it was being tracked. If it was, it would throw the trackers totally off the trail. It would lead them to wherever Gil flew. This, too, was a good idea, Jake decided.

The other major recommendation Leonard made was that special precautions be taken if Alex went on the trip to retrieve the clones. He felt strongly that the clones would be watched carefully during their vacation time. General Yuri Malashenko, he told them, was a very thorough man. Leonard told Jake that the General was now stationed at the Russian Embassy in New York City. He had to know that if the clones were going to be targeted for removal, the best time to do it was during the holidays while they were away from their usual security details. He would have eyes everywhere looking for Aleksandr Plotnikov.

Three copies of Leonard's report were printed and Jake told his roommates there would be an after-dinner meeting to review it.

"He's right about the first two primary suggestions he has made," Jake said after all three of them had taken their seats and security had been implemented. "I've already leased a larger plane to carry everyone from Grand Junction to the East coast... the Lear isn't big enough for everyone. I *was* planning to use the Lear to return the kidnapped clones back to Rifle, though. As Leonard points out, there are records from the various times we used the plane. Gil was the pilot of record. His flight plans reflect it. If they're tracking Gil or the Lear and it heads anywhere close to the East coast, they will be on it like moths to a flame."

Alex and Meredith had little to say beyond agreeing with the basic premise of the statement. After thinking about it for a moment, Alex asked Jake about the larger jet he had rented. "Do you think we should leave from Grand Junction? Will they be watching for private planes from this area?"

Jake pondered the questions. He looked into the fireplace as he thought. Maybe he could find the right answers there. "Good question. It might be better for us to leave from a larger airport... the headquarters of the plane rental is Las Vegas. It would probably be a good idea to leave from there. They have a dozen private planes a day that fly people non-stop to the East coast. We wouldn't look at all out of place, leaving from there. Gil's name won't be on the flight manifest... he won't be piloting our plane.

"The jet I've rented holds fourteen passengers. I need to go to Vegas tomorrow to make sure they'll be able to use the same plane to bring the three clones, Dr. Dean – and whoever accompanies them – back home. But I don't think we should fly the clones or you back into a major airport like McCarran International. We need a smaller airport. I'm sure we can work it out... if they can't do it, I'll make other arrangements." Jake paused. "I like Leonard's idea about having the Lear jet on the ground at the airport when we bring the clones home, then having Gil fly an empty plane to Oregon or California after they land in Nevada. We'll put the clones in a rented RV and drive them home while they sleep. If anyone's tracking Gil or the plane, they'll be led away from the ranch. That has to be a primary objective for now."

"Indeed it does," Meredith said quietly as she moved to sit on the floor between Alex's legs. His hands automatically began to massage her shoulders and it made Jake smile. They were already developing the habits of an old married couple.

Jake cleared his throat. "Which airport do we use to bring the clones home?" he asked them.

"How about using the Mesquite, Nevada airport?" Meredith suggested. "It's small and the drive from Mesquite to the ranch is just over eight hours. I'd think landing in the Nevada desert would be safer than landing close to the mountains. It's January in Colorado," she said meaningfully.

Jake paused. "I want to run this by Leonard to see what he thinks."

William Leonard had been well-fed and had showered in preparation for bed. He was in pajamas and house slippers when Jake called to him through Nancy's intercom.

"Hey, Bill, it's Jake. If you have a minute to discuss your review, I'd appreciate it. Would you press the correct computer key to let me in?"

Jake heard a chuckle before he let up on the intercom key. He smiled at Nancy and thanked her and headed to the last room on the right side of the hallway. He knocked and in about five seconds he heard the door lock click and he entered the room. Leonard was standing on his patio with a big smile on his face and his finger on a computer key.

"Okay, Bill, you can let the key up now," Jake told him. When he did, Jake told him to hit the Enter key. He did and the patio door unlocked.

"This is some system you put together overnight," he said. "The people here – Joe and Nancy – lovely people," he smiled. "My review. You want to talk about it?"

Jake walked into the patio area. "It's well done and, we're changing the plan based on your input," Jake told him. Leonard smiled broadly.

"Glad I could help," he said quietly, nodding his head.

"I want to bounce our new plan off of you." Jake took a seat at the patio table and indicated to Leonard that he should do the same. He began explaining how they were thinking of using his suggestions. Leonard listened, raptly.

"It's a good plan," Leonard said. "But I think you're overlooking one asset you have and are not using properly," he stated.

Puzzled, Jake asked him what he was talking about.

"Me," Leonard said. Before Jake could say anything, Leonard held both of his hands up in front of his chest, fingers spread. "I know, I know. You don't know enough about me and you don't trust me. I don't blame you… but let me change your scenario just a tiny bit," he said.

He then proceeded to tell Jake how easy it would be for him go with them on the trip to return the Real Things, get off of the plane with Alex in Vermont, stay there while Jake and the others kidnapped the clones, then be on the plane carrying the clones back to the Mesquite airport while Alex stayed put waiting to accompany the Redbridge clone back to Colorado the next day.

"It's winter, Jake. You are depending on being able to fly the clones and Alex back to Mesquite, fly the plane with Alex on it back to Baltimore to pick up the Redbridge clone the next morning, then fly back to Mesquite again. It would be far easier, less expensive, and more certain if you rented a second plane in Baltimore and Alex stayed on the East coast to wait for the Redbridge clone.

"Airplane seats are bolted to the floor, Jake. Alex can put the chain on me and attach it to a metal seat leg… I won't be able to go anywhere. Make the chain short enough to keep me away from the cockpit. Think about it," Leonard said encouragingly. "It will save you hours of time because your pilot won't have to make two round trips to the East Coast within forty-eight hours. It reduces your risk of uncontrollable error caused by weather or mechanical failure. Gil takes off for the West Coast in the Lear while Joe and I drive the clones home… I'll even wear your damned glasses." Leonard laughed as if the thought amused him. "That way, Alex can stay on the Coast and wait for the Redbridge clone, Joe returns to Mesquite to pick them up, and… it's a done deal."

Jake just looked at the man. What he was saying was true. "I'll talk with Alex and see what he and Meredith want to do. I'm sorry I can't say any more than that right now." Jake looked directly into Leonard's eyes the entire time he spoke.

"I understand. I want to help if I can." He smiled. "I want Arthur Redbridge back in office so we can finish what we started all those years ago! Hell, it ought to be a very quiet flight with a doctor on board to keep the three clones asleep. Mesquite's a good choice of a winter airport, by the way."

Jake stood. "Do you know which computer key to punch so I can leave?" Jake asked.

"Yes, I know how it works," he said quietly. Jake waved goodbye, heard the patio door lock then waited a few seconds for the room door to unlock. Once in the hallway, he waited to make sure the room door re-locked behind him. It did.

Alex had placed two large logs in the fireplace and the lights were turned low. Music played softly in the background. It was a warm and welcoming room, Jake thought.

After re-seating himself, Jake looked sadly at Alex. "He's right about you not taking an active role, Alex. If they're looking for you, it could endanger the entire operation." Jake let the report fall in his lap. He knew this would hit Alex where he lived. He was there at the beginning of the clones and he wanted to be there for the end of the story.

"My presence could endanger the operation," Alex said softly. He was surprised... and hurt. No one said anything in response. Jake just nodded.

Alex grunted a response. "I see what you mean," he said, frowning. "So, who will replace me? Who will baby sit the clones on the flight home? You will be watching Meredith and coordinating the Redbridge accident. Bryant will be with J.J.; Grosvenor will be with Senator Martinez. Brett will be with Justice Scott and working with you on the Redbridge accident. The clones will be knocked out at the point of the kidnap and Dr. Dean will be on the plane with them coming home to make sure they get proper fluids. He is not there to guard them, though. Who will stay with the clones for the ride home?" Alex was irritated and it showed.

Jake heaved a deep sigh, running the fingers of both hands through his hair as he thought. "Well," he said, pulling his chair to an upright position and leaning forward. "I have an even better question, Alex. If you are on the plane with the first three replaced clones, who will be on the plane with Arthur Redbridge a day later if we have bad weather or a mechanical failure?"

The room became very quiet. "Without the flexibility of the Lear jet, we're a person short, aren't we?" Alex asked.

"Someone needs to be on the first plane load of clones on the 8th, and someone needs to be on a plane with the Redbridge clone on the 9th." There was a long pause. "As long as we were using the Lear, it was no problem. That one glitch changes everything."

"Or," Jake breathed deeply, clearing his throat, "or, we could take William Leonard's suggestion and let him fly home with the first three clones."

Alex's eyes widened at the statement. "A day ago, you weren't even going to let this guy close to the ranch. Now you're talking about letting him participate in the project?" He couldn't believe Jake was suggesting such a thing.

"We need to find another person someplace, Alex. Keep in mind, unless Redbridge is successfully returned to office, William Leonard's problems can't be solved. So, he has a lot of motivation to get the clones kidnapped and back here safely. Who besides him do you suggest?" He paused and then explained the ways Leonard had suggested he might be able to help and the restrictions he was willing to endure, including chains and blind glasses.

"So, he would be on the ground with me, at a motel in Vermont, for about twenty-four hours. I would put him on the plane, chain him to a seat, and send him back to Mesquite with Gil and Dr. Dean?" Actually, the more Alex thought about the idea, the better it sounded. He would rather have Leonard with him in a motel room where he could control him than leave the man at the ranch, unattended by anyone but Nancy and Joe.

"Okay. We take him with us... as you said, he can stay with me at the motel in Burlington," Alex said.

"I think you should rent a second plane in Baltimore rather than rely on no problems with the one you lease in Las Vegas... as I keep saying, it's winter in Colorado," Meredith offered. "Flying back to Colorado with the first three clones, then using the same plane to fly back to the East coast before noon to pick up Arthur's clone and Alex is taking a chance... and, it wastes a lot of time."

Jake chuckled. "That's what Leonard said, Meredith. He made the same recommendation."

"They're both right," Alex commented. "You can spend the night in Baltimore with Meredith and Arthur," he concluded. "With the accident planned for the next morning, you'll need a good night's sleep." Again, he thought for a moment. It was always a surprise how one small glitch in the middle of a big plan meant everything had to be changed. He also realized it was better to identify the glitch now. He did not want Yuri Malashenko to be waiting for them at the Lear jet as they brought the kidnapped clones home.

"Well, I'll see what I can get worked out with the leasing company in Las Vegas tomorrow," Jake said. "You know how I like last minute changes."

They all decided that they hated these kinds of changes, but after reviewing the plan one more time everyone felt the changes actually strengthened things.

"Okay... then. I'm going to my place in Rifle to spend the night," Jake said as he headed for the door.

"Wait..." Meredith said, stopping him at the bottom of the stairs. She squirmed in her chair for a moment before asking a question she'd had on her mind ever since she met with Dr. Dean in Montrose a few days ago. "I... please don't misunderstand my question, Jake, but I want to know something." She hesitated and the room was quiet. "Why has Dr. Dean agreed to put himself and his career at such risk to help us? How much do you trust him?"

There was a long silence. Alex's head dropped and he looked at the floor, offering no response. Jake's mouth opened as if to answer, but no words were forthcoming.

"I think I see," Meredith said quietly. "For how many of his patients have you cloned new organs?" she asked Alex. When there was no answer, Meredith knew she had an answer. "I will probably never know how many people should be dead but are up and walking around thanks to you, will I?"

He raised his head and looked at her for just a moment. "I have a debt to pay." His voice was barely above a whisper.

The next day, Meredith was doing laundry and packing for her and Alex when she was startled by a knock on the front door. It was, she thought, the first time anyone had ever knocked at the door of the main house. She opened the retainer wall and peeked out the window. After turning the security system off, she opened the door. It was sunny outside, but cold air swept into the room as Bill Bryant entered carrying a large box. Bob Grosvenor came next, also carrying a box.

"Smells like food," Meredith said, smiling. "The caterer in Grand Junction again, right?"

They nodded and said they'd be back with Nancy's table. Jake and Alex wanted all of them to eat together tonight. It wasn't long before the first seven guests arrived. Arthur Redbridge, Avery Scott, John Martinez, J.J. Branchman, Brett Restov, Bill Bryant and Bob Grosvenor arrived without Alex or Jake accompanying them. They had walked to the house from the bunkhouse. This day, she realized, was going to be filled with surprises.

"Come in, come in," she smiled. "We don't have a bartender in residence at the moment, but Bob and J.J. can fill in... okay guys?" They smiled their agreement and walked to the built-in bar at the end of the kitchen counter. "Bill, can I get you to bring in a couple of logs to get the fire started?"

"No need," Alex's voice came from the front door. "I have the logs and Jake is coming right behind me with the champagne."

Everyone clapped. At just that moment, William Leonard entered with Jake close on his heels. Arthur Redbridge immediately walked to the bottom of the entryway stairs and shook Leonard's hand. Leonard did a double-take as the security wall closed. All he could say was "My, my..."

"I'd like for all of you to meet a very old friend of mine, Roger Marchman," Redbridge said. "He will be flying with us tomorrow."

Leonard was warmly greeted by everyone. Each of them remembered Redbridge's comment at the stable about a "confidential" issue involving their return. They assumed this was it. Nancy and Joe came to the door next. Nancy immediately shooed Meredith out of the kitchen and told her to join her guests. She could handle what needed to be done.

Darkness caused the patio cover to close and as it slowly pulled across the area at the back of the house, William Leonard just smiled. What a place, he thought!

Meredith turned her attention to the man named Roger Marchman. As she approached him, Alex grabbed her hand, put his arm around her and pulled her close.

"It's William Leonard," he whispered in her ear. She duly noted that his breath in her ear still caused butterflies in her stomach...

maybe even more now than a month ago. She turned her head and kissed him lightly on the cheek. She whispered to him that she had figured that out for herself. He smiled at her and took her to Leonard and introduced the two of them using Leonard's pseudonym, Roger Marchman.

"I'm one of your fans, Mrs. Plotnikov," Leonard said softly to her, bowing slightly. "I watched your video tapes with great interest. You have a very good grasp of what's happening in the world of international finance. I hope we'll get a chance to talk privately, some day."

She shook his hand and welcomed him to their home and turned to engage her other guests in conversation. Leonard watched her admiringly.

They gathered at the dining tables they had shared on two prior occasions and this time it was Alex who stood to propose a toast.

"My friends," he began, "please make sure your glasses are filled because this will very likely be our last occasion for toasts together. It is a memorable occasion. We will say 'goodbye' at this table tonight." He paused, looking at Meredith for a moment. "Though this is a moment that will never see the pages of a history book, if everything goes as planned, it is an historic event."

"No "Midnight Ride of Paul Revere' will be written here, hey Alex?" Branchman called.

Alex chuckled. He looked seriously at Redbridge, Scott, Martin and Branchman, holding the eyes of each for a brief second before moving from one to the other.

"You four men hold part of America's future in your hands. The plans you have devised to work together hold great power... positive power." The room was very quiet. "I know I'm talking too long..." he chuckled, but the room remained silent. "Let us drink to the Republic of America..." he said softly, and raised his glass. The others at the table repeated his final words and with great solemnity raised their glasses to drink in honor of their country. The room remained quiet as Meredith stood.

"The food isn't on the table yet, so don't worry about it getting cold," she began, laughing. They laughed with her. "I have to take this moment to tell the four of you what an honor it has been to meet and know you… to have shared an important moment of my life with you. I can only pray you recognize the significance of what you are about to do." She paused for a moment then raised her glass. "I toast the four of you. To the Real Things."

Glasses were raised and the toast reiterated by everyone.

"And now we can eat," Meredith said. She and Nancy began bringing in the various foods Alex had ordered for the occasion.

"I have to say," J.J. Branchman offered, "I have heard the best toasts ever made at this table – I know we'll never come back and will always wonder where we spent over three months of our lives, but I will always remember this house."

Arthur Redbridge stood and the talk quieted. "I think we should drink to what J.J. just said. We don't know the name of the place we have lived these past months, but I'll always think of it as a place called 'Freedom.' To Freedom!"

It was eight o'clock before everyone was gone and the kitchen clean-up was done.

"What time will we leave here in the morning?" Meredith asked the two men. She was determined to make their departure as little troubled as possible.

"Well, I'm flying to back to Las Vegas with the other guys in about an hour," Jake said. "They were going to go with me when I went earlier, but Alex wanted to do dinner. You guys have to be out of here by o-four-thirty in the morning," Jake's voice was quietly resolute.

"I've set the alarm for three-thirty," Alex told her. "Can the three of us talk for a few minutes before we call it an early night?"

The room was silent for a long time. Jake rose and got another log to put on the fire and Meredith slipped over and sat between Alex's legs for a shoulder massage.

"We need a topic, Meredith," her husband told her gently. "Why don't you tell us your theory about – surely you have a theory to cover this kind of… what? Closure?" He thought for a moment. "Separation?"

Jake sat down and agreed with Alex that going to bed with something philosophical to mull over would be good for all three of them. "It will be much nicer than sitting here worrying about over-sleeping," he said, chuckling just a bit.

"You're right. It is separation," she commented. "It's closure in some way for you, Alex – and it is certainly closure for those four men," she added. "What do you think our trip tomorrow represents, Jake?"

"Hmmm," he said thoughtfully, his brow furrowing. "I guess what we're going to be doing for the next week or two has more to do with truth than anything else. It has to do with Alex's truth of accepting his part in what happened and repairing as much damage from past actions as possible. It has to do with the simple truth of no government having the right to sacrifice a single human life to achieve political objectives. It has to do with the truth that there is such a thing as right and wrong. And, it has to do with a truth we discussed when you first came here, Meredith: The truth that when each individual is faced with a choice between right and wrong, each inherits a fate resulting from the choice."

The room was quiet again for a moment.

"I agree," Meredith finally said. "The reason the three of us are sitting here in front of a comfortable fire feeling nervous and on edge is because we are facing truth. Sometimes it gets buried so deeply within us." She murmured. "This entire project has been… about wrestling with an angel, hasn't it? Like Jacob's all-night wrestling match in Genesis. Was it an 'angel?' Or, was it his conscience? Are they the same thing? It's almost dawn," she continued, "and the angel is about to depart. As dawn neared, Jacob's angel – or conscience – wanted to give him a new name – a clean slate. He gave Jacob the name 'Israel.' Our angel wants to give each of us a new name. What will that name be?" She turned her head and looked up at her husband.

She noted the soft look of love in his eyes and then watched them change to embody a look of satisfaction or completion. "I think Arthur said the word tonight at dinner. For me, the name will be 'Freedom.' What about you?" he asked her back.

She thought for a long moment. "Well, freedom is, I believe, the ultimate truth. But I'm with Jacob in Genesis," she said. "To me, truth means wrestling with your conscience, facing truth and doing what you can to make sure it triumphs in the end. Jake?"

"I guess it reminds me a bit of a quote from the Bible, too... I haven't thought of it in ages," he said, "but it has been on my mind a good part of the day. It's why the word 'truth' popped into my mind when you asked what this night is all about." He paused, leaning forward and looking into the fire. "'I am the way, the truth, and the life.' It has always been my favorite Bible quote," he said quietly.

Meredith smiled. "I like that a lot," she said, pausing and smiling at Jake. "I don't know what you carry on your conscience from your days at the CIA, Jake, but I know it's something. Otherwise, you would not have become so involved with Alex in this scheme to replace the clones."

Jake thought for a moment, then rose and went to the bar and poured two small glasses of brandy. He went to the kitchen and poured Meredith a small glass of cranberry juice and returned, handing each of them a drink.

"As usual, you are very insightful Mrs. Plotnikov," he told her. "Tonight is the perfect time to deal with some of my truths. So, I want to make two toasts," he said quietly. "The first is to Jack Caldwell, one of the finest CIA agents I ever knew. He was killed in Brussels... just before you and I met, Alex. He was killed because a guy who worked for the CIA preferred deceit to truth, wanted money, and could get it by selling government secrets to the Soviet Union. To Jack Caldwell!"

Meredith and Alex both repeated his toast and tipped their glasses.

"The second toast is to Jim Danforth." Jake looked at Alex who was, in return, studying his friend's face. "Danforth was killed after Jack Caldwell, a victim of the same information given by the same CIA mole to the Russians. He had a wife and two kids... probably the reason I never married. I saw how devastated they were when he died. If you hadn't warned me that my cover had been blown in the Russian Embassy that night, Alex, it could have been me that got killed, not Danforth." He paused again. "To Jim Danforth," he said, again very quietly.

He quickly downed the remainder of his brandy and told his friends good night. He gave Meredith a hug and said he'd see them in Mesquite in the morning.

Jake waved wordlessly and departed.

Alex rose from his chair and took her hand. "Let's put these glasses in the dishwasher," he suggested.

"Listen, Scientist," she said, holding him in place, three glasses in his hands. "Experience tells me those glasses will still be there in the morning."

Alex smiled at her, put the glasses on the coffee table, and taking her hand led her down the hallway to their bedroom.

Chapter 31

Winter nights in the desert were cold and the early morning of January 7, 2007, was no exception. Joe drove Alex, Meredith, William Leonard and the four Real Things to the Rifle airport that morning. None of the men objected to wearing the glasses that prevented them from seeing where they were going. They knew their destination: Home. Once they were in the air the glasses would come off for the last time.

Gil gave them a timely takeoff in Rifle and a smooth landing in Mesquite. When the plane from Las Vegas stopped to pick them up, the rental jet, a Challenger 684, was warm and comfortable They were on time, so it was a short wait. Meredith convinced herself that it was a good omen.

As they prepared for take-off, Jake picked up the jet's microphone and began giving a pre-flight safety announcement. "Now," he began, "you are all going to learn one of the deep secrets of my hidden past. I began my career as a flight attendant with Eastern Airlines many years ago. Maybe that's why they went bankrupt."

Everyone laughed. He was doing a good job of easing the tension.

"You see, I've promised the people who provided our jet that I could and would make a full security announcement because we opted for privacy on this flight. We don't have an in-flight attendant with us. The FAA says you need to be informed about how to save yourself – or, me – in case of an emergency. So, fasten your seat belts snugly and bring your seats to a full and upright position in preparation for take-off. Make sure your trays are locked tightly against your seat... oh, we don't have trays on this plane. We have serving tables. We do have emergency exits, however..." and he went on to give a full overview of how turbulence could occur at any time and how they would be safer if they kept their seat belts loosely fastened about them during the flight. He explained what would happen if the oxygen level in the plane dropped and told them where they would find their oxygen masks. He showed them their flotation devices... a flight attendant could not have done a better job. He had them laughing, but listening.

After take-off and achieving altitude, Jake unbuckled his seat belt and walked into the small kitchen where he began putting pre-packaged breakfast meals into the microwave oven. As they were heating, he served coffee to everyone. Meredith got up to help him and as he heated the meals, she delivered them. He winked at her and told her they both missed their calling.

Once the two of them had picked up the plastic plates and cups, Meredith sat back down by Alex and reached for her purse. She pulled from it a small, magnetic chess set and laid it on the seat divider between them.

"How about a game of chess, Ivan?" she asked, smiling at him.

"I don't know," he replied, a worried look on his face. "You've been getting so much better, I'm afraid you'll beat me in front of all these men. A respectable Russian could never hold his head up if that happened."

She raised her eyebrows and picked up the two kings, putting them behind her back, and told him to choose. He chose her left hand and Meredith made the first move with her white queen's pawn. About the time they finished the match – Alex would be able to hold his head high, she told him – Jake delivered each of them a glass of champagne. Both she and Alex picked up books and began to read.

In one way, the time seemed to crawl. In another, it moved too fast. Alex would be departing with William Leonard when they reached Burlington, Vermont. This was the last time the newlyweds would be together for two or three weeks.

Jake squatted beside their seats long enough to remind Meredith that she and Arthur would be landing at Martin State Airport. The group that leased the plane to them had a permit for that airport which specialized in handling private chartered aircraft. He liked the smaller airport. Privacy was more easily achieved. He gave her a map showing the twenty mile route to the Baltimore Waterfront Marriott.

As the plane began it's descent into the Burlington area, Meredith tucked the book she brought with her in her purse and reached for her husband's hand. Jake gave them a "buckle your seat belts" sermon and she squeezed Alex's hand and closed her eyes. She hated this. At that moment in time, not one thought of the rightness of what they were going to do was on her mind. It would be later, but for now, it was not.

Just before they began the descent for landing, William Leonard went to the restroom and re-entered the cabin of the plane in his bus driver disguise. Everyone stopped what they were doing to look at the stranger among them. They had been told he would be putting on a disguise for the landing, but the complete change startled everyone. No one said a word.

They would be on the ground for an hour in Burlington. The four Real Things departed the plane first, their hats, sunglasses and scarves serving their purpose of disguise. In the cold afternoon air, they did not look out of place with scarves covering their noses and mouths. The pilot needed the time to do a flight check and refuel before they took off again. This time, the destination would be the Baltimore Martin Airport.

After deplaning, Jake, Alex and Leonard pulled the luggage the two men brought with them from the storage space in the plane's belly and Alex turned to Meredith.

"I love you," was all he said to her. His voice was strained and very quiet.

"I love you, too, Alex." She smiled at him and they hugged for a long moment. "I will see you... back at the ranch in two or three weeks," she whispered in his ear.

He kissed her softly and briefly. They hugged once more before he turned and walked to the limo. As one box was placed in the trunk of the car, it rattled. Leonard looked at Jake and made a face. It was his chains, he knew.

It seemed like no time at all and they were in the air again. It was a short flight to the Baltimore airport and this time Jake, Meredith and Arthur deplaned. After Jake got their luggage from the storage area and re-boarded the plane, they would take off again as quickly as air traffic control gave them a runway time. There would be no refueling here and they would quickly be on their way to Fort Lauderdale. Meredith envied them their destination as the humid winter chill so much a part of coastal living made her shiver. She pulled the heavy black winter coat around her, making sure her mourning hat with its thick black veil was in place. Arthur walked at her side holding her elbow, scarf wrapped around his mouth and nose. Again, the company provided a car that picked the two of them up on the flight line. The limo drove them to the car rental outlet. Arthur waited in the limo while she got their car.

All Meredith could think was: It has begun.

The plane landed in Fort Lauderdale that evening just as the sun was disappearing into the Gulf of Mexico. They all deplaned at Kendall-Tamiami Executive Airport. The group had been reduced to Jake, Branchman, Martinez, Scott, Bryant, Grosvenor, Brett and Gil. They stayed on board until their limo arrived and pulled close to the plane. They all removed their suit jackets and carried their over-coats across their arms... not an uncommon sight in the sunny South when people arrived from the cold North. The scarves could not be worn to cover the lower part of their faces, but they kept their hats and sunglasses on. It was not much of a disguise but was better than nothing. The limo from the airplane leasing company pulled fairly close to the plane to pick them up so their risk was minimal.

They were taken to the newly-refurbished Harbor Beach Marriott. Jake got out of the car and went into the hotel to rent their rooms for the night. The check-in clerk informed him that each person would have to register but he would mark them as "Paid." Jake returned to the limo and told Brett, Bob Grosvenor and Bill Bryant to register and pick up their room keys.

"You will attract less attention if you enter one at a time with your security guard," he told the Real Things about their entry into the hotel. He lowered the window between the driver and the passengers and told the driver how to get to the hotel's side door. He gave each man a handkerchief to put in front of his face – under his nose, as if he were fighting a cold. It would help keep people from seeing them as they walked across a corner of the lobby to the elevators. He went back into the hotel to make sure the side door would be open.

Jake had reserved rooms on the same floor, close together. After everyone had a chance to get settled, he called a meeting.

"I will order breakfast for everyone here in this suite at six a.m.," he told them. "As soon as the food is delivered, I'll call you. When you go back to your room in a few minutes, your security guard will order dinner brought to your rooms. When it's delivered, you will be in the bathroom. Am I understood?"

Each of them nodded.

"You will not leave your room for any reason tonight... if the hotel burns down, you can leave." He smiled, briefly, and hesitated, raising his eyebrows as a silent means of telling them if they had any questions, now was the time to ask. "At seven in the morning, after breakfast, the limo will pick you up at the same side door you came in tonight. Gil will go downstairs ahead of you to make sure the limo gets to the right place. He will call each room and tell you to come downstairs. You won't have to worry about seeing many people between your room and the car that early in the morning. People are here on vacation. You will go back to the same private airport and board the plane and you will wait there for me and J.J.'s clone to join you. Bill and the real J.J. will leave with me in a rental car in the morning."

Jake got up and paced for a moment, rubbing the stubble on his chin. He hadn't let it grow long but wore it in the fashion of the day, looking as if he had forgotten to shave for a few days – the Jack Bauer look, he called it.

"Tomorrow's travel arrangements are much the same as they were today. After we collect J.J.'s clone, we will first go to Ogunquin, Maine where I, Justice Scott and Brett will leave you. This leg of our trip tomorrow is the longest of the day. You will have to deplane as you did when we got to Burlington, today. The leasing company's limo will pick us up close to the plane, as they have at our other stops today. They will take us to Hertz. The plane – and you – will await my return with Justice Scott's clone. Bob, you will be the only security guard left on board by this time and you and Gil will assist me in getting Justice Scott's clone on board. It would be helpful if the pilot was inside the flight line building having coffee, Gil," Jake told his pilot, almost as an afterthought. "While the plane is being refueled, we will be putting Justice Scott back in his vacation home. After we refuel, we will take off for the short flight to Burlington."

Jake went through the same description of what would happen when they landed in Burlington, Vermont. Alex and Leonard – Jake called him by his "Marchman" alias – would rejoin the plane to guard the clones while Senator Martinez was taken to the Sugarbush ski area by Jake and Bob Grosvenor. His clone would be replaced and returned to the plane.

"Bob will stay with Senator Martinez and I will return to the plane with his clone. At this point, all of you will have replaced your clones. Gil, Marchman and the doctor will fly the three clones back to Nevada and be driven back to the ranch." They would arrive late. "Before heading home they will drop me off in Baltimore. We will replace Arthur the next morning." He looked at all of them, reached out to physically touch each of them in some way, and asked if they had any questions. There were none.

"A doctor will appear at each place. There will be no introductions. I hope you will forget what he looks like." Jake paused. "You know the clones have tracking devices implanted in them. They will be removed by the doctor – a very good surgeon – and will be re-implanted in you," Jake told them. "It starts tomorrow morning when Bill Bryant, J.J. and I will drive to Lago Mar... it's less than five minutes away."

He paused and looked around at the group of quiet men. They had paled a bit... it was one thing to desire their freedom, to want their lives back. It was something else to do what was necessary to re-seize them.

"Okay, it's been a long day, we're all tired and we all need a good night's sleep. Bill, you go first. Get J.J.'s room door open and I'll check the hallway. When it's clear, we'll send him across the hall to you."

When they were gone, Jake called Dr. Dean, cell-to-cell, and when the surgeon answered, Jake gave him his room number and asked him to come for dinner.

Like Meredith, Jake had a keen awareness that it had begun. Nothing would stop their efforts now. Would they be successful he wondered? He thought so. There was, however, always the unknown. Jake knew that.

*****

Jake and Bill Bryant did not have to walk through the lobby at Lago Mar at 7:30 the next morning. J.J.'s clone was staying in a unit right on the beach, disconnected from the main hotel building. Dr. Dean had been at the resort hotel for two days and saw Branchman sunbathing on his private patio. After dinner the night before, Jake and the doctor had walked five minutes along the ocean to Lago Mar's private beach. Dr. Dean was able to point out exactly which unit was occupied by the Branchman clone. Jake counted doors... third patio door from the South end of the building.

Jake would be wearing a white room service jacket, carrying food on a Lago Mar room service tray. Dr. Dean had brought the tray to Jake when he came for dinner. The food Jake would place on the tray would come from Marriott's room service.

Once inside, rather than reaching into his pocket for the food bill, Jake would take out a syringe with sufficient Phenobarbital in it to almost – but not quite – put the man to sleep. Bill Bryant would be waiting at the end of the building to bring a wheelchair into the room.

Perhaps it was sheer luck that Branchman was on the first floor of the building. It would make their escape easier.

The real J.J. Branchman stayed in the car, awaiting Jake's cell phone call. It was a cool, breezy morning and was altogether pleasant aside from the butterflies floating around in J.J.'s stomach. Branchman was dressed in white tennis shorts and a blue striped shirt, a white navy hat with brim pulled down over his head and he was wearing sunglasses. When Jake's call came, J.J. was quickly out of the car and, following directions, walked around the outside of the building to the patio doors of the units overlooking the Atlantic Ocean – or was it the Gulf? He was never sure. Only a handful of people dotted the scenic beach and J.J. met no one directly. He went to the third unit from the end of the building and saw Jake through the patio door. He quickly entered the suite.

"So that's my twin," J.J. said quietly, looking at the man lying on the living room couch. "I'd like to whop him one," he added before turning away. It pained him somehow to look at the man. He wasn't quite asleep, but appeared helpless… unable to control his ability to speak or to move. When he saw J.J., terror filled his eyes and he tried desperately to call out or to move. He could do neither.

Sweat began to pour from his brow and then his eyes closed.

Jake dialed Dr. Dean, cell-to-cell and then used the scanning technology provided by Brett to find the tracking microchip. It was right where Leonard said it would be.

"Hurry up," Dean said when he arrived moments later. "The room service cart is just three doors away… we've got a few minutes, but very few." He wore his stethoscope around his neck. Should they be interrupted, they would hide the clone in the bathroom with Dr. Dean. The doctor quickly took a vial of Lidocaine from his black bag and numbed the clone's arm at the location Jake had marked. He felt for the device, made a quick incision and slipped a small metal disc from the man's arm. He rinsed it quickly but carefully in the bathroom sink, then dropped it into a small bowl of hydrogen peroxide and waited for one minute.

"Your turn," he said to the real J.J..

Branchman held his arm out and the procedure was quickly completed. Though the cut had been a little deeper than Jake thought would be necessary, it was very small. Dean quickly put a gel over the wound, covered it with gauze and told J.J. to apply pressure for about five minutes and then cover it with a large Band-Aid. "Remember to put on a long-sleeved shirt so no one can see it," he warned the man, "but keep direct pressure on it and keep it raised above your heart for a minute, or two." There was a very brief pause.

"I'm out of here," he said to Jake. He removed his stethoscope from around his neck, pocketed it, removed his white jacket and stepped quickly out of the patio door and onto the beach.

"Okay, J.J.," Jake said. "You're on your own for about five minutes while Bryant helps me get this guy back to the car. Put on a robe so when your breakfast comes your arm is covered. Keep your arm up – scratch your head if you have to – say as little as possible, sign the tab, give the room service guy a cash tip... not too big." Jake handed him the billfold he had taken from the clone. It was filled with cash and credit cards.

Branchman, always the most emotional of the four Real Things, reached out to Jake and gave him a one-armed, brief bear hug, slapping him on the back. "If you ever need anything, Jake..." he said. Bryant helped Jake quickly lift the Branchman clone off of the couch and tie him in the wheelchair. Jake and Bill Bryant put J.J.'s white navy hat over the clone's head, covering a portion of his eyes, and the sun glasses covered the rest. A towel was quickly wrapped around the clone's neck and arranged so it covered the lower part of his face.

They had to use the hallway and risk hotel security cameras. Oceanside, a portion of the area between Branchman's room and the garage was beach sand. Sand and wheelchairs did not mix. Jake opened the front door and looked out. The room service cart was coming down the hallway of the building but stopped at the room one door away on the opposite side of the hall. "Quick," was all he had time to say to Bryant as the two of them got the wheelchair out of the door and began pushing it swiftly down the hall. When they arrived at the exit to the building there was a short walkway between the building they were leaving and the garage. They navigated that quickly, too. Bryant had scoped the garage during his December visit and found several gaps in security camera coverage. All garages had such gaps. They had plotted their escape route around that knowledge. They unceremoniously unloaded the clone into the back seat of the car.

Jake said nothing, just turned to Bill Bryant and held out his hand.

"I'll take good care of him, Jake. I promise," the man said. "Good luck." He turned and quickly went back to the ocean-side patio door of J.J.'s room. It was good to avoid the security cameras in the hallways, he thought.

Within a minute after Jake and Bryant left his room, J.J.'s breakfast was delivered. At the same time, his telephone rang. He picked up the phone and told whoever was at the other end to wait while he signed for his breakfast.

When the room server left, he went back to the telephone.

"Yes?" he said into the telephone.

"J.J.," the voice came, "this is John. I'm in the hotel restaurant having breakfast and the security guy just told me that someone was taken from your room in a wheelchair. Are you okay?"

J.J. pushed away the panic he felt. John… John… and he remembered. John was one of the clone's security guards. He fell naturally back into the role of a nationally-known radio star. "No, no," he replied. "Three friends of mine were visiting… one is disabled, in a wheelchair."

"Okay… I just wanted to make sure you're okay," the response came.

"I'm fine… except my breakfast is getting cold." Without waiting for a response, he hung up the telephone and began humming Gene Autry's old song, "Back in the Saddle, Again."

It was a fifteen minute ride to the private airport. Jake called Gil and told him to send the limo for him at Hertz. Gil rode along in the limo and helped Jake get the clone out of the back seat of the rental car and into the limo so the rental could be returned. "The medical treatments these guys get are tough, aren't they?" Gil asked for the benefit of the limo driver.

The "medical treatments" line was Jake's official story to the airplane rental place. He had to tell them something to explain passengers who were awake going one way, and sleeping going the other. Jake was glad Gil was serving as co-pilot on the trip. He had coordinated things that would have otherwise caused questions from the flight crew. Jake and Gil half-carried the clone up the stairs of the plane and placed him gently into one of the seats, fastened his seat belt, then covered him with a blanket.

Gil called the pilot on his cell phone and told him they were ready to leave, any time. The pilot was in the airport restaurant having a cup of coffee.

It was the longest trip they would make that day… aside from the return to Nevada late that night, of course.

The kidnapping of Justice Avery Scott was accomplished so smoothly that it almost made Jake nervous. Nothing should be so easy, he thought in its aftermath.

This time Jake knocked at Scott's front door telling the man inside he was his neighbor from two doors down. Hearing a dog barking in Scott's back yard, he told him he needed to talk with him about his dog. Jake got the neighbor's name off of the mailbox in front of the house two doors away from the Scott residence. Justice Scott opened his front door, frowning, and Jake pushed him back into the room. With Brett's help he quickly and quietly slapped a piece of duct tape over the man's mouth and pushed up his sleeve to put a needle in his arm. Aside from the dog that started barking in the back yard again, everything went as planned.

Dr. Dean was in the car waiting to be called and was in the house a moment after his cell phone rang. The real Justice Avery Scott came into the house with the doctor and the transfer of radio tracking microchips went smoothly. Dr. Dean had more time to get the bleeding from both men's arms stopped before leaving. The Scott clone's reaction when he saw the Real Thing was very similar to the reaction in Fort Lauderdale. It gave Jake a glimpse into the souls of the terror people who live lies feel.

Brett and Jake disguised the clone with a ski jacket, knit cap, glasses, and put one of the clone's arms around each of their shoulders and walked him to the car. His legs moved, as if he was trying to walk, but he could not.

"Thanks, partner," Jake said. "I'll see you tomorrow morning in D.C."

Brett had barely re-entered Scott's house and removed his coat when there was a knock at the door. He motioned for Justice Scott to go into the bathroom and told him to shut the door, and flush the toilet, but to listen to the conversation.

"Yes?" he said to the rather large, serious-looking man standing on the porch. "Can I help you?"

"I just noticed some unscheduled visitors," the man replied. "I'm Justice Scott's security officer. May I come in?"

Brett stepped away from the door and said "Sure, sure. I'm the unscheduled visitor… some friends dropped me off, but one of them had a bit too much to drink so they didn't stay. Justice and Mrs. Scott are good friends of my family. Mom and dad wanted me to stop by and wish him a happy New Year. I hope it isn't a problem?" Jake looked at the man directly in the eye.

"I saw four people enter," the security guard said in an almost threatening voice.

"And I'm sure you saw three of them leave. One had a bit too much to drink this evening. The other two were…. well, helping him along," Brett replied. "Are you saying there is a problem?"

"I need to talk with the Justice," the man said.

"My name is Brett Radov," he said, holding out his hand.

"Ed Rymanowsky," the other man replied, taking Brett's hand with no enthusiasm. He was suspicious, Brett knew.

The bathroom door opened and Justice Scott walked out, smiling at both of his guests. "I have unexpected company, Ed," he said to the man, glad Brett had dimmed the lights in the room. "This young man just retired from the CIA… can you imagine that?" he asked the stranger. "I met his father in law school… my God, Brett, do you realize how old that makes me feel?" He laughed, slapping Brett on the arm. "I'm sorry I didn't tell you he was coming, but I didn't know myself until he showed up on my doorstep." Scott winked at Rymanowsky. It took only a moment for the guard to figure out that the Justice's visitor was from the real Justice Scott's long-ago past.

Brett had been watching the man's eyes. There had been a reaction when Scott mentioned the CIA.

"How long will you be staying, Brett?" the Justice asked. "If security knows you will be coming in and going out of the house during your stay, it won't be a problem."

"Just a few days," Brett replied, knowing that within 48 hours the private security being provided by the KGB would be gone. "Sorry about that," he said, smiling at the other man. "I should have realized Justice Scott would have security that visitors should go through… I wasn't thinking."

The other man nodded. "I'm sorry too, but I need to see some identification," he told Brett who immediately pulled out his billfold and provided it.

He returned the ID and asked the Justice if he would be staying in for the rest of the day. When he got a "yes" answer, Rymanowsky told the Justice he would be outside until five o'clock, and would then be at the bed and breakfast down the street if he needed him for anything. Justice Scott told him to have a good day and closed the door.

Brett wrapped a large bath towel around his arm and headed for the back door.

"What are you doing?" Scott demanded of Brett.

"I'm going to deal with a barking German shepherd before some neighbors actually do show up on your doorstep to complain." He paused. "I'd suggest you get back in the bathroom until we see how friendly this critter is."

The clone capture had gone so quickly that Jake, carrying Scott's clone in the back of the car and Dr. Dean in the front, had hardly been gone from the airport longer than forty-five minutes. Grosvenor came to the car to help him get the clone into the jet. Dr. Dean would accompany them on the short flight to Burlington. They would be at that airport shortly and Jake called Alex to tell him their estimated time of arrival. "We'll meet you," was all Alex said, and hung up. It was three o'clock in the afternoon when they touched down in Burlington, Vermont.

Alex and William Leonard joined them shortly after they landed. "Two down, two to go," he said to his friend. "We'll be leaving for Sugarbush in a few minutes. The doctor is putting the J.J. clone back to sleep. He's starting a glucose drip... got to keep liquid in him. After he goes with us to Sugarbush, the Doc will be with them the rest of the way, so that will be a relief... for everyone."

William Leonard looked at the two of them with a new respect. At first he had not really believed they could pull off what Arthur Redbridge told him at Neuschwanstein they intended. It was part of the reason he had hung back.

"What a coup you've pulled today," Leonard said, grinning. "I will take very good care of these men on the trip home. Is there anything you need me to do before Alex comes back to the ranch?" He looked at the two men expectantly. He got no answer from Alex, just a smile.

"Just take care of the clones, Bill," Jake said with a tired grin.

Alex chuckled at the look on Jake's face. He still did not know quite how to take William Leonard. "He has been as good as gold for the last twenty-four hours, Jake," Alex told him. "Have you talked with Meredith?" he asked, trying to sound casual.

"No," Jake replied. "Hopefully I'll see her in three or four hours," he said. "Do you have your Amtrak ticket to Baltimore?"

"Yeah... I leave about two hours after you fly out of here," he replied. "I'll call your cell when I get there. I'm staying at a Super 8 Motel close to the airport."

The next morning after the accident, the Redbridge clone would be taken to the private airport in Maryland. Alex would fly to Mesquite with him. Jake grabbed his friend's shoulder and told him to be sure and get to the train on time.

After tending to the two sleeping clones on the plane, Dr. Dean told them he was ready to pay their last house call for the night. Jake, Senator Martinez, Bob Grosvenor and Dr. Dean headed for I-89 South where they would pick up Route 100 South to Sugarbush. It had been a long day and Jake was bone weary tired. He would be glad to land in Baltimore and get a good night's sleep.

They had the least amount of information on Martinez and that concerned Jake. As he feared, they were unable to find the Senator on their first round of public places. "He's in the hotel bar," Grosvenor said when he returned to the car after making his second visit there. They had been to every restaurant and bar in the area that night looking for the man.

"He's got his hand on some blonde's knee at a table in a dark corner... a little public display of affection with someone other than his wife," Grosvenor told Jake.

"Okay," Jake said. He pulled his ski jacket around him. It was cold... the humid kind of cold he was not used to since living in Colorado. He wore blue jeans, après ski boots, a ski hat pulled low on his face, and gloves. In short, he looked like two-thirds of the other people walking around Sugarbush.

Jake found a side entrance to the bar. The fact that it was close to the men's restroom made it the best place to do what had to be done.

"Senator when you go into the bathroom stall remove your clothing. Bob will pass you the clone's clothes so you can return to the table and tell the young woman with whom your clone was... well, you can tell the young woman goodnight." Jake looked at Bob. "We'll have to do this fast, my friend!"

Jake escorted Grosvenor, Dr. Dean and Senator Martinez to the side entrance, telling them to take a sharp left. "Doc, stand in front of the urinal like... well you know like what," he told the man, chuckling. God, he was tired.

Jake walked back out of the side door, unseen as far as he knew, and walked to the front of the bar, opened the door and entered. He removed his gloves and unzipped his jacket but left his ski cap in place. He saw the Senator and took his digital camera from his jacket pocket and began taking pictures of Martinez with his hand on the woman's knee, then kissing her neck. He walked to the couple's table in the corner and took a seat on the opposite side.

"Senator Martinez." He smiled at the man who was at a loss to identify him. "I know Fran... I don't know you. I just got some dynamite pictures of you from across the room."

"I – your name is...?"

"Jake," he replied. "The newspaper I work for is going to love the pictures. Excuse me, ma'am, but I've got to respond to a call from nature," he said. "How *is* Fran?" he asked, looking at the man with the most condescending look he could muster. He rose and left the table. As he walked, Jake looked around the room and saw who the security guard was. He was watching the table very closely but since Jake was leaving so quickly, he stayed at the end of the bar... but he was standing, not sitting.

In the mirror behind the bar, he saw the Senator rise to follow him and noted the hand he put up to tell his guard that everything was fine. He smiled. "Jake, Jake..." the clone called to him, catching up with him and putting his hand on Jake's shoulder. "Let's talk this over, man-to-man. I'm sure we can come to some agreement," the clone told him.

"I'm sure we can," he said, stopping as he opened the bathroom door for the other man to walk through. Jake took a quick look around and, once again, their luck held. No one other than Grosvenor, washing his hands, and Dr. Dean, standing in front of the urinal, was in the bathroom. Jake quickly grabbed Martinez's arms and pulled them behind him as Grosvenor almost simultaneously slapped a piece of duct tape over his mouth. Dr. Dean pushed his ski jacket sleeve up, found a vein in his hand, and injected the man. Jake and Grosvenor quickly put him in the stall next to the one with the closed door, occupied by the real Senator Martin. They emptied his pockets, stripped him and threw the clothes over the top and retrieved the ones the Senator threw back at them.

Once the clothing had been exchanged, Dr. Dean entered the clone's stall and removed the microchip, closed the wound and bandaged it. Jake quickly stepped outside the bathroom door and stood there. He held his breath as he watched the clone's guard from across the room begin the long walk to the restroom. He tipped the door open and told everyone to freeze.

"Get a piece of duct tape ready for our visitor's mouth, Bob… just in case," he whispered urgently.

"Sorry," he said to the man. "Senator Martinez asked me to let him have a private moment in the restroom and so no one's going in there for another minute or two. You know how the rich and famous are…" he laughed.

"I'm the Senator's security guard," the man retorted and started to open the door.

"Hold on," Jake told him, putting his hand on the man's chest. "Anyone can say they are someone's security guard. Show me the proper ID and I'll get out of your way and we won't have a scene that could embarrass the Senator. I'm with the media… you can ask the Senator. Remember the article about him in the Cincinnati paper?" He flashed his camera at the man.

The guard heard the word 'media' and his attitude changed slightly. "My name is Richter, Gerald Richter," he said, pulling an ID card from his wallet. "I provide security for Senator Martinez. I know he likes to be left alone when he's on vacation, but I need to check on him," the man said.

"Okay," Jake said and let the man open the door.

Richter put his head inside the door, looked around and saw Dr. Dean's back as he faced the urinal, then called Martinez's name. The real Martinez answered and told him he'd be out in a minute. "For heaven's sake, Richter, can't a man even take a crap without you interfering?"

The security guard stepped back outside the door and stood with Jake, embarrassed. "Come on, Jerry" Jake offered. "I'll buy you a drink."

He slapped Richter's shoulder and began a slow departure from the dark hallway into the main public area.

A moment later, the real Senator Martinez walked out of the restroom and headed back to the table where the clone's playmate sat. This time he sat across from her.

"That guy got pictures of us," he whispered. "I bought him off and got his digital camera," he said. "But I think we'd better call it a night."

"You've got my number," she said slyly. "Call me John. I always enjoy our time together."

Martinez was holding his upper arm, Jake noticed. He rose from the table to bend and whisper something in the woman's ear, she laughed, and then he walked out through the door leading to the hotel lobby. Gerald Richter got up, told Jake "See ya... thanks for the drink," and followed a short distance behind the Senator into the hotel. They had found the clone's hotel room key and wallet in his pants, so Martinez could get to his room and have privacy for the rest of the night.

Jake returned to the restroom and found Bob Grosvenor by himself. The door where the drugged clone sat was closed.

"The Doc went to get the car and pull as close to the side door as he can," Grosvenor told Jake. "Let's get him out of here before anyone else comes in."

The clone, wearing Senator Martinez's broad-rimmed felt hat pulled over the top of his face and a neck scarf pulled over his nose and mouth was walked from the restroom and out the side door. With one arm around Jake and the other around Bob, it looked like they were helping a drunk get home. A few people looked, but not because they recognized anyone.

With the clone's body lying across the back seat, Grosvenor grabbed Jake's hand and said nothing. He just winked and trotted quickly to the hotel lobby where he caught the elevator to join Senator Martinez in his room.

Dr. Dean moved to the passenger seat and Jake began the long drive back to Burlington.

"Three down, and you're heading for home," he said to the good doctor. "And think of the adventure you can tell your grandchildren about in twenty years!"

They were later getting back to the plane than the plan called for, but they were back with another successful removal of a clone from public office. That was the main thing.

"I was getting worried," Leonard told them. "Scott's clone is beginning to stir a bit, Doc." He turned to Jake. "I told the pilot to go to the snack bar and have some coffee... he was getting impatient. I'll get him..."

They were quickly in the air headed for the private airport in Baltimore. After they landed, Jake stuck his head in the cockpit and thanked both the pilot and Gil, apologizing for being late. "The guy's doctor was having dinner," he lied. "We had to wait. The doctor is flying home with him, so everything should go smoothly from here." He shook everyone's hand, said thanks, and turned to the passenger compartment. He shook Dr. Dean's hand and then turned to Leonard. "Take good care of them, Bill," he said softly. "Get them home safely." He was suddenly glad they had decided to include Leonard in their plans. The guy might be a flake in some ways, but he was good at this kind of thing. If he wasn't, he wouldn't be alive, Jake thought.

He walked into the cold winter air of Baltimore's Chesapeake Bay and stepped inside the coffee shop and called a taxi. As he waited, he watched the plane he had just left return to the runway and takeoff.

Only after the plane disappeared from sight did he heave a huge sigh of relief. All Jake could think of was how good it was going to be to feel a pillow under his head.

Chapter 32

It was ten o'clock at night by the time Jake got to the Waterfront Marriott in Baltimore. He stayed in his room long enough to call Meredith and tell her he had arrived. When she asked how the day had gone, he told her he'd be there in five minutes to tell her. He splashed some water on his face, got out of the ski clothes and replaced them with jeans and a shirt, then headed for her room.

"Have you seen Alex?" she asked.

"Just left him about an hour ago," he told her. "Funny thing… he asked if I'd seen you." He chuckled but the tiredness showed through his humor. "Alex will be on a train to the Baltimore area in about an hour. I put William Leonard and three clones on the plane back home and left Alex in Burlington, Vermont." He shivered. "It was cold!"

Jake walked across the room to shake the hand of Arthur Redbridge. "They're back," was all he said as he shook the Fed Chairman's hand.

Jake went to the bar in the suite, opened the small refrigerator, poured himself a drink, and spent the next half-hour filling them in on the day's events.

"You must be exhausted," she said, noticing the dark circles that were beginning to form under his eyes.

"I am tired," he said, "but I wanted you to know everything went well… as well as it possibly could under the circumstances," he added. "Are you ready for your turn tomorrow, Arthur?"

"The longer I wait, the better Sakhalin Island looks to me, Jake," the other man responded, chuckling. "It's the waiting that gets you, isn't it?"

"Yep. It's the waiting that gets you, Arthur. And it's almost over. Brett will be landing at Reagan at 0700 tomorrow. You and I will leave the hotel at 0-630. We'll meet him at 0800. We will join him in an ambulance. Doctor Nordenberg will be doing your facial update. You're scheduled for surgery at 1300. The accident is scheduled for 1100."

"How are we getting to D.C.?" Arthur asked him.

"I rented a car... we'll drive. Brett was in D.C. for two days before we left for Las Vegas. Everything is ready." He rose, looked around the room and then turned to Meredith. "Are you okay? Do you need anything?"

"I'm fine," she told him. She paused for a moment. "Here is the manila envelope and the material Jeffrey sent. And, here is the notification for the Russians." She paused again. "I won't see you in the morning, Jake... I'm going to try and sleep in. The trip tired me out. How do you deal with all of this stress?"

She was worried, he could tell. It was his turn to give her a hug. She patted his back.

"Good night," she told him. He kissed her cheek, waved at Arthur Redbridge, and headed for the pillow he had been longing for since the Burlington, Vermont airport.

Jake had no trouble falling asleep. Sometimes when he got overly tired, sleep was impossible. Not tonight. When he awoke the next morning, he smiled at the dream he'd just had... Meredith's friend, Sue, was re-decorating the kitchen at his new home and was just about to tell him something. Before she could say anything, his cell phone alarm rang him awake.

Arthur was waiting for him when Jake knocked softly on the door of the suite. The car that would change history would soon be driving around the area, never far away from where Massachusetts Avenue merged into DuPont Circle. One man in a hotel a little over a mile from "ground zero," as Brett called the site of the "accident," would call another man who was sitting at an Ethiopian café on DuPont Circle. He would keep him updated on the progress of the clone's limo. He, in turn, would contact the driver who would get his car to DuPont Circle and stall it at the Massachusetts Avenue entry, blocking the traffic behind him. Without a stalled car, DuPont Circle was a nightmare. When the clone's limo pulled into the Circle from Connecticut Avenue, the driver would suddenly be able to start his car, gun it, and run directly into the side of the limo. Hopefully he would hit the car in the area away from the back seat where the cloned Arthur Redbridge would be sitting. The mercenaries employed for the job came highly recommended by Grosvenor and Bryant. They were costly... but good help always was.

The ambulance was parked on a side street close to the restaurant on DuPont Circle. The traffic tie-up would be so bad that no emergency vehicle would be able to get to it for at least a half-hour. It would just be a coincidence that an ambulance chartered to provide service for high-ranking federal government officials was practically on site... its occupants on a coffee break. It would be a miracle, the media would say, that the emergency medical technician with that ambulance had the day's security codes with him that made it possible to treat and remove the Fed Chairman from his vehicle and take him to the hospital.

One security guard would ride with Redbridge the clone in the ambulance. The other would meet the ambulance at Bethesda. As soon as Jake and Brett got the real Redbridge into the small, private hospital, Brett would place the gurney back in the ambulance. He would take the clone to a leased jet sitting at the private Martin Baltimore airport where Alex awaited the arrival of his passenger.

After the accident, before the clone was removed from the back seat of the Fed Chairman's limo, Jake injected him with the drug that had been so effective on the other clones. His security detail was busy handling the crowd. By the time they removed him from the back seat, the Redbridge clone looked as if he might be seriously injured. People who like to rubber-neck any accident were at once quieted by what appeared to be the serious condition of the limo's occupant... the man they knew to be the Chairman of the Federal Central Bank. As they watched his inert body being loaded onto the ambulance gurney, the click of tourist cameras could be heard. He and Brett both wore ski jackets with large upright collars over their uniform shirts and cark cargo-pocket pants. They wore baseball caps and sun glasses. No one would get a clear view of their faces on the evening news.

When the time came for the real Arthur Redbridge to hide behind a curtain in the ambulance, Jake noticed him trembling. There was sweat on his brow, too. That was okay, he thought. Let him tremble.

When Jake and Brett pulled the unconscious body of his clone into the ambulance, Redbridge thought he was going to faint. He was too old for this, he told himself. He knew one of the guards would be entering the vehicle to ride with the unconscious clone. Redbridge held the curtain that hid him in the back of the ambulance carefully closed. Fear caused Redbridge's sense of hearing to become acute. His breathing sounded so loud in his own ears, he feared the clone's bodyguard could hear it, too.

Brett had to drive the ambulance over the curb and onto a side-walk to get around the traffic tie-up caused by the accident, but was able to pull onto Connecticut Avenue heading north. He turned left on Macomb, then right onto Wisconsin. Sirens blazing, he headed toward I-495 and the Bethesda Naval Hospital. The security guard was sitting by the body of the Redbridge clone. Jake quickly removed the second syringe from his pocket. He had to get the needle in a vein and to do that, he had to knock the man unconscious. Within a few moments the Redbridge clone's security guard was lying on the floor of the vehicle. Jake knocked on the driver's compartment to let Brett know everyone who was supposed to be unconscious was unconscious.

After they had gone about a mile, Brett turned off the siren, turned off of Wisconsin Avenue and, after a few blocks, pulled into a closed, deserted lot that was about to become a new apart-ment building in the area. The previous business that occupied the land was a car wash. They pulled the vehicle between two of the remaining walls and under its roof. They were not visible from the street or the sky.

Jake and Brett removed the sleeping body of the security guard and laid him on a blanket on the cement floor of the car wash. They removed the tracking device from the clone and threw it on top of the guard's body. He would not be alone for long.

As Redbridge quickly put on the clothes his clone had been wearing, he looked very pale, Jake noted. "Cripes," he finally told the real Redbridge, "don't have a damned heart attack on me, Arthur. Simmer down. Everything is going just as planned."

He nodded his head and Jake told him to come and help get the clothes that he, Redbridge, had been wearing put on his clone. As the clone's eyes saw the real Arthur Redbridge, he gasped something out loud but it was not understandable. It sounded like a word spoken in Russian, but Jake didn't catch it. Like the other clones, there was a look of terror on his face as he lapsed into unconsciousness.

Brett, meantime, was changing the license plates. He also removed the magnetic panels on both sides and the back of the ambulance and replaced them. The new panels identified the ambulance as belonging to a different company and it was no longer white and blue. It was white and beige. He slapped the back of the ambulance to warn Jake and Redbridge they were about to start moving. Jake quickly got Redbridge on the gurney in the ambulance and worked to put the body of the clone behind a couple of boxes and a medical bag. He covered him with a blanket and pulled the curtains. No one at the hospital would enter the ambulance, but they might see inside.

Admittance forms for Norman McTavish had already been prepared for the hospital by Dr. Nordenberg's office. He advised the hospital staff that a high-level government official was coming to the hospital. No one was to question his identity or try to find out who he was. They were to simply admit him. He would be arriving in an ambulance, but would need no emergency room care, procedures or evaluations. The hospital staff understood what was happening. A well-known politician wanted a face lift.

"Okay, Arthur," Jake told him, "you are about to go on stage. Just do it the way we rehearsed it and everything will be fine!"

Brett stopped the ambulance and jumped out. He went to the rear of the vehicle, opened the doors, and helped Jake remove Redbridge. As soon as the "legs" dropped under the gurney, Brett closed and locked the back doors of the vehicle. Jake knew he was to by-pass the emergency room and take "Mr. McTavish" and the completed hospital forms directly to Room 441.

The private room was across and one door from the elevator. As they had planned, this particular elevator was accessible from the hospital's parking garage. Once they reached his room, Redbridge sat up, climbed off of the gurney and went into the bathroom and emerged wearing the hospital gown required for his surgery.

"Okay, Arthur," Jake said, handing him the cell phone he had removed from the hand of the Redbridge clone as he entered the limo to drug him. "Make your first call." Jake had no idea who the clone was trying to call when the accident happened, but had grabbed the phone from his hand before the call was completed.

Redbridge pushed the "phone book" button on the handset and scrolled through the names until he arrived at POTUS: President of the United States. He looked at Jake and then pressed "Talk."

The man who answered the telephone at the other end simply said "Arthur!" Caller ID was obviously working. His voice was filled with relief. "I've been worried!"

"I knew you'd be worried, Mr. President. I have a few cuts and bruises that need some attention, but other than that, I'm fine." His voice sounded a bit tired to Jake, but that was to be expected of an accident victim.

Redbridge listened to the President's response for a moment, smiling as he spoke of the news about his accident. "People around DuPont Circle said you looked badly injured, Arthur."

"I was unconscious for a few moments... but I came to in the ambulance. Aside from a very bad headache and a few cuts that need some stitches, I'm okay. They're going to take some x-rays to see if I have a concussion. If I do, I'll need some bed rest."

He knew the President would call a press conference within the hour as he said the words. "Mr. President, I am concerned about something. I called to ask for your help."

"Anything I can do to help, Arthur... anything. You name it," the President replied, true concern in his voice. This was the man who was holding the shaky American economy together for an unpopular President, after all. If something serious happened to him, public reaction could send everything over the edge. The markets had already reacted to news of the accident. The DOW had dropped over 400 points the past hour.

"I have lost confidence in my security detail, Mr. President... in fact, I am not too sure that the accident was not part of... well, I don't want to talk about it over the phone from a hospital bed. I'm sure you understand... we can discuss the details later." Redbridge paused. It was beginning to come back to him, he realized. That sense of power one has when one can pick up the phone, dial a number and have the President of the United States answer. It was coming back.

"I would appreciate it if you would contact two people for me," Arthur said in an almost condescending tone. "I would like to have Secret Service Agent John Hunter, and a friend of his, Brett Radov – a personal acquaintance who just retired from the CIA – assigned to me. Can you arrange to have these men provide security for me while I am hospitalized?." Again, he paused, smiling. "You can?" he asked. "You will?" he queried. "Thank you, Mr. President."

There was another long pause. "No, Mr. President, I am not at Bethesda. I am at a small, private hospital... I did not trust being taken anywhere my former security team had connections. It would be better if I do not tell you where I am or why I have these suspicions. If you don't know where I am, the media can't hound you about it, can they? If there are any leaks to the media, we will both know they did not come from you." Redbridge smiled at the long pause while the President digested the meaning of Redbridge's words.

When the long pause ended, the President carefully began speaking. "It is imperative we find a way to restore everyone's confidence in the market by making it known that you are better than people seem to think," the President told him.

"I have an idea, Mr. President," Redbridge proffered in a comforting tone. "You should call a press conference. Tell the media I will be appearing on the national news tomorrow... you don't know which one, yet. Then, as soon as John Hunter meets with me here at the hospital, I will have him contact Charlie at ABN... or Bill, at FAX. I will agree to do an interview with one of them for the evening news." Again there was a pause... Redbridge was smiling and it almost made Jake laugh. "Not at all," Redbridge said in a pleasant tone. "I'm happy to do it for you... I won't look my best, but people will know I'll soon be back in my office. You will have Agent Hunter contact me as soon as possible?" Another very brief pause and then, "Thank you. Good bye, Mr. President. I'll stay in touch."

Redbridge lay back on the pillows of his bed with an almost silly smile on his face. "It's like riding a bicycle, Jake. You don't forget how to do it, do you?" Jake laughed with him.

A soft knock sounded on the door. Jake quickly put a white towel over Arthur's face as the door swung open. It was Dr. Nordenberg. "Off with the towel, Mr. Chairman. It's just your friendly plastic surgeon come to do your pre-surgery examination and fill out some hospital forms."

Jake stopped the physician and asked him to provide two forms of identification. The doctor's eyebrows raised but he complied.

Jake checked both IDs carefully and then returned them to the man. "I hope you will understand, Dr. Nordenberg. Chairman Redbridge has had a security breach. We are double-checking everything." Jake held his hand out to the man and smiled at him warmly. "Would you mind stepping out to the nurse's station with me, Doctor?"

"I... I..." Doctor Nordenberg did not really have a chance to finish his sentence because Jake's hand on his shoulder moved him gently from the room.

"Nurse?" he asked one of the women at the nurse's station. "Who is this man?"

The woman looked at Jake as if he had lost his mind, but replied "Why, it's Doctor Nordenberg. Everyone at the hospital knows him. Why do you ask?"

Jake laughed. "I was just going to ask for his autograph, but wanted to make sure it was really him," he said, still chuckling.

"Oh, you..." she smiled back.

"Sorry, Doc," Jake said to Nordenberg, "but I'd rather be safe than sorry. Please don't take it out on Arthur when you start cutting on him," he grinned. The doctor hesitated and then gave a brief smile in return.

"Can I see my patient now?" he asked, somewhat curtly.

Jake entered the hospital room ahead of the doctor. "Mr. Chairman, this man is, indeed, who he says he is." Jake reached out and removed the towel from Redbridge's face. "He's all yours, Doc," was all he said. "Oh," Jake continued. "We'll be paying cash for hospital expenses and for your services," he said, handing him the hospital's admittance forms. "There will be no insurance forms..." He removed the clone's cell phone from Redbridge's hand as he moved away.

"The before photos you sent of your face and the ones you sent from ten years ago were certainly accurate, Mr. Chairman," Nordenberg told Redbridge.

"Call me Arthur, please," Redbridge said, smiling.

"Thank you, Arthur... my name is Ken."

A pre-surgical IV was started. Good, Jake thought. Arthur needed to relax. His blood pressure was taken and a medical history was given. It was only slightly after one o'clock when Arthur Redbridge, the man who had a little over an hour ago been sweating and trembling in the back of an ambulance, was wheeled out of his room to get his face fixed. When he came out and had time to heal, Jake had no doubt the man would look exactly like the picture of the clone that had been provided Dr. Nordenberg. After all, he thought, Ken was one of the best plastic surgeons in the country.

Within seconds after Redbridge was wheeled out of his room, Jake used his own cell phone to call Alex to let him know that Brett would arrive momentarily at the airport.

"Everything is ready and waiting," Alex told his friend. "Things went well?" he asked.

"Per plan," Jake replied.

"I see the ambulance coming," Alex said, interrupting his friend. "Got to go. Take good care of Meredith, Jake."

The connection was broken and Jake picked up the clone's cell phone to scroll through all of the personal numbers listed in the directory. Which numbers could Arthur dial to reach the international banking groups that needed to be contacted? Those calls would have to be made first thing tomorrow morning, he thought. It was too late European time to place a call now.

The clone's cell phone startled him when it rang. Should he answer it, Jake wondered? The caller ID listed the name John Hunter. Jake quickly hit Talk.

"This is Jake McGregor speaking. Is this John Hunter?"

There was a pause before a voice at the other end of the line said "Yes. Yes it is."

"I'm Brett Radov's former partner at the Agency. I believe he told you I would be at the hospital with the Chairman," Jake told the man. "I know you were expecting to hear Arthur Redbridge's voice, but he's in surgery right now, John. I expect it will be two or three hours before he's back in his room."

"I am calling at the request of the President of the United States," Hunter told him. He was unaware of the clones or the kidnappings. "How can I help, Jake?"

Jake told him to meet him at a coffee shop about two miles from the hospital in a half-hour. "Take every precaution not to be followed, John, by friend or foe. It's important." The coffee shop was closer to another private hospital than to this one, Jake thought, in case the President decided to put a tail on Hunter.

"I can give you the information you need... it would be better to do it away from the hospital," Jake told him. After putting a lock on Arthur's hospital room door and locking it, Jake departed the hospital, taking his own advice about not being followed.

"Jake McGregor," he said, holding out his hand to Hunter when he entered the restaurant.

"Have you got some ID, Jake?" was Hunter's only answer.

"I do if you do," was Jake's reply. He knew it was Hunter. Brett had given him a photo of the man.

With the identity question settled, both men ordered coffee and a club sandwich. This was going to be the tough part, Jake knew. He had to gain the man's acceptance... trust would not come easily. Not if the man was truly a good security guard.

"I'm not sure I know how much Brett told you," Jake began, attempting to gain some insight into the man. Jake was, indeed, very sure of what Brett had told Hunter.

"Why don't you start by telling me what I need to know about Chairman Redbridge's circumstances," John Hunter replied. "It's not every day I get a call from the President asking me to do him a personal favor."

Jake just looked at the man, trying to carefully pick his next words. He knew the next sentence out of his mouth would set the tone for how his and Hunter's relationship would progress from this point.

"Look, John," he said carefully, "you and I can keep going with my CIA or your Secret Service training in Interviews 101 and we'll get nowhere." He paused, looking directly into the man's eyes. "The President did not call you because everything is business as usual, did he?"

Hunter broke eye contact with Jake, looking down at his coffee. "I'd say that's valid." He grinned.

"Here's what I know," Jake began. "I'm helping Brett out. He's in Maine visiting an old friend... Justice Avery Scott. He knew I was in Washington and asked me if I could provide security for the Chairman until the President got in touch with you. He told me Redbridge had been in an accident. He suspects that his security team might be involved. I agreed to help. When Dr. Redbridge and I discussed his concerns, I suggested that he could call the President and ask for you. Brett gave me your name. He says you are good at what you do and Dr. Redbridge needs someone he can trust right now. So far, so good?"

Hunter said nothing but nodded.

"It will be a few days before Brett can join Dr. Redbridge to head his new security team. Brett hopes you'll join him on that detail after your retirement." Again, there was a long pause as Jake let the carrot of a plum after-retirement job hang in the air.

"When the President spoke with Dr. Redbridge, he – Dr. Redbridge – agreed to do an interview with Charlie at ABN, or Bill at FAX. The first thing he needs is an Agreement drawn up. ABN or FAX will announce the interview on tonight's news. Redbridge agreed to do this on behalf of the President... I assume you've heard that the Dow is falling like a rock. That agreement must also guarantee that the network will not try to find or divulge the whereabouts of the Chairman for any reason. I'm sure you can understand that right now Dr. Redbridge needs anonymity so we can maintain his safety. He doesn't need a media feeding frenzy outside of the hospital. Are we agreed?"

Hunter slowly nodded his head before speaking. "So you want me to get a contract written offering Charlie at ABN – or Bill at FAX? – or is the agreement for both of them?"

"Only one person… Let's say Charlie at ABN on one copy and Bill at FAX on another – keep our options open, as it were. If Charlie doesn't agree to our terms, an Agreement is ready to offer Bill. As I'm sure you've noticed, we do not have a lot of time. I wrote a rough draft based on what Dr. Redbridge says he wants…" Jake handed the papers carefully written at the ranch by himself, Redbridge and Justice Scott to the man. "I hope it'll help."

"Okay," Hunter replied. "Oh. I see what the President and the Chairman are trying to accomplish. They want to make sure Wall Street knows that the Chairman is in a recovery mode and will soon return to his office so the markets will stabilize."

"You got it," Jake told him, smiling. "It was Dr. Redbridge's idea. He made the offer to the President on the telephone before he went into surgery." Again, he paused for effect. "Your first job is to get that Agreement put together ASAP. We need it at the hospital by three p.m. My job is to return to the hospital and make sure security is provided for the Chairman until you get the Agreement done, bring it back to the hospital for Dr. Redbridge or myself to examine, and then, from your Secret Service office, get a copy of it faxed immediately to ABN in New York."

Again, Hunter nodded. So far, so good, Jake thought.

"Oh," he said, reaching out to touch the other man's arm. "One thing the Chairman wants in the Agreement to ensure no one will find the hospital. Until we get this security team matter cleared up, John, we can't let anyone know where he is. He wants them to agree to the Chairman's terms of transport to and from the hospital where they will do the interview."

Hunter looked at Jake with a half-smile on his face. "You're pretty good at what you do, aren't you, McGregor? I read your record… interesting. I doubt the Chairman thought of these things. Can you tell me how you want transport to occur?"

Jake just returned the half-smile. "I help where I can," he said. "A panel truck, no windows. You'll pick them up, they will be driven to the basement parking garage of the hospital and taken to the Chairman's room. There will be no identifiers telling them in which hospital the Chairman is a patient in the elevators or hallways. I'll clear all personnel from the area before you arrive with the camera crew." Jake paused. "Is there anything you would add to that?"

Hunter thought for a moment. "Only that you probably need to stop somewhere under some kind of cover and change vehicles on the way to the hospital... just in case either of the networks gets cute and tries to follow the vehicle that picks them up from the air."

Jake smiled. "Great idea! Be sure and add that to the plan." The man had taken the bait and crossed the "t" that Jake had left uncrossed. That was precisely what he and Alex had planned. Now it was Hunter's plan, too.

"So, where the hell is the hospital? Which one is it? I checked the emergency rooms at all of the hospitals before I came here and none of them treated an auto accident case this morning." Hunter took the last gulp of the coffee in front of him and held up his hand when a waitress approached with a pot to give him a re-fill.

"When you get the Agreement done, call me at the same number you called earlier," Jake said, ignoring Hunter's question. "It is Chairman Redbridge's personal cell phone number. Guard it. Please do two things. First, hurry. We need to get this done ASAP. Second, make sure no one is tracking you – friendly or otherwise. The truth is, at the moment we don't know who is friendly and who isn't. Are we in agreement?"

Hunter thought for a moment, then held out his hand and Jake grasped it in a firm handshake. "Indeed we are," was all he said to Jake as he got up to leave.

Jake took a circuitous route back to the hospital and, when he arrived, unlocked and re-entered Redbridge's room. He pulled his own cell phone from his jacket pocket and called Alex. "Your plane is in the air?" he asked when his friend answered. When he got a positive response, Jake told Alex to make the call to the Russian Embassy. "When you get the address where I can put your evidence package in Malashenko's hands, call me back."

As he disconnected, Alex looked across the aisle at the sleeping clone. He had regained semi-consciousness about the time they took off. He looked at Alex curiously. He knew he recognized this man's face... but from where? Alex spoke to him soothingly in Russian and told him to sleep, that he was being given back his life by a grateful Motherland. The man smiled, drank some of the water Alex offered him, and closed his eyes.

When Jake's call had come, the plane was somewhere over Ohio. After he hung up, Alex moved away from the clone so he would not be overheard. He dialed the number of the Russian Embassy in Washington, D.C. He asked to speak to General Yuri Malashenko. When asked who was calling, he said to tell General Malashenko that Dr. Aleksandr Plotnikov needed to speak with him.

"Plotnikov?" the surprised voice was easily identifiable. It was Malashenko. He still sounded bigger than life but he also sounded skeptical. He must be wondering what he had done to be so lucky, Alex thought. He probably thought a bird he had hunted for years was falling from the skies, right into his lap.

"Yuri," Alex responded. "You sound like life has been good to you. It's too bad I cannot offer you fresh fish from the waters around Sakhalin Island, but I'm calling to tell you that the four clones we took from the island have been returned to their real lives." Malashenko attempted to break into the conversation, but Alex cut him off.

"Before you trace this call, I will tell you it is being made from an airplane. It is being made with a throw-away cell phone... the kind you buy at Wal-Mart, use the minutes, then throw in the trash. It will not be used again and any trace on it will be useless." He paused for a moment.

General Yuri Malashenko did not try to interrupt him again.

"Please listen and do not talk, General. I have no desire to put our two countries into a dangerous confrontation reminiscent of the 1960s. You and I both know that would be the result if I disclosed the cloning program. Shall I continue?" Alex asked.

It felt strange to talk in his native tongue. It had been over fifteen years. There was a long pause at the other end of the telephone.

"Da," was the man's response. "I will listen... I am interested," Malashenko said in a somewhat subdued voice.

"Tell me where you are. A document will be delivered to you. It lists all of the items, including photographs, I have to prove what the U.S.S.R. did by creating clones and how Russia has continued this deception. I will direct the courier to put this information into your hands only and no one else's. Give the appropriate directions to your Embassy staff.

"This material will tell you what you must do if Russia is to be spared what will be a world crisis. Washington, London, Paris, Brussels... they will all know how you created clones and embedded them in power positions. I did not leave Russia without sufficient information to confirm the charges I would make. Do you understand?"

"Da," Malashenko said again, his voice barely above a whisper. "I am at the Embassy in New York City." Alex wrote the address as it was given. "I will make the necessary arrangements." He paused for a moment before continuing. "Is there any way we can discuss this, Aleksandr?"

"Do you think I am unaware of the kill on sight order Russia has on me, Yuri?" Alex could not hide the bitterness from his voice. "No. There is nothing to discuss. I will tell you this and make no mistake that I am serious. If any attempt is made to harm any of the four men who have replaced their clones – Scott, Redbridge, Martinez or Branchman – any agreement will be forgotten. All of the information will be delivered not only to newspapers. We know the socialists control some – even most – of them. But you do not control bloggers on the Internet. You do not control talk radio – though you are trying. Additionally, the material will be immediately delivered to numerous government agencies." Alex paused. "If I have to print leaflets and drop them on American cities, I will make sure people learn what you have done."

There was another long pause. "I understand," Malashenko said. "But you know I need approval from...from those higher up than I am," he replied. He sounded frustrated. He probably was frustrated. He was a powerful man and was not used to being backed into a corner.

"Yuri," Alex said, chuckling, "I am sure you have recorded this conversation. How long does it take to call your contacts in Moscow and replay a three-minute telephone conversation? You won't even need to find a translator. By the way, we are just flying through the air space of the busiest airport in America. I am hanging up, Yuri. It will be impossible for you to track so many aircraft traveling in so many different directions. The information will be delivered to you in New York this afternoon. Your security details assigned to the four clones have been replaced. If I were the Russian government, I would make sure that none of these four men slips on an icy street and falls. If anything happens to any of them, I will hold you responsible and all deals are off. Goodbye, Yuri Malashenko."

Alex quickly hung up the telephone and immediately picked up another cell phone and dialed Jake's number.

"It's done," he told him. "Malashenko is at the New York Russian Embassy. I told him you would deliver the material to him by this evening." Alex gave Jake the address.

"Consider it done," Jake told him. "This puts three men on base and a heavy-hitter at the plate."

"Okay, Mickey," Alex said chuckling, "bring them home safely," Alex told his friend.

Jake left Redbridge's hospital room, locking the door behind him. Redbridge's private nursing staff had arrived. It was time to brief them and give them the key to Arthur's room. He needed to get to New York quickly.

Chapter 33

"Good evening, Mr. Chairman," said the highly recognizable voice of the man who read the evening news every night for America's most popular television network.

"Good evening to you, Charlie… and good evening, America," Arthur's face was a bit swollen and he had bandages around his head. The stitches on his face were hidden by makeup. Otherwise he looked healthy. Dressed in a bathrobe, he was sitting in a chair for the interview.

"So… what can you tell the American people about what happened to you, Dr. Redbridge?" The concerned half-smile, the sincere yet boyish look on Charlie's face was something with which everyone in the country was familiar. Somehow, it comforted people. It made what he said about the world believable.

Redbridge looked gently serious as his eyes moved to the camera. "First, since this was a very public accident, I thought I should let everyone know that I'm okay."

"And you and your security team took excellent precautions to keep even me and my camera crew from knowing in which hospital you reside," Charlie added with a bit of a smug smile on his face.

"Well, Charlie, you and I both know that if someone leaked the location of my hospital, everyone would blame you… or they would blame the President." Redbridge chuckled, trying not to smile enough to hurt his face. "So, those extreme measures benefit us all… you, me, the President."

After a brief laugh, Charlie's face grew serious. "What can you tell us about your condition, Mr. Chairman?" The answer to this particular question had been rehearsed numerous times at the ranch during the past month.

"Well… my head did get banged around and I was unconscious and I do have a minor concussion. I need to stay in bed for a week or so." He paused briefly. "As you can see from the bandages, I also have some facial cuts caused by broken glass. But I wanted to do this interview so the American people know that aside from minor injuries – which the doctors are watching – I am just fine and will be back in my office within two weeks." Arthur once again gazed directly into the camera with a look of complete sincerity on his face. Jake watched from the sidelines with John Hunter. Both were pleased.

Redbridge paused. "I'll be staying in touch with my office… handling things from here, as it were. I have very qualified people working with me at the Federal Central Bank and have complete confidence in them." There was another pause. Charlie was about to ask him another question when Redbridge continued. "I have appointed a new administrator who will be working on my behalf, making sure everything gets from the office to the hospital, then back to the office again. The American people should have confidence that nothing in the markets is going to change because I got banged on the head. Everything is fine."

"Do you have a name for us? Who is your new administrator?" This was a breaking bit of news and one for which Charlie had not been prepared.

"You will have a press release in your hands tomorrow, Charlie. It is a woman I have known for many years… someone with an impeccable reputation in the banking industry." Arthur just smiled. Charlie tried one more time to get a name, but no word came from the Chairman's mouth. He just smiled, and the interview moved to its conclusion.

Arthur looked totally relaxed but like someone who had suffered minimal injuries in a car accident.

"Thank you, Arthur Redbridge, Chairman of the Federal Central Bank." Charlie reached out to shake Redbridge's hand and then turned back to the camera. "And there we have it. Fed Chairman Arthur Redbridge is better than anyone expected after hearing witness reports of his serious injuries at the scene of the auto accident that hospitalized him yesterday."

The appropriate after-interview camera shots were taken from behind Redbridge's head showing Charlie looking as if he were listening intently to Arthur Redbridge. There were warm goodbyes and the news crew left. Arthur got up and lay back down in his bed.

Jake had cleared the halls and John Hunter took the crew down the elevator, put them in the back of the black panel truck – the one in which they had been picked up was white – and drove them back to the car that awaited them. They would fly hastily from Baltimore back to New York where the interview would be edited and run. After the exclusive appeared on Charlie's network, all of the other networks would have it available for the late-night news.

"I will stay with you until Hunter returns, Arthur," Jake told the man with the painful face, "and then I have to get back to the hotel to see Meredith. She needs to be updated on your conversations this morning with the various international banking groups. When do you think it will be safe for her to go to the Fed office on your behalf?"

"I wouldn't let her go out until day-after-tomorrow, Jake," Redbridge said. "And, you need to bring her here, first. All of the networks are going to want to interview her... I think you should let Bill at FAX do this one, don't you?" He winced again as a soft groan escaped his lips. "God my face hurts," was all he said. "Would you ask that nurse if she would bring me some pain medication?"

Jake sympathized with the man. He had done everything that had been asked of him and done it well. He called the private nurse into the room and requested some pain relief for the Fed Chairman. When John Hunter returned, Jake left for the night. Again, he was tired.

"Well," he began his conversation with Meredith, "are you ready to be seen on the business pages... on the network news? Arthur is healing nicely. He's in pain, but he'll be fine. John Hunter is spending the night with him."

He gave her a complete overview of the events of the day. Alex was back at the ranch. All of the clones were a bit lethargic and confused, but all seemed to be coming out of their day of drugging on schedule. William Leonard was helping Alex question the clones and they would be sending information within a day or two.

"And, Arthur wants to see you first thing in the morning. We will take a picture of the two of you together, write a press release, and send a copy to the *Washington Post*, the *New York Times*, the *Wall Street Journal*, the *Associated Press, Reuters*, and all of the television networks. Day after tomorrow, you are on the job." He walked to the refrigerator in the suite's living room and poured himself a drink. "How about having room service bring you some cranberry juice?" he asked. She smiled, nodding. It sounded good.

"So the international calls were made to the right people this morning?" she asked.

"Yes. Arthur wanted to make them before the interview. They went just as expected. Arthur told them he has hired you to coordinate things between his office and the hospital… that you are right under his thumb where he can keep an eye on you. You are his new administrator. He told them you brought Jeffrey's material in the envelope to him because you did not understand it, but thought it might be important. The material was sent to them by courier and they will have it in their hands first thing in the morning." He paused to take a sip of his Scotch and water. "We changed the manila envelope… didn't want to give them any insight into what Jeffrey was trying to tell you with the swan's neck," he finished.

He walked to the door of the second bedroom in the suite and told her he would be staying there for the next few days. "How about having dinner tonight here in the living room? About seven?" he asked.

She agreed.

Everyone, including Justice Avery Scott, J.J. Branchman and Senator John Martinez and their bodyguards enjoyed seeing the Arthur Redbridge interview from his hospital room. They all thought it bordered on magic that the plans they had been discussing just three days ago had been so carefully implemented. Watching it play out in front of them on their television screens helped bring into focus what a tremendous job of planning had been done to make it all happen. Now, they realized, it was their turn to put some plans into action.

The next morning there was no doubt that Meredith was nervous. As she and Jake entered Redbridge's hospital room, Arthur introduced Meredith to Hunter and told him she was now his personal administrator. She would coordinate things for him until he returned to work. Arthur then suggested Hunter leave the three of them alone for a planning session, take some time off and then return.

Hunter was grateful to get the time away. This assignment had come out of nowhere and he needed to take care of things at his office before walking away from his old job.

As soon as she entered Arthur's hospital room, Meredith frowned at the bandages that covered his head and part of his face. She bent over to give him a gentle hug.

The picture of Meredith and Arthur Redbridge holding papers in their hands and meeting in his hospital room was carried on the front page of newspapers around the country. It was given special, prominence in Colorado papers. She lived in the state and it was big news that the number one person serving the Chairman of America's Central Bank was a Colorado resident.

When Meredith went to the Fed office the first time, she took with her a video tape filmed by Jake. It was Arthur, speaking to his employees from his hospital bed. He instructed everyone in the office to help Meredith Morgan in any way they could... to understand that when she spoke they should hear his voice. The first thing she asked for was a list of all employees, their titles, and their dates of hire. She knew the message that would send to personnel put in place by the Russians and expected a rash of resignations within a day or two.

Meanwhile, back at the ranch, Alex worked all day every day with the clones. It was amazing to watch their own hormones reassert themselves and begin to dominate their relatively young bodies. The Redbridge clone was the oldest and the age began to melt from his face within the first week of treatment. At first, they had been terrified when they awoke, locked in a room in a strange place. Even so, each of them had provided important information and it had been forwarded to the four Real Things.

William Leonard was of great assistance to Alex. It had surprised the scientist. He thought of the man as mostly talk… Leonard had to be the smoothest talker Alex had ever met. The longer he was exposed to him and what was obviously a brilliant mind, the more depth Alex found in him. He had issues with trust. Alex could sympathize and relate. When you live your life hiding and telling lies to survive, trust is difficult.

Meredith's face appeared with periodic regularity in newspaper photos and television coverage on evening news shows. Her interview with Bill on FAX went extremely well. She was more than able to handle the pointed questions the famed no-nonsense news editorialist threw at her. Meredith liked the guy and admired his style. She watched him every night and had known what to expect.

During the next two weeks, the numerous jobs that were suddenly vacated at the Federal Central Bank, a New York radio station and at Senator Martinez's and Justice Scott's offices were quickly and quietly filled by applicants who had been interviewed by Jake and Brett two months earlier. They had advertised the most likely positions in large cities around the country. Alex had been sure that high-level positions at each man's office had been staffed by the Russians and was proven right.

Alex had negotiated hard with Malashenko to save the lives of the other clones on the list identified by him and the four Real Things. The Russians had agreed to use age reversal drugs on them and to support the clones' re-entry into lives in their homeland. Many of the Real Things held in captivity on Sakhalin Island had died. Alex was able to verify that claim through the same contact that had helped him steal the four men from the island and bring them to the ranch. The few who still lived would stay in Russia. Malashenko guaranteed them a comfortable life lived in relative freedom in small towns where any protestation of identity would fall on deaf ears. They would, of course, be warned to keep their identities secret… or face the consequences.

Though it was not the best possible outcome, it was certainly better than what had awaited them... death on a lonely island while living in a prison camp.

After six days in the hospital, Arthur Redbridge was released and returned to a home in which he had never lived. Thanks to Meredith, he knew where to go in the house to find his bedroom. He knew what to call the dog that came running to him as he entered the house and, as the maid expected, she was told what special doggie treat to provide for the Weimaraner. He looked for the large portrait of Helen that had been painted years before, but there was no sign of it. Jake found it in the basement. It was immediately re-hung over the fireplace where Arthur could see it every night when he came home.

Three days after his homecoming, Meredith and Jake accompanied him to his wife's grave site where each of them placed flowers. Redbridge knelt by her grave for a long time before Jake urged him to return to his car. Most of the bandages were gone and the stitches had been removed. The scars would soon recede. He already looked ten years younger. Meredith, Jake and John Hunter would remain guests in his home until he returned to his office in about a week. After that, Arthur was planning a family reunion with his children.

Things were getting back to normal. The three Real Things returned to their jobs and everyone involved with the project was close to a radio on the morning of January 22nd.

"Here it is, folks." The voice of J.J. Branchman came over the radio at Alex's lab. His bumper music followed his initial words.

"It is January 22nd and we are already seeing the hypocrisy of the promises, promises crowd in Congress. We're going to talk about that and other political issues today, but before we do, I have some comments I want to direct to a group of people from whom I have learned much about love of country and of my fellow man.

"I won't tell you their names, because they are very private people. I spent a great deal of time with them while I was away from the station... on vacation, as you all know. They reminded me that freedom cannot exist without hope and neither can exist without truth."

413

J.J. paused for a moment, making a couple of side comments on topics people related to him and his show. He kept reminding himself that he had to keep one foot on his clone's format road for a short time.

"I have a project," J.J. began, slowly. "I hope you are going to support me in this new endeavor." There was a long pause. "I am starting a national newspaper called '*We Hold These Truths.*' I have hired legal experts to evaluate each and every piece of legislation that comes before the U.S. Congress. I have hired public policy experts to analyze the impact on you and me of any legislation put before the Congress. I have hired two accountants who retired from the General Accounting Office. They will analyze the short and long-term cost of any Bill on which the Congress votes. All of these things will appear daily in *We Hold These Truths.*

"I'm looking for writers. I'm working on hiring an editor. Right now, the one I have my eye on is working in our nation's capitol, but I know she will be available soon.

"The newspaper will accept no advertising so you can be sure no corporate dollars will influence news content. The paper will be supported via subscriptions only. I guess I'm about to find out if there really are enough of you out there who want to know the truth about what's going on, aren't I?

"So... that's how I'm starting my New Year. When we come back from our commercial break, we are going to talk about the items it looks like the Supreme Court will be evaluating during its spring session, so... stay with me."

Jake and Meredith looked at one another across the lunch table at Arthur's home.

"And how much vacation do you get between this job and editing a new national newspaper, Mrs. Plotnikov?" Jake asked.

Jake and Arthur both chuckled, but Meredith remained quiet. John Hunter quietly eyed one side of the table, then the other.

Arthur Redbridge would be returning to his office the next day. For the past two days he had practically lived on his secure line talking with William Leonard. The FBI had provided new security for Justice Scott and Brett would be joining them for Arthur's return to office. John Hunter would guard the home while Brett provided security at the Fed's offices. Two additional guards would be added to the Redbridge staff. They all felt that Jake and Meredith would be able to return home within three or four days. She would have to stay close to the new, scrambled telephone at the ranch, in case Arthur needed access to a detail she knew and he did not.

Jake and Meredith knew William Leonard's fortune was supposed to buy America's currency out of danger and begin getting the federal deficit paid. Redbridge ranked the hidden tax of inflation as one of the major problems of the economy, one caused by the Fed having overprinted the currency for so many years. Meredith knew that Arthur had come to embrace totally the idea that the same game that had brought down the Soviet ruble was now being played with the American dollar. He intended to do everything within his power to stop it.

While lunch was being served and eaten at the Redbridge residence, Senator John Martinez was sitting in the private "For Senators Only" Senate Dining Room. His lunch partners were two conservative Republican Senators, one from Kentucky, another from Iowa.

"I am telling you, the immigration amnesty legislation will not pass." The comment came from Senator Scott Coomer of Kentucky. "I don't get home as much as I'd like, but when I do, illegal immigration is what people talk about," he told Martinez.

"Well," Martinez told him, the look on his face making it appear that whatever he was about to say was painful but necessary, "if I can get your support for a piece of legislation I'm working on, you just might convince me to change my vote on the immigration bill to 'nay,'" he said, his eyes looking down at the dining room table.

Senators Coomer and Silver were almost stunned into silence by the Martinez remark. One of the most powerful liberal Democrats in the U.S. Senate was willing to cross party lines and vote 'no' on the liberal cause of the year? The new Democrat Congress had promised amnesty would get passed, come hell or high water! Senator Martinez was known to vote the party line every time a vote came to the floor.

"You are joking, of course," Senator Art Silver remarked, smiling.

"Well," Martinez replied, smiling back at each and nervously turning a fork on his napkin over and over, "maybe I am. Then again, maybe I'm not." There was a long pause. Martinez could see the two men were all but holding their breath. This would be a huge break for them if he was telling the truth.

"You know, there comes a point in any statesman's life when his country rather than his party comes first. I may have reached that point. I come up for re-election in five years and Fran and I have decided to travel and see the world while we still can. I don't plan on running for reelection... I haven't really decided, but I'm seriously thinking about hanging it up. If I make this decision – if I'm willing to change my vote – I want some commitment from your Republican friends to support a new piece of legislation I plan to introduce. Hopefully, it will come up for a vote in Committee – your Committee, Scott – as quickly as possible. If I could get that Bill to the Senate floor just before the Immigration Bill... well, who knows what I might do?"

Senators Coomer and Silver looked at one another for an extended time before either of them dared answer.

"And what is this legislation you want to get passed, John?" Senator Silver asked him.

"Well, actually I think you and your Republican friends might like it," Martinez answered, smiling at both of them. "You know how you guys have been trying since forever to make the capital gains-tax disappear? My legislation would help you." He picked up his iced tea and took a long drink.

Martinez then proceeded to extract from each man a promise that not one word of what he was about to tell them would pass their lips should they not agree to give their support... not to their fellow Republicans, or anyone else. After a lot of discussion to determine precisely what it was they were committing to, both men agreed to be silent.

"I will hold both of you to that promise. It's a matter of honor now." He took a deep breath, spread both hands with fingers separated over his plate... they were still awaiting their food. "My Bill basically says the following: 'During any calendar year, any publicly traded American-based company that creates more jobs for verified

American workers living in the United States than it provides for workers in nations other than the United States will earn the right for all who invest in that corporation's stock to pay no capital gains tax on it the following year.' I haven't completed the final language yet... I was hoping you might help me, Scott. What I just gave you was a simple overview."

Martinez's two lunch companions just stared at him. They could not have heard him right. He, one of the biggest liberals in the United States Senate, was going to propose what amounted to a very conservative Bill on the floor of the Senate. Coomer and Silver both knew that every Republican who was not owned by big business would vote for such legislation and they told him so.

"That's what I thought," Martinez said quietly, "but I needed to make sure. You can both see why I want to get this Bill to the Senate floor before I vote against the Immigration-Amnesty Bill? I will be able to sell my Bill to a number of Democrats on the basis of the support it will gain from labor... not unions, but labor. It means more jobs for Americans. That's why I think with a little help from your side of the aisle, I can get enough votes to get it passed.

"Once I take the floor to expound on why the Immigration-Amnesty Bill does nothing but reward lawbreakers from another country – and explain why we do not get to choose which laws the nation enforces – my credibility with my own party may be shot. I wouldn't be able to get my own legislation passed... even though we have a slight majority at the present time. That's why I need to get this done first."

"Why?" Art Silver asked him simply.

Martinez chuckled, more to himself than anyone else. "I believe the one-worlders are going to get the job done this time if we don't do something to stop them. I am no longer going to ignore the Oath of Office I took to preserve and protect the Constitution. I am no longer going to support my party over my country. I would appreciate it if you would not let that get around. I have not become a conservative or a Republican. You guys spent more on pork barrel projects since 1994 when you gained control of the Congress than the Democrats ever thought of spending. Frankly, I don't see many conservative roots hanging around these halls. I see a lot of Republicans, and

I see a lot of Republicans who, whenever an election nears, call themselves conservatives. But I don't see many real conservatives, gentlemen.

"Over the holidays, I got to thinking about what one thing would do more to stimulate job growth than anything else. Shipping jobs overseas or giving them to illegals for slave wages has to stop. I believe this legislation will increase corporate profits and attract investors. No one wants to pay capital gains taxes on their investments. Corporations that create jobs for Americans will attract investors to their stock like bees to honey because there will be no capital gains taxes levied the next year. I'm right, aren't I, Scott? Economics isn't my strong suit... that's why I wanted to talk with you and Art."

"Out of the mouths of babes..." Silver began. "John, it's a brilliant idea. I'm sick that we didn't think of it. What else have you been thinking of... any other ideas?"

"Oh," Martinez began, thinking of the message he'd had from Arthur Redbridge on his secure telephone last night, "I've got some ideas, but I have to work on them."

"Whew," Silver said, shaking his head. "You are talking free enterprise, John. You'd best be careful or your compatriots will have you committed."

"Well," John said, a tight smile on his face, "if we counted the number of neo-conservative Republicans who understand how to spell 'free enterprise,' how many do you think could do it, Art?"

They all laughed. Coomer and Silver knew John Martinez was right.

Justice Avery Scott returned from Maine to his Washington home. His wife, Lindy, found herself surprised over and over again by his thoughtfulness... the change in him. She wondered what had happened to him while he was in Maine.

"How does this sound, Lindy?" he asked her. He hadn't asked her opinion about a legal statement in... over ten years, she knew.

"What in the world happened to you while you were away, Avery? You are... well, you are like your old self. Since you came home, you are different. Did you meet a woman or something?"

He laughed. "I certainly did Lindy, but not the kind you think. Just someone whose opinion I respect. What happened to me in Maine? Good question. You always could ask the best questions. I used to rely on you to keep me on track. What happened to me in Maine is that I found my soul again, Lindy. I found my soul. And guess what? My soul doesn't live by itself. You are part of it."

Lindy blinked the tears away quickly and asked him what he would like for dinner. They decided to eat out. Justice Avery Scott wanted some crown pork roast. He could not believe how good freedom felt.

When the Scotts returned from dinner, he told her he was going to work for awhile. He invited her to join him if she didn't mind reading in his office instead of in bed. And that is how Justice Avery Scott and his wife Lindy slipped back into the habits they had once shared.

"I'd appreciate it if you'd buy something for us for the holidays next year, my love," he told her.

"Next year's holidays? My, we are planning ahead, aren't we?"

"Well... I don't want to forget it. I want to get a copy of the video, 'Holiday Inn.' Some people call it 'White Christmas.' I want to put that knight back on that white horse for you this year. When we watch Bing and Rosemary romance, you can tell me how I did, okay?"

She just nodded, picked up a book and followed him into his office.

On March 21st, Justice Scott would show his new colors. He would join with what was usually the minority to write a majority opinion about abortion being an issue that should be decided by legislatures and voters in each state. He would use the 10th Amendment as the base for what he knew would be the majority opinion. "The powers not delegated to the United States by the Constitution, nor prohibited by it to the States, are reserved to the States respectively."

Also just before March 21st, the Court would hear arguments about a Border Patrol agent who had been sent to prison by a federal prosecutor. The prosecutor, it appeared, suppressed evidence that violated the rules of Discovery. He would write an opinion stating that the man was entitled to a new trial.

The third case really interested Scott because it spoke to the very essence of American sovereignty he had discussed so heatedly with his former roommates at "the ranch." He smiled as he thought of the experience and wondered if he would ever know where he had been held during those months of despair and rejuvenated hope.

This case had to do with a decision for the State of Idaho v. the United States of America. Idaho's legislature, along with Montana and Oklahoma, had passed laws telling its U.S. Congressional representatives to halt any work that was being done by the federal government on plans to establish a trade zone for America, Mexico and Canada. The Executive Office had no Constitutional right to make such an agreement without the involvement of the Legislative Branch of government. The agreement signed by the President of the United States drew together the nations of Mexico, the United States and Canada into a single trade zone sharing a single currency and would resemble the European Union.

Scott remembered the video tape he had watched at the ranch... the clear lines of authority regarding American currency that Meredith Morgan had explained. The United States Congress had responsibility for America's currency, not the President and not the Federal Central Bank. As he read very old precedents, it appeared to Scott the government had been in violation of Constitutional law for a long time regarding the creation of money.

The final case that would be decided had been filed by a citizen who objected to the Food and Drug Administration being given control over vitamins, herbs and other food supplements. As Justice Scott read through the materials presented by both sides, he shook his head at the multitude of conflicts of interest of those who sat on the Board of the FDA. How could people who made most of their incomes from the pharmaceutical industry make fair decisions regarding whether a natural substance rather than a pharmaceutical product might be best for people? It might be a good story for J.J., he decided.

"Come on Lindy," he said to his wife, "I've had enough law for one night. Have you had enough reading? Let's go to bed... and I think it's too damned cold for us to be sleeping in separate bedrooms, don't you?"

She tilted her head and smiled at him. "Just don't get too cozy, Avery. Remember what I told you years ago when you decided to start sleeping around with sweet young things. We won't be lovers again until you have a blood test for HIV and whatever other tests you need for STDs." She rose from her chair and took his hand. "I love you, darling, but I also love my health."

Avery Scott put his arm around the shoulders of the woman he had loved for so many years. Since their marriage, he had never slept with another woman... but his clone obviously had.

"Darling," he said, "you might not believe it, but I cannot tell you how grateful I am that you made such a wise decision. I will schedule an appointment with the doctor tomorrow... I may not be able to tell you why I know the tests will be negative, but take some comfort in knowing that I am sure they will be."

"You know what Ronnie always said," she responded in a kindly voice. "Trust, but verify."

Chapter 34

"Take good care of this man, you two. As long as he's okay, your grandchildren stand a good chance of living in a free country when they grow up," Meredith told Brett Radov and John Hunter as she bid farewell to Arthur Redbridge. She waved at them and walked happily toward the Lear jet.

It was a long flight. After landing in Rifle, the drive from the airport to the ranch seemed interminable. As they approached the ranch, Meredith took a deep breath and looked at Jake who had, she thought, a silly grin on his face.

"Mrs. Plotnikov, I believe that is your husband waiting for you on the porch," he said calmly. "It looks like he has a big red dog by his side." He paused, smiling at her. "I will be moving on after I say hello to Alex." He paused. "I'll be next door if you guys need me."

"You are the second most wonderful man I know. We'll have dinner here tomorrow night so we can have a talk… just like old times."

They stepped out of the car and Meredith walked into her husband's arms. It was at that moment she truly knew she was home. She held him as tightly as she could until Alex let her go long enough to give Jake a welcome home hug and slap on the back while she gave Rusty a kiss on the forehead. The dog would pout for a few days… he always did when she left him for longer than a day.

As Gil turned the SUV around to take Jake home, Alex feasted his eyes on this woman he so loved. He took her hand and they went inside. The security wall that usually covered the downstairs from view was open and she feasted her eyes on what had been so dominant in her thoughts these past weeks: Home.

Meredith walked to the center of the living room, took in the blazing fire, and turned to him with a look he had never seen in her eyes.

"I need to get your bags," he told her. "I'll be right back." Alex decided he would wait until Jake had time to get over the cattle guards before he turned the security system back on.

She nodded, realizing she had not yet said one word to him. After depositing her bags in their bedroom, Alex walked back into the living room and picked up the stereo remote. He took her hand.

"I would like this dance, wife," he told her softly as the strains of "Lara's Theme" filled the room. When it ended, he placed a hand on each side of her face and looked her straight in the eyes. "Someday, we'll meet again my love... And there are dreams, all that your heart can hold..." he repeated the lyrics from the song. "You have said nothing," he told her. "Are you okay?" His thumbs wiped the tears that spilled from the outer edges of her eyes and he smiled gently and reassuringly at her.

"I... think... I'm a bit overcome," she said quietly, sobs permeating her words. "You could not have given me a better homecoming," she said after gaining control of her tears. "I will never forget it. Oh, Alex," she said as the sobs started again, "I cannot tell you how happy I am to be home... how happy I am to know that wherever you are *is* my home." He had never seen her cry so hard and it startled him. He remembered her telling him that she usually showed little or no emotion because the turmoil of her life had caused her to build such big walls around her heart. She feared breaking down the walls because she had so much emotion stored up behind them. Maybe the day of Jericho had arrived for her.

"You look like a banker... a beautiful banker, but a banker," he said gently. "Why don't you take a shower? Then you can take a short nap."

She smiled agreeably and walked down the hallway. Meredith looked tired. She had been off of the IVs for almost three weeks. He knew it was too soon for that to happen. As she showered, he put her luggage on the bed to make unpacking easier for her. He was going to get a DNA IV ready for her while she napped. They would go out for dinner. As he walked back to the living room, the idea of going somewhere in public together was pleasing.

"So, Dr. Plotnikov," the Russian words came from the doorway above him, "you gave up being a prominent scientist in the Motherland to become a cowboy out West in America."

The hair on the back of his neck stood up as Alex recognized the voice of General Yuri Malashenko. He turned slowly and faced the nemesis from his past. Malashenko was dressed in full military attire. He had grown into a striking older man.

"I don't recall inviting you into my home," Alex replied in English. "I knew I should have kept the security system turned on but..." he shrugged his shoulders.

"But I am in," Malashenko replied as he walked slowly down the stairs, his boot heels clicking rather loudly against the wood as he descended each stair. "I am in and you and I have some unfinished business." His voice was not threatening or ominous, just a horrid reminder of a past Alex wanted dead. "I come in peace, scientist," he finally said.

A growl sounded from behind Alex and Malashenko's eyes widened as he saw a large red Doberman standing in the entry hallway, white fangs showing.

"You had better come in peace." The voice came from the behind the dog, further down the hallway. Meredith walked into the room holding the shotgun Alex kept in their bedroom. It was pointed at the Russian. She wore a purple silk nightshirt that came halfway down her thighs and buttoned down the front. Her hair was dripping water. She put her hand, fingers down, in front of Rusty's nose, telling him to 'Stay...'" then moved slowly toward the stranger in their home. She instinctively knew who he was. "It's Yuri Malashenko, isn't it?"

"So," Malashenko said, smiling, "you have a cowgirl to protect you? Alex... what has become of you? What kind of future can you build here with uncivilized people who threaten guests in your home with weapons?"

"The way I heard it, Yuri, my husband said you were not invited into our home. Now, I suggest you unbuckle that belt and put your firearm on the ground. I warn you that if you take one step towards me, that dog will be all over you like beets in borscht."

Malashenko did as she requested. "You have a wife, Plotnikov?" He looked at her more carefully. Under the wet head he recognized the front page pictures of Arthur Redbridge's new administrator. "Please tell your wife to put down the shotgun and restrain the dog, Alex. I have three armed men outside and if one of them should walk in and find me in danger, someone might get hurt."

Alex moved slowly toward Meredith and took the weapon from her hands. Meredith quickly walked toward Malashenko and told him to step away from his weapon. When he did, she picked up the belt and the weapon in it and handed them to Alex.

"Why are you here?" Alex asked in a tone Meredith had never heard him use. His voice sounded like ice.

"Good question, my friend. I am doing a favor for your Secretary of State because it is an action with which your Department of State can have no involvement. Can we sit down and talk?" Malashenko walked slowly towards the living room. "I am going to reach inside my jacket for an envelope, Aleksandr… don't get nervous, now." He pulled out a legal-sized manila envelope, bent slightly, and placed it on the coffee table. Alex nodded to Meredith and she walked to the opposite side of the table and picked the envelope up, opened it, and a total look of surprise came over her face. Her eyes darted back and forth, from Malashenko to Alex and back to the paper.

"These are your citizenship papers," she told him in a raspy whisper. "You are a citizen of the United States of America."

Meredith wanted to cry out in joy, but did not know how to behave with a perceived threat standing a few feet from her. She did not trust Malashenko enough to move close to Alex, but she did think to put Rusty in her old bedroom. Malashenko was right. It would not take much to set the dog against an intruder, and Malashenko had a very deep, rather loud voice. There was no sense in having three armed military men come barging into the house, guns blazing. As she returned to the living room, she heard the Russian General's voice speaking in a bit of a monotone.

"I was asked by the President of your country to bring these papers to you personally. The request was made of the President by your Federal Central Bank Chairman, Arthur Redbridge, and by Justice Avery Scott. I have been instructed by the proper authorities in Moscow to tell you that the kill on sight order for Dr. Aleksandr Plotnikov has been burned and no record of it exists. Not anywhere... not even in anyone's memory."

All Meredith could do was cover her face with both hands, utter a noise that sounded like an extended "Ohhhh," and she collapsed in a chair.

"We have no arguments, scientist," Malashenko told him, a half-smile on his face and grateful the dog had been put away. "Put down the weapon and tend to your wife."

Meredith had been under too much pressure for someone who was still in a health recovery process. She was overly tired. He went quickly to the kitchen and got a glass of water. He carried the rifle with him.

"Here, Dorogoi," he said gently, putting the glass to her lips. "Take a sip."

Meredith recovered quickly but when she looked at Malashenko her eyes grew dark and wide. She did not know what to think of him. If he had brought papers that made Alex a U.S. citizen, he was more friend than foe, she decided. At least, he was for the moment. And the blessed news that Alex would no longer have to worry about that damned kill on sight order... it deserved thanks.

"Can we offer you a drink, General?" she asked after thinking about it for a moment. She still looked pale but had a smile on her face. "Alex, get the man a glass of brandy... you might want to have him sit down, too – over there, away from the guns," she said, again unsure of just how much to trust this bear of a man.

Malashenko chuckled. He accepted the drink from his former comrade and raised it in a toast. "Here is to Dr. Alex Plotnikov, an American citizen, and to his lovely wife," he said and gulped the brandy down in three large swallows.

"Moscow asked me to come because they want me to ask you a question, Aleksandr Mikhail." He paused, put his glass on the coffee table and stood. "Do you become an American of your own free will?"

"Of course," Alex responded immediately.

"Would you like to have dual citizenship? American and Russian?" Malashenko asked. "It can be arranged."

The response was not immediate this time. Meredith looked at her husband curiously.

"America is my home, Yuri. I think not. I want to be an American citizen. If I ever take my wife to Russia for a visit, I will have to go through the same Visa nightmares all Americans who visit Russia suffer." He smiled at the man and held out his hand. "But I thank you and those in Moscow who made the offer. It puts balm on a sore spot in my life." He hesitated. "You are sure about the kill on sight order?"

"Da," was all the man said. He nodded his head affirmatively. Then, after a moment, "I am sure."

Meredith watched Malashenko. That he respected Alex was apparent from the look he gave him. "Can we get anything else for you – or for the men outside – General Malashenko?" she asked.

"No, Mrs. Plotnikov, my men will be getting cold out there... and restless. We will be driving up to Aspen for a weekend of rest before returning home," he said, smiling. "Things have changed since you left, good Doctor. Can you imagine even saying the word 'Aspen' in the old days?" He laughed the belly laugh that Alex remembered so well and walked to the stairs. "I wish you both well," he said, his voice serious. "You bore a terrible burden while on Sakhalin Island, Aleksandr." He suddenly turned around to face them. "I'm sorry we lost you," he said sadly.

Alex looked at Meredith as Malashenko shut the door behind him. She was still a bit pale and shaky.

"You must admit" he said wryly, "I throw the best welcome home parties of anyone you know."

"How do you suppose he found you?" she asked him.

Alex shrugged. "He probably followed you from the airport... Gil called to tell me he was about to file a flight plan... it would have gone into the computer system about two hours before you departed. They had plenty of time to leave New York before you left Washington, D.C., to get the Rifle airport ahead of you. William Leonard was right. They had identified the Lear jet as key to our involvement with the clones. They were tracing it. Bill's insight probably saved our hides when we returned the Real Things and took the clones."

He walked up the stairs to the security system and turned it on. "I think we'd better keep our security status high. As for you, I am going to fix something to eat and you are going to go to bed. You are tired and it shows. In another six months, you won't need the IVs, but until then…" he raised his eyebrows, gave her his 'don't fool with me' look, pointed his finger at her and said "you are back on them. Today."

After a good night's sleep, Meredith was rested and calm.

"Well, cowgirl with a shotgun, would you like to meet the clones today?" Alex asked her, chuckling. "After you've had an IV, of course."

There was no response. He had not expected one. Alex knew the thought of seeing clones of close friends would upset her. He wanted her to think about it. Now she would. He rubbed the stubble on his chin.

"How did you know Malashenko was here? You appeared out of nowhere."

"Rusty kept growling at something as I got out of the shower. I heard someone speaking Russian and opened the door and let him out… I grabbed the shotgun and followed him," she answered.

Alex shook his head and told her what good instincts she had and how grateful he was.

They invited Jake and William Leonard to join them for dinner. It was a steak and baked potato night. Alex made shrimp cocktails and Jake, who was surprised William Leonard was joining them, brought a bottle of wine.

As they seated themselves at the table, Meredith stood and raised her glass. Both of their guests grinned, wondering what new emotional experience would be added to the list of toasts made at this table.

"I have something to say to my husband in the form of a toast." She picked up her wine glass and faced Alex, her glass raised. Jake and Leonard expected a toast involving the success of the project.

"To Aleksandr Mikhail Plotnikov, the best and the smartest – and the handsomest – new citizen of the United States of America!"

Meredith's eyes were locked with those of her husband as the two of them tipped their glasses together, then turned to their two guests at the dinner table to touch their glasses, too. The other glasses had not moved. Jake recovered quickly and asked what it was Meredith was telling them. He remembered wondering why Alex looked like he owned the chicken coop when he'd come to invite him to dinner earlier in the day. He realized this was probably why.

Alex stood, walked to his wife's side, put his arm around her, and told them that for now, they would have to trust what Meredith had just said and drink to her toast.

William Leonard and Jake moved their glasses to touch the other two, repeated the last part of Meredith's toast then sipped their wine.

"Alex, please, for God's sake, get on with it," Jake said. He was not laughing.

"Right," the Russian said, unrolling a legal-sized piece of paper he held in his hand. "This piece of paper grants me my citizenship," he said, handing it to Jake.

"I would say we should drink a second time to Meredith's announcement," Leonard advised. And they did. "And now can we hear your toast?" he asked Alex. "My steak's getting cold."

"Bill," Meredith said. "This one may take a minute. We may have to re-heat the food." Her comment merely raised the level of curiosity that already permeated the room.

Alex waited for Meredith to take her seat. She knew what was coming but could not head it off and so just waited for the words to come.

"To my wife, Meredith, a Colorado cowgirl, who yesterday pointed a shotgun at General Yuri Malashenko and made him remove his side arm. She and Rusty saved her husband's life – at least we both thought so at the time."

There was a long pause and he turned to his wife and raised his glass to her. "Here's to Meredith. And, here's to the removal of the kill on sight order which, until yesterday, has hung over my head since 1991."

Again, there was stunned silence around the table.

"Does anything mundane ever happen in this household?" William Leonard asked quietly. He quickly repeated the toast adding Rusty's name and the four of them touched glasses, drinking to the words. They knew a story would follow.

"Now we can have our dinner while Alex tells you the rest of the adventure," Meredith told them.

There was no lack of dinner conversation on this night and the events of yesterday continued into their after-dinner talk in front of the fireplace.

"She actually told Malashenko that if he moved, Rusty would be all over him like beets in borscht?" Jake asked. He laughed so hard his sides hurt.

William Leonard was being very quiet for him, Alex realized. He finally turned to ask him why he had so little to say tonight.

"I have heard from you, Jake, and also from Arthur about the chats held around this fireplace," he chuckled. "I must say, this has got to be one of the most unusual households in which I have been a guest." Leonard paused to sip his brandy and then looked directly at each of them as he spoke. "I do have some things I would like to say, but it is almost anti-climactic to what has already been said."

Jake got up, put another log on the fire, and told William Leonard to put his feet up and sit back. "We all know that nothing you have to say will be anti-climactic to anything or anyone, Bill."

Chapter 35

After talking around what he wanted to say and being given permission by everyone to move the conversation to different topics, William Leonard became more serious than Jake or Alex had ever seen him. His intensity surprised them.

"Arthur and I have some recommendations we want to pass by you. We want to see how you react to our plans to use these trillions of dollars I have sitting in banks around the world," he began.

Jake told him to wait a minute as he went into his former bedroom and pulled from it the scramblers. They were put in their usual place on the coffee table. As Jake turned the scramblers on, the panel truck sitting on the road just outside of Alex's land suddenly lost the sound he had been getting from the house. He did not know where General Malashenko had placed the listening device, but until a moment ago it had been broadcasting to his truck just fine. At least he got the first part of what they were saying recorded.

"I believe Arthur talked with you yesterday morning before you got on the plane to come home. He said he mentioned one project we want to implement, Meredith."

Alex looked at her, eyebrows raised and chin tilted down. It was his 'so you are keeping secrets from me, already,' look. She just smiled at him.

After explaining in depth what the objective would be, Leonard said casually that they thought $500 billion would be a good budget to start that program.

"We want to establish some kind of credit agency outside of the banking industry to make loans to individual investors," he told her. "Since we won't be taking or holding deposits, we should have no problems getting properly licensed... we'll just be a glorified loan company. You know how engraved in stone bank loan policies are. We don't want that. Neither do we want bad loans that result in losses... we want the money to work for us and the country. First, we want money in the hands of those who create rather than manage wealth. We want to loan to people who do things like rehab low-cost housing... turn older areas into decent neighborhoods for the elderly and the poor – and it's not contractors who do that kind of work. They build subdivisions. Individual investors do rehabs. I've read your speeches, Meredith, and you used this example many times," he said, again stopping to sip his brandy. "The tax laws Ronald Reagan signed brought low-cost rehabs to a halt... as you said would happen.

"Anyway, there are dozens of other examples of the kinds of loans we mean... you know what they are." He paused. "Your wife wrote the book on this, Alex. We also want the money to be repaid at a fair interest rate so, as money should be, it can be re-used to further invest in business growth that will strengthen the economy. We want to fund businesses that will build and sell American, not Chinese or Indian. We need your help with that program." He put his hands up as if to defend himself as he saw her getting ready to give him the same response she had given Arthur Redbridge. "Wait, wait... our plans will not take you away from your husband or your ranch. Please, let me finish.

"Alex, we are going to start a cancer research center in the little town of DeBeque, Colorado – yes, Jake, I know where I am. The center will focus on using DNA and genetically engineered – yes, cloned – body parts. In the 1960s when the war on cancer began, only one person in thirty-three contracted the damned disease. Today, one in three people are likely to be affected by cancer. The medical establishment focuses entirely on surgery, chemotherapy and radiation therapy. In some cases that can't be helped. Even so, we feel your DNA IVs can help people regain healthy immune systems when chemotherapy is required. We want to make a cancer treatment center available for the doctors who wrote the book about cures available from alternative medicine rather than prescription drugs. They need a research center that will not undermine their work to focus the medical world's eyes on non-chemical treatments. And, they need lawyers to defend what they are doing.

"It will take legislation, but Senator Martinez feels he has made the right contacts to legalize cloning body organs from one's own body tissue to save one's own life. Justice Scott thinks this kind of science can be legally justified under the pursuit of life clause. The cloning will be of organs only and restricted to life-threatening diseases. It can be used for more than cancer. Infants born with heart or organ problems can benefit, too. We'll make DNA organ growth available to the poor so there will be no complaints about civil rights abuses. We should be able to get insurance coverage for the procedure within two or three years – first, because it works; and, second because it costs only a tiny percentage of what chemo costs.

"Over time, we hope such a research facility will find a more intelligent approach to the prevention and treatment of all disease than is currently available. As you know, Meredith, we have to back slowly out of that driveway. If we chop the chemotherapy business off at the knees without doing it gradually, the economy couldn't withstand it. Hard decisions, hard decisions…"

Leonard paused before continuing. He rose and for a brief moment paced in front of the fireplace. It reminded Jake of a Russian scientist he knew.

"We will, of course, want you to run the center, Alex. Again… you will have a staff of sufficient size so you won't have to relinquish the life you have just begun as a happily married man. Rather than driving down the road to your lab here at the ranch, you'll just be driving down the road to DeBeque. And you will finally be able to get the recognition you deserve for the scientific innovations you've achieved – as well patents and monetary rewards for the techniques you've developed."

Alex took the last sip of brandy from his glass and asked his guest if he would like another… or would he prefer coffee or some other drink. The room was so quiet, Meredith thought, if a hair had fallen from someone's head, it would be heard.

"I would like another brandy, Alex… thank you." He turned to Jake and smiled. "So, you are going to build an earth home at your new place, I hear?"

"That's the plan, Bill," Jake smiled in response.

"How would you like a few thousand acres to work with instead of just forty plus the hundred and forty Alex has here?" Leonard asked.

"I'm happy with what I have, Bill," Jake replied. He paused before continuing, looked at the floor for a moment, then looked Leonard directly in the eye, grinning. "You may not know it, but I have trouble every month spending enough money in business enterprises I own around the world to keep my tax accountants happy. I plan to grow as land becomes available."

Meredith's eyebrows rose at the disclosure. She knew Jake had money. She did not know he had that much.

"I know how much money you have, Jake," Leonard responded. "I am not referring to money and I'm not trying to give you any. What I'm referring to is life purpose."

Leonard paused and Jake could not help wondering if the man had been reading his mind the past few months. The thought of a life purpose had been weighing heavily on him. "What I'm talking about may be a good business investment…"

"Why does it not surprise me that you know how much money I have?" Jake interrupted him, chuckling.

The man smiled at Jake before continuing. "Arthur and I want to start an education center… a place where young people can be taught about the history of America and how free enterprise works – or, how it's supposed to work. We all know kids today are not learning what they need to know about the Declaration of Independence, the Constitution, the Bill of Rights, and the Amendments to the Constitution. We know today's kids are so wrapped up in themselves and have been so dipped in political correctness they couldn't smell real subterfuge if it came in the form of cow droppings on their shoes. And, we all know this government is going to fight to keep getting bigger and bigger and more and more intrusive. All governments do.

"We want to train young people in survival… how to be responsible gun owners, how to hunt, how to make soap and candles, how to weave fabrics, how to generate electricity, how to spin wool and drill their own water wells. We want to teach them how to live independent of utility companies. We want to teach them how to survive no matter what happens in the world around them. They need to know how to butcher an animal – kind of a Girl and Boy Scout graduate school."

Meredith smiled at him. "You would be so good working with kids, Jake!" she told him, enthusiastically.

"In fact," Leonard interrupted her, "putting together a home school curriculum on the Internet is one of our objectives. Home schooling is the only way we'll ever solve America's education problems. We want to prepare young people to know the difference between a Republic and a Democracy. We want to motivate them to choose the former and reject the latter – but they need to be informed about both and make up their own minds. We need to train journalists and lawyers whose first priority isn't liberal or conservative or politically correct. Their first priority needs to be facts. It needs to be truth.

"J.J. needs unbiased reporters… he doesn't care if they have a degree from Columbia's journalism school. I think he'd prefer they did not. We can provide them… and we can do it quickly. We need to train law school graduates – and pay them – to counterbalance the ACLU and its lawyers. We need to train political science majors about how free enterprise works and help them become successful in their communities so they can run for office and get elected in five years. And, we want to teach kids about competition… healthy competition.

"You would have a lot of help… me, for one. This is what I want to do with my own money. I want to be involved in it. So, too, do those other intelligence operatives I told you about who became disgusted with the world's intelligence agencies."

He paused for a long time, as if considering something. "I guess I should tell you, I'm personally buying as many acres as I can here in the valley. That won't come from the money Arthur and I are using. It will be my personal investment."

Jake just looked at him for a moment, his head tilted curiously to one side. "How much of those trillions of dollars did you, personally, keep, Bill?" he asked quietly but very seriously.

"Let me answer you with a question, Jake." Leonard returned the smile. "How much in honestly-earned money do you think I would have if I'd charged President Rory McCoy the going brokerage commission rate for my work?"

Jake furrowed his brow and thought seriously about the question for a moment, but could find no answer. He shook his head. "I have no idea," he finally replied.

"Billions and billions of dollars," Meredith contributed. "Billions and billions."

"To answer your question, Jake, I kept five billion dollars from the total, so the American people got a bargain. I'm actually glad you asked because I want this out in the open. Aside from the brokerage commissions I earned, what I did kept America from long, expensive years of the cold war. It may have prevented untold losses in human life had it turned into a hot war. The last fifteen years of my life, I have dodged just about every government on the face of the earth. There were many times I thought I wasn't going to live through the day, let alone the night." Again, he paused and then looked directly into Jake's eyes. "I hope that's a satisfactory answer. I appreciate the fact that you asked the question. It needed to be asked and answered."

Leonard rose, took the final sip of his brandy and thanked his host and hostess for their hospitality.

"I won't bore you with the long story about what Arthur and I are going to do with the rest of all that money... pay down the deficit, eliminate foreign debt, gradually eliminate the Federal Central Bank. I do want you to know that I have created a trust. Since I have no family, I have named you, Jake, and you, Alex, as the Successor Trustees of my trust. If anything happens to me, you guys – with Arthur – will be managing a lot of money. It sounds like you, Alex, are out of the woods and on safe ground. Until all of my accounts around the world are emptied by funding Arthur's programs, I'm not safe. As I begin to identify those accounts, my personal danger will increase. That's why I wanted to tell you about this tonight... just in case."

Leonard's four companions just looked at him, overwhelmed.

Jake looked at the floor and shook his head. Though he had disliked Leonard's behavior, he had always respected his intelligence. Jake realized that he had underestimated the man's sense of patriotism and willingness to sacrifice for the betterment of his country. He truly was a patriot.

"You're going to go into the history books as Cecil Rhodes equal and opposite by doing this," Jake told him quietly. "You will be the man who took America away from the British Empire a second time."

Leonard walked slowly towards the stairs to the entry and was reaching for his coat when Meredith's voice stopped him.

"You are not going to go back to the bunkhouse to sleep, Bill. Let me show you to the guest room here at the main house. The security is good where you are. It's better here. Please, Alex..." she turned to her husband for support.

"She's right, Bill. You don't have Meredith and Rusty there to guard you with a shotgun." They all laughed, easing the tension in the room. Alex waited until it was quiet again. "Malashenko found this place by tracking the Lear jet. He must know you are here or somewhere nearby. You *will* be safer here, with us. I'll drive you down to the bunkhouse and you can retrieve your things and bring them back here."

Jake rose, unlocked the gun cabinet, picked out a rifle and grabbed a handful of ammunition. He handed them to Leonard. "I never thought I'd be doing this," he said, chuckling. Bill Leonard smiled broadly as he accepted Jake's offering. It represented the trust one man gives another he respects and considers his equal.

After the two men left, Meredith and Jake sat quietly looking at the fire.

"I really like Bill Leonard," Meredith said quietly. "He's one of those people who is so bright no one can really understand him. He must be very lonely. My guess is he's a very good guy to have on your team." She paused, stretching. "I'm ready for bed already," she yawned.

"Are you going to edit J.J.'s paper? Or, are you going to help with the loan company they want to start?" Jake gave her a serious look as he spoke. "It seems your career opportunities are beginning anew in your 60th year."

She laughed, thinking of the times she'd had to leave jobs she loved because it was the only way a woman could get ahead... the days before equal employment.

"I have a friend in Arizona who is a newspaper editor and can coordinate J.J.'s newspaper better than I," Meredith said quietly. "I told Arthur I'd sit on J.J.'s Board. I'll help make sure J.J.'s objectives are achieved because I think they're important." She yawned and stretched again. "And Sue knows my loan policies as well as I do... probably better, since she's been using them more recently than me." She smiled at Jake. Meredith Morgan Plotnikov was, for the first time in her life, totally happy. She had no intention of upsetting that apple cart with a new career.

Jake smiled. "What are Leonard and Redbridge going to do?" he asked. "Bill's plans are good for the long-term, but we need immediate short-term solutions to save the country."

Meredith thought for a few moments before speaking.

"Arthur and I talked a lot about it while I was with him. I know it involves buying back ownership in the Fed from foreign investors... they now own more than half of the Federal Central Bank System. That makes it possible for political strings to be pulled by foreign governments in a way that controls our economic policies. The ongoing objective will be to reduce all foreign owners of the Fed, a little at a time, year-after-year.

"I know they will do away with the nonsense of banks creating money by making loans... fractional reserve banking. It has caused us to become a debtor nation – a debt-dependent economy.

"Arthur and Bill will use gold to buy dollars caused by our international trade deficit... money that some nations are holding. If they decide to cash it in or start buying land and businesses in this country – as China has already started to do – it can cost us the legal ownership of America's land and economic base. Should we have a severe recession, those trade deficits and the money those nations are holding could be the death of us. I know they plan to restore the U.S.

dollar to a precious metals plus productivity standard, reduce federal spending, lower income taxes, and eliminate taxes on savings, dividends and capital gains. People need to save, not spend. Subsidies and other special interest protections and transactions must cease. They will solidify the bond market. And, I know Arthur plans to begin eliminating the power of the Federal Central Bank."

Meredith paused and sipped her cranberry juice. "That is the real test... he has to do things in such a grandiose way that he looks like a super hero to the public. He has to bring jobs back to the country and increase the value of the dollar. As the dollar strengthens, our exports will go down... that's why they want to do the 'buy American' thing. Arthur will have to be so big and so popular that the government will be afraid to touch him when he begins cutting down the power base. And, that is when he will be in real danger." Meredith paused for a moment. She frowned. "It is also when the nation could be in real danger from him."

Alex and Bill returned as she finished speaking. Leonard did not have many personal possessions. Alex quickly turned the security system back on. Meredith guessed they were back on high alert. Maybe in today's world, she thought, that was not such a bad idea. It would take time to weed out all of the evil that had been growing in America's gardens for many years. The weeds – Gramsci's foot soldiers – had, indeed, almost taken over the garden.

As Bill Leonard reentered the room, he walked to where Meredith sat and offered her a rather large, heavy package. "I want you to have this," he said quietly. "It was all I brought with me in my backpack when I snuck on board Jake's plane in Munich..." he paused, looking at Jake and told him, "I hid it in open sight on the Lear, Jake." He knew the former CIA agent was thinking of how many years he could have gotten in prison for smuggling had Leonard been caught.

As he handed her the package, the weight of it almost caused her arms to fall.

"Oh, my goodness!" she said, startled. Leonard grabbed her hands, helping her support it as she lowered it to her lap. Meredith unfolded the canvas from the gift it concealed and gasped at the gold swan. It was about eighteen inches high and even her untrained eye could see its value.

"Bill," she said breathlessly, "I can't accept such a valuable gift from you!" She looked at him and for the first time since she had met him, noticed that his eyes were smiling at her. They looked gentle and calm.

"It belongs with you," he said, almost shyly. "Its body is twenty-two karat gold, but the body is not solid... if you ever need a really good hiding place, the neck of the swan screws off. You can't see it because the break where the neck can be removed is covered by these little decorations... see here?" He bent and twisted the neck of the statue. As he removed the neck of the swan, she noticed a protruding piece of paper in the lower part of the swan's hollow body. "This is where for almost fifteen years I have hidden a list of all of the bank and investment accounts I have around the world and what's in them. Even Arthur doesn't have this information. If anything happens to me, he'll need it, so I need to share it. I think you are the person closest to him, Meredith. That's why I'm entrusting it to you. I ask that you do not touch that paper unless something happens to me."

Leonard lowered his head for a moment then looked directly at her. "I have to admit that I have not trusted many people in my life. I trust the people in this room and I know the swan and what it represents – which I've had enough of, frankly – but I know it will be safe here."

Meredith finally realized that her mouth was gaping just a bit and looked at Jake and Alex. She was not the only one suffering from the malady.

"How were you able to keep such a valuable item hidden while you were running away from all of the governments that were trying to track you down?" Jake asked. His face and voice were serious, but his blue eyes held a kind of respect he had never before bestowed on this man. He sometimes liked and admired Bill Leonard. Other times, he was tempted to strangle him.

"It was a part of the collection of swans you saw on display at the castle, Jake," Bill said, smiling in reply. "That's why I had to go to Neuschwanstein to meet Arthur... that's why I had to do it on

New Year's Eve. Going there to welcome in a New Year had become a ritual. It didn't raise suspicion. Every year, I'd go there to update the information about my accounts. When we met, I snuck back into the castle and took it, knowing I was going to leave. I'll have a new one made and return it to the castle. This one is special and it deserves a place of honor. I can't think of a better place for it than right here where our nation's second chance for liberty may have been born, can you?"

Exhortations and protests to the contrary, Meredith finally and with some small amount of grace accepted the historic, beautiful gift. She excused herself momentarily and returned to the room carrying Jeffrey Lund's manila envelope. Wordlessly, she handed it to William Leonard.

He took the envelope from her hands and studied it for a moment before asking her where she got it and what had been in it. She suggested that he take a seat because it was a long story.

"So," she said as she finished describing to Leonard how much difficulty they'd all had trying to figure out the significance of the drawing, "it appears one of the international banking conglomerates for whom Jeffrey was consulting put this material where it got confused with Jeffrey's. Picking up the material got him killed. They found out about your swan, Bill. This has to be what it was about," she said, looking to Jake and Alex for confirmation. Neither man said a word. They both nodded their heads at her, slowly. "Thank heaven you found a safe place to hide this. Otherwise, you would have been killed long ago."

It was late and Jake wanted to get to his new home. He wanted to sit in front of his own fireplace and think of the alternatives offered to him this night. As he left, Jake walked to Leonard's side. Leonard sat, still looking at the drawing on the back of the envelope. When he noticed Jake's boots on the carpet beside his chair, he looked up, smiled, and stood.

"A few weeks ago when I found you sitting in the toilet on the Lear," Jake began, "I never thought I'd say this. I sincerely look forward to getting to know you, Bill Leonard. I hope you'll come with Alex and Meredith to dinner at my place tomorrow night." He started to leave, but turned quickly back to Leonard. "I will warn you Bill… if your hostess mentions the word 'theory,' be sure you are wide awake before going any further in the conversation."

Everyone laughed. William Leonard raised his eyebrows and wondered about this new mystery. This house seemed to be filled with them.

Jake turned to Meredith and gave her a big hug. He merely slapped Alex's shoulder and said "Good night, fellow citizen." Jake chuckled. "You are going to be surprised at how many sentences I'm going to think of that start with 'you Americans' over the next few weeks…" Jake said, and laughed. "It's pay-back time." He turned on the full security system. The patio walls and the retainer wall slid silently into place.

Meredith and Alex showed their new guest to Jake's old room and helped him get settled for the night. They returned, hand in hand, to the living room and the warmth of the fire.

"You know our lives are going to change rather dramatically, don't you?" he asked her.

She sat on the floor between his legs and he began to massage her shoulders. "My darling husband, our lives began to change rather dramatically the day we met… the day you and Jake saved my life. Please tell me when the change that started that day has ever stopped?" She sighed deeply. "Bill Leonard is giving us some great opportunities. We have no Real Things to return to power, no more crises to handle. We both need to find a new life purpose that goes beyond dedicating ourselves to our marriage."

Alex hit the remote button for the stereo and once again the sound of Lara's Theme filled the room. "One more time," he said softly in her ear before biting her ear lobe. Meredith knew how to fight back as she blew softly in his ear.

"Are we still on simmer?" he asked her suddenly.

"No," she told him, "I think we're dancing to the song that suggests the back burner is turned to high heat." This time, she whispered the words of the song to him.

*****

As Jake drove home from a night he would never forget, he pulled the SUV to the stop sign where the road to Alex's ranch met a county highway. A turn to the left would take him to DeBeque and I-70. A turn to the right would take him home. He smiled at his own thought. He liked the sound of "home." For a moment he studied what appeared to be a deserted panel truck sitting across the road with no lights, no signs of life.

He exited the car and walked to the driver's front door and jerked it open. A man suddenly appeared from the back of the truck and Jake felt the handgun against his temple.

"I'm a friend of William Leonard," the man said quietly in Jake's ear. "I don't know the name of the man who was recording whatever was said at the ranch tonight, but we have him tied up in back. We haven't met, Jake, but I know you."

The man removed the gun and Jake stood, not moving. The guy with the gun got to make the rules… for now.

"Bill Leonard told you who we are… his friends from the intelligence community?"

Jake nodded.

"Here's the tape from the machine," the man said, handing the reel-to-reel tape to Jake. He put the gun in a shoulder holster. "We'll keep the equipment. It'll come in handy. This guy overheard too much to send him back to Malashenko, but we'll deal with it. You need to check the house for bugs because you've got at least one." He looked at Jake's car with the headlights still lighting the area around them. "Sorry you caught us… another minute and we'd have been out of here. Have a good night…"

The man's accent was reminiscent of Alex when he had first arrived in America, Jake thought.

Jake quickly turned the car around and returned to the ranch. The lights were out but he unlocked the door and entered.

"My God, Jake, what are you doing back here? Is something wrong?" Alex carried the same shotgun into the room with him that Meredith had threatened Malashenko with the day before.

"Get Meredith. We need to talk… now!"

Alex had heard that tone of voice before and knew Jake was deadly serious. He went to the bedroom and brought his surprised wife back with him.

Jake told them what had just happened and began going over the living room, searching for bugs. He found one under the rim of the coffee table where Yuri Malashenko had placed Alex's citizenship papers.

"Bill and I will go over the place more thoroughly tomorrow," he told them, "but, until then, no conversations without the scramblers."

"We need to talk about never forgetting to be vigilant," Alex said quietly, but firmly. "We won't forget again that the fight's not over. It just felt like it for a moment. Apparently, it's just begun," he said. "We need to have a long talk with Bill tomorrow night about how we can help him with his plans."

Meredith had never seen a more intense look on their faces.

"Help him how?" she asked.

"What Leonard was talking about tonight is using Gramsci's theories of hegemony against those who have been using it against us. We're going to create our own foot soldiers. We're going to wage our own war of position in the short-term and Arthur Redbridge is setting things up to wage a long-term war of movement," Jake said solemnly. It had taken time and an unpleasant experience for him to figure it all out.

"What we just accomplished was winning a battle in a war of position," Alex said quietly.

"The elitists – or, one-worlders or whatever you want to call them – are now the dominant class… they enjoy hegemony, or dominance," Jake added.

"Yes," Meredith said thoughtfully. "You're both right. Bill's plans will create our own hidden class… one being trained to become the new moving force in America. We'll be using their very effective Gramscian tactics against them." She chuckled and both men looked at her, rather startled.

"I love it when the worm turns – and it is turning," she offered in way of explanation. "I have a theory about that."

CPSIA information can be obtained
at www.ICGtesting.com
Printed in the USA
FSHW04n0649050418
46595FS